19 YEARS

Ellie Thompson

19 YEARS

Vanguard Press

VANGUARD PAPERBACK

© Copyright 2021
Ellie Thompson

A CIP catalogue record for this title is
available from the British Library.

ISBN 978-1-80016-043-9

*Vanguard Press is an imprint of
Pegasus Elliot MacKenzie Publishers Ltd.*
www.pegasuspublishers.com

First Published in 2021

**Vanguard Press
Sheraton House Castle Park
Cambridge England**

Printed & Bound in Great Britain

Dedication

To Dad

Chapter 1

So, the day had arrived. The day Ellie had been looking forward to, for what seemed like forever. The fine spitting rain had slowly subsided and the warm July sunshine was peeping through the scattered clouds. Ellie kneeled on her childhood bed and leaned over to the windowsill, looking up to the heavens and silently pleading for the rain to stay away. The photographer had assured her a little fine rain wouldn't be noticeable on the wedding photos but Ellie was more worried about her hair falling flat in the damp and her beautiful, not to mention expensive, white silk stockings getting wet through her dainty, shoestring style white stiletto heel sandals.

For her, today was the beginning of the perfect fairy-tale life that she and Curtis had talked about and planned for almost four years. She leaned back on the bed and looked up at some of the childhood posters that still decorated her side of the bedroom. Although she had left home almost twelve months ago, she wondered if her mum had left the posters in situ as the wallpaper underneath did have very unattractive tears where she had swapped pictures over the recent years.

Since meeting Curtis at school and their

relationship becoming very intense very early on, he had expressed his dislike for her posters of male pop stars, going as far as to insist she took them down. Even in the first few weeks of them becoming boyfriend and girlfriend, he had professed his undying love for her and informed her they would get married as soon as they had bought their own house. At only fifteen Ellie was blown away with the affection and attention that Curtis enveloped her in. She clearly remembered him taking her into town, on the bus, two weeks before her sixteenth birthday, to choose an engagement ring. He never actually proposed but merely informed her that once they were sixteen, they could do as they pleased and they *were* getting engaged on her birthday.

"You belong to me now and I will love you more than anyone else possibly could," he had said.

Ellie looked down at the engagement ring on her finger, now accompanied by an eternity ring that Curtis bought her on her seventeenth birthday. He had placed it on her finger and said, "This ring is a symbol of my eternal love for you. I will love you with all my heart until the day I die, you will be mine forever. We will have two children and a beautiful home and everyone will be jealous of me for having the perfect wife and the perfect life."

"Ellie," called her father from the foot of the stairs. "Car will be here in twenty minutes, you okay?"

"Okay, yes thanks, Dad," Ellie replied, being abruptly dragged from her thoughts of yesteryear.

James Thompson was a doting father to Ellie and even with two other children, he didn't make too much effort to deny he had a favourite. Her slightly older brother, Lloyd, and her three years younger sister, Suzie, had constantly, throughout their childhood, nicknamed Ellie 'pet'. It was all very light-hearted name calling, as the three siblings were always quite close, especially Ellie and her brother. But Ellie was most definitely a daddy's girl. She could wrap James around her little finger and everyone knew it. Apart from the odd extra pocket money given in secret, the way James spoiled Ellie was more of an emotional bond. He would hardly ever say no to a request from his pet. Whether it be a lift to a friend's house, out of school activities Ellie wished to pursue, or even just something as small as what television channel was on. She knew just how to get her own way whilst making her dad smile and give her a hug for good measure.

Now, counting down the minutes to leaving her parents' home, to marry the man of her dreams, Ellie was feeling melancholy and very emotional. This feeling gave her a lump in her throat and she felt a tear welling up in her eyes.

Her sister, Suzie, burst into the bedroom flapping that her flower wouldn't stay in her hair. "Ellie! Do something. This stupid hair slide won't stay in my hair, I knew I shouldn't have agreed to be your bridesmaid. If you don't sort it out, I'm taking it out and it's going in the bin." Rolling her eyes to herself, and definitely shaking her out of the private moment she was having, Ellie told Suzie to sit on the bed so she could take a look at the offending hair slide.

Suzie, at the age of sixteen, was a totally different character to her sister. Wearing a dress, for one, was not something she would normally agree to. As much as Ellie had persuaded her to be her bridesmaid, Suzie would not be seen dead in a traditional bridesmaid dress. She told Ellie, "If I can choose my own dress, and you pay for it, then I will agree to wear it. But only until we get to the reception, then I'm getting changed."

Ellie agreed and the dress was a calf-length, white shift dress with dainty blue cornflowers. Very summery and matched with a hair comb of blue and white silk flowers. That was Suzie's limit to any kind of headdress. Ellie secured the comb as tight as she could and gave it a good five-second blast with the hair lacquer. "All right, all right, Jesus, what you trying to do, choke me before we even set off? Come on, Dad's shouting us again, car's here." She grabbed her small silk bouquet, a matching round version of Ellie's own which was a larger cascading one, containing blue roses, cornflowers and lily of the valley and, after throwing Ellie a look of complete distaste for the whole affair, she shot off down the stairs.

Taking a last look at herself in the mirror and lifting the sheer veil over the Juliet cap and over her face, Ellie smiled to herself. She had chosen a very simple calf-length wedding gown. Shoestring straps and a plain fitted bodice, accentuating her small waist. The skirt was several layers over a crinoline underskirt. Very full and plain but exceptionally chic. All finished off with a see-through, lacy bolero jacket. She was very happy with the Audrey Hepburn look she loved so much.

Approaching the top of the stairs, she looked down to see her father gazing up at her. He looked handsome and proud in his silvery-grey suit she had chosen for him. He watched her descend the stairs, took her in his arms giving her a strong, meaningful hug and said, "You look absolutely gorgeous, Ellie." She could hear the catch in his voice as he continued, "You know it's not too late to change your mind." His eyes never left hers and his smile was, she could tell, a little forced. She knew he was just making sure she was sure.

She paused and gave it a millisecond thought but knew this wedding would be going ahead. She knew her life wouldn't be worth living if she wasn't at the alter where Curtis was waiting for her. She was surprised at the way in which her father's words had come across. She felt an uncertainty on his part at giving his daughter away to be married. Ellie had never given her father, or anyone, for that matter, any reason to dislike or distrust Curtis. And now, as she stood here, it was as if her father were looking into her soul and questioning this day.

He broke the silence by reminding her that this would always be her home and she should keep the key to their house on her at all times. "I know, Dad, and I will, please try not to worry, I love Curtis and he loves me," she said, smiling. She knew this statement was true, they were very deeply in love and had been since they met at the age of fifteen. Cutis told her he loved her every day and craved reassurance that she loved him too. In fact, she had asked herself on a few occasions if it were possible to love someone too much, to be too possessive. Surely not, was all she came up with. Curtis was, after all, tall, dark, handsome and very charming to everyone. What more could she want? There had, however, been a couple of occasions over the past four years when he had had to apologise to her for his behaviour. These did play on her mind. Just a little niggle she couldn't shake. Maybe he would be better once they were married, not so scared of losing her like he keeps saying. He did like to set boundaries and have things his own way.

One such embarrassing occasion, Ellie recalled, was when she left her first job for a better position and increased pay. She loved her job in the fashion shop she worked in and was proud when she had been offered one of the sixteen positions available. There had been over three hundred candidates and Ellie didn't think she would stand a chance.

In the back of her mind she always remembered the advice her dad gave her years ago… *If you don't ask you don't get.* This he constantly repeated to her. Now at the forefront of her mind, as she stood up to leave the interview, she extended her hand to the interviewer and said, "I would love to be a successful candidate and given the chance to prove that I will be a valid member of your fantastic team."

She worked there for almost two years and, for the most part, really enjoyed the work. This, however, didn't stop her from always being on the lookout for a career move-up. So, one hot August day when the opportunity presented itself, Ellie grabbed it and acted immediately. She had just been out in her lunch hour and noticed a new funky fashion shop across the road, advertising in the window for staff. She took the details and later that day had a letter of application in the post. Sadly, when she mentioned it to Curtis, he was quite put out about it and said she should have consulted him before applying.

Ellie recalled the argument it caused… "Seriously, Curtis, what is your problem? This is a great opportunity; the money is almost double what I earn now and you're the one who wants us to buy a house so we can get married. If I got this job we could start looking now!"

His reply was as unreasonable as it was infuriating. "I like you working where you are now. All the staff are women and I'm happier with that. There may be guys working in this new place and I'm not gonna be happy if that's the case. I love you, Ellie, and I always worry that you will meet someone else."

Ellie was shocked at this outburst and, whilst she felt a little flattered, she was also a little cross. "Curtis, you are being ridiculous. I love you and we are going to buy a home, get married and have a family and be happy ever after. Why would I even look at another man?" She felt irritated and thought that Curtis sounded pathetic, expecting her to only ever work with and speak to women.

But Curtis turned snappy and came back with, "I know, I know." He took a long slow breath. "Look, Ellie, it's not you I don't trust, it's all the blokes out there. You are so pretty and I know what blokes are like. They will be all over you given half a chance."

Now Ellie felt a bit sorry for him and said, "Curtis, you have no need to worry at all, I love you and I would never let that happen and, anyway, maybe they will all be girls working there. Let's wait and see how it works out, eh?" She then kissed him passionately and held him tight.

After securing herself a position at the new fashion shop, Ellie was feeling the nerves on her first day. Not because of the actual work but nervous of who her colleagues would be. She was proud of getting this job and excited to start work, just keeping her fingers crossed for an all-female work force.

Her heart-sinking moment arrived as she joined the other seven members of her new working team. They were meeting in the staff room downstairs from the shop floor and, as there was no natural light, it seemed dark having come in from the bright sunshine, but she immediately noticed a very handsome guy at the back of the room. They all proceeded to take turns in introducing themselves and Ellie's face lit up when Pete told them all about himself and his partner, Simon, who was a male nurse. Hallelujah... Pete was gay, how fabulous.

She couldn't wait to get home and tell Curtis the only male member of staff was gay. Unfortunately, unbeknownst to Ellie, Curtis had been in the shop already and had a sneaky look round for himself. He had obviously seen Pete and his anger had had all day to fester inside him. Now he wasn't even giving Ellie a chance to speak, he had just jumped to the wrong conclusion and took her roughly by the shoulders shaking her and threatening her to keep away from him.

Ellie was furious. "Yes, Curtis, he is very good looking and a really nice guy, too. He is also gay and has a partner. And if you don't believe me, do your worst, go on into the shop and ask him yourself. You're the one that's gonna look crazy!"

Curtis struggled to believe this and thought she was lying to save herself. The following days they were hardly speaking to each other until Curtis realised he was wrong and broke down, asking Ellie for forgiveness. "I'm sorry, Ellie, I love you so much. I am so afraid of losing you. Please say you forgive me. I can't help the way I feel."

And there it was, the beginnings of a pattern. A pattern that Ellie failed to see. A pattern that would not only repeat itself but intensify in the process.

"Right, you all set, my lovely?" James said to his

daughter. "Let's get to that church and get you married. I am so proud of you, Ellie. You are a good girl. I am so lucky to be your father." He leaned down and kissed her cheek through the veil.

"Hey, hey, stop… Don't you make me cry and ruin my makeup," she teased.

Chapter 2

That's me, Ellie Thompson, as was. Now Ellie Parson. Our wedding day went to plan, more or less. Shame we couldn't say the same about the honeymoon. That was a total cock up.

We had booked a week in a guest house on the east coast and planned to sleep off the wedding day alcohol and leave on the Sunday morning. Even with hangovers, we were both in quite high spirits. A week off work was enough to be excited about and here we were getting away from it all on a beautiful warm and sunny day, laughing as we pulled out of the drive at all the ridiculous decoration on the front of the house. There were good luck messages stuck to the front window, silver plastic horse shoes hanging everywhere and toilet rolls streaming down the garden attached to the upstairs windows.

"Do you think we should move them before we go?" I asked Curtis.

"Nah, leave them. Give the nosey neighbours something to talk about," he laughed.

With that we drove off and I pulled the massive AA road map book out of the glove compartment and folded it over on the correct page for our journey. I had only a few days ago highlighted the route we were taking in the hope it would avoid any wrong turns.

Although the drive was only about an hour and forty-five minutes, we weren't in a rush and stopped off half way for a cuppa and a bite to eat. We even managed to laugh about taking headache tablets to shift the hangovers. "Do you know what?" I thought out loud to Curtis. "Nice walk on the beach when we get there. That's what we need, that'll blow the cobwebs away." He grunted under his breath but nodded in agreement.

When we pulled up at the guest house it looked very cute and colourful. Bright yellow glossy painted door and a matching picket fence either side of the pathway leading to it. Pretty flowers of all colours adorned the small front garden. "Aww, looks cute, eh. I'll go and get us checked in, shall I? And you can get the cases out of the boot," I suggested.

Curtis took off his sunglasses and rubbed the bridge of his nose and across his eyes. "Yeah, go on, then. Don't know about walking on the beach, I could do with a lay down," he mumbled.

I walked up to the door and, expecting it to be open, I pushed the handle down. To my surprise it seemed to be locked. So I knocked on the door and stood back a step. Nothing. Then some movement at the bay window caught my eye. An elderly lady, at least in her eighties, poked her head round the net curtain. "Hello, duckie," she mouthed to me through the window. Then a few more elderly faces joined her. All smiling their best smiles and showing off their chipped dentures. "I'll get somebody... Hang on," said the first lady. I looked back at Curtis who was wearing an unamused look on his face. I put my hand over my mouth in an attempt to stifle the giggle that was fighting its way out.

I ran back to the car and Curtis stopped in his tracks of taking out the luggage. "I thought we'd booked a guest house not a bloody care home," he grumbled. "I'm not stopping here with all those old cronies. Quick, get back in the car, let's get the hell out of here." I shot back into the passenger seat and by now couldn't hold the laughter. Curtis just didn't seem to see the funny side. "Now what?" he demanded. "I hope we haven't paid a bloody deposit."

"No, we didn't actually, so we can do what we like," I replied. "Let's find somewhere to park and have a walk on the beach. Then we could get some lunch and decide what we want to do."

We did just that. Curtis then decided he'd have a beer and made a suggestion that we head back home. "Just think, Ellie, we can spend all the money we put aside for this week on a new kitchen. We'll go to Macro tomorrow morning and choose some new doors and stuff, and we've got all week to do it."

He was quite pleased with his decision-making and had another beer, telling me I would be driving home. We had put aside five hundred pounds for our honeymoon, this would be more than enough to upgrade the kitchen. Curtis was in good spirits as I drove home.

"I know, let's not tell anyone we're back home," he suggested happily. "When you pull the car onto the drive, Ellie, just go right up as far as you can so the car is a bit more out of sight. Then we can have a nice lie-in tomorrow and I can have you all to myself all week." He leaned over and put his arm around my shoulder and kissed the side of my face. I felt quite flattered that he wanted me all to himself; it gave me a warm happy feeling and made me smile.

That was exactly what we did. Never told anyone we had ditched the holiday and spent the next day kitchen shopping. A couple of days later, still in full swing renewing the kitchen, Curtis popped out to the DIY store for some bits and bobs. I was just about to put the kettle on when there was a knock at the door. Opening it, I was faced with a guy from around the corner. Geoff was his name. I'd never really met him properly but Curtis had and I had waved to him a time or two when he had driven past with his wife. "Hello," I said in a surprised manner.

"Sorry, didn't mean to disturb you. Ellie, isn't it? Er... Hello, I'm Geoff. I live around the corner and was just passing when I noticed your front windows open so I thought I'd chance it." He held out his hand and I shook it, smiling back at him.

"Oh, right, OK... Well, come in, Geoff." I really didn't know what to think. Why was he here. I didn't have to wait long to find out. "Er yeah... Sorry, it's just that I saw Curtis in the pub last week and he said your telly's on the blink. I'm a television repair man. I said I would pop in when I had time and have a quick look. See if it's salvageable."

Now this was making more sense. "Well, Geoff, I have just put the kettle on, so, fab, why don't I show you where the telly is and make us a brew. It's a right old black and white telly, mind. I wouldn't be too surprised if it's ready for the scrap heap," I laughed. I showed him through to the lounge and went back to make a drink for us. "Tea or coffee?" I shouted through to Geoff.

"Ooh, coffee for me, love. Strong and two sugars, please."

"No bother, just how I like my coffee, too," I said conversationally. I sat on the sofa and chatted to him while he took the back off our old dusty telly. It was quite nice to have a bit of company after our non-honeymoon period. I hadn't spoken to anyone other than Curtis in days. We chatted about his wife and his kids. He said they had gone swimming and that was his cue to get out.

" I hate the swimming baths. The kids love it but I hate the smell and the thought of all those kids peeing in the water. Just turns my stomach." He pretended to balk and made me laugh. I told him about our holiday disaster and the subsequent kitchen shopping. "Ah, good idea. A lot more practical. Now, let's see if we can get this telly working for you." We continued to chat easily and I was enjoying his company. To be honest, being alone with Curtis was okay but I craved someone

21

to chat nonsense to.

When he got the telly working, there on the screen was Olivia Newton-John singing 'Summer Nights' with John Travolta. "Ooh, I love her," he said as his eyes lit up. "Told my missus I'd never leave her but if Olivia came knocking... Well Julie would be history... No danger. She's just gorgeous, don't ya think?" He looked at me with a big grin on his face. I started laughing at him and the next thing Curtis is standing there, hands on his hips. I jumped up, wiping tears from laughing off my face.

"Hiya, Geoff." He walked towards Geoff with his hand outstretched. "Good to see you again, mate," he schmoozed, all over-friendly. He turned to face me for a millisecond and the pure look of hate was palpable. "Make us a coffee," he ordered, turning back to Geoff, all smiles, chatting away like they were best buddies. "Would you like a coffee, Geoff?" he asked.

"No, cheers, Curtis, Ellie just made me one. Perfect, just how I like my coffee. She was telling me about the honeymoon not happening," he continued "Mind, if you ask me, I'd say money well spent on the kitchen, eh? Looks lovely."

They chatted easily for a few more minutes until Geoff said he had to get off. Something about a shopping list that Julie had left him. He refused any payment for fixing the telly, said he'd only been ten minutes and Curtis could buy him a pint next time they met in the pub. With that, Geoff left and Curtis showed him out, politeness personified, he was, until Geoff had actually driven away from the house.

I had, during the last couple of minutes, put up the ironing board and plugged in the iron. I was just pulling one of Curtis' shirts over the end of the ironing board when he returned to the room. "So… Just ten minutes, eh, Ellie?" he asked in a very slow and sickly-nice voice.

"Yeah, 'bout that, ten or fifteen minutes." I looked at him with a questioning frown.

"Well then, tell me this." He spoke quietly and came very close to me and then making me jump he slammed his fist down onto the ironing board and bellowed at the top of his voice. "HOW COME HIS CAR BONNET WAS STONE-FUCKING-COLD?"

The shock made me feel a bit panicky and my heart was beating out of my chest. *Jesus,* I thought to myself, *what's going on here? So he was here half an hour, what the fuck!* But I chose the actual words I spoke more carefully. Also, trying to look calm, I continued to iron the shirt while I spoke. "What… What's up, Curtis? Listen to yourself, would ya? You were the one who asked him to look at the telly, not me. I mean, honestly, do—" But I was interrupted mid-sentence.

Again shouting, he carried on his crazy accusations. "Yes, but I didn't ask him to lie about how long he had been here, did I? And WHY did he lie, Ellie, WHY? Ten fuckin' minutes my arse, I saw you through the window, all nice and cosy having a little chit-chat, laughing together, eh… Yeah, so what was that all about, Ellie, tell me what you were talking about, what was so funny?" He was snarling the words out now and bits of white spittle were forming at the corners of his mouth.

I was just in shock but angry at the same time. I didn't want to shout back. I knew only too well that was not how to deal with this. So I continued ironing and said, "Oh, I get it… What you're saying is that whenever anyone is… No, wait, I'll rephrase that, whenever any bloke calls here and you're not in, I'll just hold a sign up at the back door saying, 'Sorry I'm not allowed to speak to anyone of the opposite sex cos my husband is an unreasonable, jealous control freak. Try coming back when he's in!' shall I?" I tried to not sound sarcastic or belittling but I suppose the choice of words weren't helping my cause.

As I placed the iron on the asbestos plate to rearrange the shirt, Curtis immediately grabbed it and held it up towards my face, about four inches away. I could feel the heat from the steam escaping and panicked. I froze and looked him directly in the eyes. He was glaring at me and practically screamed, "DON'T YOU DARE speak to me like that. I am a good husband to you, Ellie, and don't you ever forget that. You don't know HOW lucky you are." His face was red and he moved the iron a touch closer, enough for me to feel the heat intensifying.

Jesus Christ, I thought, *would he really stick the iron in my face?* I didn't know whether to move, argue

24

back or just stay put and call his bluff. As these options raced through my mind, I found myself saying, "Go on then, Curtis, if you've got the bollocks… Do it." I lifted my chin slightly in defiance.

With that, he roared like some crazed animal, yanked the iron backwards with such force it ripped the cord from the plug. He waved the iron around like someone demented for a couple of seconds and then, marching through to the kitchen and opening the back door, he threw the iron at a wall outside. I heard it smash into pieces. I was still standing behind the ironing board but could picture the scene. He stamped back into the room, his face still red and the veins in his neck bulging. He was out of breath and tears were slowly falling down both cheeks. In a quiet, guttural voice, he spoke. "Let that be a lesson to you, Ellie. Do not cross me EVER."

And with that, he left the room stamping his feet on every stair up to the bedroom. I heard what must have been him slinging himself onto the bed and, standing, wondering what to do next, I heard him sobbing. My heart was racing and, without even realising I was doing it, I was clenching my teeth and now felt a sharp pain in my temple. I let out a deep sigh and felt the beginnings of a pounding headache. What the hell had just happened? I was scared and angry at the same time. I sank back onto the sofa and tried to regain my equilibrium. Looking down, my hands were visibly trembling. I just sat trying to get my breathing to slow down for maybe six or seven minutes. I couldn't hear any movement upstairs and was contemplating my next move when I heard, "ELLIE... ELLIE... Come up here, I need you." I was clenching my teeth again.

Chapter 3

I think I did try to justify Curtis' behaviour to myself, by blaming his dysfunctional family. His parents, John and Stella Parson, were a million miles away from my parents in their personalities and ways. They had been married nineteen years at the time of our wedding and Stella was always non-committal about her previous marriages. She made everyone believe she had previously been married once but told me in private there had been another quick one she doesn't like to talk about. She had a five-year-old son when she married John, his name was Steven. She was pregnant when she married John and Curtis arrived in late 1961. The cutest little boy you could possibly lay eyes on, was Curtis. Stella was totally smitten with him from day one and their bond was extremely strong. Just when Steven, who had had his mother's undivided attention for his full five years, was starting full time school, along comes Curtis to fill the gap. She was so happy.

John was a busy businessman and worked long hours. He was an old-fashioned gentleman, very family orientated and very strong values and morals. When the beautiful, trendy Stella, eleven years his junior, started to show an interest in him, he couldn't believe his luck.

He was well aware he was not what you'd call handsome and had never had a serious relationship by the age of thirty-four. Stella was twenty-three and to say she was stunning was an understatement. She worked in the beauty industry and had once even had her face on the front cover of *Vogue* magazine.

She, in comparison, had had a string of relationships and was never short of male attention. She was quite a vain person and very materialistic by her own admission. And here lied the attraction to John. Older, sensible, hardworking and a very nice bank balance, thank you very much. She knew he was in shock at having landed himself a bride that was the envy of any red-blooded man, but she had felt hardship in the past five years.

Bringing up Steven through rocky relationships and financial struggles meant no extra money for herself, she would be relieved to leave that all behind. John's bank balance, coupled with his generosity, were enough for Stella to say 'yes' to his marriage proposal. He was an honourable man and she knew he would take care of Steven and herself. She lavished in his attention and, being pregnant so early in their relationship, wasted no time in giving him a nudge to buy them a new family home for starters.

Curtis came along and even though he was off-the-scale cute, he was also off-the-scale hyperactive, and this made him a difficult child to manage. He hardly slept more than a few hours and, once he could walk, never sat still for a moment. Stella saw the positive in running around after him all day as a way of keeping herself fit and trim, especially dreading her upcoming thirtieth birthday.

John was forever busy and also had to fit in his twice weekly visits to his elderly mother as a priority. This over the years led to Stella and Curtis having a very close relationship. He went everywhere with her and was in awe of his popular, attractive, kind and loving mother. Not to mention the fact that he never heard the word 'no'... He was spoilt, getting his own way financially, too.

Dealing with a demanding teenager took its toll on Stella and a bit of retail therapy was her answer, always. Once she got bored with shopping perhaps a holiday was the answer. As much as Curtis had everything and more than he asked for, Steven was the opposite. Happy to be out of the house and spending time with his mates. Never asking for anything more than he needed.

I was first introduced to his parents one day after school. Both Curtis and I were fifteen years old and I was giggling as he introduced me as his girlfriend but added that we were going to be married one day. He was so proud of his mum as he introduced her as 'the best mum in the world'. He hugged her and she kissed his cheek and then he pulled us in for a group hug. He looked like he could burst with happiness and I could only think how differently this would play out when I introduced him to my parents. I told myself not to think about it, just enjoy the moment. Stella was thirty-eight when we met but looked (and dressed) about twenty-five. She had an amazing figure, fabulous skin and a bit of a beehive kind of hairdo, she looked very chic. She was very gushy with me as if we were new best friends and, I can't deny, I loved being in her company and, from that day on, just looked forward to any time I could spend with her.

Curtis was about to leave school and some days, if he wasn't in school, he would walk and meet me and we would go to his house. Even if he wasn't there for any reason, I would still go to his house after school, rather than go home. Spending time alone with his mum was just the best. Comparing it to spending time with my ordinary, normal, average, dare I even say 'dull' family was a guilty thought I kept to myself. I was always whipped into an excited frenzy in Stella's company. She was like a celebrity and a soap opera all rolled into one. Always full of stories about her personal life. Really, she made my toes curl with some of the stuff she told me, including bitching about John and how boring he was. She really treated me like a mate, making us a coffee and encouraging me to stay longer.

She was a very flirty person, dressing for maximum attention and getting it. Her see-through black negligee was not off the agenda on the window cleaner's day. He was an ex-professional footballer who lived on the estate and he didn't look like he was ready to complain about her attire. The same black number even brought a very broad smile to my own father's face one Boxing Day morning as he was dropping me off. That... I didn't find funny. That wiped the smile right off my face. I relished her brash personality when it didn't directly involve my family. Secretly I'm sure my dad was a little flattered. As you can imagine, on the rare occasions she was in the company of my mother, it was a different story altogether. My mum didn't even need to speak. Her face did that thing, a bit like when you're eating something you wish you hadn't put in your mouth.

Never the less, Stella and John had lots of friends and acquaintances. The closest ones being Dave and Sue. They saw them regularly, even going on holidays together, but Dave and Sue were as mismatched as Stella and John. Sue, as nice as she was, was very old-fashioned and dull — she even made my mother look exciting. Quite the opposite, Dave was a jolly, round-faced, stocky guy. He was funny with a very loud presence but he was charismatic and always smiling. Hard not to like. He had been a business contact and close friend of John's for many years. The bond between them was palpable. Curtis and I were very often invited along for meals out or day trips with the four of them and readily accepted all offers.

By the time we got married, I had a job in the town nearer to where we lived and Stella had taken a job on the same street at a nearby fashion shop. We would often meet for lunch and she would regale me with colourful stories of her past and present. Never a dull moment when she was around. Her unhappiness with John was one of her top subjects of late, so when our meetings started to dwindle, I giggled one day and asked if she was up to no good, cancelling our lunch times together. She was very defensive and dismissive of my comments but now a seed had been sown. I wasn't going to rule out the possibility of another affair. She practically bragged about the amount of men she had had flings with and I always enjoyed the stories. After all, they didn't affect me.

However, when for the third time in the space of a week, I had spotted Dave's shiny red sports car pulling up outside her workplace, I started to feel suspicious and nervous. The first time I saw his car I assumed it was an innocent reason, but three times in almost as many days… I toyed with the idea of sharing this with Curtis and decided to confront Stella first. Give her the chance to explain or come clean. When the next day I broached the subject, she vehemently denied it and the only problem was, I knew her so well by now, that I knew she was lying!

From that day onwards she started going out for lunch, allegedly, alone. She said she was struggling with issues with John and wanted to be on her own. She seemed to be distancing herself from me and this made me believe I was right, so that's when I decided to say to Curtis that she was unhappy. Later that week, when John was at his mum's, we went around to see her. She broke down into Curtis's arms and sobbed. Telling us how miserable she was and said she was leaving John as soon as she had somewhere to go. Curtis was so upset for her. He idolized his mother and seeing her this upset was clearly heart breaking for him. Between sobs she said how bad things were and how she felt John was repressing her personality. She was only forty-two and, although John was fifty-three, he acted like a seventy-five-year-old.

"He complains if I buy new clothes and pulls a face if I even mention going on a holiday," she wept. "I promised myself I would never break up the family while you and Steven were still at home. You are with Ellie now and Steven's moving in with his girlfriend soon. I can't be on my own with him."

This all happened three weeks before our wedding and we promised to be there to support her. She decided to wait until after the wedding to leave, for the sake of the top table, the photos and, of course, the drama that would unfold. So, until then we kept her secret between the three of us. Still there had been no mention of Dave.

Chapter 4

With a deep breath, my heart hammering and clenched teeth, I tentatively made my way upstairs. A million and one scenarios playing swiftly through my mind as I made the step onto each stair. Was he going to attack me physically, as he had just shown he could be capable of? Was he going to scream and shout and break more things we could ill afford to replace? Or maybe he was just going to cry like a baby and feel sorry for himself. God knows, but I was now about to find out.

Slowly opening the bedroom door, he was, as I had imagined, laying the wrong way across our bed, sobbing into a pillow he had dragged from the top of the bed. "So… What do you NEED?" I emphasised on the word need. I was standing arms folded and feet slightly apart, subconsciously, I suppose, trying to look braver than I felt. I did feel threatened.

"Mum's left Dad," he blurted out. "I just called round at theirs while you were here cosying up to Geoff." He spat the end of the sentence at me. I didn't move a muscle or say a word, the only sound was Curtis's snivelling. He sat up on the bed and raising his voice. "Did you hear me?" he demanded. I had, over the years, learned the hard way not to reply with sarcastic comments so, yet again, I had to bite my tongue.

"Yes, I did," was all I said.

"Is that it… Is that all you've got to say? What, are you glad? Or are you just not interested? Suppose you already knew, eh, you two are as thick as bloody thieves. Been giving you some tips, has she, how to get away from your husband. Stupid bitch, telling us all how sad she is and what a crap husband Dad is, when all the time she's shagging his best mate."

So it was as I had suspected, it was Dave. I wasn't shocked, more surprised, that she had denied it to me and then admitted it to Curtis. "Did she admit that to you herself?" I asked.

"She didn't need to. When I got there, she was arguing with Dad and just stormed out. She put loads of stuff in her car and when I asked, she just said she had found a little flat somewhere."

"Well, then, that doesn't prove anything. I thought you were all for her leaving your dad. You said to me he was boring and miserable and she would be happier without him, so why all this, don't you want her to be happy?" I sat next to him on the bed and relented, putting my arm round his shoulder and pulling him toward me. It was hardly a shock that she had left John but it was obviously hitting Curtis a lot harder than I'd imagined. I found myself wondering if it'd been my parents would I be this upset.

He calmed down slightly now and continued… "Yes of course I want her to be happy, and Dad's made her life a misery for years, but after she had gone, Steven told me what he had heard. He shouted downstairs to me to put the kettle on and filled me in on what he had heard. Dad shouted at her, calling her a whore, a cheat and a home wrecker. He even said she was a terrible mother and that he was proved right about his suspicions all along. Y'know, about the Dave thing. Then, then, he even threw some of her stuff at her."

Curtis held his head in his hands while he took a breath and wiped his face on his sleeve. So, I spoke in the pause. "I know, love," I started, with my arm still around him ,"but we did think maybe there was someone else. And I know it's not very nice, both families are going to be affected, but if they love each other and want to be together, surely it's better than living a lie." I knew who I'd rather spend my life with, I thought to myself.

"That's not what I'm mad about." He raised his voice again, making me withdraw my arm from round him. "You have no idea, Ellie. Typical, you're all the same, you women. You're probably just like her, deceitful, lying, cheating treating your husbands like they are as thick as shit." He stood up, his voice getting slowly louder, his speech faster and, opening his eyes wide, he stared at me as if I were the one having an affair and practically screamed, "TEN YEARS... ten bloody years she's been sleeping with Dave behind Dad's back. And Sue, don't forget her. How did he not see this? How did he not suspect? How did we not know? I didn't know... Did you, Ellie?" He paused but barely long enough for me to draw breath, let alone say anything. "Did you know? I bet you've known all along, haven't you, in on her dirty secret, were you? Answer me, Ellie." He was now leaning down, shaking me by my shoulders as I still sat on the bed.

I just started to cry. I felt... Well, I don't even know how I felt. Even though I suspected Dave... Ten years. Ten years, I just was in shock. It kind of felt like a betrayal, even to me. I thought we were close and she told me everything. It seemed to put a whole new dimension on the infidelity. Now we were both crying and hugging each other. After a couple of quiet minutes, we agreed to go back downstairs and put the kettle on. Have a calm conversation about what we knew and what to do next. Steven, it seemed, had heard quite a bit about the longevity of the affair, during the exchanges between his parents and had heard it from his own mum's mouth that it started about ten years ago.

Curtis was a wreck. The more we talked the more realisation of what had been happening behind their backs for all these years. The betrayal of his mother to him absolutely infuriated him the most. He talked and talked and cried in-between as it all dawned on him. The family holidays they had had with Dave and Sue. The weekends away, the nights out. Oh my God, the six weeks his mum had spent abroad visiting her sister and family. Dave had shown up there for a week saying he was on business close by. Stella had even shown photos with Dave on them as if it were just an amazing coincidence that he was there. Curtis was beside himself with anger. Besides making a mockery of her marriage he was really struggling with the fact that his wonderful, kind, generous, beautiful mother had lied to him for the past ten years. He loved her unconditionally and thought they had a very close mother-son bond. This level of betrayal had broken him totally.

Two cups of tea and almost two hours later, going around in circles, he was spent. He went to lay down on the sofa and just looked like he was in a daze. Eyes open, staring into the middle distance, but I knew the cogs in his head were working overtime.

Chapter 5

We both went back to work after our non-honeymoon and the weeks started to hurry by. Our DIY kitchen was complete and we were very happy with our efforts. The only thing we couldn't afford to replace was the washing machine. An automatic was a little out of our budget, and anyway, the twin tub, which was my mother's previously, worked fine.

Curtis was still stewing over his mother's revelations but we didn't seem to talk about it much. He had made it clear to me that it just rocked his trust in women and that didn't exclude me. He was already possessive and jealous but this had just added suspicious to the list. Thankfully my current job, in a small bridal shop in the nearby town, was acceptable to him. I had only three colleagues and they were all women. Other than work, I wasn't allowed to go anywhere alone. He would ask me if I needed to go anywhere without him and made me feel like I was the wrongdoer if I wanted to spend time without him. It just wasn't worth the aggravation so I just played ball with his insecurities. Many weekends we would visit my family. Usually on a Sunday, as we could incorporate a Sunday lunch, which was always a bonus. I wasn't allowed to call in and see them on my own and, as much as him dictating to me what I could and couldn't do was annoying, I really didn't feel the need to see my parents more often than we did. I loved them very much, undoubtedly, but being at theirs wasn't exactly drama central. Boring and predictable was a more accurate description.

Although, just recently, my brother's wife had just up and left him. That was a shock. They had only been married for eighteen months and there had been no tell-tale signs. My mum was really upset and worried about him. He had just gone quiet and hadn't been round to see them for weeks. He was her favourite child, of this I was sure, and I felt sorry for her and for my brother too, but also, I couldn't help thinking inside that, *Jesus, this was just another shitty wife fuelling Curtis' thought process*. He already tarred us all with the same brush.

By the by we spent most of our spare time with friends. Going out for drinks on a Saturday night, eating out or even them coming around to ours for an evening. Even with our friends, though, I had learned to keep all males of any description at arm's length. Not to make eye contact for too long, no general harmless touching and certainly not to be in a room alone with any bloke. The three exceptions to this rule were my dad, his dad and my brother. These were all unspoken rules but, nonetheless, rules that would have consequences if not adhered to.

We had some really great friends and always had a laugh and a good time when we saw them. Curtis' behaviour when we were with friends was impeccable. He was the perfect husband. Loving, complementary and really great fun. No one would have guessed his personality behind closed doors. So early on in our marriage I just accepted all this as 'our way of life'. As long as I played my part, stuck to all the rules, I knew just how to make Curtis happy and keep him happy. I knew what to tell him and what to keep to myself. I knew that all the rules didn't apply to him, he was the dictator in this relationship and best I didn't forget it.

We had been married for little over six months. Christmas had been and gone and it was a cold dark January evening. Curtis was always home about an hour before me and tonight, as I walked in, I felt the warmth from our new gas fire. It wasn't actually brand new but my dad had bought it second-hand for us as a wedding present. He knew that Curtis was useless at making the coal fire we originally had in the house and this gift was, I'm sure, to make my life easier. Curtis would sit in the cold and wait for me to get home to make the fire. He would not scrape around in the coal bunker for coal and he couldn't make paper sticks to save his life. All these skills I had learned from my dad. The gas fire was an absolute blessing.

"Hi," called Curtis. I took off my coat, scarf, gloves and boots and went to kneel down in front of the fire. I rubbed my hands together and was just about to ask what he fancied for tea when he came out with, "I've decided we are going to have our first baby now!" He said it like he was actually deciding what to have for tea. "So, when your period is finished, that's it. We will get going. I have thrown your pills away. I reckon we could have a baby before Christmas this year."

"Wow... Well, not how I thought this conversation would go but... Yeah fine. In fact, great. Fantastic, let's do it." I was a bit peeved that it had, in fact, not actually even been a conversation, more an order but, hey, why should that be a surprise. I was happy, though, as having a family was my absolute dream. The most important thing in the world to me and Curtis knew I would not want to go back to work after giving birth. We had in the past discussed this and he was happy for me to be a stay-at-home mum.

"Are you sure we can afford to live on your wages alone if we start a family now?" I asked.

"No, but if we wait 'til we think we can afford it, we'll never do it. It's what we planned all along. So, let's enjoy making a baby and start the family we have dreamed of for almost five years." He smiled and sat beside me on the rug. "Let's have a takeaway and a bottle of wine to celebrate, shall we?" he suggested, whilst nuzzling my neck. I laughed and agreed. I couldn't wait to be pregnant.

Luckily, I didn't have to, either. My next period never arrived and after we counted three weeks overdue, I decided to make an appointment at the doctors.

"What will they do?" Curtis asked me.

"Dunno," I replied truthfully. "Maybe a urine

sample or a blood sample. It's all new to me, never been pregnant before," I giggled.

"Mmm… Well we can go together one evening after work. Don't want some doctor thinking it's all right to have his hands all over you." This comment made my heart beat quicken. I knew if I commented negatively on this it would only provoke an argument so I had to think before I spoke. The thought of Curtis kicking off in the doctor's surgery filled me with dread. I hatched a little plan. "Okay, I will call the surgery and make an appointment for us," I said with the right amount of excitement to convince him I would do just that.

"Great, not on a football training night though, eh?" Curtis was getting more and more involved with football and really enjoyed coaching the kid's local teams.

"Okay," I replied. I knew he would be taking a bath; this was regular practice on a non-football night. I would get dinner ready while he had the first bath, making sure he had a full tank of hot water. Then, after tea, I would top up the bath water with the kettle. Yes, I know, I know, but really it was just easier and I had fallen into this routine. Submissive wife keeps unpredictable-tempered husband happy. So, while he was running the bath, I phoned the surgery, and this was how it went.

"Good afternoon, Doctors Group Practice."

"Oh, hi, yes, I would like to make an appointment,

please, to see my doctor for a pregnancy test."

"Okay, let me have a look." I heard quick page-turning noises. "How about tomorrow at eleven thirty a.m.?"

"Thank you, that sounds great, my name is Ellie Parson." I continued to give her the rest of my details, thanked her again and hung up. I waited for a few seconds to be sure the receptionist had hung up and then leaned over to open the door to the stairs. Then, raising my voice enough for Curtis to hear, I said, "Oh really, so if I just drop off the urine sample into the reception tomorrow and that's all I need to do, brilliant. Well, thank you very much for your help, bye."

I replaced the receiver, more loudly this time, and made my way upstairs to tell Curtis about the appointment. Predictably he was already hanging over the top of the stairs smiling at me. "So, I suppose you heard all that?" I asked.

"Yeah, yeah I did, that's great, so you can just drop a sample in tomorrow? Good job it's your day off." We hugged and held each other tightly. "Oh God, Ellie, let's hope it's positive. I love you so much having a baby is just gonna be the best news ever." He gave my tummy a little excited pat and kissed me hard on the mouth.

The next morning, I handed him his packed lunch, gave him a kiss and bid him goodbye. "So, you're dropping off the sample and then coming straight back home. Remember all the old wallpaper still needs scraping off the bathroom wall. I will call you later."

I just knew he would ring the house phone whenever he got the chance, whether it was from the office at work or whether he would use a phone box out and about. His present job was with a marketing company and, as much as he didn't really like it, it paid the mortgage. So until he landed a job at the city gym, which a mate was instigating on his behalf, it would have to do. Curtis had had a number of jobs since he left school, due mainly to his arrogance and temper. It wasn't that he didn't work hard, more that he wasn't really good at taking orders from anyone at work, or anywhere for that matter. Diplomacy was not something Curtis possessed. He was a very narcissistic person, add that to someone who thinks they are never wrong, and, hey presto, you got Curtis. This led to many a disagreement and alpha male behaviour at work.

He was, however, very forthcoming with his feelings towards me. He would always profess his undying love on a daily basis. Constantly saying he was the luckiest guy in the world, and how he couldn't live without me. I loved him too. He always made me feel special and said he was nothing without me. I was now so used to our way of life and, as time went on, I just got so good at being me, the wife Curtis wanted and needed. It all seemed so normal.

The doctor's appointment went well, he told me to come back in three days for the results. That would be a Friday so I asked if we could both come after work at about six p.m. He said he could make me his last appointment at 5:50 p.m. Great, I thought, but I had then realized he might mention to Curtis that we had the appointment on the Tuesday. So, on Tuesday evening, I had told Curtis that I'd bumped into the doctor in the reception while handing in my sample and that we spoke briefly to decide on an appointment for Friday. Dishonest, some might say, but trust me, my dishonesty was frequent and necessary for us to have a normal married life.

There was only one person (although we had never had a discussion of any kind about Curtis or our marriage) who actually felt like an ally, that was Simon. Simon had been Curtis' best man. They had met a couple of years ago through Simon's girlfriend, who worked in the office at the same company as Curtis. Angie was a lovely girl and Curtis met her boyfriend quite by chance in the car park one day. They had all had a coffee together and the rest was history, as they say. The four of us became firm friends and we socialised with them on most weekends, whether it be going out to eat or staying in at ours for dinner, drinks and a bit of telly.

On the Thursday, during my lunch hour, I literally bumped into Simon as I stepped out of the Mothercare shop. It was only a few shops further down from where I worked and, even though I hadn't had my pregnancy confirmed yet, I was just loitering around the newborn section in there, as you do... We bumped shoulders slightly as I misjudged the step out.

"Hey, you," he said with a smile. "How's things? Sorry we missed you last weekend, Angie had a bad migraine, not much fun, as you can imagine, but, hey, what have you got planned for this Saturday evening? There's a new wine bar in town do you fancy a look?"

"Aww, poor Angie," I said. Having never suffered a migraine and being the kind of person that just got on with it whatever the circumstances, I really thought it was a poor excuse. Nevertheless, I made all the right noises. "Yeah, sounds great," I replied.

At the same time as I said this, Simon looked behind me to acknowledge the nature of the shop I was exiting. His eyes widened and he had a big cheesy grin on his face. "Whoa, wait a minute, are you... Is there something you want to share?" He held out his arms like he was going in for the congratulatory hug.

I immediately put a hand up to stop him, fighting for the right words to stop any public displays of ANY kind of affection. Way too risky in public. "Well, not really, not just yet, anyway."

"Oh my God," he said excitedly. "What's that supposed to mean, tell me, come on, what's the score?"

"Look, let's not stand here," I said, looking around all the time for unsuspecting tell-tales that may know Curtis.

"OK, come on, I've got time for a quick coffee if you have," he offered.

I chose the darkest coffee shop around; one I'd never been in and slunk into the table right at the back.

Simon was such a lovely guy, we had a really nice chat and I explained we were getting test results tomorrow.

"Shall we pop round tomorrow night then?" he asked.

"God, no," I chirped up rapidly, "and have to tell Curtis that we saw each other today? What, are you trying to do get me locked in the house?" I laughed.

"Oh yeah, course, I forgot for a minute then... Ha ha, Mr Jealous would put two and two together and get five hundred, eh!"

"Oh, you know him so well," I laughed through my teeth whilst rolling my eyes upwards.

"Tell you what, why don't I ring him about football practice tonight and then if we have a quick pint afterwards, we can arrange to go to the new wine bar."

"Sounds like a plan. Thanks for being an understanding mate," I said. Simon squeezed my forearm gently and gave me a knowing look. "Right, back to work for me," I said. "Oh, and don't tell Angie about the..." I touched my tummy. "Wouldn't want you both to have to fake a surprised look."

"Mum's the word," he said and laughed at his own pun. "You go on ahead, I will leave in two minutes to save you having to ask me to." Now he rolled his eyes. I smiled at him.

Results day and we were both really excited to be rushing home in time for our 5.50 p.m. appointment. When we arrived, there was one gentleman still waiting to be seen by my doctor. We still, however, managed to be in and out by ten past six. The doctor confirmed the pregnancy and with me knowing the last period dates he gave us a due date of October twenty-seventh, but told us to expect it anytime around the end of October / beginning of November.

We thanked him for everything and went home to discuss the exciting news, all the things he said we would need to think about the main one, of course, being our choice of hospital to give birth. We went home and I stayed in the kitchen to put the kettle on. Curtis looked at me with wide, excited, happy eyes. "Oh, Ellie, I can't tell you how happy I am." He hugged me in a proper strong bear hug and kissed me all over my face and neck. "How lucky are we, we're going to start our own little family this year and everything is gonna be just perfect. I love you so much, you are my world, Ellie, I am the happiest man alive." He had tears in his eyes and seemed really emotional, which was lovely and I loved him so much when he was this version of himself.

I, on the other hand, was happy but nervous in equal measure. We would have a few months to wait to find out that everything was fine and perfect. I was little pessimistic maybe, but a work colleague of mine, last year, had a baby with a really bad cleft palate and a large facial birth mark. I know these are not life threatening but, nonetheless, a shock when the baby arrives, if you have no idea. I would be happy when the baby was in my arms, safe and sound.

"And... Guess what else I found out today?" He

paused for effect. But looked excited.

"Tell me, tell me… What?"

"Tony called me earlier, he's only gone and secured me the job at the gym." He was grinning from ear to ear.

"That's amazing, Curtis. Congratulations, how fab. I'm so happy for you… For us… All three of us." I touched my tummy.

"I know, and the money is great, much more than I get in this wanky job. And I start next month so we will have loads of time to save up for all the things we need for the baby. It will be spoilt and you won't need to go back to work at all, I know you wanted to be at home… It's all gonna work out just perfectly." This all came out at a hundred miles an hour, with Curtis gesticulating wildly with his arms. He was well aware that I didn't want to go back to work. We had discussed it many times and the one thing I wanted more than anything else in life was to be able to stay at home with my children and not miss a thing. It would have been a struggle on Curtis' wage at the moment. Things were looking up.

Chapter 6

It was what felt like the middle of the hottest summer ever. Seven months pregnant and I was blossoming out everywhere. Still working full-time but now Curtis had allowed me the use of our clapped-out little car, it was much easier. He bought himself cheap moped and seemed happy with this. In fact, he seemed a lot happier all together these days, saying he loved me being pregnant, said it showed that I was taken and other men wouldn't look at me. Very shallow, I know, but he was happy so I was happy too.

Over the past few months we had done all the visiting — parents, grandparents, best friends — to tell everyone our wonderful news. My parents were happy for us, even though the raising of my mum's eyebrows and pursed lips expression made me think the real reaction she wanted to shout, out was, "Well, I hope you know what you've let yourself in for!"

My dad, on the other hand, was really happy. Happy that I was happy and said he couldn't wait to meet his first grandchild. He said all the right things to me, about how his life was complete and how lucky he was to have three wonderful children who were all safe and well. I just knew he was going to be the best grandad ever.

We took a fish and chip supper round to Curtis'
dad, to tell him the news. A completely different
reaction. "Well, I hope you can afford it, " were the first
words to leave his mouth. "Don't be coming around
here looking for handouts. I've got at least another ten
years before I retire and, the way things are at work right
now, looks like I will have to sell up and downsize."

"I think 'congratulations' was the word you were
looking for," spat Curtis. "We don't want any money
off you, thank you very much, I have a new job, not that
you'll be interested, so we will be just fine, thank you."

"Oh yeah, another new job, Curtis? How long will
this one last before you start losing your temper and
threatening the boss. I hope for Ellie's sake that this
baby coming will, if nothing else, make you grow up
and start acting like a responsible adult and hopefully
then you'll learn to respect other people."

The bickering session between Curtis and his father
continued, with Curtis throwing in the 'no wonder Mum
left you' card. I just sat open-mouthed as it all played
out. But secretly I was punching the air and awarding
ten points to John for saying what I wished I had the
guts to say. Not really paying too much attention to the
ongoing match, and even feeling a little smile creeping
onto my lips… Then, as quick as it started, it was over.
Curtis grabbed my hand and the Fish and Chips still
wrapped. "Come on, Ellie, we're off no point hanging
around here with Mr Happy, maybe Mum will be

happier for us." And with that we left. I managed a quick sideways glance at John that he knew meant 'sorry' and also 'good on ya' at the same time.

"Why did you say that?" I asked, whilst almost being dragged back to the car.

"What?" he replied.

"About your mum. We don't even speak to her. I thought you had done with her?"

"It's my mum and I will decide who we see and who we speak to. If Dad wants to be such a dick about everything, well, like I said, no wonder she left him. Jesus he's such a miserable twat."

We were silent driving back home in the car and, in the five minutes it took us to get home, Curtis had cooked up a little plan he was about to share with me. We ate most of the fish and chips, including the extra we had bought for John, and opened a bottle of wine (yes, having a glass of wine wasn't so frowned on in the 80s).

"Right, this is how we are going to play it," Curtis instructed. "You can telephone Mum, you will have to ring Steven first for her number. Tell him you're calling to tell them we're having a baby and then get Mum's number. If he says anything about me not speaking to her, just say you want the number because you think she has the right to know... Okay?"

I followed out all the instructions to Curtis' satisfaction and got Stella's number. Now I was receiving a new set of instructions as to the conversation

I was about to have with her.

"So, tell her you're ringing with good news, and say you really miss her, but make out like I'm not here and I don't know you are calling her. She's bound to be really happy to hear from you and she will probably start crying. So, let her blub a little and then tell her all our good news. Tell her about the baby first then tell her about my new job and then tell her about Dad being a dick. Then, if you can get a word in edgewise, (because, after all, Stella was a world-class talker) say that I would go mad if I knew you had done this behind my back but that you feel we should be trying to patch things up now there's a baby coming. She's bound to agree and want us in her life, so you can finish off by saying that you will try your best to talk me into making up."

This had all played out exactly as Curtis had predicted. She cried, filled me in on her circumstances at the moment, begged me to talk to Curtis so we could all be a family again, blah blah blah. Forty-five minutes later I said, "Ooh, Curtis has just pulled up outside, Stella, I've got to go. I'll be in touch." And I hung up.

So, Curtis, as always, got his own way. He was still angry with his mum, there was no denying that, but he missed her and his love for her was stronger than his anger. To be honest, I missed her too and, also, I missed seeing Dave. He was such a jolly, happy person to be around and, over the years, I'd become quite attached to him.

Tentatively, over the remainder of the summer, we

got back into a good relationship with Stella and Dave. The situation had totally reversed. We were now, according to Curtis, never going to speak to his father again. He said that it was my prerogative to make decisions that involved my parents and his prerogative where his family were concerned.

What he didn't know was that I called his dad once a week to make sure he was okay and to keep him up to date with things. I didn't lie to John, he knew how Curtis worked, so I let him know we were in contact with, and visiting, Stella and Dave. I said that I just did as I was told and John seemed to agree that that was the best thing for me to do. "Just you take care of yourself, Ellie," he always finished with and reminded me that, if I should ever need him, he would always be there for me and for this I was very grateful.

John had sold the marital home and was now a couple of miles away in a quiet village, in a lovely appointed bungalow. He seemed resigned to his single life and, though not 'shouting from the rooftops' happy, he was certainly getting on with his life. He assured me he was okay and this was how our weekly calls went. He knew I always called from a phone box, couldn't risk getting caught at home, so we only stayed on for a few minutes to catch up with each other.

Meanwhile, with Stella, Curtis had resumed his position of blue-eyed boy. He had also settled into a closer friendship with Dave. Dave had always called Curtis 'son', it was not an uncommon title for an older man to refer to a younger man, it just seemed to hold a little more weight in the dynamics of this new emerging family. Curtis had now done a full three-sixty, he was like a purring cat that rubbed up against your ankles, he couldn't seem to get enough of his mum. Though he still maintained that living a lie for ten years is the lowest of the low.

We had many a discussion over the dinner table, including everyone's opinions of the break-up, however, Stella was steadfast in her statement of not wanting to upset her two sons' family life and that was why she kept it a secret for so long. She was adamant about how none of us had any idea how bad it truly was living with John and should therefore respect her decisions.

Stella and Dave had both had their divorces finalised and they were now talking wedding plans. Looking at early next year if possible. They did a lot of traveling for Dave's work, much of it in India, and were discussing having a ceremony there. Dave was a very successful businessman and Stella was happy, right back in there, living the lifestyle she craved. They bought a cute bungalow out in the sticks and were very happy.

We did, on my insistence, try and visit my parents as often as we could. Whenever the opportunity presented itself, sometimes on a weeknight, we would pop down, especially during the summer months as it was much warmer and lighter in the evenings.

Curtis's new job was going great, he really seemed to love it. Never stopped talking all things training and exercise and this was carried over into the youngsters he took for football training. He was down to one night a week, though, now, as his new job had more unsociable hours, but, nonetheless, he put everything into the teenagers he trained and took it very seriously.

The two people we always made time for, though, were Simon and Angie. They were such good mates and we always had a good laugh when we were together. Sometimes a cheeky pub meal during the week, or, if we all had a spare evening, maybe tea at our house. But, if these failed, we almost always spent Saturday evenings together.

Late September, on a Saturday afternoon, I wasn't feeling too great. Getting bigger by the minute, I felt, but now backache seemed to be getting more regular and today had knocked me right off my feet. "Curtis, can we call Si and Angie and take a rain check on tonight, please? I really don't think I can be bothered to get ready to go out. My back is killing me."

He could see the pain in my face but I knew he really wanted to go out, and considering my feelings wasn't something he was familiar with. "For fuck's sake, Ellie, you're pregnant not ill," was his sympathetic reply.

" Well, you know what then, you go, coz really I can't, I've been on my feet all day at work and I just need to sit down."

He could see I was upset and in pain and relented by saying, "Okay, okay, I'll call Si and we can have a Chinese takeaway and a few beers at home instead. That do you?" I really could have done with an early night, but even the compromise to stay in I was grateful for. So I called them and made arrangements.

We had a lovely evening, considering how uncomfortable I felt, and during a minute when Curtis popped upstairs to the loo, Simon asked me if I was okay. "Yes," Angie agreed, "you look really pooped and in pain." She screwed her face in sympathy with me. "Why didn't you just get an early night and cancel altogether? We had no idea you were this bad."

"Oh, you know, a total cancellation could have proved even more painful," I laughed, raising my eyes to the upstairs.

"Yeah, we know," said Si, "but, listen, we will make our excuses and be out of your hair early, so don't worry."

"Oh, you're a gem, thanks," I said. And, true to their word, they cried off just before ten o'clock on the pretence that Angie had a bad headache. They would usually stay well past midnight, so ten was good for me.

"Oh, you two, a right pair of lightweights," half-joked Curtis. "Well, I'm having another drink."

"Ha ha, yeah you do that, bud," replied Simon. "Let Ellie get some rest, though, you don't want to put the baby at risk if she's not feeling well."

"Yeah, don't worry, guys, I'll look after her," he

said, pulling my head over towards him and kissing the top of my head, which really didn't help the pain in my back. I winced and so did Simon and Angie. I sucked the air in through my gritted teeth and rolled my eyes.

Sunday morning and still no respite from the back pain. Curtis, his usual sensitive side shining through, called me a 'killjoy' because I didn't feel up to visiting his mum and Dave. "You get yourself off there if the prospect of spending a day at home fills you with that much dread," I commented, with an edge of sarcasm. To be perfectly honest, I would get more rest and peace and quiet if he was out of the way. If he stayed at home, he would expect me to cook for him and I really wasn't up to it.

"I will," was his decision, "no point spoiling my weekend too, eh?"

"Yeah," I laughed. God forbid Curtis would have to share my suffering in any way.

"Tell you what, I will ask Mum to plate you a dinner and then when I get back you can warm it in the oven." I noticed he said 'you' can warm it in the oven. All heart, was my husband.

On Monday, although my back felt slightly better, there was still a twinge and I took a big decision to take the day off work. This was the first sick day I had ever had so it was new territory for me, but I felt another rest day would be a lot more beneficial than being on my feet all day. Curtis said he would go out later and get a chippy dinner for tonight's tea, which I supposed was something. Not that it had occurred to him to get up and make his sandwiches to take to work that morning. He just said how I shouldn't go to too much trouble so he would just have cheese today instead of cheese and pickle. His cup of thoughtfulness overflowed.

I spent most of the day horizontal on the sofa. No daytime television in those days but I had a book that I was reading, recommended by a colleague from work. She had said it was like a baby Bible and every expectant mother should read it. *Dr Spock's Baby and Childcare* was the title, originally published in 1946, but had had countless revised editions, year after year. I was really impressed, I have to say. I did attend all my antenatal classes and read every leaflet I was ever given from any doctor or midwife but this book had details you couldn't even imagine. I was so happy to be getting nearer to the baby's birth. I had experienced a brilliant pregnancy so far, even with the back pain, no morning sickness, nothing.

I took a tentative stroll to the kitchen, late morning, to make a cup of tea and, whilst leaning on my elbows on the worktop waiting for the kettle to boil, trying to find the most comfortable position to stand, there was a little tap on the back door. As I looked up, slowly the door opened to show me Simon's cheeky little face, smiling but with a sympathetic grimace across it at the same time.

"Hiya, mate," he almost whispered. "How's it going?" I laughed and thought what a complete mess I must look, hair unbrushed, baggy pyjamas and standing there the size of a beached whale.

"Don't think I really need to answer that, do I, Simon, just look at me, I really don't know whether to laugh or cry." And as I said this, a few tears squeezed from my eyes.

"Aww, Ellie, stop it, you look amazing. You're, what, five weeks from having your baby and have a bad back. You're going to be fine, don't worry, come on," he said and walked across the kitchen to give me an awkward hug. The kettle started to boil, the whistling getting louder and louder. "All right, all right," joked Simon, looking across on the kettle on the gas cooker. "I'm coming, I get the message."

I went to wipe my tears on the sleeve of my pyjamas and ask Simon if he had time to stay for a cuppa. "Truthfully, not really, mate, I'm actually working on a job further up in the village but I'm not about to leave you like this. I was just passing and Angie got this for you this morning." He waved an envelope in front of me. "She knew I was passing so she wanted to get this card to you." He handed it to me. "I was going to post it but I saw your car in the drive. So you go and get yourself comfy and open this, and I will make us a brew." I did as he said and while we were sat having a cuppa, we got into a conversation about my back pain. The card from Angie and Si was a blank card inside, with flowers on the front but she had written a lovely message inside…

Dear Ellie
hope you are feeling better
hang on in there, mate
not long to go now
if there's anything we can do to help
please you only have to ask
lots of love Angie and Si xxxx

"Wait till Angie knows you've taken a sick day," laughed Simon. "She will pass out, I'm sure. She knows you never take time off, even if you are ill."

"I know, I know, but honestly, Si, the pain, it shoots from my back and down my right leg. I feel like I'm going to just collapse sometimes and I'm worried I will fall and hurt the baby."

"Can't you go to the doctors?" he asked

"Well, I asked at my last antenatal class and they say back ache is normal during pregnancy, so I didn't want to make a fuss." I shrugged my shoulders.

"To be honest, Ellie, the way you describe the pain, it sounds the same as my mum had last year. She had sciatica and was in agony. The only thing that helped were some exercises I remember her doing. I used to help her with them, wait till you finished your cuppa and I will show you," he offered.

He really wasn't able to stay too long, I realised that, but he quickly showed me how to lay flat on my back and bending my right knee up, push it over my straight leg as far as possible and hold. He explained how sciatica was a trapped nerve and doing this as often as possible would help to open the joints in the lower back and, hopefully, un-trap the nerve that was causing the problem. I was willing to try anything on while it was a little awkward, of course, I was going to keep trying throughout the day.

Simon shot off and said to tell Curtis that if we didn't see them in the week, he would definitely be at football on Friday night. "Right you are," I said and thanked him again full the card and the exercise tips. I kept trying the exercises all day and they really started to help. Simon had helped to put the pressure on my bent leg when he showed me and that made a big difference, so I was hoping Curtis would be up for giving it a go when he got home.

Funny, but it never crossed my mind it would be a problem that Simon had called round. Since I had been pregnant, Curtis had not been half as bad as he usually was. He seemed more relaxed and the past few months had gone by without incident or even any arguments. Anyway, I knew Curtis didn't see Simon as a threat. We were such good friends, the four of us, and, besides, I'm sure Curtis felt that Simon was not any kind of competition. He was a good five inches shorter than Curtis and physically nowhere near as muscular and not generally interested in his outward appearance.

Curtis was nothing short of being in love with himself, he was very handsome with a body that was the envy of most of his male friends. Now he was working at the gym he was undoubtedly pumping weights at every opportunity. He couldn't walk past a shop window without checking himself out, not to mention the time he spent flexing his muscles in every mirror in the house. He had recently bought a full-length mirror to put at the top of the stairs, facing the long hallway, so he could see himself from top to bottom. I just let him get on with it, it wasn't hurting me, as long as he was happy, which he seemed to be these days.

I heard the sound of his motorbike coming up the driveway and walked over to the window to wave, he jumped off his bike and waved and smiled as he wandered over to speak to the new neighbours. He made a 'T' sign with his hands to me, which I knew meant put the kettle on. I smiled back and rolled my eyes and made my way to the kitchen.

About three or four minutes later, Curtis came through the back door with a face like thunder, he slammed the door behind him and hissed through gritted teeth. "Just been talking to the lovely new neighbours, guess what? They were waiting for the builder to turn up today and he never even showed up." Where the hell was he going with this, I thought, surely that can't be my fault.

So, I shrugged my shoulders and said, "And?"

"And… I'll tell you what 'and', Ellie… And they said they thought he had actually arrived earlier than planned, eleven fifteen this morning, but no… No… Ellie." He was shouting now. "They were mistaken, that was the builder that came around here! Ringing any bells now, Ellie?" he shouted.

"Oh, that was Simon," I said, a little relieved. "He was in the work van, he came by to drop off a card from him and Angie, but obviously I was in so he popped in for a cuppa." I was just about to get the card from the front room to show Curtis and said, "Look, let me show you the—" And that's as far as I got when he grabbed me literally by the throat. He was holding my throat with one hand and pointing an inch from my face with the other.

"What the fuck was he doing here for more than half an hour, according to our lovely new neighbours?"

"Are you for real?" I screamed. "Jesus Christ, it was Simon, what do you mean 'what the fuck'? What the fuck… Yourself." I couldn't believe this reaction at all.

"Don't be smart with me, Ellie." And with this, he pushed me backwards into the door, slammed the back of my head against the door and tightened the hand on my throat. This made it very difficult to talk, also, with the shock of what was happening, my mind was racing. I couldn't decide if I was more scared or angry.

He put his mouth right next to my ear and slowly and quietly said, "I've seen the way he looks at you, he might be able to fool everyone else but I am not a fool. Just because you are pregnant…" And now his voice was all sweet and sarcastic sounding. "Oh, poor Curtis, won't have a clue what's going on, best cover in the world being pregnant. Oh, and his best friend and best man, no, Curtis will never suspect. DO NOT insult my intelligence, Ellie, so help me God, you will both live to regret it if I find anything has been going on here."

With this last outburst, he let go of my throat and said, "Go on, then, tell me, why was he here, what did he have to say, what did you do for more than half an hour?"

I was totally speechless, in shock and angry. I was gasping for air and panting loudly holding my throat that was really painful. "You fucking idiot, Curtis, don't even come near me and do not speak to me," I stammered through my tears. I dragged myself upstairs, locked myself in the bathroom and sat on the toilet seat.

What on earth had just happened? It felt like some person had broken into my home and attacked me. I sat in the bathroom for ages. I just sobbed and sobbed. Here I was about to have a baby, and this abuse was starting all over again.

Chapter 7

Only moments after his outburst, Curtis had taken off on his motorbike. I slowly made my way downstairs after waiting for about twenty minutes, nervously I walked into the kitchen checking to make sure he had actually gone. I put the kettle on to make myself a coffee, with mixed emotions running wildly inside me. I felt sad, angry and even deflated.

Just while I was holding my head in my hands the phone rang and made me jump almost out of my skin. It was Stella, saying that Curtis had just turned up at their house in tears. "Good," I said. "Tell him to fucking stop there if he knows what's good for him." He would have obviously told her what had happened but Stella was well aware of her son's misgivings and probably realised she was getting his version of events. I told her the absolute truth of the situation and she was deeply apologetic on his behalf. I didn't really want her to be apologising for him. "Do you know what, Stella, just have a word, would you, because this cannot carry on." I implied that even an apology from him would just not cut it this time, he had better have a serious think about his actions. She said he could stay there but only for one night. I was thankful for this at that time.

I returned to work the next morning, it wasn't really polo neck jumper weather, but in light of the fact that my neck was covered in marks from the previous day, I didn't really have any choice. I was not in the mood to have to explain this to anyone. It was bad enough that my eyes were still a bit red and swollen without everyone seeing what they would assume were marks caused by Curtis, and be correct in their assumptions. I tried to keep busy, which stopped me from dwelling on the state of my marriage. I felt out of my depth and, being on the brink of starting a family, I just felt trapped without a get-out scenario.

Wednesday evening and Curtis returned as if nothing had happened, the atmosphere was cloudy to say the least and, even though I had said an apology wouldn't fix it, I was still waiting for one. I wasn't really speaking to him and trying to avoid him as much as possible but he was chatting to me like he had done nothing wrong. This was how it continued almost until the weekend, thank God for work.

My back had improved enormously over the few days, and when Simon rang to see if we fancied a meal out on Saturday evening, Curtis accepted without a second thought and without even consulting me. Jesus, he was so infuriating. I was too embarrassed to share with anyone what had happened and time just carried on, as it does, and we went to the new rib diner that Simon and Angie had invited us to. The evening was very pleasant, Curtis acted like nothing was wrong and, although a little quieter than normal, I didn't arouse any suspicion. I suppose, at eight months pregnant, I could get away with a little moodiness. "How's your back pain?" Simon asked me. "Did you keep doing the exercises?"

I swallowed hard, remembering the attack I suffered and Curtis jumped in, quickly replying, "Oh yes, mate, she's a lot better, thanks, aren't you, Ellie? Thanks to the exercises that you showed her, they were brilliant, Si, thanks. We are really grateful, eh, Ellie?" I just nodded and tried to smile belying feelings of anxiousness pulsing through me.

"Yes, I did continue to do them, Simon, and it helped a lot, thanks. I'm glad you stopped by on Monday morning." I made a swift side glance in Curtis' direction and he knew exactly what it meant. "And thanks for the lovely card, Angie, it's nice to know your friends really do care." I gave her arm a little squeeze. The weight of my comment wasn't wasted, judging by the sheepish look on Curtis' face.

Seeing out my last two weeks at work was pretty mundane, to say the least. I was feeling very heavy and very tired but, on the last day of work, I was celebrating my twenty-first birthday. This definitely was the highlight of the week. My work colleagues had a bottle of champagne and some fresh orange juice on ice and we planned a quiet drink and some nibbles after work.

This should have been a Saturday but we`d planned it to the Monday as Saturday was always a busy day.

Curtis was at work anyway and, being my actual birthday, I decided to spend it with my workmates. We had a laugh and talked all things babies. I had two weeks until my due date and I was really, really excited. The girl who had left work to have her baby came in to have a drink with us and said the actual birth was like shelling peas. Debbie, the oldest member of staff, who had two teenage children spat her bucks fizz all over the place in response to this comment and we all duly fell about laughing. "I'll reserve judgment on that for now," I piped up, "but I will come in and let you know how shelling peas feels."

I left work early that day and, with Curtis working late, I had told him I was going to have tea that evening at my mum and dad's. Notice I say 'told' him. Without ever getting an apology from Curtis, and the matter never having been spoken of since, we seemed to settle back into a familiar routine although he did seem a little sheepish at times. I wondered if Stella had actually given him a proper bollocking the day he stayed there. I just hoped this had been the case.

Mum and Dad had bought me some lovely birthday gifts and Mum made me a really nice birthday cake. We had a cosy evening in and talked baby names. I said we had picked two boys names and two girls names and when we met the baby we were going to choose then. I had a shower at theirs before I left as we only had a bath and it was almost nine p.m. I didn't fancy the struggle in and out of the bath, at home alone. The past week,

Curtis had had to help me in and out of the bath as I was huge. Dad tapped on the bathroom door to check I was okay. "Yeah, good thanks. Lovely to have a shower again," I laughed. "But I can't reach to dry my legs and feet, don't suppose you could do the honours, after all, it is my birthday."

"What have I been saying for years? That I will still be drying your legs when you're twenty-one, and look, here I am. I didn't really think it would come true." We laughed in unison.

"Thanks, Dad, you're the best, I love you."

"I love you too, Ellie," he replied.

I was at home, tucked up in bed by ten p.m. Curtis have given me a beautiful gold, heart-shaped locket for my birthday. He had put a small photo of us in either side. We had had breakfast together and I left him something in the fridge to have when he got home.

The gym didn't close until ten p.m. on weeknights and, although they rotated who worked late, it seemed to me that Curtis did more than his fair share. However, he didn't complain so why would I. He never worked late on Friday evenings as it was football training and he never missed that.

I felt him slip into bed although I didn't know what time it was and we cuddled up together him nuzzling the side of my neck. He had made a point of nuzzling my neck often these days as if he were kissing better the damage he'd caused. Nonetheless, it wasn't mentioned. The next thing I knew I was rudely awakened by a sharp stabbing pain in my upper belly. "Ouch," I said, sitting up abruptly.

"What, what is it?"

"Aww, ouch. I don't know. That was a really sharp pain."

Curtis just sat up and turned on the bedside lamp. "Christ, Ellie, it's only just turned four in the morning. Go back to sleep, I'm knackered."

"Oh, well you go back to sleep, then. If the baby's coming, I'll drive myself to the hospital, shall I? Don't worry I'll call you and let you know what it is," I retorted in an angry manner.

"Stop overreacting, Ellie, you've got two weeks to go yet and that's if you're lucky. Didn't they say at the antenatal class that the first baby is usually late, even up to two weeks?"

"Oh yeah," I snapped, "well perhaps the baby didn't hear that PAAAART." I yelled out as another pain stabbed through me.

"Maybe it's a bit of heartburn you're having. What did you eat yesterday? Did you have too much to drink, seeing as though it was your birthday?"

"Maybe you should quit with all the suggestions, Curtis. Heartburn! Do me a favour and shut up."

I got out of bed, turned on the main light and looked around for the small suitcase I was going to pack this week. I hadn't bothered to get my hospital bag ready, knowing I had two weeks or possibly more to kill after I had left work. "What are you doing? Turn the bloody light off," snapped Curtis. "Some of us were at work till late."

"Some of us are having a fucking baby," I yelled, and started throwing anything I could remember into the bag. Both the pains I had experienced were like nothing I had ever felt before. I had had friends talk about crippling period pains but I had never really suffered with any problems regarding my periods. I had not had any morning sickness at all and had enjoyed the whole pregnancy experience (minus the back pain), until now, that was! Surely it doesn't hurt this much, this early, I asked myself.

I found the phone number I'd being given to call the maternity hospital. Can't hurt to call and ask, I thought. I looked at the clock on the mantelpiece: 4:23 a.m. I made the call and gave all my details. Then answered questions fired at me. No, my waters hadn't broken. And then, all of a sudden, another pain seared through me. I kept hold of the phone but knelt on the floor trying to pant through the pain. When it subsided the woman on the other end of the phone said, "Good girl, Ellie, well done, sounds like you may be in very early labour, or it could be a false alarm, given your due date. So, what I need you to do is make a note of the times of all the pains."

False alarm… Early labour… The thought of this getting progressively more painful, and over God knows how many more hours, just totally filled me with fear. "So don't come to the hospital, then?" I asked, with a noticeable waver in my voice.

"Not at this stage, no, but, as I said, keep a note of each pain and how long they last and that will be a good indication for us. We can make a decision at five thirty to save you having to come in and go home again." What was she talking about come in and then go home. "Ellie, are you alone?"

"No, my lazy bastard husband is in bed cos he thinks I have heartburn," I almost shouted at her.

"Okay, that's good," she cooed, as if I had said he is here stroking my back. "Call us back in one hour and let's take it from there." Then she hung up and I replaced the receiver at my end.

"Un-be-liveable," I said under my breath. "UN-FUCKING-BELIEVABLE," I almost screamed. Curtis opened the door from the stairs with my bag in his hand. I had struggled downstairs with it but dumped it at the foot of the stairs.

"What's happening, then? You okay?"

"Yeah fine, me, yeah, I'm just fine. Got to sit here for an hour and see how much pain I can suffer and then call back."

"Oh, okay, that's good, then. Put the kettle on, may as well have a brew now you've woken us up, eh?"

"Put it on yourself. I am going to get dressed, bloody woman doesn't know what she's on about, bet she's just a receptionist," I muttered under my breath as I headed for the stairs.

I was getting dressed, having a wash, cleaning my

74

teeth and then remembered to take my toothbrush and toothpaste downstairs to put in my bag. On my way back downstairs, there it came again. "Yeoow!" I shouted, squeezing the handrail in one hand and the toothbrush and toothpaste in the other. I slowly lowered myself down to sit on the stairs. "Curtis!" I yelled, panting from holding my breath through the pain. "Quick, look at the time on the clock and come and help me downstairs."

"4:55," he said, as he offered me his arm for support. "Is it really that painful?"

"No, course not, darling, I just thought I'd milk the attention. Course it is, you idiot, fetch me a hammer let me break all your fingers and see if that hurts."

"All right, sarky, no need to take it out on me. Here, come and sit down and have a cup of tea, it might make you feel a bit better."

"Curtis, I don't want a cup of tea and this won't get better, it's just going to get worse, surely even you know that?" I slumped on the sofa and just stared at the clock. Just sitting, waiting for the next pain. It felt like forever but at 5:28 I could feel it. It was here.

Curtis looked at little afraid as I bent over and swore loudly through gritted teeth. The second it started to subside I picked up the phone, called the hospital again and told them the times of the pains then said we were on our way. I didn't wait for a two-way conversation. This baby was coming. It was in my body. I felt it and I knew it was coming. "Curtis, get dressed and let's get going," I instructed. He ran upstairs and came back with his kit bag that he used for work.

He picked up my bag and said, "Come on, then, let's go." He smiled like he was about to win a prize. I was terrified and secretly hoped it would all be over in a couple of hours. Shelling peas, eh. Well let's see. Then my fears about the baby being okay came flooding back. *Oh God, I hope it's all right please let it be perfect.* We set off and the fear of the unknown washed over me. I felt shaky and emotional.

Chapter 8

It was absolutely pitch-black outside as we sped along the deserted roads towards the city. Not having suffered another pain yet, my mind started racing through thoughts that I didn't want to think. What if I'm being a total wuss and it's only a false alarm? Does it really hurt as much as I'm making out, or is my pain threshold zero? Worst of all, is Curtis gonna flip out if they send us back home?

"Oh my God, Ellie," Curtis shouted at me, which cut through my thoughts like a gun shot. "There's no bloody petrol in the car. Why haven't you kept your eye on the petrol. What are you, stupid? You're expecting a trip to the hospital any day now and you didn't even check the bloody petrol in the car? And you didn't have your bag ready either, I thought you were supposed to be bloody organised."

"Oh, fuck off, Curtis, I was expecting it two weeks late not two weeks early. Thought I'd got plenty of time, anyway, there's a petrol station just up the road, we can put some in there."

"Well fine, you're the one in agony not me," he stated nonchalantly. Little did he realise I was now doubting myself.

A few minutes later we pulled into the petrol station. Curtis jumped out (which I can assure you was not common practice, he usually sat there and made me get out) and, after filling the tank, strolled into the little shop to pay. I saw him pick something up and put it on the counter while he chatted happily to the young girl on the till. She smiled at him and they chatted easily, laughing as they got into a conversation. I was just watching them when... "Shit... Oh, God, no, not another pain," I cursed. I grabbed the interior handle above the door on the left-hand side and leaned forward clutching the dashboard with my right hand. The pain just swam into my stomach making me hot all over and I bit my teeth together hard. I let out a little scream to the empty car and bent my head over my knees panting to try and get through this and out the other end. As I looked up, Curtis was now leaning on the counter towards this pretty young girl and she in turn looked over to the car. Her mouth fell open as she saw me in obvious pain. She said something to Curtis. He looked across to the car, not just as if he had forgotten it was there, but even as if he had forgotten that I was in it... In labour.

He dashed back through the shop door and legged it to the car. "Oh my God, is it coming? Are you okay?"

"Just drive," I countered as the pain started to subside. "If you paid more attention to your pregnant wife instead of flirting with teenagers."

"I wasn't flirting," he butted in, "that's Gary's

sister and she was asking about football training. Their Gaz trains with us on a Friday and he's told her that we have quite a few girls there now. She was just saying she might start coming too."

"Ooh," I said with obvious sarcasm. "How wonderful. Well, that's way more important than your pregnant, in labour, wife, isn't it? Maybe we should turn round and go back for a chat now my pain has gone?"

"Oh, don't be ridiculous, Ellie, I was only being nice to her."

"Mmm, I wonder how nice you would've been if she were ugly."

He laughed. "You're just being paranoid because you're having a baby. You're the only girl for me, Ellie, don't I tell you this every day? I love you, look how pretty you are, even at this time in a morning with no makeup, and not to mention your 'Not tonight Josephine' hairdo." This made me laugh too. I hadn't given a second thought to my appearance. "But you will always be beautiful to me, Ellie." And he said this with such sincerity and love that I felt quite emotional. A stray tear made its way down my cheek. I looked across at Curtis and he asked me what was wrong. After the turbulent times we had shared, I couldn't help but feel vulnerable and afraid of what lie ahead.

"I'm scared," is all I said.

"Hey, hey…" he cooed. "It's okay, darling, everything is going to be just fine. This time tomorrow we will have a beautiful baby in our arms. Our baby,

Ellie. It's going to be perfect and you will fall in love straight away." He continued, "We will be the best parents and perfect family." He squeezed my hand and then kissed his fingertips and planted the kiss on my lips. Then proceeded to open and munch the sausage roll he had just bought at the petrol station.

"I love you, Curtis, and you're right, I'm sure everything will be fine. I will just be glad when this part is over, if these pains are going to get worse I just don't… I'm not sure… I can take it," I said, stuttering. I really was afraid of what was yet to come.

On arrival at the maternity hospital I was checked in and answered all the questions that were being fired at me. "When did you last eat? Have you had a drink this morning? When did you last open your bowels? What's your due date? Have you booked an epidural?" the woman asked me. I was hooked up to the monitors and given an internal examination, to be told I was in labour. This was it, I was three centimetres dilated.

"Three?" I questioned. "That's not much, especially if I've got to get to ten," I exclaimed. My labour pains seemed to still be every twenty minutes or so and the midwife said they were going to give me an injection in the top of my thigh. An injection of pethidine. This was a pain relief and would last up to four hours. She said it would start working in about twenty minutes I looked up at the clock it was 7:20 a.m. "Let's hope it kicks in before the next pain," I said to no one in particular.

The midwife smiled at me and said, "Don't worry, Ellie, we are going to look after you. You will be much more comfortable when the pethidine takes effect, and don't worry when it starts to wear off, we can go onto gas and air."

I had expressed vehemently that I wasn't having an epidural. I have heard things from other people, and my mum had said to me, "We never had anything like that, can't be good for the baby, pumping drugs and into your spine like that, not to mention your own health." This alone had made me want to go through as natural a birth as possible, easy to say this before the event.

"Okay, Ellie, so that's thirty minutes gone by," the midwife said, "so I'm going to take you off the monitor for a while and you can have a nice bath and shave as much pubic hair from between your legs as possible. Don't worry about the front, that's not going to get in the way."

"Er… Can I just ask a question?" piped up Curtis, who was sat in a chair going through some work papers. "Do you have any time scale on how this will all pan out? I mean will the baby be here this morning?"

The midwife seemed a little amused by this question and retorted, "Why, Mr Parson, do you have somewhere else you need to be?" She smiled as she asked this.

"Well, no, not exactly," he answered with a serious look on his face. "But I'm sure I'm not going to be much help and, to be honest, I'm starving. Also, I'm on the rota to work this morning and was wondering if I could fit my shift in before the baby comes?"

The midwife looked at him like she couldn't tell if he was joking or not. "Well…" she started to say slowly and was interrupted immediately by Curtis.

"I mean, obviously I want to be here to see the baby come out, but if it's going to be hours, I only work across the city. I could give you the telephone number and you can call me when it's getting closer." It just came out of his mouth like it made sense.

"Oh, cheers." I jumped in before the midwife even had time to draw her breath. "Just piss off and leave me, why don't you?"

"Oh come on, Ellie, I'm starving and you know I'm only ten minutes away. Now you've had some pain relief and you're going for a bath you'll be fine. It means I can sort things out at work." I just started to cry. "Don't cry, love, you try and get some rest and I'll be back soon."

The midwife just looked like she didn't know what to say but then diplomatically said, "Yes, Ellie, we have plenty of time, baby will definitely not be here before lunch, why don't you try and rest after your bath?"

Curtis had a 'there ya go' smug look on his face like he was right and being reasonable. Then he added, "So, how long will she be in hospital after the birth?"

Directing this question to the midwife, she frowned at Curtis and was quite abrupt with her answer. "Let's get the baby delivered first, shall we?"

Curtis had the good grace to look a little abashed by his question. "Yes, of course, sorry, right, well I'll get off, then. Here's the gym telephone number and if you haven't called before two p.m. I will make my way back." Then he kissed my cheek and turned to leave the room. The midwife followed him out and closed the door, she returned almost immediately.

"Don't worry, Ellie, he won't be that long. I told him he'd better have his backside back here before twelve noon or he will have me to answer to." I liked this midwife; she wasn't going to take any nonsense from Curtis. She smiled and raised her eyebrows as if to say, 'I come across dickhead husbands like this all the time, just leave him to me'. I smiled and thanked her, adding that he could be a bit of a twat sometimes. We both laughed but I could definitely see pity behind her eyes.

A couple, or even maybe three hours later, I was laying back in the bed when the midwife came back in. She asked me how it was going and said that, because the labour was not progressing as it should, they were going to break my waters. She explained that doing this would help to make the contractions more regular and hopefully lead to more active labour. I was still only a little over three centimetres dilated and, as the time was now eleven fifteen a.m., I should be starting to progress. Breaking the waters would hopefully induce the labour somewhat. They did this and we waited to see what the effects were.

It was now after midday and I noticed the phone number Curtis had written down and left on the side, was gone. My pains became much worse and, with the pethidine wearing off, I asked if there was anything else they could give me. I was absolutely knackered and, watching the paper graph spew slowly out of the monitor, I could see the little humps it was drawing start to increase again. "Oh, Jesus, please no more," I cried. I knew another contraction was coming and I really had had enough.

"I will get the gas and air for you, love," said the midwife. "Then we can have another little look and see if you are dilating any more. I'm sure hubby won't be long, either," she said with a knowing look.

Curtis walked in five minutes later while they were checking my cervix to see if I was any further on. "Ooh… Is it going to be soon?" he asked as he walked around to give me a kiss. I had the mask on, drawing in gas and air like my life depended on it. "How's it going, love?" he asked.

"Yeah, fabulous," I replied. "I think I'll have another one next week." I could barely speak properly, I felt that weak, but managed to summon up enough energy to swear at him. "Where the fucking hell have you been? It's almost two o'clock. Are the baby and I really that unimportant?"

"Oh come on, I have responsibilities at work. I just wanted to make sure everything was all right and let them know what was happening."

"Mmm," I muttered, "because you couldn't possibly do that over the phone, eh? So instead, it takes nearly six hours to explain in person. Just don't even try and justify it cos I'm definitely not in the mood for your bullshit right now."

"Okay, okay, if you could just sit down over here now please, Mr Parson, that would be great. We don't need Ellie getting upset, thank you." She smiled politely at him and nodded her head towards the chair, but she looked as if she wanted to head butt him into the sitting position.

Another couple of hours ticked passed and I was just feeling weaker and weaker. The last time I had eaten was about seven p.m. last night and it was now four p.m. The pains came quicker and more intense. I was sure I was going to die. I had had another couple of checks on the dilation and, at four thirty, I was nine centimetres. "Almost there, Ellie, soon be ready to push."

Is she kidding me, was all I could think. I didn't even feel strong enough to push out a fart, let alone a baby. I started pushing at 4:45 p.m. All the encouragement and good intentions were not having the desired effect. I was sweating, crying, screaming, moaning and, not least of all, swearing. Seriously this was just agony. Shelling peas, my ass. Good job she wasn't standing in this room I'm sure I would have had her by the throat.

"Come on, Ellie, good girl, doing well but you

really need to push harder, when I tell you, on the next contraction. Come on, you can do this."

"I can't," I wept. I felt delirious like I was wavering in and out of consciousness. " I can't do it, I just need to sleep," I cried. The baby was just not coming out and, at five thirty p.m., they said they were going to give me an episiotomy. I said I didn't care what they did, just get it out.

With local anaesthetic injections in my nether regions, the cutting started. I could hear the skin being cut but felt nothing. One more push, nothing. "Okay, let's cut the other side," I heard a man say.

"Forceps," someone else shouted. There were few people milling around me and I was aware I had been wheeled into another room.

"Okay, Ellie, listen to me," someone said, "the baby's head is stuck and we can't get the forceps in, we are going to have to do a ventouse extraction. This means... Blah, blah... Blah... Blah." I wasn't even listening. I heard someone send Curtis out of the room; he protested loudly and she protested louder. He was escorted out and I was asked if they could let some training students in to watch the delivery.

"I don't care what you do, just get it out before I die." I wasn't paying attention to what was happening around me. I was totally exhausted and, as I turned my head to one side, I saw Curtis' face at the tiny square window in the door. He looked ashen.

"Right, we're all set, Ellie, last push and baby will

be out. Okay, now… PUSH… PUSH." I tried to call on any reserve energy I might have stowed away and made a final attempt to have this baby. "That's a good girl, well done, here it comes." I just thought to myself, surely even dying can't be this bad. "Here it is, it's a little boy, congratulations. Someone let Dad back in, please. There you go, Ellie, a gorgeous baby boy, do you want to hold him for a second before we clean him up?"

"No, I don't care if it's a monkey, just take him away," were my actual words. She started explaining things to me but I was totally spent, odd words floated in and out of my ears, cord wrapped around the neck, large head, next contraction, afterbirth, jaundice, heat lamp, another doctor coming to do the stitches, blah blah blah. I felt like I had truly been hit by a bus, I couldn't move and I couldn't speak. The room seemed to clear of most of the bodies. "Cup… Of… Tea," I whispered, hoping someone, anyone, would hear me.

"Okay, lovely, I will get you a cup of tea," said a female voice. My eyes were closed, sleep was blanketing me, I didn't resist.

What must have been, I don't really know, sometime later, a man walked into the room. "Hi, Ellie, is it?" said the soothing male voice. "Just stay as you are, I'm just going to ease your legs back into the stirrups so I can stitch you up and make you more comfortable. Then you can have your cup of tea." I remember seeing a massive circular light being pulled down from the ceiling and I could just make out a reflection of the damage, in the doctor's glasses. I turned my head to one side and saw blood smears and splats all over the place. I closed my eyes and the smell of carnage hung heavy in the room. When eventually the needle work had been completed, and my cup of tea placed on the blanket near my hand, a midwife said she would leave me to rest for a few minutes. I cried silently as I couldn't even summon up enough strength to hold the cup. I just lay there and watched the skin form on the tea I so badly wanted.

Chapter 9

I had absolutely no idea what the time was when I opened my eyes. I was obviously on a ward, three beds opposite me and one to either side of me. Just trying to take in my surroundings… Curtains at the window were closed. Was it night time? Two of the women opposite were sleeping, one was breastfeeding. The woman to my right was changing the nappy on a tiny baby and I couldn't be bothered to put the effort into turning to my left. Then it hit me, right between the legs, the painful throbbing sensation. It felt like it should have been flashing red and pulsating, like a hammer-smacked thumb on a *Tom and Jerry* cartoon. Woo, this did not feel good. I felt like I was just existing, invisible, in the middle of a nightmare. I was starving but felt sick, tired but in too much pain to sleep, wanted to speak but didn't know who to.

Just when I thought crying was the only thing I could manage without any effort, I was pulled from my thoughts by a squeaking, gurgling cry that seemed to drift up from my feet. Looking down, I saw at the foot of the bed a tiny plastic cot… With a baby in it! That can't be mine. I'd asked them to take it away, him away. Yes, him. A boy, I had had a baby boy. The bundle wriggled and grunted and within ten or fifteen seconds it started screaming. Now what do I do. All those antenatal classes and I felt totally out of my depth.

To my relief, a nurse walked in and took the decision (that I couldn't make anyway) out of my hands. "Hello, Ellie, how are you feeling, love? You've had a lovely long sleep but I think baby is ready for feeding. He's been under the lamps to help with the jaundice but sounds like he's hungry now. You did say you wanted to breastfeed, yes?"

"Er, yes. Yes, definitely, I do, yes."

"Have we got a name for the little chap?" she enquired politely.

"Yes, we chose some names but agreed that if it was a girl, I get to choose but if it's a boy, my husband would choose."

"Sounds like a good plan." She smiled, picked the baby up and sat on the edge of my bed. "Well, hubby will be back in the morning so you can tell us then." She loosened him slightly from the tight cocoon he was swaddled in to expose him a little and said, "There you go, Ellie, now you're a little more compos mentis, say hello to your gorgeous son. And look at all that dark hair, he's a proper little stunner, eh? Seven pounds eleven ounces, he weighed, and was born at six thirty p.m. Seems like you had a bit of a struggle getting him out, but he's here now, safe and sound and doing well. Guess he wanted to make sure you remembered his birthday," She laughed at her own joke.

"Bit of a struggle… I'd have cheerfully put a gun to my head if there'd been one available." I rolled my eyes at her.

"Well it's all over now. Now for the hard part." She cooed at the baby.

"Do you have any kids," I asked "Yes, three. Eldest is fourteen and eleven-year-old twins."

"Blimey, I can't think I will ever do this again. You must be crazy." She made a humming sound in response, as if to say, you have no idea.

Helping me to sit up and easily holding him to my breast, to my surprise, I seemed to be totally naked. He opened his tiny dark blue eyes and seemed to look straight into my eyes. Oh God, I was totally smitten. Love at first sight. He got comfortable and started sucking hungrily, little snorting breaths coming rapidly from his cute little nose. His skin was a beautiful olive colour (which, as yet, I had no idea was due to his jaundice) and his dark hair so long it was just past his eyebrows. I held his little flailing hand and he gripped round my thumb. As he wriggled slightly, his tiny foot popped out, bearing a blue plastic ankle bracelet. It had 'baby Parson' written on it along with his weight and birth date. Wow, what an absolute miracle he was. My miracle. Well, our miracle, I thought, as, for the first time since I'd woken up, I thought of Curtis. "Er… What's the time, please?" I asked.

"Two thirty a.m., we gave baby a bottle earlier as we couldn't wake you. But it's up to you now, love.

We'll try ten minutes on this side," she chatted. "Then we'll see if we can get some wind up and swap for ten minutes on the other side."

It was three fifteen a.m. when I finally put him down to settle. I'd taken more pain killers and was whacked out. So, when I'd just managed to nod off, hearing another screaming baby in close proximity, was rather annoying. Why isn't anyone seeing to that baby, I thought. I looked round to see if I could see anyone. The woman on my right was breastfeeding so I asked her. "Who's is that baby crying, why doesn't someone pick it up, for God's sake?"

"It's yours," she replied, looking up for a split second.

"WHAT... Can't be mine, I only just fed him," I objected. I tried to sit up at the same time as the nurse walked back in.

"Come on, Ellie, time for baby's next feed. When you're breastfeeding we say feed on demand, that can be anything between two to four hours."

"But I only just fed him not ten minutes ago." I was so confused.

"That was at two thirty a.m., love, its five forty-five now," she laughed.

"I didn't think I had even been to sleep," I offered apologetically to the woman on my right.

"I know what you mean," she laughed. "But you definitely have, unless you snore when you're awake," she giggled. "Don't worry, I remember my first born.

It's all a bit of a shock. You'll get used to it and soon you'll be a dab hand. Takes over your life, mind, but they're worth it." She kissed her little pink bundle on the head. "Fourth." She nodded her head towards her baby.

Psycho, was all I could think in response. We smiled at each other but my smile soon left me as the down below throbbing started again. Mental note to ask about more painkillers, I thought. I fed, winded, changed and settled baby back down. Even dragged myself out of bed to put him in the cot. The pain down below was immense. I felt the need to wee so shuffled slowly towards the bathroom.

The ward was now becoming a hive of activity. It smelled of bleach and food, which was a funny combination but managed to make me realise how hungry I was. After breakfast had been and gone and I had had instructions from the nurse to let her know when I had opened my bowels, I was feeling ever so slightly more normal. Though I couldn't imagine the 'opening bowels' was anything to look forward to. It felt like if I did, all my stitches would pop open and fifty percent of my body would fall out, down the loo.

Jill, the woman in the bed to my right, cheerfully informed me, "If you don't open your bowels in two days, they will give you something that will make you go." She put emphasis on the word 'will'.

Fabulous, was all I could think. Having lived through my delivery from hell, I kind of got the feeling that anything else life wanted to throw at me couldn't even be half as bad. It was a little bit empowering, I have to admit.

I was expecting Curtis around eight a.m., as the two visiting slots for the day were eight 'til ten in the morning and six 'til eight at night. I thought he would come and see us before work and then again after work. He arrived at eight fifteen a.m., with flowers and a card. I was so happy to see him and he looked equally excited to see me.

We chatted about the horrific birth and how angry he was about being sent out of the room. I discovered that I had had thirty-six stitches in all, to close the layers of skin they had to cut through. Also, they had told Curtis I would be in for seven days if everything went well, so, with this news, he had decided to work this week and take a week off when I went home. "Can I pick him up?" he asked.

"Sure, go ahead," I answered.

He gingerly lifted the baby out of his plastic cot and stood staring at his sleeping face. "Oh, he's so cute, I thought we would call him Scott. He looks so different today. Last night his face was all screwed up and frowning. Today he just looks perfect and happy. How are you feeling now? Jesus, I didn't expect it to be that traumatic, did you?"

"No I bloody didn't, if I'd have been able to have a five-minute trial of that kind of pain, I would never have got pregnant." I smiled. "It was a nightmare and I've still got this car crash to get through." And pointed down below.

"Oh, you'll be fine, love, made of strong stuff, you are. I love you, Ellie, well done, you were so tired and it just seemed to last forever."

"I know, never again, that's for sure," I chipped in. "Ah... We'll see, you know we plan to have two, you'll soon forget the pain."

"Er, I don't think so, if I live to be a hundred with Alzheimer's, I will never ever forget this birth. Truthfully, Curtis, it was horrific, I really thought I was going to die."

"Give it a couple of weeks and we can start practicing for the next one," he laughed.

All I could think was, *are you for real? Two weeks, try two years, more like.*

Curtis stayed for about an hour and then said he was going to get off to work. "I won't bother popping in tonight," he said, like it was no big deal. "I've arranged to go out with some of the lads, you know, wet the baby's head and all that. And tomorrow I thought I'd come at six p.m. instead of in the morning as I'm on the late shift at the gym." All came out like it was a sensible plan and I was really taken aback.

"You're kidding, right?" I laughed, expecting him to laugh too.

Instead he frowned and said, "no," without further explanation.

"Curtis!" I exclaimed and found tears starting to

spring into my eyes. "Please, you can't do that, I feel so alone, I thought you would be here every chance you got. The other dads stay for the whole two hours morning and teatime."

"Yeah well, I'm busy, Ellie, and, anyway, who cares what everyone else's husband's doing. I'm providing a good standard of living for you and Scott, that's what counts." And with that he kissed me, said he loved me and waved goodbye.

I just laid there a bit stunned but very emotional about his attitude. What's more, Jill had overheard the whole conversation. I looked across to her, she was packing her bits away as she was off home in an hour or so. "Woo, no wonder baby Scott is so cute, your bloke's a right stunner, isn't he, Ellie, lucky old you, eh?"

"Mmm," I muttered under my breath. "Shame he doesn't have a moral compass to go with his good looks," I spat.

"Oh, he's just excited, Ellie. Let him go and be the macho proud daddy to his mates, it's just how men work." She said this as she was folding a nightie that she popped it into her bag. "Listen, love, you're only a young girl, trust me, you take care of yourself and your baby. This experience will enhance your life and being a good mum is the most rewarding thing that will ever happen to you. Yeah, sure, men are great and they have their uses but, trust me, look at Maggie Thatcher, women are the backbone of the world. We have capabilities that far outweigh any man. Remember that,

Ellie, you are a woman and you are strong."

I looked at her, my mind ticking over. That was one of the most profound things anyone has ever said to me, it seemed to make sense and I knew Curtis would be useless without me, so why then did he make me feel so inferior? "So what's your husband like?" I asked her.

"Useless," she replied immediately. "In fact, less than useless. This is our fourth child and he still can't do a nappy change properly. He is shit at cooking and he's never done a supermarket shop in the ten years we have been together."

"Really?" I was shocked. "But you love him and you're happy?" I asked.

"Well, let's put it this way, we love each other and all our children, but he thinks he's the boss. I let him think he's the boss but I know that I'm the one that's in charge really. I can do anything and everything. I don't rely on him but he relies on me and I just know that knowledge is power. I might not have a paid job but being a mother is one of the hardest jobs there is and he works because I look after his children for him. I read a lot and study when I get the chance. It's a good feeling to know yourself that you can cope with anything. Look what you just did." She pointed to Scott. "This is just the beginning for you love, be strong for your family but always keep something back for yourself." And this advice was abruptly cut into by the nurse asking if I could get settled in bed for a visit from the doctor.

The curtains were pulled around my bed and the

doctor came in to see how I was. He talked about the birth and explained the baby had started getting distressed as the cord was round his neck. He confirmed I had indeed had thirty-six stitches and said it would take some time to heal. Not to attempt intercourse for at least six weeks. He left as fast as he had arrived but not until he made me roll onto my side and lift up one leg so he could inspect my stitches. Well, what the hell, I'd lost my dignity now anyway, it certainly smashes any tendency to be shy out of you, that is for sure. As he was leaving, so, too, was Jill.

"Ta-ta, love." She waved and winked at me. She nodded towards her husband who was five steps in front of her. He was carrying a plant someone had brought in for Jill, Jill was carrying her baby in one arm and her overnight bag in the other. She rolled her eyes and laughed. "Useless twat, what did I tell you?" And with that she was gone. I felt a little bit sad knowing that I would never see her again. Although she was probably ten or more years older than me, I would have loved her as a friend. She was so confident and seemed to have this whole 'life' business sussed out. I felt like a total beginner but her resounding words would always stay with me.

Days in the hospital were very routine. Feed, change nappies, bath time and lots of cuddling and kissing, then thinking about yourself. My parents had been to visit on day two and my sister came with a friend on day three, in the morning. After she had left, day three seemed to drag. Curtis didn't come in, in the morning, so I was really looking forward to his visit at tea time. So, from five thirty onwards, I kept strolling over to the main window. It overlooked the main car park and, with Scott all fed and watered, I thought I'd watch for Curtis arriving.

At twenty past six I saw his car driving in through the entrance. By now I was more than a little pissed off. By the time he got up here it would be halfway through visiting times and, when I asked him yesterday evening why he didn't seem to stay very long, he'd just shrugged his shoulders and said, "Well I don't really like hospitals and, besides, it's just boring sitting around with a room full of strangers, just not my cup of tea." I was hurt more by his selfish attitude than anything else. I knew that there were a hundred things I could have said in reply, most of them were not pleasant and would most definitely have caused a row. Not what I wanted, least of all in public. So, I just told him that he was right, it is boring in hospital but it's even more boring when you're stuck here all day. I said I missed him and would have thought he'd want to be here as much as possible. "Nah, you know me, Ellie, but I can't wait for you to get back home, it's not the same being on your own. There's nothing in the fridge and I'm getting sick of fish and chips, think I'll get a Chinese tonight. I miss you in bed, too, don't like sleeping on my own." Gosh, how awful for him, my heart bleeds.

Now, as I watched him park up, I noticed some

other person in the passenger side. At first, I was just mildly curious, as he jumped out and swiftly ran around the front of the car to open the passenger door, I was thinking, this must be an elderly person. But no, even from eight floors up, my eyesight was good enough to see a girl with long blond hair step out of the car. He opened the door, gave her his hand to help her out and stepped aside for her. He closed the door behind her locked it and proceeded to catch up with her as they walked easily together towards the hospital entrance. Now I was fuming. Who the hell was she? If he's just given her a lift or something he'd better not come in here and deny all knowledge of her.

My blood pressure was at boiling point by the time he got to the ward. And to my utmost astonishment, not to mention disappointment and anger, he walked in with her. They approached Scott's cot and the blond girl 'oohed and aahed' whilst looking up at Curtis to say how much he looks like his daddy. "Oh, he's gorgeous," she said. "HI, I'm Katie, nice to meet you at last. I've heard so much about you… All good." She smiled as she extended her hand for me to shake.

I just stood there open-mouthed and frowning, looking at Curtis and said in reply to Katie, "Oh funny, Curtis has never mentioned you at all!"

"Oh sorry, love, yes, Katie runs The Spa Centre at the gym. Have I not mentioned her before?"

"No you definitely have not. How funny." Now I was really angry. "And you brought her here today with you because…?"

Curtis was obviously not receiving the reaction he'd expected and, while his face started to colour up, he started stuttering out a sentence. "Just wanted her to see the baby… And, besides, she is visiting her granddad… He is in a ward just close by." He smiled at his own answer and continued to walk over and kiss me on the head. He handed me a small cuddly toy of Snoopy the dog holding a red heart shape and then turned to pick up Scott. He held him up and gave him a kiss on his cheek and proceeded, to my astonishment, to hand him to Katie. I was stunned. "Here, hold him and I'll take a photo, we can show the guys at work." She took the baby and stood there, all glamorous and pretty, and smiled whilst posing for the photo.

Something inside me just died at that precise moment. I was sitting there, no makeup, hair unbrushed wearing a milk stained nightie. I'd never felt so vulnerable and so low. I was crushed. Curtis took Scott from her arms and asked if I wanted a photo with him and the new cuddly toy he had brought. I just shook my head in answer and took Scott from him. "He's due for a feed now," I said, "so, if you wouldn't mind!" I looked in Katie's direction. She had the good grace to look uncomfortable and said she would meet Curtis at the car after she'd seen her granddad.

She left and I put Scott back in his cot. I was in a state of shock. What did this mean? Surely, he wasn't sleeping with her, he wouldn't bring her here if he was,

101

or would he? I just felt deflated and unhappy. "Why did you bring her here?" I asked.

He just looked at me. Putting Scott down, he replied, "I thought you were going to feed him?"

"Well, I'm not. I wanted her to leave and thankfully she got the message. What in God's name made you do a thing like that? Are you sleeping with her...?" It just came out.

"Ellie, please... Don't be ridiculous. She's only eighteen. She's just a work colleague. She's a lovely girl and when I said I was coming straight to the hospital, she said her granddad wasn't well and could she have a lift."

"Bollocks, Curtis, and you know it. If you were going to make up some bullshit reason for galivanting around with a tart, at least get your story straight and get your facts right."

"What do you mean?"

"In a ward close by, my ass, this is a maternity hospital, you absolute twat."

He looked a bit shaken and his face took on a pink glow. He breathed in and stumbled out his next sentence of bullshit like I was a total half-wit. "Well, I don't know, do I? She didn't say this hospital maybe he's in one next door. I will have to ask her when I drop her back at work."

"Yeah, you do that and, while you're at it, just think on. We are just supposed to be embarking on a dream life with a new family member. Don't let me and Scott down. I'm sure you would live to regret it."

"Oh don't be so dramatic, Ellie, she's just a kid. I was just being kind, giving her a lift, and you are just overreacting."

"Kettle… Pot… Black." I raised my eyebrows. "Go on, you get yourself off. I'm sure she'll be waiting at the car by now."

I turned my head away from him and slowly climbed into bed and when I looked back, he was just exiting the ward. I scrambled out of bed over to the window and there she stood leaning on the boot of my car. I waited and watched Curtis arrived back at the car, he unlocked his door and leaned over to let her in. She jumped in and off they drove. To say I was mad was an understatement but, as I returned to my bed, I thought through the words of Jill, my ex-bed neighbour.

Chapter 10

Sleep my new best friend. We were never very far from each other. I couldn't ever remember feeling so totally and completely whacked out. If Scott was awake, I was awake, if he was asleep that's exactly where I wanted to be. A lot of the time, this was possible if no one else was in the house.

I had served my full week in the hospital, I say served, it really was like enduring a prison sentence. You'd think that a hospital would be the ideal place to get some rest, but no. Up two or three times in the night to feed the baby, lights on at six thirty a.m., cleaners in and out like a noisy army, banging every piece of furniture they pass, nurses constantly in and out with meds and the tea and coffee trolly, audible from at least five or six wards away. The chinking of the cups and saucers on the metal trolley, getting louder and louder. By the time they got to me, I needed the strongest coffee they could produce just to settle my shredded nerves. Then there was the doctors' rounds, coming to see those of us that need checking on… Can't be asleep for that. A continual sound of at least two or three babies crying, the worst of which was a woman's in the opposite bed to me. I say this was the worst, her little boy was, by no means, the loudest crier, but he sounded like a mini Rod Stewart, all croaky and gravelly. He had been born on the same day as Scott and the very next morning, his mum had been informed that he had a hole in his heart. She still smoked continually whilst in hospital. She spent most of her time in the sitting room, where smoking was allowed. The cry from her baby was heart-breaking and really hard to listen to. When he cried, and she was off smoking, I would waddle across and pick him up for a cuddle and walk up and down with him. So, add all that to four hours of visiting times a day, and six portable televisions in the room, getting some quiet downtime to catch up on much-needed sleep was almost impossible.

Getting back home and into my own bed was heaven. The trauma of Curtis' unwanted visiting colleague seemed to drift into the past. He didn't want to talk about it. He said I was totally unreasonable and put it down to me being emotional because I had just had a baby. To be honest, just being home and feeling solely responsible for my baby was a daunting enough task in itself. I didn't really have the energy to argue with, or even think about, Curtis. He was now a few days into his week off and he was out of the house more than he was in it. Which, on the one hand, was really annoying and very little if any help to me at all, but, on the plus side, at least when Scott was sleeping, I could sleep too. If Curtis happened to be in during Scott's sleeping hours, he was even more demanding.

Constantly complaining because there was not enough food in the house. He even commented to me how the house looked a mess and suggested I might feel better if I got dressed and went out and did some shopping.

My mum had been round with my sister and brought us a massive shepherd's pie. It lasted us for two days and was amazing. Curtis, well, he would go out and pick up a takeaway but spent most of his time visiting friends and his mum and eating whilst he was out. I was meanwhile existing on cereal, toast or a quick cheese sandwich.

When the fridge and cupboards were starting to look decidedly empty, I called my mum and reeled off a basic shopping list. I asked if she could drop it in for me. I was embarrassed that Curtis was so useless so I made an excuse that his mum wasn't well and he'd gone to see her. Whether my mum saw through this excuse, she didn't say anything at the time. She did arrive two hours later with tons of shopping and wouldn't take the money for it. This made me cry. They were probably a lot worse off than us, financially, and I'm sure the shopping would have put a big dent in their weekly budget. Mum stayed for a while made me some lunch and put away the groceries. Then, after Scott had had a feed, she nursed him off to sleep and put him lovingly in his wicker Moses basket before she left. I then had a meeting with my new best friend.

Later that day my lovely midwife, Chris, came on her daily visit. She would check how I was, how the breastfeeding was going, weigh Scott and check him over. She was a local lady and such a lovely woman. When she knocked on the door and let herself in (which was quite normal) she marched into the front room with her usual positive step and confident manner. Leaning over the Moses basket, she smiled and cooed at Scott, exuding natural warmth. "Oh he's so darling, isn't he?" she commented as she came over to me on the sofa. "And how is Mummy today?" she asked, sitting beside me. She only had to stroke my arm and that caring, genuine look on her face just reduced me to tears. "Hey, hey, hey, what is it? Has something happened or is this just an emotional mummy moment?" She smiled with obvious concern and waited patiently for me to stop blubbing and to speak.

"Oh I don't know, Chris, I just think I'm tired. Scott seems to be awake more than he's asleep, I thought it would be the other way around. Feeding on demand is very... Demanding... Too demanding. Is he not full enough? It's really hard to know how much he's actually getting but, judging by his nappies, he's not starving."

"Okay, love, listen, don't worry and try not to be upset. We can start writing down his feed times and then, if you feel like you want to do a bit of bottle-feeding, we can give it to go. At least then Curtis could take turns in the night and share the responsibility." And as she spoke the back door opened, signalling Curtis' entrance. My mind was working overtime on her suggestions. Keep a diary of feed and sleep times, okay, I can see that being beneficial, slotting in some bottle-feeding so Curtis can help. Help! Helping and Curtis we're not really words that you came across in the same sentence.

"Oh, hiya, Chris," he said jovially as he entered the room. "How's tricks?"

"Hi, Curtis, yes, good thanks. You?"

"Tip-top, thanks. Who couldn't be feeling great, with my gorgeous, brave wife and my perfect baby son, all is well in the world, eh?"

"Oh, how nice," said Chris in answer. She followed it with, "Yeah, we were just chatting about whether to try Scott on a bit of formula to top up his feeds. Ellie needs a bit of a break during the night, you'd be really doing her some good to let her get some extra sleep."

"Yeah, absolutely, I agree, she's been a bit teary and I'm sure she's just overtired. Anything I can do to help." He smiled his most charming smile at Chris and walked across to me, leaned down and kissed my cheek. "Anything for you, love," he said.

I couldn't even speak. Really... Really... Curtis was willing to get up in the night and feed the baby. I just smiled at Chris and she proceeded to lift Scott out of his basket and arrange the terry towelling nappy on the floor, which she placed him in once he was naked. She pulled all four corners of the nappy together and pierced a hook through them. The hook was attached to a mobile handheld weighing device. "Well, baby's weight is fine so all good there."

Curtis had walked back into the kitchen. "Can I get you a cuppa, Chris?" he shouted through. "Ellie, what about you, tea or coffee? Chris declined the offer, saying thanks, but she couldn't stay too long. "Actually it's getting on for tea time. Let's see what we have in here," he shouted from the kitchen.

Chris continued to go about her business, and, just as she was getting her bits and pieces together to leave, in walks Curtis with a cup of tea in one hand and a plate containing an omelette and salad in the other. "Here ya go, love, grab that while I get the salt and pepper and a knife and fork for you," he said, in a calm, matter-of-fact way, like it was a normal regular occurrence for him to cook. "Salad cream?" he shouted.

"No thanks," I whispered in a daze and he reappeared with a knife and fork and salt and pepper on a tray for my knee.

"Well, no need to ask if he is looking after you properly," stated Chris as she smiled at Curtis like he should be nominated for a 'Husband of the Year' award. "Lucky you," she said to me. "Not all new dads are this attentive. Enjoy him while he's off work, I'm sure you'll miss him next week." She smiled at him. I felt like I was in a scene from a soap opera where everyone had learned their lines really well and the acting was brilliant. Inside I just couldn't believe what was happening. So much so, that I took the dinner and just agreed with Chris.

"Yeah," I said quietly. "Yeah, I'm really lucky, aren't I?"

Curtis showed Chris out and thanked her profusely for all her help and two minutes later, when she had driven off, he completely exploded. "WHERE," he demanded, "did all that fucking shopping come from?"

"Shh, don't disturb Scott, he's only just gone down," I said quietly, putting my index finger to my lips. "My mum bought it, and just as well, cos you've not exactly gone out of your way to make sure there's food in the house, have you?" I placed the omelette on the floor and walked into the kitchen with my cup of tea.

"Nosey cow, how the hell did she know what we needed?" he snarled.

"Because I rang her and gave her a list. Oh, and don't worry about your shining reputation, Curtis, as usual I covered for you with a bullshit excuse you were at your mother's because she was ill. How in God's name am I meant to get out and do a food shop, especially when you keep disappearing in the car?"

"You've got legs, haven't you, not broken are they? And all the money we spent on that fucking buggy, well get him in it and use it." I couldn't believe my own ears, was he really saying these things just after his Oscar-winning performance to Chris?

"And as for running crying to Mummy that we needed shopping, why didn't you write a list for me?"

"Write a list... For you! Why didn't you write a list for yourself, you live here as well, don't you? Not that you wouldn't be forgiven for thinking otherwise. God knows where you manage to slope off to ten times a day. You're supposed to be off work to give a hand, not swan off out with your mates all day." Now I was really mad but it all came out attached to floods of tears.

"Oh, quit your crying, Ellie, you sound like Scott and, as for calling your mum to come here, you know what I've told you, nobody visits here unless I say it's okay." He marched angrily back into the front room, picked up the telephone cable that led to the socket on the skirting board and, after wrapping it round his hand a couple of times, yanked it as hard as he could and ripped the wires straight out. "There, now try and contact anyone to come and stick their noses in," he yelled.

With that, Scott fidgeted around and started to cry. I picked him up and, wiping my eyes on my dressing gown sleeve, left the room. I took Scott upstairs and laid on our bed with him by my side. There I stroked his beautiful little forehead and sang quietly a lullaby in his ear, trying to abate the tears fighting to be released. We lay there for some time. Curtis had long ago slammed the door and driven off... Again. I wasn't even thinking about him at all, or the fact that we no longer had a phone. As far as I was concerned, his way of thinking had absolutely no substance or merit. Was he suffering from some kind of postnatal depression? Was that possible? I had no idea, and, to be honest, my only concern right now was Scott. Keeping him safe was my priority. And suddenly, again Jill's words came back to me, 'strong, be strong, I had to be strong'.

When Curtis returned later that evening, I had had a shower, tidied the house, washed the dishes and was sat breastfeeding Scott, whilst watching the telly. He came in with his head down and a crumpled look on his face. "You look nice," he offered. I was wearing a maternity dress but had washed my hair and attempted to blow dry it into some kind of order.

"Thanks," I replied.

"Oh, Ellie," he cried. "I'm so sorry." He knelt on the floor beside me and reached up to touch Scott in his blanket. "I don't know what happened," he offered. "I'm so sorry. I love you... And... I don't even know, please say you still love me, I need you to, Ellie." He started to cry.

I looked down at him and thought how pathetic he looked. It was like living with Jekyll and Hyde. I tried to gather my thoughts before I spoke. "Curtis, you know I love you, you shouldn't have to keep asking but your behaviour scares me. What's going on? Speak to me and tell me what's happening. I have a tiny baby here and I'm scared when you get angry. Talk to me."

"I don't know, I just feel useless, and you just said 'I' have a baby, not 'we', like he's only yours and not mine. I'm not a necessity in your life and, when you really do need me to do something, I can't even do it. Then your mum rocks up with shopping and makes me look even worse. Bet your mum and dad hate me. Even

Scott doesn't like me, he just cries whenever I hold him."

Now he was properly sobbing. He snivelled as his nose ran and inched his way up onto the sofa. Sitting next to me, he started to try and kiss me, first on the cheek but then forcefully on the lips. I was still feeding Scott and tried to carefully unlatch him from me and place him gently on the sofa. Now didn't seem an appropriate time to be kissing passionately, but, equally, I felt that if I rejected Curtis at this moment, he would go into meltdown. We kissed a while and I held him in my arms.

As Scott had been fed, I picked him up and offered him to Curtis. "Here," I said, passing him gently across, "hold him on your knee like this." I demonstrated. "And put this hand under his chin. Come on, you've seen me do it. Then lean him forward slightly and pat his back like this." He gingerly followed my instructions and after a few seconds a little burp came up. Curtis laughed a little and kissed Scott on the head two or three times. "There you go, look, see how good you are at that." It was then followed by a dribble of milky sick which ran down the back of Curtis' hand.

"Aww yuck… Quick, Ellie, wipe it off." He pulled a face. I laughed, picking up a muslin to wipe them both with.

"Comes with the territory, I'm afraid. Now stand up and try rocking him to sleep," I suggested.

"No, I can't do that. He'll cry as soon as I move,

watch." He stood up and gently but awkwardly rocked him back and forth. Scott stayed relaxed and slowly but surely drifted off to sleep.

"See," I whispered, "anything's possible if you just keep trying." We stood there for a minute and just looked at our beautiful son.

"Yeah, you're right, Ellie. I'm sorry, why do you stay with me? I know I'm a dick, you deserve better. I will try harder, honest, I will. I love you."

We sat for a while quietly until Curtis sat bolt upright and said, "I know, let's invite Si and Angie round for a take away at the weekend." Simon and Angie had been to see us at the hospital but we hadn't seen them since. Curtis jumped up as I smiled my approval at the suggestion. He merrily picked up the phone to call but the realisation hit him when there was no dialling tone. He looked so ashamed as he traced the wire in his other hand and it swayed loosely around with ragged wires hanging out of the end. He replaced the receiver and, looking towards the floor, he said to me, "Please don't tell anyone I did that, will you, Ellie?" He pulled open the top drawer of the nearby unit and took out a screwdriver. Unscrewing the small connection box from the skirting board, he came to an instant decision. "I'm so sorry, I really am. Let's just tell everyone we have decided to save on the expense of a phone. Anyway, now you're not working it's not a bad idea to save some money. Also, it'll stop all the nosey busybodies ringing all the time." He looked quite pleased with his decision.

"Really, Curtis? We have a new born baby, remember?"

"Yeah but the phone box is only thirty seconds away and also Walter next door will always let us use his phone." Walter was our joined-on next door neighbour and we got on with him really well. Curtis had talked himself into it. Saying we would save around forty pounds a month, he smiled and rattled the change in his pocket. Pulling out a ten pence piece he held it up and said. "There… I'll nip and call Si at his mum's. Love you."

Chapter 11

The first baby months were not to be sniffed at. How can one tiny little addition to the family change the dynamic to such a degree? My new best friend, sleep, was constantly avoiding me. Breastfeeding on demand just seemed to blur into one long stint of having my boobs out, I have never seen so much of them. I actually really enjoyed the breastfeeding, per se, it was just the regularity that was killing me. I felt so drained. I couldn't find the energy or, indeed, the enthusiasm to do anything constructive. Just keeping the house tidy was a mammoth task, let alone washing nappies, getting myself dressed, having a wash, etc.

Some days it would be past lunchtime and I would suddenly realise I hadn't even cleaned my teeth. This sometimes made me want to cry but I would have a word with myself, be strong and think to myself, *who is going to look after Scott if I crumble into a heap?* The answer was nobody could look after him like me, so just eat a piece of chocolate or even a few chocolate digestive biscuits, have a cup of tea and pull yourself together — best foot forward. Generally, this would work and I did little things to make my mindset better.

One thing that really, instantly made me distressed

was waking in the night to Scott crying and thinking I had only been asleep for, like, half an hour. I would jolt awake, get angry, then once I had him latched on, I would scramble around to find my watch on the bedside table to see what the time actually was. Sometimes, only occasionally, I would be pleasantly shocked to find out he had slept for over three hours, then subsequently felt guilty for being cross. So, to combat this, I bought a white plastic kitchen clock with big black numbers and fingers. I put a nail in the bedroom wall about three feet away from the bed, and hung it there. It looked ridiculous but I didn't care. It was perfect. As soon as I opened my eyes, it was the first thing I saw. I looked at that clock and it felt like such an important thing in my life.

Unfortunately, one of the days, around the four-month mark, got the better of me. Curtis had gone to work in a really bad mood. That had stemmed from the night before when there wasn't really much food in the house so I had done bacon, eggs, baked beans and chips for tea. Curtis just exploded. "What's that supposed to be?" he demanded. "If I'd wanted breakfast for tea I would have asked. You've got all fucking day to get a decent meal together, and this is all you can manage?"

"Have you seen the weather? I was not going out on foot with Scott to get shopping, I'm sorry but it's all we had in so it will have to do," I bravely retorted.

"Well it might 'do' for you, but I'm in training so it won't 'do' for me," he spat back at me. It was mid-

February, the rain had never stopped it was freezing cold and windy.

"But, Curtis, you keep taking the car to work, what do you expect me to do?"

"You'd do well to try that thing called an umbrella and stick the plastic cover on that you insisted on buying for the damn buggy. Jesus, Ellie, some women have three or four kids and they do a better job than you. When I get home after a hard day at work, I expect a decent meal to be served. Just because you don't care about your body and don't mind being fat, well, I'm afraid I do." And with this, he put on his coat, slammed the back door and left.

I looked down at my post-pregnancy jelly belly and felt so ugly. How hurtful his words were. I walked over to look at myself in the mirror. My long brown hair looked un-styled and tired. I made a mental note to call a mobile hairdresser tomorrow.

Tomorrow came and Curtis, even though he had clearly been somewhere to eat the previous evening, was still in a really bad mood. He walked into the bedroom after having been in the bathroom for half an hour and just shot me a real look of disdain. I was sat chatting, cooing and tickling Scott, who was smiling up at me from our bed. I had just finished feeding him and he was such a cutie, with a gorgeous cheeky face, you couldn't help but smile back at him. Curtis didn't even acknowledge that Scott was in the room. "Yeah, don't mind me, I'll just get my own breakfast, shall I?"

"Aww, look at him, Curtis, how can you resist that smile? Don't you just want to eat him?" I crooned.

"Mmm, you might, I prefer breakfast, thanks, and have you done my pack up for lunch, or is that too much trouble?"

"Well I haven't done you anything, no, because I really need to go shopping, so just grab something on your way to work and I'll get stuff for tomorrow." I tried to make it sound like it was no big thing but I could even just sense Curtis getting angry.

"Great… Didn't think having a baby would take over your life to this degree, you really need to get your shit together, Ellie. I'm off." And the familiar slamming of the back door followed.

Right, I thought to myself. I wasn't going to let him put me down, making me feel inadequate. *Today I will take control, if it kills me.*

I thought back to a couple we met a couple of weeks ago. Andy and Jenny. Andy was in the police force, this impressed Curtis — that in itself was a small miracle. They met at the gym. He had paid Curtis lots of compliments about his physique and his commitment to the training sessions he ran. Add a few beers to the mix and a firm friendship was sealed. I had only met them by pure chance when we were out walking Scott. They did seem a lovely couple. Andy was tall, dark and very handsome, with perfect teeth and a beaming smile. He and Curtis chatted football, and Jenny took a sneaky peek at Scott, who was wrapped up like an Eskimo. She said he was adorable and commented on his lovely long eyelashes. Laughing she exclaimed, "Hey, Andy, he has eyelashes like yours." And, indeed, on closer inspection, he did. Andy's were very long and dark, looking like he had mascara on but I'm sure he didn't. Changing the subject, I asked Jenny about her hair. It looked fab and I told her as much. She said she had just had it cut yesterday by a friend of hers who had her own mobile hairdressing business. "Might suit you better, Ellie, being at home with baby, do you want her number?" she asked, scrambling round in her bag. "Can't seem to find her card in my bag but I'm sure I have one at home. Shall I drop it in when I'm passing?"

"Ooh, yes please." The opportunity for a haircut at home was certainly appealing. I told her our address and Curtis, on top form, invited them to dinner sometime. Obviously, no skin off his nose as he wouldn't be doing any of the cooking. Andy and Jenny both noticed the fleeting look of panic on my face and considerately offered to bring a takeaway. We set a date and said our goodbyes. Jenny, true to her word, dropped the card off two days later.

So, today, I picked up that card, bundled Scott into his buggy and grabbed some change for the phone box. As luck would have it, Alison said she could fit me in later in the afternoon. Brilliant. While I was out, and Scott was now asleep, I nipped back for my purse and seized the opportunity to do a bit of shopping.

By the time Alison was gently tapping on the back

door, Scott was not sleeping but he was fed and content in his bouncy chair. Kicking his legs around happily and making intermittent grabbing gestures for the toy mobile hanging over him. I made a cuppa for Alison and myself and, within ten minutes, Scott was nodding off and hair-cutting started. "Wow, your hair is really long and in great condition," she commented. "What were you thinking of doing to it?"

"To be honest, I hadn't given it much thought but, this morning, my husband wasn't backward in coming forward, telling me to pull myself together, tidy myself up. He thinks, just because he works, he doesn't have to help me at all. Like a 'get out of jail free' card. Anyway, I met Jenny the other day and she gave me your number. So, today, I'm on a mission. I've been shopping and done an hour's cleaning, now for the chop," I laughed, enjoying having someone new to talk to. "I will do some washing later on and probably be on the floor by tea time. But he can do one if he thinks I can't cope. Lazy bastard that he is, I'll show him." Phew that felt liberating. Just offloading to a stranger.

Alison laughed and raised her mug of tea, saying cheers. "You go girl, good on ya," she giggled. "You know, my husband is great with all that stuff. We have two kids, Joshua will be two in a couple of months, and Tanya is coming up three." She was happy to chat. "He's a great help but drives me mad with his penny pinching. Questions every penny we spend. That's why I now do my hairdressing, got my own money and don't

121

have to answer to him when I want something."

I laughed and raised my mug. "To us girls," I toasted.

"Ha ha, so what are we doing with your hair, then?"

"Well I wish it were more like yours, all lovely and curly. Mine's as straight as an ironing board. To be honest, I trust you, so just do whatever you think will look the best. Top priority is easy to manage, other than that, fill ya boots, you're the expert." We had a really great couple of hours. Alison chatted away as she chopped off half my hair and we became friends.

I was just starting to arrange the washed, terry towelling nappies over the huge fire guard we had, when Curtis arrived home from work. I heard him comment immediately from the kitchen. "Ooh, someone's been busy." This was probably directed at the pot of chilli con carne, bubbling away on the cooker top.

"Yeah, your favourite for tea," I replied, as we both entered the dining room from opposite doors.

"Jesus Christ, Ellie, what the fuck have you done to your hair?" It was a toss-up between his eyes and his mouth as to which was open the widest.

"Do you like it?" I asked happily. "Jenny's hairdresser came around and did it here."

"Are you serious? You know I like you with long hair. You never said you were gonna get it all chopped off. No... No, I don't like it. I like it long. Why didn't you ask me first? You'd better hope it grows quick."

I was so taken aback by his cruel and biting

comments and tears welled as I bit my lip and held my chin up. "Well, it's my hair and I really like it and—" My reply was cut short and I was stopped in my tracks as I turned to walk away, by Curtis yanking me backwards by my hair.

He pulled a fist full of my newly cut short bob towards himself and snarled in my face, "Don't try and be cocky with me, and you do not have your hair cut EVER again, without my permission. You ask me if you want to make changes to anything, ANYTHING, do you hear me? I'm the breadwinner who pays for everything, I make the decisions. Got it? Now get dinner served, I'm starving."

We ate dinner in relative silence. He said the chilli was nice, I didn't speak. He questioned who had been in his house to cut my hair. I didn't comment. Then, the straw that broke the camel's back was his final statement... "Don't put the nappies to dry round the fire like that, makes us look like scrubbers." This just pushed me over the edge and I couldn't stop myself from responding.

"What the fuck do you expect me to do with them. The radiators are drying the clothes and it's not exactly summer outside. Honestly, I don't know what you expect from me. Today I have cleaned the house, been shopping, cooked, done the washing in an eighteenth century washing machine, all whilst looking after your four-month-old son. I am bloody knackered and all you do is complain. Where's that happy family we dreamt of being? I'm trying my best and… And…" With that, I burst into tears and ran upstairs. I heard Curtis opening a can of beer and then the telly went on.

I stayed upstairs until I heard Scott crying, then went down to collect him and all his paraphernalia. I decided to feed him and bath him upstairs. He was now just starting on some solid foods, which, thankfully, helped with his sleeping. He had gone as long as five hours in one hit, which was a vast improvement for him. I did all the necessities then ran myself a bath.

I had just started to relax when in walked Curtis with a glass of wine and a can of beer. "I'm sorry, love. Here, I've brought you a glass of wine." He held it to me and it looked so appealing, I took it without a word and swallowed a couple of large mouthfuls. He knelt down at the side of the bath and started stroking my shoulder. Progressing down to my breasts and round my waist. He smiled a sad puppy dog smile at me. "I love you, Ellie, I know I get cross and I shouldn't. You're a great mum and a great wife. And when I said yesterday about you being fat, I didn't really mean it. Look at you." He continued the stroking lower down and under the water. "You're gorgeous and I'm a very lucky man." With that, he took the glass from my hand placed it on the bath side, stood up and lifted me from the water, grabbing a bath towel on his way through the door. He carried me to our bed.

Our sexual intimacy had improved over the past couple of months. The first time we tried, about six weeks after Scott's birth, was a disaster. I wouldn't say it was as painful as childbirth but it was still pretty eyewatering. Curtis, however, was never going to take no for an answer, so he just verbally cajoled me into basically just sucking up the pain and working through it. He assured me it would get easier and practising was the answer. Now it felt back to normal and Curtis, as ever, used this as his way of apologising and demonstrating his love for me. He even refilled my wine glass after the event and brought it to the bedroom.

"Andy came into the gym today," he started. "I invited them round for a Chinese takeaway this weekend. Andy says they will pick it up and be round here for about seven-ish."

"Mmm, lovely, that's nice. They are a lovely couple, aren't they?"

"Yeah. Andy joined the gym today. He says it's better than the one he's been using. He has to work out for his job but he loves the football training too. He reckons I'm a lucky guy. Says he wants to have kids but Jenny's not ready. Don't you think she's a bit stuck up? He says she works for a building society and she's expecting a promotion anytime soon. She told him there's no rush, and she wants to wait for a few years." Curtis didn't facially hide the fact that he didn't like Jenny.

"Well, everyone's different, I suppose, a lot of people will think we are too young. Depends on the individual."

"S'pose, yeah, she'd be daft to piss him off though, a good looking bloke with a good job."

"Yes, he is definitely a handsome guy."

"All right, Ellie, that's enough." Curtis sat up and a frown creased across his forehead. "Steady on, you're as bad as the girls at the gym, all swooning over him."

I just laughed and said, "Ooh... What's up, Curtis, don't you like a bit of healthy competition? Don't worry, he's not even in your league. My sexy husband, no one could even come close." I kissed him on his toned chest and suggested we top the bath up with hot water and get in together. He smiled at this.

"OK, you do the bath and I'll get us some refills."

It didn't seem to matter how often Curtis attacked me, verbally or, even, on occasion, physically, he still possessed the charm to win me over. I was mad with myself for being so easily bought with an apology. I so desperately wanted the happy marriage, gorgeous children, genuine and supportive friends. I felt as though I had to suffer Curtis' shortcomings as a trade-off to get my ideal life. But, inside, the truths I was locking away, never to be spoken of, were starting to scare me.

Chapter 12

Everything seemed to be getting back on track. Our relationship, as on and off as it was, seemed to be reignited. The passion was back and this encouraged me to put a little more effort into my appearance. Curtis had got used to my haircut now and said that when I made an effort, wore makeup and dressed a bit better, instead of wearing comfy mummy clothes, I was looking great and even used the word sexy. This spurred me on to try and curb eating anything fattening and Curtis said he would bring me a diet sheet from the gym. "Just follow the dos and don'ts on the sheets," he advised, "and the pounds will drop off. I know you're not exactly working out, but looking after Scott, and getting out to walk him, will be a great bonus. You'll be back to your beautiful, trim self before you know it."

"So you still fancy me, then?" I asked, giggling.

"You know I will fancy you till the day I die. We belong to each other, Ellie, nothing will ever, ever come between us. And, you know what? Now that Scott's getting a little bit older and you're feeling better, we should go out more."

"Yeah, that'd be great." I smiled and felt so happy. The three of us, a proper family, going out together.

"So why don't you ask your mum and dad to come and babysit next weekend? I know we're having Andy and Jenny over this weekend, but we haven't been out with Simon and Angie for ages. If you fed Scott and we went out as soon as he's asleep, we could at least get three or so hours out, it would be nice to get time out."

I hesitated; I didn't want to put a dampener on the mood but there was no way I was leaving Scott with anyone else. Not at four months old. I wouldn't be able to relax and enjoy myself. Especially with no phone to be able to check in on him. What if Mum and Dad had a problem and there was no phone? The overwhelming, powerful thoughts steamrolling through my mind were endless. All those 'what if?' scenarios popped into my head. Absolutely no, not a chance I would leave him. But I would have to tread carefully with my answer.

"Yeah, I suppose it would be nice to see Simon and Angie. I will ask Mum next time she pops in." Which wasn't that often, to be fair. To say she disliked Curtis would be an understatement. Problem was, unlike Dad, who played the game, Mum just said it as it was and managed to piss Curtis off almost every time they were in the same room.

Dad was quiet, observant and reassuring. He would be polite to Curtis and, whenever he had an opportunity to speak to me alone, he would check that I was okay and that Scott was okay too. He tried coaxing me into speaking to Curtis about getting the phone put back on. I always assured him everything was fine and we were both really good, even when we weren't, but he knew. He listened to me, but still came back with comments like, "Well, you've still got your key to home and, you know, you can ring me anytime of the day or night, and I will be here in five minutes. I would kiss him and we'd have a lovely hug and this always happened when Curtis was not in the vicinity. It was very reassuring for me and, although I always insisted everything was okay, I felt loved and protected by my dad's concern. He was a comfort to me.

We had had a great weekend, Andy and Jenny came over and we had a lovely meal, a few drinks and a good laugh. The only awkward moment was when they arrived. I was just putting Scott into his Moses basket and Curtis let them in. Jenny, carrying the takeaway, stopped to put it in the kitchen. Andy walked into the room with Curtis and Andy took one look at me and said, "Wow… Wow, Ellie, I love your hair like that. It reminds me of how you looked when I first saw you at school." He chuckled. I immediately felt my cheeks flush and, whilst enjoying the compliment, for the life of me, I couldn't ever remember seeing or meeting Andy before these recent months.

So, when we were all sat to the dining table, eating and having a glass or two of wine, Curtis just asked him how he remembered me from school. I was dreading the answer. Turned out we had both been at the same party one night and, unbeknown to me, Andy had been there with an ex-girlfriend and I was with an ex-boyfriend.

"Yeah," he laughed, "if only I had known then, eh? I split up with my girlfriend a week later, and I was just leaving school, so our paths never crossed again. Looks like I missed my opportunity. Best man wins," he added and gave Curtis a matey slap on the back. Curtis laughed and joined in with the whole conversation, but knowing him as well as I did, I knew for sure this wasn't the last I was going to hear about this. "And don't think you can make me suffer at training for my school memories. Your training is punishing enough, as it is. You'll have Jenny to deal with if I get any debilitating injuries in the gym," he warned in jest. Jenny was in stitches. She was laughing so hard and taking it all in good humour. So, I just joined her.

We chatted about Andy's job in the police force and his stories ranged from hilarious to heart-breaking. Whatever the story, it was always interesting and his obvious love for the job shone through. He was also basking in the attention, so I changed tact and I asked Jenny about her job. She was vying for a promotion at the building society. Seemed the interview was in a couple of weeks' time. Branch manager in the town centre branch. Although Jenny was a couple of years older than Andy, she was still only twenty-four and had worked at the same place since leaving school, the last four years in a supervisory position. And now hoping for manager's position. This was very impressive and I told her so. "You must be really good at your job, Jenny, and very well-respected to even be considered for an interview. I really hope you get the job. I can see how much it means to you. Good luck with the interview and keep us posted, won't you?"

"Sure, I will, yes, and thanks, Ellie." She smiled sincerely. At the exact same moment Andy leaned back in his chair and with exaggerated animation raised his hand to yawn. "Yeah, yeah. I know, Andy, very dullsville, eh, talking about my job. We can't all have such exciting work lives."

"Ha ha, I'm just kidding, baby. You know I'm very proud of you." But I caught him do a secret eye roll in Curtis' direction. I had the feeling he might just have been a tad jealous. I could have been wrong but women's intuition, and all that.

A little underlying tension was now in the air. Clever Scott must have felt it, because at that exact awkward moment, he started to stir, giving us a reason to change the subject. All in all, the evening went very well. And it was only after they had said their goodbyes and left us, that I could feel some questioning coming on from Curtis. He didn't disappoint. Within minutes, he was asking me about the party that Andy had remembered me from. I told him truthfully that I couldn't remember the party or Andy. In actual fact, I couldn't even work out who would have been my boyfriend at that time. I had probably had three or four boyfriends before Curtis but being only fourteen/fifteen years old at that time, they were easily forgotten. This part of the discussion however was of no consequence to Curtis, but he kept banging on about Andy.

"I can't believe you don't remember somebody that quite clearly fancied you. And I'm not even sure that this is not still the case. The way he 'wowed' about your haircut and all those compliments. Good job you were with some boyfriend at the time or you could have ended up getting together with him."

I laughed at Curtis' flippant summary of a teenage party six years ago, ending in me being married to Andy. "Yeah, a lucky escape for me," I said.

"Well, depends on what you think of him now. He's definitely got a better job than me and what girl doesn't fancy a handsome guy in uniform. Bet you wish things had turned out differently, eh?" Curtis had a real look of deflation on his face.

"Okay, cheer up and stop talking nonsense. This is not even up for discussion. Andy is married to Jenny and very happy and I'm married to you and very happy." A little ultra-quick thought of being married to Andy flicked in and out of my mind in a millisecond. "So let's just leave it right there." To be perfectly honest I had more important things on my mind, like getting out of going out and leaving Scott at home.

As we got ready for bed, I was trying to concoct a plan in my mind. Something plausible but realistic. It was funny, but I was physically within inches of Curtis knowing he had no idea what I was thinking. It made me smile to myself. *Good job our private thoughts are just that,* I thought. Some of the things that went through

132

my mind on occasions would be enough to get me hung!

Because Curtis had had a few drinks, he was totally up for a night of passion. Well, I say night, after a few beers, his idea of passion was him just getting exactly what he wanted. A five minute 'thanks-a-lot', that's all he needed, and off to sleep. But I didn't really feel up to it and when I said, "Mm? Really, Curtis, I'm not really bothered, to be honest. I'm knackered."

I went to kiss him and have a little cuddle and, to my horror, he held me roughly by the shoulders and said, "Good job I wasn't asking ,then, isn't it? Now turn over and do your wifely duties."

"No," I replied. "Just cos you've had a few, what's wrong with you? No means no, and I'm so tired. It's been a really long day, now I want to go to sleep."

With that, he yanked me back to face him and started kissing my mouth hard. I tried to pull away, saying I didn't want to have sex but Curtis was determined to have his way. He grappled with my nightie, pulling it up high enough to expose my breasts and violently moved his mouth to them. Unrelenting, he parted my legs and did exactly what he deemed to be his right. It must have lasted all of two minutes and, whilst I tried to resist for a few seconds, I just thought it would be easier and more comfortable if I just let him get on with it.

He rolled off me and was asleep within seconds. I went to the bathroom for a wash and then went back to planning. Curtis forcing me to have sex with him, surprisingly, didn't seem to worry me. How terrible was that?

Simon and Angie both lived at home with their respective parents. Angie's parents, on the odd occasion that I had met them, were pretty normal. Her dad was a little bit of a pushover, her mum definitely wore the trousers. On the whole, they seemed supportive of Angie but weren't a touchy-feely kind of family. Simon's parents, on the other hand, were cute and lovely. They were both about the same height, pretty similar to myself, around five foot, four inches. I would have said they were smiley, friendly, laid-back people, including his younger sister. Whenever we had been around, that may be to pick up Simon or drop him off, they would always stick their head out of the door and wave us in. Simon insisted it would make their day. So, as not to disappoint, we would pop in. Immediately the kettle would be on and they both dished out hugs and cheek kisses. I really like them a lot.

So, when I had made a plan and I knew I needed an ally, Simon was my first choice over Angie. I knew, first of all, that he would understand my predicament and, secondly, I trusted him to keep a secret. I went to our faithful phone box on the corner and called his mum's house. I thought my plan was fool proof. I'd been over it so many times. I was calling to see what was a good time for them if we popped over to let them meet Scott. Simon brought a gift from his parents months ago and we kept saying we needed to take the baby over to say thank you in person.

When his mum answered the phone, she was delighted I had called. We talked all things babies for a minute and then planned an evening next week when we were all free. "Oh, I can't wait to hold him and have a cuddle. I'll make a cake, I know coffee cake is your favourite, Ellie, I'll do an extra one for you to take home."

"Oh, you're a gem, Shirley. Everyone should have a mum like you. How lucky Simon is." The phone pips started beeping and I put another coin in the slot.

"Oh, yeah, try telling him that," she laughed. "Here, he's just sorting out his work stuff, he'll be off soon. Do you want to say hello?"

Bingo, I thought, just as I had hoped. I had a rough idea of the time he worked — looked like I was right. "Oh, yeah, why not, if he's around, a quick hello won't hurt," I laughed.

"Hi there, Ellie, how's things?"

"Yeah, not too bad, Simon, thanks. Listen, I need a really big favour, but don't talk or repeat anything I say." I didn't want his mum asking questions if she overheard anything, couldn't risk her mentioning it, albeit innocently, in front of Curtis. "Curtis thinks it's a great idea to have my parents babysit so we can have a night out with you and Angie. Now, as much as I'd love that, I'm not leaving Scott at home with anyone when we have no phone. I would be a wreck all night. So, before he contacts you to suggest it, why don't you call around to ours, say tonight or tomorrow evening, just quickly to ask if Curtis fancies is a night out with you and the lads. You can suggest that Angie and I stay home and have a girly night in. And while you're here, please, please say what a nightmare it is not to be able to phone us, say something to shame him into getting it reconnected." I was rushing the whole plan.

"Wow, okay. I think I've got all that. Ellie, are you okay?"

"Yes, I'm fine. But you are the only person I trust to do this for me so that Curtis won't find out."

"No pressure, then?" he laughed. "Okay, I will stop by tonight. Leave it with me."

"Thanks, Si, what can I say, you're a proper mate, thanks." And with that, the pips were going again, but this time I didn't put more money in, I just let it disconnect.

True to his word, as I knew he would, Simon pulled up at ours. I saw his car through the window, so, with quickening pace, I nipped upstairs on tiptoes, thinking it would give Si a chance to say whatever he was going to say, without me being in his way. I knew this little plan could go either way, but I have to admit to feeling a frisson of excitement. Though nervous, the anticipation of getting my own way was a pending sense of triumph. I waited a few minutes just sitting on the closed toilet lid. I heard them move from the kitchen to the lounge and when the voices change to a higher level, I realised they were talking baby-talk to Scott. I had left him dozing in his baby swing.

I decided to go back downstairs and, entering the room, the first thing Simon said was, "Oh, hi, Ellie, how's mummy getting on? Wow, you've had your haircut, it looks great, it really suits you."

"Yeah it's great, eh?" chipped in Curtis, unexpectedly.

"Thanks, Simon, yes I'm good, you? And how's Angie?"

"Yes, we are all fine, thanks. In fact, I came around with a bit of a proposal... Of sorts," He laughed.

"Sounds interesting, I hope it's not just about boring football." I rolled my eyes in mock despair.

"No, Simon and Angie are coming round for dinner next weekend but after dinner me and Si are off out for a pint with the lads while Angie stays in with you for a girly night!"

"Well, that sounds fab." I feigned a look of surprise.

"Simon requested your wonderful chilli con carne for dinner," continued Curtis, all smiles... As if the compliment on my cooking would soften the blow of being left at home. If only he knew. "Sounds like you have it all worked out, does Angie know?" I enquired.

"Yep, all sorted. I just called to see her, she wanted to come now to see Scott but she already made plans with her mum."

"Well, cool, sounds like we have a date." I smiled at Simon and gave Curtis a little kiss on the lips. He looked like the cat that got the cream. I excused myself and took Scott up for a bath, leaving them to chat.

I was just snuggling up to Curtis on the sofa after getting my pyjamas on, ready for bed. He put his feet up and pulled my head onto his chest. The television was on but we weren't really watching it. Curtis gave a small cough to clear his throat and started. "Ellie, I have been thinking. If we are gonna get your parents to babysit now and again, it's only fair that we get the phone reconnected. Don't you think?" He took a small pause. "After all, Scott is our priority and you would be able to relax more if you could check on him while we're out, yes?"

"Er, yeah sure." I tried to sound nonchalant to hide my euphoric feeling inside. "Good idea. Plus it would be easier when the weather is awful, eh?"

"Sure, that as well. Well we can get onto the phone company and get it sorted. As long as you try and cut down on spending, Ellie. I mean, the phone bill is almost forty quid a month so, I'm thinking, if you could shave a tenner off the shopping bill every week, we won't miss the money."

That, I was not expecting, and I sat up straight and tried to hold back my anger. I was seething. The cheek of asking me to shoulder the cutbacks. I had a good mind to suggest we don't buy beer and that would do it. But I had got better at handling these situations now and just replied, "Sure, no problem I can do that." He patted me on the shoulder like I was being a good girl. I'd deal

138

with that later, for now I was having a celebratory dance inside for pulling off the plan. With help from Si too.

The weekend plans went without a hitch. I was learning not to be so reactive and argumentative with Curtis. I was embarrassed by the way I allowed him to treat me but mostly he saved his coercive and controlling behaviour for behind closed doors. In the company of others, he acted like the model husband and perfect father, just never when we were alone.

I had learned the main reason for his behaviour was his all-consuming jealousy of *any* male person in the vicinity. No matter how much I reassured him of my love and faithfulness. I continually went out of my way to minimize any reason to give him doubt but he still struggled with it. He was, without question, not my parents' favourite person. Mum totally kept her distance, and Dad, being the loving, doting father he was, just wanted to extend that love to his first grandchild so popped up quite regularly. He was aware Curtis worked some evening shifts and, knowing he would leave at five p.m. to pick up Tony, the mate that got him the job there, Dad would arrive about five thirty p.m. Weather permitting, he would take Scott for a walk, to feed the ducks or the horses nearby. If it was too cold, he would stay in and play with him. He was totally smitten and this was reciprocated one hundred percent by Scott. All in all, it seemed an unspoken rule that mum and dad just tolerated my marriage as long as they could see I was okay and happy. They had their own code of ethics but I never felt pressure of any kind where expectations were involved. I knew they loved and cared for me and Scott, just at a safe distance.

Chapter 13

The summer of 1982 will always be remembered for the Falklands War. It lasted for approximately ten weeks, from the beginning of April to mid-June. Curtis and I both had friends from school that joined the forces and a couple of them actually fought on the front line during the Falklands War. One morning, in August 1983, we had bumped into one of these friends. His name was Mark. He had been a close school friend of Curtis'. Mark had served six years in the army and Curtis, not having seen him for over two years, did a double take when he spotted him across the road. We were out walking Scott, in the next village to ours that morning.

"Hey MARK... MARK..." shouted Curtis. Mark turned slowly and spotted Curtis. He gave a half smile and an unenthusiastic wave. We caught up with him and Curtis just jumped in, all guns blazing, asking how he was and saying he'd heard that Mark had fought on the front line. Mark looked very forlorn and quite pale but Curtis seemed to notice none of this. Instead, slapping him on the back and asking if he actually shot anybody. Mark shrugged his shoulders and asked if we wanted to walk with him home and pop in for a coffee. We both knew his mum well and therefore accepted the offer, feeling, myself, that the addition of Scott to the entourage would lighten the mood. I could see Mark was not the guy we knew of years gone by and I hoped that seeing his mum would shed some light on this. The hour or so we spent there were quite trying.

Curtis and Mark went to the lounge to talk and I staying in the kitchen to drink my coffee, while Mark's mum fussed over Scott. She told me he had been to the doctors and they said he was suffering from 'shell shock'. He had left the army and she described how she would find him just sitting on his bed, crying. I just listened to her and tried to understand how she was feeling. She was so worried about her son and when the time came to leave, she hugged me and thanked me for just listening.

As we walked back towards home, Curtis expressed his hatred for the foreign soldiers that had reduced his friend to a shadow of his former self. I didn't really understand much about the war, except that it was a fight against Argentina to claim the Falkland Islands, but if Mark's condition was anything to go by, there must have been a lot more people who were now suffering the consequences of it. My feelings were shock at the severity of how it had left Mark and sadness for all his family, particularly his mum. As I started discussing with Curtis how sad it made me feel, he just gave a guttural growl and punched a street sign that we were walking past. "Fuckin' bastard Argentineans," he swore, but quickly recoiled his hand and cradled it in his other hand. It all happened so fast and, looking down at his hand, all his knuckles were bleeding.

"What on earth are you doing?" I couldn't believe what I'd seen. "Please, Curtis, not in front of Scott. Children pick up on anger. Look how he's looking at you." Scott just had a little frown creased across his tiny eyebrows.

"Oh, shut up, Ellie, for fuck's sake, he's not even one yet."

"Well, nonetheless, I'm sure he doesn't need to be subjected to that kind of behaviour."

"I have just had to sit with a good friend and watch him cry as he told me about the past years and how he feels like he doesn't want to live any more. How he shot a man that stood feet away from him. He said they looked at each other in the eyes for a millisecond, before he pulled the trigger to save his own life, and now all he can think is how the other guy maybe didn't even want to fight and probably had a wife and kids, not to mention parents."

"Oh God. Curtis, I know. I spoke to his mum and she told me everything but please don't be angry in front of Scott, being angry isn't going to fix Mark, he needs help and support."

"You don't understand, Ellie, I just need to take it out on someone, I just feel like I need to hurt someone." He had tears in his eyes. I leaned in and gave him a hug. He held onto me and I could feel how tense his body was.

"Come on, we have arranged to pop over and see Simon's mum and dad this afternoon. We've only been a couple of times in the past few months and she's always buying little gifts for Scott. It's time we went for a visit." This was my attempt to pull Curtis from this angry tirade.

Whenever we visited Simon's mum, she always managed to drag Simon's name into the conversation and say how she couldn't wait to be a granny. Simon and Angie had got engaged during the summer but didn't plan on a wedding until next May. This hadn't stopped Shirley getting excited about the prospect of a grandchild. It was most definitely her favourite topic of conversation at the moment.

After we arrived home, I asked Curtis if he still wanted to go. He had calmed down somewhat, now. He said yes. It was a warm day and, just before we left, I took an ice pop out of the freezer, with the intention of letting Scott try it. He had a little taste but wasn't overly bothered. So, I finished it off and grabbed another to eat on route. "What's with the ice pops?" laughed Curtis. "I always think you're pregnant when I see you eating those." I had had a proper craving for them when I was pregnant with Scott, and not just during the summer months, practically the whole nine months. I had munched my way through hundreds of them. As soon as he was born, I hadn't touched another one. However, with the weather warming up, I thought Scott might enjoy one. I had recently bought a box and now I had eaten two. I really wanted more. We laughed about the craving and Curtis said I constantly had cold lips I ate them that often. We got in the car and, as I made my way through the second ice pop, I started trying to think when I was due to have my next period. Curtis mentioning being pregnant made me wonder. While I sat there, going through the dates and thinking, *actually I am a couple of weeks late.*

"Actually Curtis," I broached slowly. "I think I am late on my period but only a couple of weeks."

"Ha ha, that would be funny if you were pregnant, wouldn't it?"

"Not sure funny is the right word. It would be a shock but not a tragedy."

We had a lovely afternoon visit to Simon's house. He and Angie were both there and Curtis told them he predicted I was pregnant, just on the strength of me eating ice pops. We had a laugh about it but it didn't stop me having a couple of glasses of wine with the fabulous cake Shirley had baked. "God, Shirley, your cakes are just heaven," I complimented her.

"Aww, thanks, Ellie, it does help when I know you appreciate them so much, and there's a coffee and walnut cake in the pantry for you to take home."

"Yay, you spoil me but I love it." I gave her a hug.

Another month on, my period still hadn't made an appearance. I was positive that I had to be pregnant. Ice pops were taking over fifty percent of the freezer space and I didn't even feel I needed to get it confirmed by a doctor. Except that I did need to get it confirmed by doctor. I knew the drill, so when it had been confirmed and, in fact, totally planned into my life, we told everyone our happy news. Baby was due around the end of April next year and I had booked myself into the same maternity hospital as before. The fear of the birth crept in and out of my thoughts but, well, it was going to happen, so I just tried to keep busy and keep any fears to the back of my mind.

A few months ago, Curtis had bought himself, what he called, a decent camera. We had a very old instamatic, the ones that took the old 110 cartridges and every few weeks we filled in the 'True Print' envelopes that came through the letterbox. We had albums full of photos of Scott's life, captured right from the morning after his birth. Now Curtis had a 35-millimetre camera, with better quality pictures. He said he was going to take it to the hospital for the next birth and actually get photographs of the baby being born. *Good luck with that,* was all I could think.

It was coming up to Scott's first birthday, and the pregnancy was just starting to show. We had a little party for him with a couple of friends who had kids of a similar age. Curtis was like a man possessed, with the camera. He was quite good, to be fair, at capturing a good picture, and taking some portrait pictures for friends and family had become his passion. At Scott's party, he took as many photos as he could and tried to get some good candid shots of the other kids there.

Later that night, he said there were half-a-dozen frames left on the third film he had used and he was going to use them up at work on the new reception and coffee bar they had just had built. He was really enjoying work and never complained about staying late or going in early to help with all the refurbishments they were undergoing. The gym had been doing really well with a very successful influx of new memberships and Curtis was enjoying the financial benefits of this with his end of month bonuses. He was very proud of the gym's success and wasn't shy when talking about it to anyone. I was happy that he was happy.

He didn't seem quite as insecure as he had done in recent months and I suppose me being pregnant had helped with that. He didn't seem as moody as he used to be but one thing that hadn't improved, in fact, it was worse, was the intimate side of our relationship. He had such an inflated sense of his own importance and this had carried over into the bedroom. He didn't bother with any kisses or niceties in the lead-up to bedtime. He just demanded sex whenever he wanted. Once or twice, when I had tried to resist, he had got really narky, brutish and quite vulgar. He wouldn't take no for an answer. Just treated me like I was his property. Like it was his God-given right to have sex whenever and wherever he chose. It was tiring and also made me feel cheap. But not worth an argument.

One morning, not long after Scott's birthday, Curtis was at home for the morning. Even when he didn't have to be at work until teatime, he tended to pick Tony up and disappear hours earlier than he needed to. I never questioned this and he had said, once or twice, that he and Tony were working hard to make the gym a success. He had even mentioned he might start his own business in the near future. Buy a gym in the neighbourhood and get the football training down there, do some photography in the daytime. He anticipated this would be a very lucrative opportunity. I thought it was a bit of a pipedream, but just agreed because I knew it was the right thing to do.

So, one particular morning, he was showing me photos he'd taken at Scott's party. "Look, Ellie, some of these photos are really good. I reckon I could get them enlarged and framed and sell them to the kids' parents. Look, what do you think?"

I looked at the pictures. There were loads of them. "Wow, yeah, there are some really brilliant ones, Curtis. I didn't even know they had come back. I never saw the envelope come in the post. When did they arrive?"

"Oh, yeah, yesterday, but I had them sent to the gym cos I wanted to show the staff at work the ones I took of the new fittings at the gym."

I picked out the photographs of the gym. They were super impressive. All the old reception had been ripped out and the new coffee bar looked really stunning. It was all in black, gold and silver. Mirrors everywhere and the few tables and chairs were really sleek and modern looking. Dotted around were lamps, shaped liked naked bodies, not in detail, but tasteful shapes with outstretched arms. They were painted black and the hands held a white ball which was the bulb. "Wow, Curtis, it looks amazing. They have done a real good job."

He looked super proud and lapped up the praise. "Yeah, me and Tony designed it all and chose all the fittings and décor. You like it, yeah?"

"I do. Well done, it looks really upmarket and professional. I love it."

He was now in an upbeat mood and said he was popping out to buy a couple of cheap frames for the best pictures of the kids at the party. "If I take them round to their mums' and dads' as a little gift, they might want to order some bigger ones and I can make a bit of profit on them."

"Ha ha. Okay, very enterprising, Curtis," I laughed. "Tell you what. I will pick out the best ones and then you can pick from them when you get back."

"Okay, cool." And, with that, he kissed my head, grabbed the car keys and shot off.

Scott was walking by now and much happier that he could get around and enjoy the freedom of the house. This morning, however, he was happily sitting playing with his new wooden garage that Curtis had made him. It had been gloss painted and had a sign on the front — 'Scott's Garage'. A small ramp at one side and lots of spaces for the massive amount of Matchbox cars he had acquired over time.

So, while he was engrossed, I flicked through all the photos, separating ones of Scott on his own and group ones that were nice to keep as a memory of his first birthday. Then I separated any that were really good of the other kids on their own. The ones of the gym, I put to one side for Curtis. Gosh, there were loads. I recalled he used three films and each one had thirty-six photos on. That's, what? Over a hundred, yeah, a hundred and eight to be exact. I don't even know why I did this. I then proceeded to count them. I got to a hundred and three and thought, *well, that's a bit strange*. So, I counted them again, slower, so as not to make any mistakes about the total. No, definitely one hundred and three, for sure. I thought that it was a bit strange. So, I went over to the dining table, where Curtis had plonked his work bag, and looked inside for the envelopes that the photographs had come in. I thought maybe he had missed a few. But the envelopes were empty. As I closed them to put them back in his bag, I had a thought that maybe they didn't print any that were under- or overexposed. So, I took the plastic pockets that contained the negatives and held them up to the light of the window. I scanned through them slowly, but they all seemed okay to me. Except… When I got to the film he had finished off at work. Yes, there were the half a dozen negatives of the gym, which he had shown me, but what were these last five frames? They looked like photos of someone in a pool, or was it a large jacuzzi? I couldn't quite make it out, but definitely someone was on these photos that hadn't been printed. Or had they been printed but removed from the others, I wondered. I removed the whole set of negatives from that envelope and put the envelope back with the other two and replaced them all back into his bag and the zipped it back up. I felt a little shaky and nervous. But I knew if I questioned Curtis today it would start a massive row. I wanted to know what was on these photos. So, I hid them upstairs with the intention of sending them off later to be printed. Luckily, I had my own chequebook, so I put the strip of negatives with the five missing prints on it into a 'True Print' envelope, filled out the order form and wrote the cheque. Then, knowing Curtis may notice the cheque stub and question it, I tore it out and ripped it up.

I felt very apprehensive over the following few days. Although I was afraid of being found out, I was also, in a strange way, a little excited at having done something so secretive and sneaky. I knew there would be no post on Saturday or Sunday so I could relax a little then. Monday, I got up earlier than normal to make sure I was downstairs in time for the post arriving. Monday… No photos. Tuesday… No photos. Curtis got up just after me and questioned why I had got up early again. "Just needed an ice pop," I answered, opening the freezer compartment door.

"Bloody ice pops, it's November, you nutter."

"I know. I can't help it, have a word with your second child, would you. He or she is the one to blame."

I smiled rubbing my belly in circular motions.

"Well, at least you're not blaming me," he laughed.

We sat and had a coffee and decided to have a drive over to see Stella and Dave. We hadn't seen them for ages and Stella asked us to call by and pick up Scott's birthday present. Curtis called them and made arrangements to go out for a pub lunch while I tackled getting Scott washed and dressed. As I was just finishing off dressing Scott, Curtis shouted to me, "I'm just gonna go through these negatives and pick out the ones that want enlarging. I might not send them to 'True Print' cos there's a Jessops near work and I can get them done there."

"Oh, okay... I'm just taking Scott upstairs to clean his teeth." My heart was hammering in my chest as he started to pull open the zip on his work bag.

I was almost at the top of the stairs when I heard Curtis swearing. "Ellie... ELLIE..." he called at the top of his voice.

Oh, Jesus, I thought, *he's seen one of the negative packets is missing.* I felt sick. Quick, think... Think. Do I lie or have it out with him. "What, what's up?" I shouted back downstairs.

"I can't find the empty photo envelopes. Have you seen them?"

"No, I haven't touched them. When did you last see them?"

"Well they were in my gym bag and I took the work photos out... Shit, I think I could have taken all the envelopes out at work. Bet they're in my office drawer or something," he grumbled as he came upstairs.

I turned to face him, saying he should check later when he went in. He took one look at me and in a shocked voice said, "Oh my God, Ellie... Are you okay?" His eyes were wide open, staring at me.

"I think so, why?"

"Your neck and chest. Look, you have a really bad red rash. Look in the mirror." He ushered me to the bathroom.

Looking, I knew it was nerves from the anticipation of when he shouted to me. I thought he'd discovered the missing negatives. "Ooh, yes, it is red, isn't it? Happens a lot when I've just had a hot drink. Funny, only when I'm pregnant, though. Must be something to do with hormones." I lied and, scarily, very easily, too.

"Okay, as long as you're okay. Jesus, being pregnant got a lot to answer for." He smiled. I gave a sigh of relief, which thankfully came out as a little laugh.

Wednesday... No photos. In fact, no post at all. Thursday... Yes... Yes. The 'True Print' envelope and the phone bill. Curtis was still in bed. He had been particularly late home last night. He said he'd found the photo envelopes at work but made no mention of the missing negatives.

I put the phone bill on the dining table and took my photos into the kitchen. My hands were trembling as I opened the envelope and took out the five prints inside.

153

Each one was a picture of the massive new jacuzzi at the gym. In the jacuzzi was a young girl in a bikini. She was posing in different places. In one, she was laying on the side with one knee bent and leaning on one hand. The other hand was slightly pulling down her bikini bottoms to reveal an area of white skin against her very tanned body. On another, she was midway through jumping out of the water. Both hands on the jacuzzi side, with her ample breasts squashed between her upper arms. Another she, looked at the photographer with a sexy half-smile and her forefinger provocatively in her mouth, gently pulling down her bottom lip. And, yes... Yes, I recognized that face. It was Katie. Fucking Katie that Curtis had brought to the hospital over a year ago. I was fuming. I lined all five photos up next to the phone bill on the dining table.

I went back into the kitchen and, in a trance-like state, I put the kettle on and lifted Scott into his high chair. I made him Ready Brek for his breakfast, and just moved around the kitchen like a zombie, doing mundane jobs. I even let Scott have a spoon to feed himself. As much as his attempts to feed himself were improving, this morning he had it everywhere. Down his baby grow, on the floor, it was even splattered on the kitchen cupboard doors. I just looked but didn't react. It was as if I hadn't seen it. Scott looked quite pleased with himself and took advantage of the moment by sticking his hand in the bowl and sucking his fingers. Curtis walked in rubbing his eyes and yawning loudly. Scott smiled at him and said his one and only word, "Dada."

Curtis laughed and ruffled his mop of dark brown baby hair. "Morning, yes it's Dada. Wow you're making a bit of a mess there, buddy. Ellie, sort him out. Bloody hell, aren't you watching him? He's getting shit everywhere."

"Not everywhere!"

"What, what you on about?" He looked confused.

"Not everywhere," I repeated pointing through to the dining table. He clearly had walked straight past it and not seen. "There…. On the table. That's just YOUR shit on there," I spat.

He turned and stepped back through the door. A second or two for him to focus and the colour drained from his face in an instant. He picked up the photos of Katie, all lined up. "What the… Where the hell did these come from?"

"Yes," I shot back, "fucking good question. And that's exactly what I'd like to know."

"Well you obviously put them there, Ellie, so where the hell did you get them from. I had already given these prints to her before I brought the others home. No point bringing them here just to cause a row." Throughout this sentence, he gained bravado and his voice now took on an accusatory tone.

"Don't you dare turn this round on me, Curtis. What the fuck are you doing taking photos like THAT, of her? She looks a proper tart and I want to know what the hell is going on," I demanded, but tried not to raise

155

my voice for Scott's benefit.

Curtis tried to look like the injured party, even though I knew I'd struck a poignant chord. "For your information," he started in a hushed voice, "she... Katie asked me to take some photos of her for her modelling portfolio. So, I used a few of the spare shots left after I had done the ones for work." He nodded at me and this action alone said 'there, put that in your pipe and smoke it!'

"And you expect me to believe that bollocks?"

"That bollocks is the truth, so please your fuckin' self." And, with that, he ripped them all in half, strode into the kitchen and slammed them in the bin. "Don't bother doing me breakfast, I'm going." He turned on his heels and left in the direction of the stairs, to get dressed, I presumed.

Once again, I was left feeling like I was the guilty party. Once again, this Olympic-class manipulator had destroyed a little piece of me.

Chapter 14

My swollen belly was getting bigger by the day and, suddenly, Christmas was upon us and I really didn't feel like doing anything super special. We did the usual dropping off and picking up of gifts and spent a lovely Christmas Day at Stella and Dave's but, other than that, it was quite quiet.

Curtis had a few days off work, but that didn't mean he spent any more time at home with us. He seems to be spending an awful lot of time with Tony from work. Tony and his girlfriend, Kelly, had just found out they were having a baby, and Curtis kept telling me how he was explaining everything to Tony on what to expect being a new dad. Like he was the perfect husband and father, fully qualified to give advice on these matters. "Tony asked if we wanted to pop round to theirs one night, not too late, say teatime-ish, and Kelly was going to do a curry. We thought about renting a video to watch. What do you think?" Curtis asked one morning.

"Yeah, sounds good," I answered. I liked to take Scott when I went out. And they only lived at the other end of the village. "You seem to spend a lot of time with Tony these days, might have to have a word with him when we go round. Keep taking my husband off to work a couple of hours earlier than necessary," I laughed.

I was just teasing him but Curtis' head shot round to face me and he looked very alarmed at my comment. "No... No, don't say anything about us going to work early. Kelly doesn't know, I don't think she'd be very happy."

"Why?" I asked. "I don't complain. I know how hard you both work."

"Yeah. Well, she's not quite as understanding as you and, since Tony had an affair last year, she's been on his case."

"You what!" I exclaimed. "He had an affair last year? And she stayed with him and now they're having a baby, is she mental?"

"Yeah, I know, mental isn't it? I keep telling him he's lucky she forgave him and he should be careful. But, well, he just can't help himself."

"What do you mean, he can't help himself?"

"Well, when we go to work early, we stop off on the way and he calls in to see this girl that he was having the affair with. I wait in the car and he goes in to see her. He said it's complicated, but he has to see her. That's why we started setting off to work early. But, Ellie, you can't say anything, please, it's his business and he's my boss. So, I just don't get involved."

"What do you mean, you don't get involved?" I argued. "You take him there in your car and wait outside. That is involved, Curtis."

"I know, but now they are having a baby, he says

he's going to finish it and he says he's going to change. He's off work at the moment with a broken ankle. So, he can't really get out."

"Oh my God, Curtis. What the fuck. And you believe him? She deserves to know. And kick his ass right out of that home. Jesus, don't let me near her, I won't be able to stop myself from telling her. What an absolute bastard he is. If you did that you would be gone, finished, divorced."

"Ellie, you can't tell her. Tony will know I've told you and I need my job," he pleaded with me. I just looked directly into his eyes and he made a grab for my wrists. Squeezing them tightly he pulled me close to him and spoke slowly. "You breathe one word of this to her and I swear to God, Ellie." His voice changed from pleading to warning.

"What, you will do what?"

"You don't want to find out, trust me. We will go round there and be normal and have a nice evening and then leave. Do you understand me?"

I was mad with myself for nodding and backing down. But his menacing character scared me. By the time we went round, two days later, I had calmed down. We had had a few discussions about infidelity and I made no bones about the fact that I would never give a second chance. Curtis said he would never dream of being unfaithful and I liked to think I believed that little statement, one hundred percent. But he had, over time, given me reason for doubt. I felt really sorry for Kelly,

Tony's girlfriend, and, while I felt like I had no option but to agree to keep quiet, I wasn't happy about it.

While we were there a little opportunity presented itself... And, well, I don't like to miss an opportunity, especially to out the truth. We had only been there about thirty minutes and Tony was so obviously trying to get Kelly and myself out of the way. I asked Curtis if he knew what was going on and he whispered back that Tony needed to call Julie (the other woman) and it was urgent.

"Just take Kelly and go for a walk to the shop, get a bottle of wine or something."

"Yeah, I bet it's urgent." I could hear my own voice dripping with sarcasm. Kelly seemed oblivious to everything. "Come on, Kelly, let's go and get a bottle of wine to have with dinner. The three boys can all stay here together. I will just nip back into the kitchen and put my boots on."

Their house was an old semi with a really long driveway. The back door was right round the back of the house, and the front door, a good distance apart. Kelly opened the front door and shouted to me to pick up her purse on the kitchen worktop. This was the opportunity that presented itself. I purposely left the purse and joined Kelly, all the time chatting to distract her from checking I had the purse. After thirty seconds or so walking I feigned a look of surprise and said. "Oh, bloody hell, Kelly, I didn't pick your purse up. What an idiot, sorry. I did pick it up when you shouted but put it down while i fastened my boots." I rolled my eyes and suggested we just stroll back and shout Curtis to get it."

"Ha ha, looks like we both have baby-brain," she laughed.

"We can shout to Curtis through the front letterbox, he can pass it, save walking round the back," I suggested.

"Good thinking," she countered.

We strolled back chatting and laughing and, as we approached the gate, I could see Tony's figure through the opaque glass in the front door. "Ooh, look, Kelly, Tony's on the phone," I giggled. "Bet it's his overprotective mummy, checking up on her little boy's broken ankle." Kelly put her hand over her mouth to stifle her giggling. "Let's creep to the letterbox and have a listen." I held her arm. She pushed the letter box slightly and we both heard.

"No, Julie, listen to me, please. Look, I'm doing what I can. Of course I want to be with you and the baby. I can't leave Kelly right just now, especially with my leg in plaster, I can't drive or anything. Please, I love you, let me get sorted. Honestly, just another couple of weeks until the plaster is off, please."

Kelly had slowly slid down the wall and sat on the front door step. Her face was drained of colour. She looked ashen. Oh my God, what have I done? I had absolutely no idea there was another baby involved in this mess. I felt sick. How fucking dare he… What a bastard. Looking again at Kelly, her mouth limp and open and unshed tears balancing, just waiting for her to blink. She put her head in her hands and wracking sobs came, guaranteeing the tears to fall. I sat beside her and pulled her to me in a tight embrace. She started to moan like an animal in pain.

"Oh, Kelly… I'm so sorry. Please, let me help you. Keep crying as much as you can. Get it out. I'm here for you. I won't leave you." I had no idea what I should be saying, all I did know was the guilt consuming me felt like being trapped in a house fire. I felt so responsible. God, what a mess. "Listen, Kelly. Why don't I grab your purse and I will get Scott? We can walk to my house and give you space to decide what you want to do. Either that, or you go inside now and it will be a total shit fight."

She raised her head, sniffing her runny nose, and said, "Yeah, thanks, Ellie, I'm sorry to drag you into this. Maybe we should go to yours, I need to think. I know that Julie was the name of the woman he was having the affair with last year but he told me it was nothing… She meant nothing, he said. He even told me she'd moved away and he had never seen her again." She was wiping tears and snot on her hands as she stammered her way through this speech. "Oh God, Ellie, do you think the baby of hers is his? How could he lie to me so much and pretend he was all happy to have a baby with me?" She was talking too fast and breathing too fast. "He said we would get married when the baby was about a year old, why would he say that?" She shook her head and burst into another flood of tears. "Oh God, the house, Ellie… The house. We only just bought it. We have a mortgage together."

"Don't you worry, love, he's gonna have to pay. In more ways than one. Let me grab Scott and we can bugger off out of here."

We walked slowly down to our house, stopping every ten paces for Kelly to blow her snotty nose. Poor girl, she really was in a shitstorm. I just kept telling her she would be okay, that we'd work it out. That I was there for her and I wouldn't let her down. Words, just words. I was talking for the sake of talking and didn't even have one idea as to what would happen next. I felt completely out of my depth. If this had been my life, I would be having a total meltdown.

I put the kettle on and asked her if she minded if I rang Curtis. I felt like I needed to let him know what was going on. He was under the impression I had just changed my mind about taking Scott with us for the walk. Now he had the lowdown and Kelly said to tell him everything she had overheard. Curtis was like a headless chicken. He drove straight home and tried to sit down to talk with us. He said, to cover his own sorry ass, I'm sure, that he'd only just found out that Tony was seeing someone. He was blown away that there was a baby involved. A three-month-old baby, he'd just discovered. What a complete and utter catastrophe.

Despite the fact that it took Kelly almost two hours of deliberating, she made a decision and asked a favour of Curtis. She wanted him to take Tony out of the house for an hour so she could go in and pick up as much of her stuff as she could physically carry in the car. She expressed that she didn't want to have to speak to him or see him at all and she was going to her parents' home, around forty miles away. To be perfectly honest, I was in complete awe of her. After the initial shock, she seemed to go into 'deal with it' mode and calmly returned to the house to get her things.

We did what we could to help her on that fateful day but, ultimately, it wasn't an awful lot. "Why do these things always seem to happen near Christmas?" I asked Curtis, a couple of days later. I felt exhausted and overwhelmed after the recent revelations.

"Yeah, I know, as if it's not shit enough, as it is. It just seems ten times worse. Have you heard from her at all?"

"No, not a thing since she left. I'm not really surprised though, are you?"

"Suppose not."

"What about Tony, has he said anything?"

"Only work stuff, you know. I think his mum is staying with him until the cast is off his leg."

"Fuckin' mummy's boy," I spat, "hope she kicks his sorry arse into shape."

"Ha, yeah but she probably won't," Curtis said, smiling. "Ooh, by the way, I bumped into Andy, they're having a New Year's Eve party on Saturday night and we're invited. Do you fancy it?" He seemed eager.

"That's in two days, let me give mum and dad a ring and see what they're doing."

"Okay, let me know if they can babysit and I'll call Andy."

Mum and dad didn't have any plans for New Year's Eve and were happy to oblige with babysitting duties. I made sure Scott was all tucked up asleep in his cot before eight p.m. and wrote down Jenny's number, just in case. We were only walking five minutes up the village and I promised we would be back for twelve thirty, after we'd seen the new year in. Although Scott was now fifteen months old and sleeping a lot better, he was still sure to wake up in the early hours. Despite being pregnant, I was still breast-feeding him on the occasions he woke in the night. They seemed happy with our planned time to be home. I felt more nervous, Mum being there. Usually Dad would come and do any babysitting stints on his own. He was *the* best grandad, with so much patience and love. I think Mum's dislike for Curtis kept her at a distance. She really didn't have the time of day for him and keeping them as far away from each other as possible was fine by me.

When Dad came alone, I insisted we be home by eleven p.m. and, as much as it really annoyed Curtis, he knew that if he didn't adhere to this request, I may not go out at all. So, he would put on his 'Mr Perfect Husband' hat, in front of my dad and talk to him in an unctuous manner. I only hoped Dad didn't detect his insincerity like I did.

Off to the party we went, Curtis downing three or four cans of beer within the first hour. I thought he would be bladdered or even asleep before midnight. There was around thirty or so people crammed into Andy and Jenny's small, new build, semi-detached house. Quite a few friends from the building society that Jenny now proudly managed. She had been good friends with a lot of the staff before her promotion so they didn't have any inhibitions about letting their hair down in front of the boss. They all looked as though they were competing with each other in the dress department. Or maybe I should rephrase that to 'as little a dress as possible department'. Not that Curtis was complaining. I felt a bit frumpy and mumsy. I had made an effort with a floaty, sparkly top but, accompanied by maternity trousers and flat ankle boots, I wasn't quite rocking it. We were walking home, was my excuse.

The music was pumping out loudly and, coupled with the singing/shouting, it made for quite a noisy affair. I made myself a cup of tea and bagged a comfy chair that I strategically pulled close to the telephone table. I was just being prepared in case I was needed. Obviously, Curtis had no such concerns. His attentions were well and truly taken up with the scantily clad, eighteen-year-olds that worked with Jenny. Not wasted attention, either, more like reciprocated with gusto. Curtis, there was no doubting, was a good-looking bloke. His black, wavy hair, olive skin and very dark brown eyes were among his best assets. He took care with his clothes and was fit in more ways than one. But isn't it funny how someone's actions and personality can turn them into an ugly person.

It was barely past ten thirty and I was really ready for home. I looked around for Curtis and someone pointed upstairs in the direction of the bathroom. I thought I would wait outside the bathroom door to speak to him as it was relatively quieter than downstairs. Some random guy was sat on the top stair opposite the door and said to me, with a distinctly drunken, slurred voice "If ya want the loo, love, get behind me, I'm next." I just looked with obvious distaste at him. "Mind, ya could be in for a bit of a wait. That arrogant twat, mate of Andy's, is in there... Ya know, the football trainer guy. Took some bird in with him."

It only took me a millisecond to explode and start banging my fists on the locked door. "OPEN THIS FUCKIN' DOOR, CURTIS... NOW," I screamed.

I heard laughing as the door opened and Curtis exited wiping his lips. Then a young, totally inebriated, girl, who could barely stand unaided, wobbled out, clinging onto Curtis' shirt. I dragged her off him by her clothes and helped her in the direction of the stairs, where the waiting drunk caught her mid-flight. He started swearing and shouting but I didn't hang around to listen. I pushed Curtis back into the bathroom, followed him and slammed and locked the door behind me. "You dirty scumbag. Not only are you a total embarrassment to me, but to yourself, as well. Acting like I'm not even here, or worse, like you're not even married. You repulse me, Curtis, and not even the decency to look ashamed or apologise." With that I drew back my hand and slapped him as hard as I could across the face. He went flying sideways and crumpled in the bath in a heap. "And don't bother coming home," I added for good measure, but not before he managed to scramble out of the bath and land a slap awkwardly across my face and head.

Buoyed by alcohol and his own narcissistic sense of self-importance, he followed the slap, which had sent my head reeling into the bathroom cabinet, by saying, "Yeah... Go on. You piss off home, you boring Mrs Perfect. Just because you don't know how to enjoy yourself, don't think you can stop me." He opened the door and forcefully shoved me out. "Go on, run home to Daddy, you miserable bitch." He slammed the door and locked himself in.

I was mortified. Angry. Embarrassed. Hot fury rose inside me. I felt like ripping out my own hair. As I stepped downstairs, I was met by jeers and comments being thrown at me by onlookers, words all flying around, un-listened to. The bleeding wasn't visible from the outside but I could feel it in my heart. I was sure. I cried all the way home and then had to convince mum and dad that my runny eyes and red nose were due to the cold wind. I then lied, saying I didn't feel too good, but that Curtis had walked me to the corner and then gone back to the party. They left, I'm not sure how convincing I actually was but, well, they said nothing.

I went up to check on Scott, he was sound asleep and my love for him felt stronger than ever, if that was possible. I had to stop myself picking him up. I just felt like I needed to hold onto something, someone. I sat on the edge of our bed and just cried. Overwhelming feelings of deflation and despair. Here I was, sat alone, seeing in a new year while my devoted husband was blind drunk at a party full of teenagers throwing themselves at him. I felt so sorry for myself. I ran a bath and poured myself a glass of wine.

As I lay there in the hot bubbly water, large glass in hand, I made a conscious decision to pull myself together. I hoped Curtis didn't come home that night and I would get up early and go out. Yes, I would drive to his mother's and tell her what a twat of a son she'd raised. Yep, that's what I would do. I climbed into bed, happy I'd made a plan. *Why wasn't I brave like Kelly*, I thought. Just pack his stuff and kick him out. Was I afraid of how that would play out for me? Or was I more scared of Curtis? I knew he would come home, apologise, blame being drunk, promise not to do it again, apologise again, cry and profess his undying love for me. What had I done to deserve this life? All I could think was how disappointed my dad would be if we broke up. Or would he?

Chapter 15

I really did have a good relationship with Stella and, for that matter, with Dave too, so when I had driven to see them the very next morning, they made me feel more than welcome. They hadn't seen Scott for a while and wowed at how much he had changed. We had a lovely morning there and even stayed for a little New Year's Day lunch.

Curtis had not materialised at home before we left at nine fifteen a.m., so when we returned at three thirty p.m., I didn't really know what to expect. I felt much better after having spilled my guts to Stella and Dave and I really felt supported by them. Their feelings about Curtis' behaviour were pretty much on par with mine, they said they were there for me any time, any day and really understood my issues with Curtis. Funny how I couldn't admit to anyone else how bad his general behaviour was but his mum was definitely on my side. Her warmth reached into my heart.

When we returned home, Curtis was in bed and, having already made a decision not to speak to him, it was probably the best place for him. When he eventually surfaced, true to form, he begged for forgiveness and cried. I had seen it all before and, after telling him in no uncertain terms exactly what I thought of him, I continued my silence. He blamed the drink, he blamed Andy for giving him the drinks, he blamed the girl for 'throwing' herself at him and then he blamed me for leaving him there all alone. Good God, talk about not wanting to take responsibility.

My cold shoulder lasted well over a week. Curtis had returned to work, so daytime and his night shifts were easy, but when he was home he acted like a petulant child. Swearing to himself and banging doors, etc. He only stayed in long enough to eat and get dressed and then he would disappear off somewhere. I have no idea where and I didn't even care.

Around the middle of January, he came home from work really early one day. He ran into the kitchen where I was battling washing the bedding, in my archaic, twin-tub washing machine. This was no mean feat, but, despite it being cold outside, the sun was out and there was a bit of a breeze so I had to 'strike while the iron was hot', as they say. Curtis didn't even say hi. He ran past me and legged it upstairs at breakneck speed.

Five minutes later, he was bellowing my name. "Ellie… Ellie… Please can you come up here?" He didn't sound normal. This made me a little uneasy but I went upstairs, grabbing Scott on my way. As we reached the top of the stairs, I looked down the hallway, past the bedroom doors, to see the bathroom door open and Curtis sat on the toilet with his trousers and pants around his ankles and his head hanging over the sink beside the toilet.

"Jesus Christ, Curtis, what's up? What happened?"

He was white lipped as he stammered to speak. "I'm not well, Ellie, I didn't think I was going to make it home. I spent all morning at work throwing up and on the toilet. I feel like I'm going to die." He sounded panicky.

"Yuck, that's gross. What have you eaten? Or do you think it's a bug you have gotten?"

"No, I've not eaten anything out of the ordinary. But the pains I keep getting across my middle, God, honestly, Ellie, I've never felt this bad, help me, please. I don't even know what to do with myself." He was leaning his forehead into the crook of his arm, which was resting on the edge of the sink.

"Well, I'm not wiping your arse but if you sort yourself out, put some pyjamas on and get into bed, we'll see what we can do."

He said he felt cold, but as he got undressed, he was clearly sweating and shaking. I pulled the bed covers up to his neck, closed the curtains and put a cool flannel on his forehead. "Right. I'm going to sort the washing out and then I will have a walk to the chemist and see what I can get. If you don't improve over the next few hours. I'll call the doctor out." His eyes were already closed and his face was positively green.

After some Dioralyte, and twenty-four hours of fasting except for water, he seems to be feeling a little better. He had been up three times during the night and was fragile and very wobbly on his feet. I helped him to the loo. I was relieved that the throwing up had finally abated.

By the following afternoon, he said he actually felt hungry, so, I made him a slice of toast and a small cup of tea. We sat on the bed together and I just looked at him. I wanted to say something along the lines of 'yeah, I wonder how well the eighteen-year-old slapper from the party would have looked after your sorry ass', but I didn't. Instead I said, "Do you feel like getting up yet? I can get some blankets on the sofa if you want to come downstairs and watch a bit of telly. It's almost tea time the news will be on soon."

"Thanks, Ellie. Yes, I think I will," he mumbled. "What would I do without you? I really don't deserve you," he continued sheepishly.

"Oh well, at least we agree on something." I smiled. It was a bit of a crooked half-hearted smile.

"Yeah, my mum and Dave agree. I got a right dressing down off her last week. Even Dave stuck his two pennies' worth in. He said I didn't know how lucky I was and warned me if I carried on being an idiot, I would end up losing you." He had a couple of tears now crawling slowly down his cheeks.

"Yeah, well, best you take heed, eh? We are about to have another baby in three months, I don't want to be a single mum, but don't let that make you think I couldn't do it. I didn't get married to contend with this kind of behaviour."

"I know, I'm sorry, Ellie. I need to stop drinking… I'll just drink when I'm home with you." He quickly amended his words. "I'm nothing without you, can we leave the past in the past? I just want to make you happy."

"Best concentrate on getting better, then, and we'll take it from there," was all I could offer in reply. He leaned over to kiss me and I turned by mouth away so he kissed my cheek. "No way," I said. "Clean your teeth if you want a kiss," I laughed.

Our following weeks where much improved. Curtis really was trying hard not to be a dick. I'm sure it wasn't easy for him but, seriously, his mum told me later that she'd used the word 'disappointed' with him. How is it that the word 'disappointed' cuts a little bit deeper than if they just say they are cross with you? She also said that when she told him to grow up, he was really reactive. So, I banked that one for later.

Weeks passed by and so my belly just got bigger and bigger. I kept talking to Scott about the baby. Everyone kept telling me to be careful and that Scott would be jealous when the baby came. So, I was determined to make sure it didn't happen. I kept letting him feel the baby move and telling him I was having a new baby for him. I said he would need to help me to change the baby's nappy and he would have to put the baby powder on the baby's bottom. Although he was only just putting a few words together, at eighteen months old, he did seem to understand everything I said to him. He helped me to get my bag ready for the hospital. We also washed and folded all the newborn-size baby grows, ready for the baby's arrival.

Knowing my parents feelings about Curtis, I was hoping and praying that the baby would come first thing in the morning, and I could be home by teatime. I had been told, with the second baby, if everything was okay, I could go home the same day. I knew that if I ended up in hospital for any length of time, Curtis would have to stay at my parents' house with Scott. This thought absolutely filled me with dread. If he put one foot wrong, my mother would be down on him like a ton of bricks, but he didn't want to leave Scott overnight and still wanted to be able to drive to the hospital at any time. So, we had all decided, if I ended up staying in, he would sleep at their house. *I just cannot let this happen,* was all I could think. But someone up there wasn't listening.

It was Friday afternoon and I was three days overdue. It started with a stabbing pain going through to my back. Curtis was supposed to be home from work by four p.m., and, by the time he came, I had had a few pains. So, we took Scott to my mum and dad's and went to the hospital, thinking this was it. By the time we arrived at the hospital the pains seemed to have subsided. I just said, "Look, let's give it an hour and, if there's no more pain, we'll just go home."

"No, sorry, Mrs. Parson. It doesn't quite work like that. Let's get you in here," said one of the midwives on duty. "We can check you over and see what's happening." She saw us into a delivery room and asked me to jump on the bed. "I'll be back in a minute," She continued, and, with that, left the room with my papers in her hand.

"What do you think, Ellie?" asked Curtis. "Can they make you stay even if you are not in labour? God, I hope we're not going to be stuck here for hours," he grumbled. Before we had left home, Curtis had insisted I make him a pile of sandwiches to take. He'd remembered the last time that he had felt hungry, probably because of the boredom of waiting, he had said.

"Well, whatever I have to do, I have to do," I replied. "Let's just wait and see what she says when she comes back."

"I'm not sitting here all night if nothing's happening," he announced.

"Sure you're not, Curtis. I mean, why would you want to stay and support your pregnant wife when you could be doing something much more interesting?"

"Oh, come on, Ellie. You know what I mean. It's all right for you, you get a bed and I just have to sit here on this crappy chair. And, besides, I need to call back home. I forgot my camera and they already said I could take the pictures of the birth."

Before I had a chance to say anything in response, the door opened the same midwife entered, along with another woman. "Okay, so we're just going to have a little look and see if anything is happening. Have your waters broken at all, or even been leaking?"

"No, nothing," I replied.

"Okay, so let's get you into your nightie and we can have a look." I got changed and, after a bit of prodding and poking, she picked up my notes and said, "Right, Ellie, so you're about one and a half centimetres dilated, but it looks like the labour has slowed right down. I know you are a little overdue so what we are going to do is keep you in over the weekend and see if you go back into labour. We'll keep a close eye on you and, if nothing materialises, well, you were due here on Monday anyway for antenatal class. So, make yourself comfortable and we'll take you up to a ward."

"No, no… I can't stay here all weekend. They said I would be able to go straight home the same day with this baby. It's my second and my eighteen-month-old son is at my parents' house. I can't stay here." I felt a wave of sheer panic at the thought of Curtis at my parents' house for a whole weekend without me to mediate.

"Look, can I go home?" piped up Curtis. "Is this baby coming tonight, or what?"

"Whoa, whoa, whoa," said one of the women. "You don't really have a choice, I'm afraid, Ellie, you have started dilation and could go back into labour at any time, or it could take a couple of days."

"Fuck that," said Curtis under his breath, but loud enough for all to hear. "I'm going to get my camera and then I'll sleep with Scott at your mum and dad's. You can let me know if anything happens." And, with that, he kissed my cheek picked up his car keys and left the room.

I just started to cry. "Hey, come on, look, don't get upset. We can call him if anything happens. You get some rest and I'm sure he will be fine with your son at your parents' home."

"Really?" I said sarcastically. "You have no idea." I was still crying. "They hate each other and it will only end badly," I sobbed.

"Oh, come on, Ellie. Let me get you a nice cup of tea and I will introduce you to Kathy, she's going to be your neighbour on the ward."

I was wheeled up to a ward and put into a bed next to a large lady, who was almost flat on her back. She looked about thirty-ish and positively excited when we arrived. "Hi, Kathy, this is Ellie, she's come to keep you company for a while. I'm just going to get her a cuppa, would you like one too?"

"Oh, yes, please. Never say no to a cuppa," She chirped with a broad smile on her face. "Welcome, get yourself settled, Ellie," said Kathy, "and then you can tell me all about yourself. It's so good to have some company."

"Why, have you been here hours, too?" I asked. Kathy laughed a proper loud, belly laugh. "It wasn't meant to be funny," I said, a bit confused.

"Oh, sorry, love, no, it's not your fault. You

178

weren't to know."

"Know what?" I really was lost now.

"I'm seven months pregnant and I've been here for about four of those months and I will be here until the baby comes."

"Blimey, why, what happened?"

"Well, it's a long story, here have a biscuit." She opened the cupboard beside her, it had more food in it than a corner shop. "Help yourself, Ellie, open whatever you fancy and I'll have a dozen custard creams when the cuppa comes. Then get comfy. There are only a couple of hours before the film starts. It's *The Graduate* tonight. Have you seen it?"

"No, no, I haven't," I answered whilst rifling through her goodies. I chose some biscuits and some crisps, and also chose to stop crying. I mean, she has been here forever. I got settled in my bed and the tea arrived.

She told me in detail about how she had a threatened miscarriage at thirteen weeks and then ended up never going home. Apparently, the baby kept going too low down and so she had to have a few stitches inside. "I've been put on complete bed rest. Even now there is a chance the head will get engaged and it's much too early. So here I am, bored out of my skull, until I give birth. I suppose it could always be worse. I've kind of got used to it now. Every extra week I keep baby inside, it's safer for them. Anyways, tell me, what's happening with you. You look really ready to drop but

179

why are you so upset?"

I filled her in on, well, everything. I told her about having Scott and how horrendous the whole ordeal was. "Can't believe I have gone and done it again. They say you forgot the pain. Well, let me tell you, that is a load of bollocks. I will never ever forget that day. I just wanted to die. Oh sorry... Is this your first? I didn't mean to put the fear of God into you."

"Oh, don't worry, can't think it will be that bad for me, little bugger's been trying to get out for the last four months," she laughed, rolling her eyes. "But yes, it is my first time. They say I may not be able to have any more. I will be grateful if this one is okay, so I just count my blessings."

"Yeah, I suppose you would be," I agreed. Then I carried on and told her all about my marriage to Curtis, what a first-class twat he could be. I found myself telling her about Tony and Kelly splitting up and then the whole sorry mess at Andy and Jenny's party. She really did seem so happy to have a distraction and, when the film was about to start at ten p.m., I quickly told her of my fears of the situation right now with Curtis at my parents' home. That made me start to worry again and I made a decision. I wasn't going to hang around here all weekend. I was having this baby tonight. I shared that decision with Kathy.

"You can't just tell it to come out," she laughed.

The film started and I laid there holding onto the underside of the mattress at either side of my bed as

180

tightly as I could. Then I hooked my feet on the last rail at the foot of the bed… And pushed. I pushed for about six or seven seconds and then rested. I kept repeating this right through the first hour of the film (which, incidentally, was very good).

Kathy thought I was crazy. "You shouldn't do that, you know, you might hurt the baby," she warned.

"The baby is fine, and overdue, so should be bloody well out by now. I'm just giving it a little prod to help it on its way." It was ten minutes past eleven. "Ouch." I felt a pain. "Come on," I encouraged. "I had a contraction. I'm sure it was," I said excitedly. "Let's time them… How long till the film finishes?" I didn't want to miss the end.

"About half an hour, I think," she replied.

"Okay. I'm going to keep pushing a bit until the pains are regular and then I'll call the nurse. Then she can call Curtis and he will have to come back." I felt really pleased with myself, and my plan ran like clockwork. The film finished and I had had two more contractions. I rang for the nurse She had to look down below and confirmed that I was four centimetres dilated.

They called Curtis at twelve thirty a.m. and our second son was born at three thirty a.m. And yes, Curtis took photographs of the whole bloody mess. The birth was a million times better than the last time. I had a couple of small tears down below that only required eight stitches. Hallelujah. I felt amazing. A bit sore but elated I had managed to pull it off tonight. Tyler weighed exactly the same — seven pounds, eleven ounces — as his brother. He was two centimetres longer, which was neither here nor there, but his head circumference was two centimetres smaller, which was a big deal for my body. I felt absolutely fine and was allowed home later the same day. So, within twenty-four hours, we were all back home, with a plus-one to the family.

Chapter 16

Having Tyler and 'having' Tyler were both a breeze in comparison to Scott. Having, in the sense of the birth and, also, just having him there at home to look after. He seemed to sleep a lot longer after his feeds and, when he was awake, he didn't really cry much. He seemed a lot more contented than I remember Scott being. Scott was loving having a new baby in the house. I did what I had planned to do and, on the day we took Tyler home, I told Scott that I had been to get a new baby for him. He was excited and whenever Tyler needed changing or bathing, Scott was there, helping. The only real obstacle was the breastfeeding. Scott had still been having a comfort feed at bedtime, or if he woke in the night, which thankfully had almost stopped, but he struggled to get his head around passing on my boobs to his little brother. I told him that he had to teach Tyler how to do it and that he should hold his hand whenever he fed so that he felt safe. It seemed to work and Scott was like a mini mummy to Tyler.

During the first three months of Tyler being home, Curtis was quiet and spent as much time as possible out of the house. And whilst Tyler could not have been any better behaved at all, I still found my days were a bit of a struggle and a lot of hard work. Fighting with the washing machine and the million Terry towelling nappies we got through. Long three-mile walks to the big supermarket to get the shopping in with a double buggy. Then half a dozen full shopping bags hanging off the handles and a three-mile walk back. Hoping the boys would sleep for most of it and not kick off. Although there was a great bus service, actually using it with two boys and a double buggy was physically impossible. Scott was down to one afternoon nap, so I always timed this into any outings.

Still, I had what I had always wanted, my two perfect boys were, without question, the apple of my eye. My love for them was so strong it was palpable and ever present. This didn't improve my relationship with Curtis, however. He didn't offer to do anything to help and was always moody when I was busy tending to the children and not him. He started going out more often to the pub on the evenings when he wasn't at work. He was also trying to set up everything to become self-employed. I hardly ever saw him. He used the only car we possessed, so I just plodded along, doing the best I could on foot.

It was, by now, mid-summer, so the weather was easier to contend with. I had the odd visitor now and again during the daytime and my wonderful, loving, caring father came up most evenings to put Scott to bed and read him bedtime stories. Scott obviously idolized his grandad. He would sit in the window of the front room with his beaker of milk watching for my dad's car to pull up. My dad would always give me a hug, a little kiss on the head for Tyler and then swoop Scott up into his arms, shower him with kisses and whisper in his ear, "I love you, my darling big boy, come on, let's go up and find a book to read". My father was such a reliable constant in my life; he was always full of wise words and just having him in my day-to-day life made me feel happy and safe.

Curtis was always grumpy about my dad's influence in our family. It almost felt like he was jealous of everyone at all times. If he came home and dad was there, he would mumble under his breath and swear, saying he was here all the time. If he wasn't here, and I asked Curtis to do anything to help me, he just complained and went out. If he came home and Tyler was sleeping, and Scott and I were playing and laughing, he would say I was only happy with anybody else but I hadn't got any time for him. This was all so physically exhausting and emotionally draining.

It felt like the spinning plate act, trying not to let any crash to the floor. If we were having any intimate time in bed and one of the boys cried for me, he would have an angry fit and tell me to leave them to cry because he wanted to finish what he had started. This I found very difficult and very upsetting. How did people juggle the ups and downs of family life? I wished someone would tell me the secret. None of our closest friends had any children, so even the times I spent in the company of Angie with or without Simon, and the same with Jenny, didn't give me anyone to compare notes with. We hadn't seen anything of Tony and Kelly since the day she left him.

The one person that had recently taken to dropping by unannounced was Andy. He had popped in earlier in the new year, after his party, to apologise about... Well, about Curtis, to be honest. He said that if he had known Curtis would end up getting shit-faced and make a total fool of himself he would have made an effort to limit the amount of alcohol he'd consumed. He told me that Curtis passed out on the spare bed so he shut the door and left him there. Much to the distress of Jenny, who was woken at four a.m. by a noise that sounded like someone vomiting. She had got up and bumped into Curtis outside the bathroom door. She had no idea anyone was still in the house and, in the dark of the night, she had freaked out. She didn't speak to Andy or Curtis for a couple of days, she was so mad with them both.

After the initial apology-visit from Andy, he made a habit of calling by whenever he was walking past our house to the village shops. He was proper smitten with Scott. He loved playing cars with him or building blocks, and Scott was always happy to see him. Andy had, on one occasion, said how he really wanted to start at family and thought Jenny would too now they had been married for quite a while. But she was too engrossed in her new position at work. Her promotion had proven a great move for her and the building society, alike. Her boss, the area manager, had been making noises about applying for a regional manager's position, which would leave his job open. Jenny got on really well with him and he told her to keep her head down work hard and she would have a good chance of getting the position. Andy told me all this information and, apart from knowing it scuppered their chances of starting a family, he was very supportive of his wife and understood her wanting to move up. He confided in me that, as much as he supported Jenny's career moves, he was sad about having to wait to start a family. He was prepared to wait another couple of years but then he would be putting his foot down.

Until then, he was enjoying being Uncle Andy to Scott, and his surprise visits increased during the summer. I had mentioned to Curtis that Andy had called in on his way past one day just to test the waters and see if he would have a reaction. He was a bit annoyed but didn't make a big thing of it. I mulled it over and thought, if Andy kept calling in, he needed to know how jealous Curtis could be. I didn't want it to affect their friendship, they did see each other a lot and had a good relationship.

So the next time Andy dropped by, I spoke about it to him. "Curtis can be a very jealous person, Andy, and I don't want any of us falling out because of that. So, if you worked your visits here into the times when Curtis is home, that would be good." I smiled as I made the suggestion, not wanting it to come across wrong.

"Yeah, funny you should say that, Ellie. I was at the gym, training with Curtis, the other day and when I asked how the family was, he was gushing about how lucky he is and what a great mum you are. So, when in reply, I mentioned how much Scott is coming on with his talking, Curtis asked me if I'd been around. I didn't think to lie and just said that I popped in on the odd occasion, when I'm passing. He didn't really say much but didn't look pleased, either. Now I see why."

I told him the mornings and afternoons that Curtis was at home and suggested he came round, if possible, on those days. "In fact, you could always suggest a little walk around to the park — he might be up for that with Scott. Can't imagine him offering to take Tyler, though," I laughed.

"Yeah, good idea, I will look out for the car on the drive, then I know he's at home."

With that conversation out of the way, the visits from Andy were well-timed and Curtis was always pleased to see him. Same for Scott, he didn't hide his delight at Uncle Andy's visits, much to Curtis' annoyance. He would just moan to me later on that Scott never looked as pleased to see him as he did Andy. I replied it was only because he saw Curtis everyday it wasn't unexpected, like when Andy called round.

His reply to this was, "So how come he sees your dad everyday but he's always squealing happy to see him?"

I thought about this and just shrugged my shoulders, he had me there. I don't suppose the truthful answer would be well-received, so better to say nothing. He was definitely not in the running for any 'Dad of the Year' trophies, that was for sure.

But, in late September of that summer, his fatherly responsibilities were put to the test. It was a warm evening, mid-week, and Tyler had thrown up after his feed. This was very unlike him, he had fed very similarly to Scott, contented with breast milk and never really had any problems. Certainly not being sick. They were both very rarely sick at all. On this particular evening, Tyler projectile-vomited his whole feed, after about five minutes of being latched on. He fell asleep straight after so I let him be and waited to see how the next feed went. At ten p.m., after only two minutes of feeding, he did the same thing again. "Right, I'm calling a doctor," I stated. "He can't keep doing this, he will dehydrate. I will call and ask what they suggest." Curtis didn't even answer me, he just looked at me with his eyes wide open and pulled a face that meant 'yeah, whatever, I don't know'. Also, Scott was still not in bed, he was a bit moany and quite warm, but I just thought it was due to the hot weather. I called the doctor's number and she said it was better to be safe than sorry where babies were concerned and she was sending a doctor to check up on Tyler.

We sat up in the front room and waited, both the boys seeming to waver in and out of sleep, and, eventually, at eleven fifty p.m., a car pulled up outside. The doctor tapped on the back door and let himself in. Curtis met him halfway to the front room. He was a small man, wearing a stiff suit and tie. His dark hair slicked back; he was definitely a man of Indian origin. His voice was quiet and gentle and he spoke slowly and methodically, asking questions.

He took Tyler's temperature and rummaged in his bag, producing some sachets of powder. "These are packets of Dioralyte, they are to keep Tyler rehydrated while he can't keep the milk down." He continued with instructions and said he would probably start feeling better in a day or two. Then he turned to look at Scott laying on the sofa. "And what seems to be the problem with this young man?" he asked.

"Oh, no, nothing," I answered. "He's just a bit hot and moany so I thought I would put him to bed when we go."

"Okay, little man, let's have a look." He sat beside Scott on the sofa and asked him if he hurt anywhere. Scott just stared back at him and then raised his hand to the back of his head. "So just here?" he asked. "Is your head hurting here?" Scott nodded in reply and the doctor proceeded to take his temperature. He then started pressing the skin on Scott's arm and asked me to lift his top up so he could look at the skin on his back. All the time this was happening Curtis and I looked back and forth to each other with questioning furrows across our brows. "Mmm," announced the doctor. "I'm not too happy with these symptoms we have here, and we can't rule out meningitis."

This statement meant absolutely nothing to me at that moment. "Oh," was all that came out. "So, what are you saying?" I asked.

"Well, he's going to need a lumbar puncture," was his reply. Still nothing was registering in my brain about a situation.

"I'm sorry," I stated, "but I really don't understand what's happening here. Are you saying he's ill? What do I need to do?"

"Okay," he said, "just let me call an ambulance and I will explain everything to you."

"Ambulance!" I repeated. "For who? Is Tyler okay? Do we need to do anything else with him, or is it Scott? What's wrong?" I started to feel a little panicky. He called 999 from our house phone and calmly explained that he needed an ambulance to our address for a child just under the age of two with suspected meningitis.

Curtis just looked totally out of his depth, turning to the doctor as he replaced the receiver, he asked, "Who is going to hospital and what is meningitis?" The doctor explained that with Scott's temperature, and him complaining about pain in the back of his head, he couldn't take any chances. He couldn't rule out meningitis.

"So one of you will go with Scott to the hospital where they will perform a lumbar puncture. This is a needle in the bottom of his spine. But it's not to put anything in, it's to take a sample of the cerebrospinal fluid so we can check it for meningitis." He reeled off all this information like we should understand. I had never even heard of meningitis. I was starting to feel scared and out of control. "So, Mum, probably best if you go and Dad can stay home and look after baby. Just give him the sachets as I instructed."

The statement came out calmly and my brain was just going into overdrive. Wow, wow, wow... I didn't know what to panic about first. Hospital. Leaving Tyler with Curtis. I wouldn't even do that if Tyler were well, certainly not when he was ill. "Really... Are you sure? I'm not really happy about this. I can't leave my baby at home."

"Yes, yes, he will be fine with Dad for a day or two. He will be taking the Dioralyte for the next twenty-four hours, so we can get some down him now and then Dad can look after him tomorrow. We should know more about Scott's results then." He rattled this all off like it was normal while, to me, everything seemed to be happening in fast-forward and, before I had chance to process everything, it was fifteen minutes past midnight and an ambulance was pulling up outside.

The doctor walked me out and spoke briefly to the two men in the ambulance while they helped Scott and I into the back. As we sped off, all I could see was the scared look on Curtis' face. He was scared for the very same reason I was scared. Not for the children being ill but for the fact that he would have no clue how to look after Tyler. I couldn't do a thing about it and just kept telling myself that Curtis would just have to man up and deal with it.

The lumbar puncture was performed at one thirty a.m., while I helped to hold Scott as still as possible in the foetal position. It was quite a traumatic experience and one young nurse had to leave the room. She asked if I wanted to leave, to which I vehemently declined. Scott was obviously distressed; I wouldn't dream of walking away. When it was completed they said they understood that I would be worried and wouldn't be able to sleep but, nonetheless, had put a foldaway bed next to Scott's cot in an isolation room for me.

"I'm sure you'll be awake so I will come and see you as soon as we have the results," said a smiley nurse as she held my shoulder. I just nodded and placed Scott into the cot after she had given him, what I would have considered, an overdose of Calpol. She assured me it was fine. I crashed out on the bed and fell asleep instantly. Next thing I knew I was being prodded awake by the same nurse saying, "Hi, Mrs Parson, just come to let you know the test is negative, so nothing to worry about. Try and get some sleep and we will see how Scott is in the morning." And with that she was gone.

I looked at my watch. Three forty-five a.m. Seriously, she woke me up to tell me that? I was more annoyed at the time about her waking me. Clearly, I was totally unaware of the seriousness of the situation. Now

I was lying awake, worrying about Curtis being alone with Tyler. I managed another couple of hours sleep and, at six thirty a.m., someone came around with a cup of tea. My breast milk was overflowing with not feeding Tyler overnight, so I decided to let Scott have a comfort feed. It killed two birds with one stone.

The doctor came by at about eleven-ish and, after checking him over, said we could go home. I phoned Curtis from the pay phone and could hear Tyler crying in the background. This instantly wrenched at my heart. "Oh, Ellie, thank God you called. How's Scott and when are you coming home?"

"Yeah, they just gave us the all-clear — we can come home. The meningitis test was done last night and the results were negative, they gave him about four spoonful's of Calpol and he slept all night. Why's Tyler crying?"

"Jesus, if only I knew. He's probably just sick of me."

"Did you give him some more of that stuff?"

"Yeah, at about seven thirty this morning. He just seems really restless but he must be tired."

"Well, just get him in the buggy, make sure he's wrapped up well, and go for a walk. Even just up and down outside the house will do. He will go to sleep, I'm sure. I'm gonna call my dad and see if he or Mum can pick us up. We'll be home soon."

"Okay, okay… Hurry, please."

I rang off and called Dad. Mum answered, Dad was

out, so I gave her a shortened version of why I was in hospital. She agreed to come and get us and I assured her on the journey home that everything was fine and she needn't come in.

"Well, if you're sure. Call me if you need anything, otherwise I'm sure Dad will be up later."

"I will," I called, as I waved her off. I was quiet as I went into the house, and smiled as I saw Curtis asleep on the sofa and Tyler asleep by his side in the buggy. I put my index finger to my lips and signalled *shhh* to Scott. We bypassed them and went straight upstairs. I was desperate to have a wash and clean my teeth.

When Curtis woke, he let me know, in no uncertain terms, never to leave him home with a child alone again. "Jesus, Ellie. That was the worst night of my life. Trying to get that stuff into him and all the crying. Not to mention the nappies." I just laughed and said I didn't think he would have been enthralled with the alternative. I filled him in on the details of my night and he looked almost sick. "God, I don't know how you cope all the time, Ellie. You're such a good mum. I feel like a completely crap dad compared to you. All that crying just drives me totally insane. The walking outside was a good call, though. It really worked."

"Dad told me that trick, says it works every time."

"You'd better check his nappy when he wakes up, I made a right pig's ear of it this morning."

I checked it later and, yes, Scott would have made a better job. The safety pin had missed half of the layers

195

and the whole thing was half hanging off. It was held in place mostly by the rubber pants on top and, incidentally, they were on back to front. "I called work and said I wouldn't be in today, so I'm gonna see if Andy's in. I need a beer," he said, seriously.

I wasn't in the least bit surprised at him running out of the house at the first opportunity. "Okay, well get a loaf of bread on your way back and we can have fish and chips for tea later."

"Will do. Anything else or just bread?"

And as I slumped back onto the sofa, completely drained, it just came out of my mouth without any warning at all. I shouted back, "Ooh yeah, get some ice pops!"

He leaned back through the door and just looked at me with eyes almost popping out of his head.

Chapter 17

I don't know if it was the mention of ice pops that sent him over the edge but that day, I didn't see Curtis until eleven at night. First, I heard the back door and then muffled male voices. I was now awake and wondering just who, in fact, was downstairs. I didn't have to wait long to find out. Stumbling footsteps came up the stairs and Curtis opened the bedroom door. "Ellie, Ellie, wake up. I've brought some of the lads home for supper, I said you wouldn't mind making us all some cheese toasties."

"Are you for real?" I asked, rubbing my tired eyes. "I had about three hours sleep last night and the minute I'm back you do a disappearing act." I was beyond angry and my next words were trying to get out of my mouth and tell him to fuck off and get rid of his mates before they woke up the boys. But his actions beat me to it.

He grabbed me by the top of my arm and pulled me menacingly into a sitting position. He leaned down and spoke quietly, very close to my face. His breath absolutely stank of alcohol. "I'm not asking, I'm telling. Get up now, me and my mates want a toasty and you're going to make 'em, and you're going to be happy to do it cos that's what I told 'em. So, get up and shut up." He pulled my arm and threw my dressing gown at me. He was very rough and whispered to me that I wouldn't like the consequences if I didn't do as I was told.

I had no desire to wake up the boys and I was embarrassed that his mates might see how badly he treated me so I quietly went downstairs. The guys had grabbed a loaf of bread from one of their homes, as Curtis, true to form, had forgotten until it was too late to buy one. I didn't even recognise any of the blokes in my house and even though they were apologetic about this late-night intrusion, they were all too drunk to probably really care.

I put the kettle on and made the toasties, all the while wiping away the odd tear tumbling down my cheek. They all stayed in the front room, making too much noise, and I was silently praying the boys wouldn't wake up. Thankfully my prayers were answered and they slept through the whole ordeal. When I took the toasties and cups of tea through to Curtis' little entourage, they were very thankful and all agreed that their wives or girlfriends weren't nearly as understanding as I was. They said they would have gone ballistic if they had been woken to make supper.

"Yeah, well, Ellie knows how to look after her man, eh, Ellie? She's a proper good girl, aren't you, Ellie? Now you run on back to bed and I'll be up soon for a quickie so don't go to sleep." He joined his mates in laughing at this comment and gave me a sly look that I knew meant 'keep your mouth shut'. Then, as I left the room, he slapped me on the bottom. I felt a mixture of sick and anger. I could hear them all laughing at whatever Curtis was saying. That just made me feel humiliated. I could imagine what derogatory and chauvinistic remarks were coming out of his mouth. I hated Curtis when he had had a drink, his attitude made me feel powerless to change him. I felt helpless.

They stayed until well after midnight and I stiffened in bed with the anticipation of Curtis' arrival. I had toyed with the idea of nipping into the boys' bedroom and pretending to feed Tyler or just laying as still as possible and feigning sleep. Again, the decision was taken out of my hands when I heard Curtis trip at the top of the stairs. He pushed the bedroom door open with force and awkwardly fumbled to get out of his clothes. He must have overbalanced because I heard him crash to the floor. He swore out loud and I tried to keep as still as possible. Pulling back the bed covers he unceremoniously dumped himself beside me. I gripped my pillow tightly with both hands and tried to steady my breathing. In my head I was repeating the sentence, *please fall asleep, please fall asleep.*

"Ellie," he whispered. I ignored him. "Ellie." A bit louder... Still, I didn't answer. "Wake up, Ellie," he demanded. I tensed my body in fear. "Ah, fuck you, I know you're not asleep, but if that's how you wanna play."

And, with that, he grabbed my hips dragging me backwards towards him. He lifted my nightie and proceeded to penetrate me in a selfish and violent manner. I knew that no amount of screaming and shouting was going to stop him and possibly even make the situation worse. He thrust into me whilst talking to himself, making vile comments under his breath. Said he knew I wasn't asleep and I was getting what I deserved for not doing as I was told the first time. I didn't move throughout the duration, which was only two or three minutes. I just cried to myself and waited for it to end. Within thirty seconds of him finishing, he had rolled over and was fast asleep.

I waited a couple of minutes to ensure I didn't disturb him and then made my way to the bathroom, where I sat and cried. What had I done to deserve this monster who treated me like this? I thought I was a reasonably good wife and mother. I always put my family before myself. I just wanted us all to be happy and have a good life. I tried really hard to appease Curtis with his demanding outbursts and tantrums. Why couldn't he just be normal and kind like he was when I met him? He had, over time, just become worse and worse. My feelings, not to mention my nerves, were all over the place. The overriding concern, for me, was feeling scared. I couldn't talk to anyone except maybe his mum, but we very rarely saw her these days.

The next morning, I was up with the boys at six thirty a.m. Just looking at those gorgeous, happy faces was enough to lift my spirits. Scott was jibber-jabbering away to Tyler. They were so good together, making each other giggle. You wouldn't believe that only just over a day ago they were both not having such a great time. Scott had all but forgotten his hospital ordeal and now, with a normal temperature, he was back to his energetic self. Tyler had done twenty-four hours of Dioralyte and was much improved, keeping his milk down. In fact, I had planned to introduce solids as he was now over five months old and, so, with the chirpy mood this morning, I tested the water with half a rusk biscuit mashed into breast milk. I sat Scott in his high chair and he fed himself Ready Brek with honey on it. Yeah, okay, he did make a bit of a mess but he was definitely improving. They both made me smile and my heart swelled with pride and love for them.

By half past eight we were all fed, dressed and tidied up. Curtis was still sleeping and I had no intention of waking him. Quite the opposite, I intended to get out while he slept. I had no idea what his plans were for the day and cared even less. We put our coats on and I trussed the boys up safely in their double buggy. A walk would blow the cobwebs of last night away. I walked and walked, but, no matter how hard I tried, the events of last night were clouding my mind. We arrived at the park and Scott squealed with delight to see other young children already playing there. Tyler had nodded off to sleep, so I parked him up and helped Scott on and off the slide, the swings and the roundabout.

A granny arrived with a little girl and, as she got closer, I recognised her as one of the doctors' surgery receptionists. She smiled and nodded in brief recognition as she followed the little girl around the park. And then... A memory jog. Thinking of the doctors' surgery reminded me about the ice pop craving returning. Surely not, not so soon after Tyler. I had only had three periods since his birth and they were all a little haphazard in their timings. Was I due on now? Probably, yes. I couldn't even begin to contemplate managing with a third child when Tyler would be barely one year old. I knew, equally, that if I were pregnant, there was no way I would ever consider getting rid of it. I sighed and tried to push the possibilities of this being real to the back of my mind.

As the morning wore on, the sun popped out, warming up the air. We walked on into the next village where the main high street of shops were. I battled the double buggy round the few shops that were wide enough and bypassed the ones that were clearly inaccessible to me.

We enjoyed our morning and arrived home just in time for lunch. My heart sank as I noticed the car still on the driveway. I opened the back door and released Scott from the buggy. He went running into the house and I heard him shout, "Daddy, daddy." He had an excited edge to his voice. Curtis was flat out on the sofa, hand over his forehead.

"Jesus, would you shut his shouting up, Ellie. I'll have a cup of tea, now you're back, and bring me some paracetamols, too. Where the fuck have you been 'til now?" he complained. "I didn't know where you were. Bit inconsiderate to just piss off out while I'm in bed."

"Well, when you have finished with the bad language in front of Scott… I was letting you sleep off your hangover, or would you rather have listened to the boys making a noise all morning?" I asked, with triumphant sarcasm.

"Don't try and be clever, you know I won't tolerate that from you. You could have woken me to say where you were going or even left a note. If you are out, I want to know where. So where have you been?"

"Park," I shot back. "Walking around, hoping to God I'm not pregnant again, if you really wanna know."

I returned to the kitchen and finished the cup of tea. When I brought it into the room with the tablets for him, he just shook his head and said, "You won't be pregnant, I'm sure."

"Let's hope you're right. I did tell you to be careful and use condoms for a while. Look how quickly Tyler was conceived after Scott."

"I'm not using condoms, I don't like them."

"Yeah, what, just like you don't like helping with the kids. Well what if I am pregnant, who the hell's gonna help me then? My family won't want to come up any more than they do because of the way you are with them. So, what, eh, what are we gonna do if I am?" I started to cry and I really had tried hard not to. It just made me mad with myself.

"Oh stop your whining and blubbing. for God's

sake. We don't even know if you are pregnant…" He swallowed the pills and continued, "And anyway, your dad practically lives here, I'm sure you will manage."

That final comment just lit the blue touch paper. I was raging. "My father is a bloody saint compared to you. We would have been lost without him. I don't see you going out of your way to help, in fact, quite the opposite. Good job my dad doesn't know the truth about ALL of your bad behaviour, Curtis, otherwise he would knock you right out and me and the boys would be living back home with him."

He leaned his head back and let out the loudest laugh. Smirking, he said, "Yeah, course he would, I'd like to see him try. I'd pulverise him in two seconds flat and anyway… You breathe one word of our business to anyone and you'll be the one getting it. You belong to me, Ellie. You're my wife and my property. Our life is our business and no one else's. NEVER forget that." He said this with enough aggression for me to know he was serious.

I felt much more afraid of him than I used to. I would never let my parents know how he treated me, just because, apart from being embarrassed and ashamed, I would be afraid my dad would kick off and, if push came to shove, literally, I know Dad would end up worse off. No. I had made my bed and I would now have to lie in it. I would just have to figure out how to make it work. Make sure Curtis was always happy and this, in turn, would make our home a nicer place to be.

My priority was the boys. I was happy to make any sacrifices I had to, to make sure they were safe and happy.

It was only another three weeks later when my pregnancy was confirmed. When we were teenagers, and I was wearing rose-tinted glasses, I'm sure having half a dozen kids seemed a great idea. The reality was a whole different ball game. I seriously did, however, only think we would have two. Seems I was wrong. I hadn't foreseen Curtis being a less-than-useless dad, but he had definitely earned that badge. Oh well... c'est la vie. I knew I just had to suck it up and get on with it. I had started telling myself all the quotes in the world were correct... Like 'what doesn't kill you makes you stronger'. Let's hope so.

The baby was due mid-May the following year. Scott would be little over two and a half and Tyler, barely one. As much as I knew I would have my work cut out, I was determined to make it work. We got used to words like 'crazy' and 'mental' when we started telling our family and friends. We took it all in good humour and said that, even though it wasn't exactly planned, we were very happy. The twelve-week mark came and I had a show. I told Curtis and said I was going to call our midwife, Chris. She was lovely and had been a regular visitor of Scott's and Tyler's. Her advice was put your feet up as much as you can and rest. She didn't know that that was never going to happen.

Curtis didn't seem in the slightest bit interested and

made no effort whatsoever to help in any way. Standing in the kitchen, making lunch, two days later, and I had a really bad haemorrhage. I had no pain but the blood just came in massive clots. I called the doctor. He said I needed complete bed rest and to see how it went. The bleeding got worse and I spent a few hours in hospital the next day. Curtis took me and my parents came to stay with the boys.

I was lying in a hospital bed feeling, to be fair, fine. Then a nurse turned up and started asking questions, filling in papers. All the expected questions… How many weeks were you? When did you start bleeding? How many pregnancies have you had? And then she took me by surprise. Was it a planned pregnancy? This made me sit up straight, but I answered honestly and said no. Then I felt upset and guilty. "Why did you ask me that?" I quizzed her. "What difference does it make if it was planned or not?" I didn't wait for an answer, just drew another breath and continued with, "What do you think I've done, thrown myself down the stairs to get rid of it?" I started to cry and she started to backtrack, trying to explain it was just a routine question.

But it was too late, the seed had been sown. I felt like I had not heeded the advice of the midwife and doctor and it was my fault the baby had miscarried. My thoughts went from the initial, *everything happens for a reason*, and, *it's nature's way of telling you something is not quite right*, which, I have to admit, was accompanied by a slight sense of relief, To now thinking, *I did this. It's all my fault. I made it happen because I didn't plan the baby, that must mean I didn't want it.* Jesus, my head was all over the place.

We arrived home later in the day and I was completely inconsolable. My mum was very flippant and said I had enough to contend with, adding a sideways glance at Curtis, which didn't go unnoticed. My dad hugged me and said not to be upset, think about the boys, they need you and love you. It will upset them if they see you crying.

His words always made sense and when they left, he kissed me and whispered in my ear, "You're only young, Ellie, you have plenty of time. This was just nature's way of saying that now was not the right time."

"Thanks, Dad, yes, you're right. I love you."

"I love you too, Ellie, always remember that. If you need any help this week just call me. I'll be up tomorrow evening to see the boys and read to Scott." What would I do without my dad?

Curtis carried on like nothing had happened. I tried to tell him how I felt. The guilt and the sadness. He acted like I'd had a headache. I knew I was going to be dealing with this alone, so had to pull some inner strength from somewhere. To be honest, the boys were my strength. I knew I had fortitude. My emotional strength would get me through this. And it did. Nothing changed. Scott's second birthday was almost immediately upon us and this sapped my attention for a while. He was such a beautiful child. Beautiful to look at, for sure, but so loving, happy and cheeky. His development was amazing and, from the minute he could string a sentence together, it was question after question from, waking up 'til going to sleep.

Funny, I remember one particular sunny day; I entered the boy's bedroom. "Hey, my big boys, time to get up. Look outside, the sun is shining."

"Mummy, why is the sun shining? asked Scott, stretching his arms.

"Well, because there are no clouds today, so it's going to be a lovely sunny day."

"Where have the clouds gone?" He sounded indignant and held his arms out, hands upturned.

"They must have blown somewhere else," I tried, smiling at his inquisitive mind.

"How did they blow away?" he challenged.

"Maybe it was windy while we were asleep."

"Is it windy now?" He wasn't easily satisfied. "I don't know, Scott, why don't we get washed and dressed and then we can go downstairs and find out?" He agreed to this.

His constant need to know the whys and wherefores of everything. He loved his little brother and did whatever he could to help with the day-to-day routine of Tyler's. Tyler was the most placid, happy and contented baby possible. He very rarely cried, usually just cute gurgling and nonsense chattering. He chuckled at Scott who danced around in front of him, singing and being silly.

Yes, having the boys was my saviour. They melted my heart and I gave them my undivided attention, trying to be both parents to them. Curtis was too wrapped up in training, starting his own business and going out with his mates. He was hardly ever in the house these days. He complained if the boys made any noise at all, even playing happily. He didn't like me leaving the house at all and constantly acted like a jealous child around the children. Almost blaming them for him not having my attention one hundred percent of the time.

He was happy when they were in bed and treated having sex as his right. He would just demand it whenever he felt like it and that was often. I just found it easier to comply. I still bore the guilt of losing the baby and it made me need to get pregnant again. That took just a matter of three months and I knew I was pregnant again. I tried really really hard to take it easy. Mostly I was at home alone with the boys and made an effort to sit with them but not pick them up so much.

Curtis said he was happy to be having another child but didn't show that with a helping hand. I asked him if we could buy an automatic washing machine as pulling out the twin tub is not something I should be doing. He complained about using money to replace something that worked perfectly well but relented and bought one anyway. It felt like a significant win for me. By now, Scott was out of nappies during the day and disposable ones had just become very affordable, so I switched to these for Tyler. This made life for me a lot easier. Curtis just thought they were a waste of money but I didn't argue with him on the subject. I knew if anything got to argument stage, there was only one loser. So, I kept quiet and carried on buying them and hoped he wouldn't notice.

I had barely had my pregnancy confirmed officially and, by nine weeks, I had another miscarriage. It was a Sunday afternoon and again there was no pain at all. I had gone to the loo needing a wee and when I had finished the whole toilet bowl was covered in blood. I felt something like a blood clot fall away and, when I looked to see, there, on top of some toilet paper, was what I could only describe as a tiny skin sack, about the size of a grape. I immediately knew this was a tiny foetus and, after the last miscarriage, I also knew it was important that the hospital knew this was complete. I knew, as before, if there was any doubt, they would do a D and C to make sure there was nothing left inside me. So, with this in mind, I just thought practically and fished it out if the bowl and wrapped it in some plastic from the bin. I shoved a hand towel into my pants, cleaned up the mess, went downstairs and called an ambulance.

I told Curtis what had happened, he seemed totally unperturbed by the whole thing. The boys were both asleep after a long stint in the park so I told him to either manage on his own 'til I got back, or call my dad for back up. The ambulance arrived and two guys knocked and came in, asking where the patient was. "That's me," I answered.

They looked a little shocked. "Okay, love, can you get on the trolley, then?"

"No, seriously, I'm fine. I can walk. I already lost the baby."

"Sorry, love, but it's more than our jobs worth. You need to lay on here and we'll get you to the hospital."

It just felt ridiculous but I just wanted to get it all over and done, and get back home, so, reluctantly, I got on the trolley.

They were even more shocked when, on the journey to the hospital, I produced the foetus I had fished out of the toilet. They were filling forms in and I explained I knew the drill and didn't want to be hanging about. "If the foetus is intact, they will let me back home. I have two young children and a useless husband, I haven't got time for lying in a hospital bed, much as I'd relish the rest," I laughed.

"You are absolutely correct, love, but that's definitely a first for me. You seem to be handling it all pretty well."

"Yeah, like I said, have to be organised and proactive in my life." This was when I thought to myself, *that's it, this won't be happening again. I have two perfect little boys at home, why would I put myself through any more of this?*

I decided, there and then, to ask at the hospital about options available to us for permanent contraception. While I was waiting for the green light to leave, I asked. They said I could have a chat with family planning, but that they would be reluctant to sterilise me at the age of twenty-three, and being healthy. The other alternative was Curtis getting the 'snip'. Mmm, couldn't really see him agreeing to that.

When I had the conversation with him later, the outcome left me floored. Once back home Curtis did ask me how I felt and offered to make me a cup of tea. This, in itself, was very out of character. I said I was fine and made the tea myself. Apparently, my dad had been up and taken both the boys for a long walk. Even taking that into consideration, it meant Curtis had had to deal with them for a couple of hours on his own. He said, "I don't know how you do it every day, Ellie, even if they are being good, which they were, I felt like one pair of hands just wasn't enough. It is just constant chasing them around. Tyler can crawl as fast as Scott walks, and did you know he's standing with the sofa and starting to step round with the furniture?"

"Yes, I saw him do it for the first time the other day, I reckon he'll be walking soon. He just wants to be wherever Scott is," I laughed. I sat down next to Curtis and broached the subject of contraception. "Look, Curtis," I started tentatively, "I was asking at the hospital about making sure this doesn't happen again."

"Oh yeah?"

"Yes, I don't know about you, but I really don't want to get pregnant ever again. I can't go through this any more and I am more than content with our boys, aren't you?"

"Yeah, definitely, I am. We never really planned for more than two, I'm happy to call it a day if you are."

"Brilliant, then we just need to agree on me having a sterilisation, and, if we sign the papers sooner rather than later, we can get booked in."

"What, you get sterilised?" He looked at me, frowning.

"Well, yes, they say we are still very young and would have to talk to someone first but—"

"Wow, hang on a minute," he interrupted, "you think I'm going to agree to you getting sterilised?"

"Well, it doesn't hurt cos you're asleep, they just tie your tubes up and then I can't ever get pregnant again." I made it sound simple.

"I'm not worried about whether it hurts or not, I'm more concerned that you think I would let you do that. Oh yes, I can just imagine knowing that you can't get pregnant. You could sleep around without a care in the world."

"CURTIS." I was astounded. "Are you kidding me?" I questioned him. "What do you take me for? I am trying to have a serious conversation of how best to stop any unwanted pregnancies and you come out with that shit. You know what? You go get the snip, then. Maybe you will be happy with being able to put it about without the worry of getting some pool girl up the duff." I couldn't believe this was even a factor in the conversation but, clearly, I was wrong.

"I'm just saying…" He tried to justify his thoughts but I was not even listening any more. What actually went on in his mind? Jesus, I'm so glad no one was in earshot of that conversation.

"You know what, yes, you just go out and sort it out yourself. Have the snip and let me know when it's done." And with that I left the room.

He literally took me at my word and, within days, he had made all the necessary arrangements to enable him to go forward and have it done. He didn't seem in the least bit perturbed about it and when the time came, he went alone and did just that. He milked it, afterwards, for what it was worth. Not that he didn't already spend his life milking it, where I was concerned.

His controlling behaviour and his warped mind just gradually took on another dimension. I sometimes felt like I had a stranger in the house. As soon as he came home, it was like walking on eggshells. Sometimes he was in a foul mood and I had to try and keep my distance. Other times he would sidle up to me, all happy and suggestive. It was draining but he had it down to a fine art. You just never knew what was coming.

I just kept learning how to deal with his unpredictable ways. My priority was my two boys. I was going to concentrate entirely on them and their well-being. I loved them unconditionally, nobody was ever going to come between me and my boys. I knew we would always be tight together, the three of us.

Curtis could be part of the family… Or not. I wasn't really bothered. I just knew, for the sake of my children, I would toe the line and try to keep the home as peaceful as physically possible. It wasn't going to be easy but it was worth any hardship, on my part, for their welfare. I was adamant to keep them safe and happy.

Chapter 18

Our life in general was now slowly taking on a new dimension. Curtis moved totally towards being self-employed and all things training and football. He had decided to utilize his photography skills and equipment to add another string to his bow. Someone had spoken to him about a new scheme that had been introduced by the government. It was called the Enterprise Scheme and it awarded anyone starting up a small business forty pounds per week to help get them up and running. It was available for unemployed people who had been out of work for twelve months or more. So, this was exactly what Curtis decided to do. He became unemployed and spent the next twelve months planning everything to make sure his business would be successful.

My life was totally centred around the boys. All the trials and tribulations of getting Scott into nursery school was mentally and physically trying. Curtis commandeered the car one hundred percent of the time, that left me and the boys on foot. Which wasn't a problem in decent weather. A fifteen-minute walk to the nursery in pouring rain was no fun at all. Then, of course, fifteen minutes back (uphill) home, and all repeated a few hours later to pick him up. With Tyler in tow, this did take up a large portion of our week. It wasn't even a pleasant experience for the first few months. Scott cried every single day when I dropped him off. The funny thing was, if I hung around for anything longer than two minutes, I would lose Tyler. He was by now running around like a Tasmanian devil. If I let him out of the buggy, he just legged it. So, I learned the hard way not to hang around. Just drop and go. The odd days that Tyler escaped into the nursery class, he just caused havoc. He could destroy a play area in the time it took Scott to hang his coat up.

The upside to all of this new experience was meeting the other mums. Very rarely was there a dad amongst us, and making new acquaintances was something I cherished. I think also because they were people that didn't know Curtis, I felt like I had a little secret side to my life. Sometimes, if I was positive that Curtis was out for the whole morning, I would take Tyler and go for a coffee with one of the mums. Or sometimes we would go back to their homes and let Tyler run free while we had a girly chat. It was so nice to have a couple of new friends who didn't know anything about my home life. I never mentioned these friends to Curtis. He thought I walked to nursery and came straight home. I didn't lie to him but, equally, I just never told him anything.

Anyway, he was hardly ever home. He said he was throwing himself into the whole training and football thing, which also involved a lot of the kids' dads, so that when he eventually sorted having his own gym, he would have a good chance of getting the numbers in there. He was also planning for the gym to double up as a photography studio and, therefore, bring in more revenue. I had to say that his vision and determination were commendable. I never asked him questions on a day-to-day basis, on his whereabouts, or anything else, for that matter. He would tell me at the end of the day if there was anything he wanted to share. He always seemed busy and would often turn up back home with some friend or other in tow.

A lot of the time it was Andy. He never needed any encouragement to come around. He loved spending time with the boys and very often came bearing some sort of little gift for them. Jenny now the manager — and more — of the branch she worked in was always at work. She only took Sunday as a day off and so sometimes, on Sunday, we would walk around with the boys to visit them. She too loved the boys and we always felt welcome at their home. We still had a great friendship with Simon and Angie, though, as they both worked full-time, it was usually on an evening after the boys had gone to bed that they would pop round for a drink. They had got married in the May of 1984 and, much to the disappointment of Simon's mum, there was no sign of a grandchild yet. In fact, quite the opposite.

Whenever we were together and the subject cropped up, they both seemed pretty clear about not wanting any kids. Well, each to their own, I thought, but

I couldn't get my head round it. To me, it just seemed the most natural thing to start a family, but they were adamant about it and so it just became a conversation of the past. Simon was a great guy and, over the years we had known each other, he had seen and heard more than most of Curtis' bad behaviour. He was always a reliable ally if I needed one and, sometimes, I almost felt like I could see in his eyes that he had grown to dislike Curtis more and more over time. He always tried super hard to make me laugh and any time we spent in his and Jenny's company was always pleasant and enjoyable. They made a big effort to have fun when they had time off work and, if it was something doable with children in tow, they would always invite us to join them. I, in return, would have my dad up to babysit now and again, while we all went out for a meal and had some quality adult time with them.

In between the day-to-day stuff and seeing our friends, we did see Curtis' mum and Dave whenever we had the chance. Not so much effort was put into visiting my family. Mum's dislike for Curtis was obvious and made for uncomfortable and awkward visits and, besides, Dad was always up at our house anyway. Curtis' mum, Stella, was one of the very few people I didn't mind telling my grievances to. She, of all people, knew him well enough to know how he could be. And since the New Year's Day I had spent round there ages ago, letting her know exactly what a bad husband her son was, she seemed the obvious choice to keep on my side.

So, when one day I needed to vent, off I took the car and drove over to see her. It was a chilly winter's day but, as usual, Curtis forbid me to take the car for the nursery run. He said he had something important on. "Why don't you walk to see your parents after dropping Scott at nursery, Dad will probably drive you back to pick him up later," he suggested.

"Yeah, I think I will," I said. "It will give Dad some time alone with Tyler for a change," I laughed. "I will ring him in a minute before I set off."

"Okay, well I'm off now, see you later." He smiled and came over to give me a kiss. *Mmm,* I thought, *not what he would usually do but, hey, if he was happy.*

I waved him off and continued to get the boys ready. Picking up the phone, I called Dad to say I was on my way, walking up to see them from nursery. Mum answered and said Dad had gone off to an interview for a job. So I decided not to mention that I was thinking of walking up. Instead, I just said a quick hello and added that we may pop round over the weekend. "Hope he gets the job," I added. "Tell him to call me and let me know how it went," I asked.

"I will… Okay… See you soon, bye."

I felt so sorry for Dad in the work department. He was only fifty-three and had been made redundant at the age of forty-eight. Since then, with a very small redundancy pay-out, most of which he spent on our wedding, he had had a couple of jobs but nothing he really enjoyed. I really hoped this time it would be different for him.

I set off to nursery and, due to the drizzling rain, I walked faster than I usually would. No one seemed to be hanging around for the very same reason, so, as soon as Scott was inside, I re-hooked the plastic rain apron back over Tyler in the buggy and set off back home. As I approached the corner of our road, I noticed that Curtis was back home. The car was in the driveway but, as I looked closer, I also noticed that the front lounge curtains were closed. We had full net curtains at this window so we never pulled the curtains across. I let Tyler out of the buggy and opened the kitchen door. Folding the buggy to get it through the door, and taking off my raincoat, Tyler just took off into the lounge. Before I even got through the kitchen, he was running back with a look of... Shock? Surprise? Fear? I wasn't quite sure which. He had his arms up in the air for me to pick him up.

I entered the room to find all of Curtis' photography lighting equipment set up, his camera on a tripod, the gas fire on full blast, and... AND... A half-naked girl lying on a blanket on my floor. "What in God's name is going on?" I almost screeched.

"What are you doing back?" said Curtis, his face turning the colour of a ripe tomato. "I thought you were going straight to your mum and dad's?"

I totally ignored the question and repeated, "What the fuck is happening and who is she?" I demanded, pointing to the topless teenager on my lounge floor.

"Oh, chill out, Ellie, her name is Jackie and she wanted some modelling shots for her portfolio."

"I bet she did. Well, NOT in my house, she doesn't. Get dressed, Jackie, and get out." I was enraged. "Curtis, turn the fucking fire off, it's like a greenhouse in here."

I turned to walk back into the kitchen. He followed me and, even though I still had Tyler in my arms, he grabbed me by the back of my neck. "STOP embarrassing me, Ellie, kicking off like that," he muttered in a cautionary low voice. "That poor girl is only sixteen and she's really upset now you have come in swearing at her," he said between gritted teeth at the same time as tightening his grip on my neck.

"That poor girl," I scoffed, "and does her mother know she's here, topless, with a married bloke on her own?" My eyes widened in question and, at this point, Tyler started to cry.

"If I'm going to do photography as a business, I need all the practice I can get and she offered when she brought her little brother into football practice."

"So, apart from the fact that her parents don't know, you haven't arranged it as a proper job, either? You're not getting paid and yet our heating bills will go through the roof just because you don't want her to get cold because she's no bloody clothes on. Curtis, have you any idea how this would look to anyone else?"

Before he even had chance to reply, Jackie walked

into the kitchen. He quickly recoiled his hand from my neck and, Jackie, who was wearing nothing but a black, skimpy thong, put her hand on his shoulder and let it slide down his arm seductively, her breasts almost touching his arm, and said, "So are we carrying on, Curtis, or is she in charge around here?"

"Yes," he replied, "we are carrying on, sorry, Jackie, I will be back in, in a minute."

"You are fucking kidding me," I growled angrily. Tyler was really crying now and my whole being was shaking with rage. Curtis turned away from me and returned to the lounge. With Tyler in my arms, I grabbed the car keys from the kitchen worktop and left the house. I started the car after securing Tyler in the back and, as I drove away, I had no idea where I was going. I therefore hesitated at the junction just around the corner. *Think, think...* I just turned towards the nursery and stopped on a side road before I got there to think and make a plan. I didn't want to go to Mum and Dad's because I knew how mad Curtis would be that I had taken the car. He would probably ring them, expecting me to be there, and I didn't want them to know anything about this.

My instincts told me to go to his mum's house, but if I drove there now, I would have to come back to get Scott in a couple of hours. *Oh, sod it*, I thought to myself and I rammed the car into gear and went to pick up Scott early. I just made an excuse I had some family issues and, once he was settled in the car with Tyler, I sped off to Stella and Dave's.

Thank God they were in. They were very supportive and I knew I could tell them the absolute truth about what I'd seen and how Curtis had treated me. I also filled them in on how bad our relationship actually was and admitted to them that I was scared of him. Stella said she wanted to just ring him quickly to let him know where I was. I didn't want her to, I thought he deserved to know nothing about where I'd gone. But when she explained that if he started trying to find me, he could call my parents and then they would be worried, I gave in.

"But just say that I turned up here. Don't have a conversation with him. I am so angry and I just need time to work out what I'm going to do."

"Okay, love," she replied, and I listened as she called our house. She literally just said I was there and not to worry then she hung up.

We stayed for lunch and, later in the afternoon, when the phone rang, I knew it would be him. He was demanding I speak to him but I flatly refused. I heard Stella telling him he would have to wait until I was ready to speak to him. She replaced the receiver and looked at me in shock. "Oh gosh, Ellie," she whispered. "He just threw a right tantrum on the phone to me. I can't believe what he said, well. shouted." She looked grey.

"Yeah, I'm not surprised at all, Stella, he just seems to get worse, honestly. And walking into my own home with our son and seeing a half-naked girl… And I mean 'girl', on my lounge floor. What was I supposed to do? I am just so angry and he acts like it's me who's being unreasonable. I really don't want to go home but I know I have to."

"I know, love, I'm so sorry. I would talk to him myself but just listening to the abuse he hurled at me a minute ago, I really don't think I will be helping you."

"Listen," chipped in Dave, "I know he's not my son but we've always got on really well and I'm sure he wouldn't hurt you or the kids. But obviously he needs to understand he can't carry on like this. So, I think what you should do is call him now and tell him you're on your way home. This will stop him getting angrier because he doesn't know what you're thinking or planning to do. The next time you come up on a weekend, I will take him out for a pint and have a chat with him. How's that sound?"

"Oh, would you, Dave? thanks. That'd be great, he might listen to you."

With that, I called him and asked if the girl had gone. He said she had and apologised for not telling me about the arrangement beforehand. I said I was on my way home and he said he loved me. "Same bullshit, different day," I sighed.

When I arrived home, he came outside to meet us and helped me get the boys inside. We didn't discuss anything and we all went inside like a normal family. The atmosphere felt surreal and the charade continued.

I made some tea and helped the boys with theirs. Then I took them upstairs for their bath. Curtis sat and watched television and opened a can of beer. My dad's car pulled up outside and I felt an icy chill run right through me. When I went downstairs, he was sat, laughing and chatting with Curtis, who was being a model son-in-law. They looked like they were best buddies.

"Oh hey, love," said Curtis. "Dad's here to read to Scott. We were just saying we wondered if Tyler will sit with them too."

"Hi, lovey," said my dad, "How's things?"

"Hello. Yeah, great, thanks, how did your interview go today?"

"Yeah, really good, thanks, it's only a decorating job in the local community. Helping families on benefits to get their homes tided up. Though the money is quite good and, more importantly, it's local. So, ten a.m. start and finish at four p.m., so keep your fingers crossed for me, eh?"

"Oh yeah, course, Dad, that would be brilliant. You'll get it — they would be really lucky to have you." I beamed at him.

"Thanks, Ellie." He gave me a quick hug and took Tyler out of my arms. "Is Scott in his bedroom?" he asked.

"Yes, he knows you're here and he is pulling all his books off the shelf to find one for you to read," I laughed. "Just shout me, if Tyler gets too much."

226

"Oh, and there's cold beer waiting for you, James, when you're ready," added Curtis. "Reckon you'll need one after half an hour with them two." He smiled.

I made my way through to the kitchen and put the kettle on. Curtis came in, two minutes later, and put his arms around me. He kissed me all over my neck and cheeks and eventually on my lips. "I really do love you, Ellie, you know that, don't you?" I nodded a very small nod. Why did I feel nervous? "When your dad's gone and the boys are asleep, we can open a bottle of wine and have a good talk, yes?" I sensed the calm before the storm and just agreed. I wasn't about to cause any arguments while my dad was still here.

By eight thirty p.m., Scott and Tyler were both sound asleep and we were alone. Curtis opened a bottle of wine and poured us a glass each. He placed them carefully on a small coffee table beside the sofa and smiled at me as he sat beside me. He didn't sit too close and turned slightly to face me. "So, Ellie," he started slowly. "I think what we need to do is just have a little discussion about what happened today, don't you?"

"Well, if you mean about bringing young girls into our home (I stressed the word 'our') and taking photos of them naked, then yes," I replied, trying to sound confident and preparing to fight my corner.

"NO," he shot, "not about that at all, Ellie, about YOU. You and your big mouth running straight to Mum and Dave to tell tales." His voice just got louder and he pronounced the word 'you' very precisely whilst poking his index finger into my upper chest area. "If you think for one minute that I am going to put up with you blabbing your mouth off to anyone you feel like, well I'm afraid you're very much mistaken. So now I'm going to tell you exactly how it's gonna be, okay?" He questioned me whilst he was nodding at me. His eyes were open really scarily wide and his breathing was gathering pace.

"Okay," I muttered back whilst mirroring his nodding motion.

"Good. Good girl, Ellie, so listen carefully. You will never ever embarrass me again in front of anyone, like you did this morning in front of Jackie. You will not be running to anyone ever and sharing our private business with them. I am working very hard to start a successful business for us all so we can have a good standard of living... Yes? And I would appreciate some respect. From now on, we will not be having anything more to do with my mother and Dave. I make the decisions in this house... Got it?"

I nodded with my lips firmly pressed together. "This is my house; you are my wife and they are my kids and I say what happens around here... Me." He leaned his face to within an inch or two of mine and continued, "I love you and we are going to have a happy life together and you are going to learn, here and now, today, that this can only happen if you remember these rules. Do you understand? There's not gonna be any arguments and you will just be doing exactly what I say."

He took the level of his voice down and started stroking the side of my cheek with the back of his hand. "You're my girl, Ellie, I will always love you, don't ever think we won't be together. Never think you can leave me because I will find you and I will kill you!" And then he kissed my lips. "You know I mean what I'm saying, don't you, Ellie?" I gave a very tentative nod and tried not to let a tear escape from my eye. "Good, so we are all clear. Now drink up your wine, gorgeous, and let's see what we can watch on the telly."

My whole body felt exhausted. Was this it? Was this the rest of my life? Afraid of my own husband and treated like I was some kind of house slave. I sat, trying hard not to let any tears fall. My mind was just in complete meltdown and, even though I fought myself to try and keep a strong positive mind, deep down I knew he meant what he said. I knew he was capable of carrying out his threats. The thin line between love and hate was coming nearer. Thoughts of Jill, my hospital bed neighbour, crept into my mind. "Stay strong and always keep something back for yourself," she had said. I had always taken this statement as her meaning keeping things mentally back but, now, I was wondering whether keeping back financially was her advice. I knew I was going to have to dig deep and be the mum that my beautiful boys needed. This much I was sure of. Plan, that's what I needed to do. Plan.

Chapter 19

The weeks and months following that game changing day were very same-same. Curtis was happy and it showed. He spent most of the daytimes out of the house. Sometimes he told me where he was going and what he was doing, sometimes he didn't, but I never asked if he didn't volunteer the information.

My daily and even weekly routine with the boys was my salvation. I would daydream about what lovely young men they would grow up to be and just hoped they would be able to judge for themselves about their father. I never disrespected him to them while they were young. To be honest, I was too scared they may repeat something to him and I now really did live in fear. Generally, if I did everything, he told me to, our life ran quite smoothly.

He started to criticize my general appearance. Said I needed to keep on a diet and that if I went above a size twelve, he wouldn't be happy. He didn't like me to wear jeans so they were forbidden. He told me to grow my hair long and have it a lighter colour. He said I needed to put makeup on every morning and always look my best.

We never went clothes shopping separately and,

whilst he wasn't stingy about buying new clothes, he would choose mine as well as his own. Nine times out of ten, what he chose for me was black. Daytime tops may vary but were always baggy and very bland. In contrast, any clothes bought for me to go out with him were tighter, shorter and with lower necklines. Strappy and more revealing was what he chose. He said I needed to look 'sexy' when we were together but unnoticeable when we weren't.

He ordered an itemised phone bill and checked every single phone call that was made. Then he would question me if I had made a call. If I had a reasonable answer, that was okay, but I only really ever called Mum and Dad's house. If I made a rare call to Curtis' dad, I would still do it from a phone box and not the one outside nearby in case I was seen.

Curtis never lifted finger to help me. He never went supermarket shopping — that was always my job. If I was very, very lucky, I got to use the car to go to the supermarket. But that didn't mean he would watch the boys, I still had to take them with me. He never had the boys on his own. Not even a ten-minute walk to the park. He said they were far too much like hard work. He had no idea how to use the washing machine and chose never to use the cooker. The one omelette he made me on the day Chris the midwife called round was the one and only meal he ever made me. He would not dream of doing any washing up after a meal and never laid a finger on the Hoover or a duster. I actually felt like a single mother with one overly needy child and two normal ones. Curtis was like a jealous older child. He constantly demanded my attention and was very insecure in his nature.

He still maintained his constant questioning, like, 'Do You Love Me? Do I look muscly?' He even stooped low enough to ask me if I loved him more than I loved the boys. How was I supposed to answer a question like that? Of course, I loved the boys more. In light of the direction of marriage and the turn for the worse in Curtis' personality, anyone in their right mind would say it was a no-brainer.

I really had to work hard to keep up the pretence of being the wife that Curtis wanted to be married to. The kids had to be quiet, not make too much noise or I would have to take them for a walk to avoid Curtis getting angry. The house had to be spotless and tidy, in case he brought anyone around. He was very much a show-off about having a nice house. He watched whatever he wanted on TV and never asked my preference. He would even turn it over if the boys were watching children's programmes. If he walked in and they were quietly engrossed in *He-Man,* or some cartoon or other, it wouldn't faze him to turn it over and tell me to take them upstairs to play.

If he wanted sex, we had sex. I knew better than to refuse now. He once accused me of sleeping with someone else just because I didn't feel like having sex with him on that occasion. It was just easier to do as he wanted in every aspect of our life. Curtis was perfectly happy with his life like this. The master manipulator at work.

I appreciate now that all this sounds appalling when written down and listed in a fashion that is just digested in one go, but it really didn't feel all that bad, living it, at the time. Because I knew how to conform, and did it well, we just seemed to roll along, having a happy existence. Curtis was charming if anyone else was in the vicinity and everyone really liked him. I made sure, as much as I could, that he had no cause to be unhappy at home. Still, he threw himself into the football training and looking for the perfect place to start a gym. He had quite a few small photography jobs on the go and, when the time came, he did go onto the Enterprise Scheme and set up being self-employed.

As well as seeing all our friends, of many years, regularly, we also had made new friends. Through all the children that played football, Curtis had a very big circle of friends and acquaintances. A couple of these families we saw regularly and one in particular turned out to be the family of Alison, the woman who had cut my hair years ago. They had a boy who was a couple of years older than Scott and a daughter a year or so older. Their names were Joshua and Tanya. Her husband, Ben, seemed to really hit it off with Curtis and Curtis never stopped talking about this family. In particular, Joshua, as, apparently, he was an amazing football player. Another family we became regular visitors of was Gary and Susan. They had only recently moved to the village and had two girls, Gemma and Lucy, who were the same age as Scott and Tyler. We would pop round to see friends at their homes and, likewise, they would call in on us for a cuppa, at random times and days.

Our circle of friends were fabulous. I loved spending time with them all and their children. Scott and Tyler loved the other children too. Curtis was a perfect husband to me in public and even came across as a good father. During summer months, we would have outdoor birthday parties for any of the children of all the families. These would last for hours later than a general children's picnic or party, as the adults would all sit outside, having a drink and chatting. Everyone involved in football seemed to enjoy the camaraderie. Curtis had found a unit to rent in the village next to ours. He kitted it all out and had it primarily for gym use but with room for all his photography equipment to be utilised.

We had much the same relationship with my family that we always had. My dad, the number one babysitter. He had got the job he applied for and it changed him immensely, meeting poorer families in the surrounding villages. One time he asked me for any old clothes and toys that my boys had outgrown. I packed him loads and he would tell me about the families he distributed them to. There were some really sad stories. One single mum had been so grateful she cried and said she would wrap one or two of the toys for her child for his birthday and save some for Christmas. Dad tried to do as much as he possibly could for the less fortunate children he met.

We had, over the past few years, either been speaking to Curtis' mum and Dave, and not his father, or the other way around. While he had sent his mum to Coventry, we would pay the odd visit to John. When John annoyed him, by voicing his opinion on anything, Curtis would get angry and tell me I was forbidden to see him or speak to him. It was horrible for me and the boys and I knew he continually hurt his parents' feelings by constantly playing them off against each other. It was an impossible situation for me to have a verbal opinion on. Curtis wouldn't have listened to me anyway, I just did what I did best.

By the time Tyler was coming up for infant school age, we had a discussion about what I was going to do about working. Over the past couple of years, Curtis had become even more materialistic. He was always trying to outdo our friends in any way possible. He made sure we had everything before anyone else. We had even recently moved home, to a more desirable part of the village, where we bought a bungalow with lots of potential. We had at least one holiday abroad each year, either just the four of us, or, on the odd occasion, with friends. He even went as far as buying a second car to outdo everyone else. And when it became common for families to have two cars, well, Curtis just went out and bought a third. He had to be top dog and the adoration he received from his football kids was just sick to witness. There were lots of teenage girls now training and they all wanted to impress him constantly. He was like the handsome school teacher all the girls had a crush on.

Because Curtis' working day was as flexible as he wanted it to be, it made sense for me to go back to work and for him to drop off and pick up the boys from school. They were now old enough to know boundaries and, like me, they had learned (sometimes the hard way) not to cross the boundaries if they wanted a quiet life. Curtis said that, now he could manage the boys, I should go back to work and that way we would have even more money to show off to our friends.

After six years, more or less, of being mum and housewife, I was torn as to my feelings about returning to full-time work. On the one hand, the prospect of meeting new people and doing something with my time, was appealing, on the flip side, I was wary and nervous about leaving Curtis in charge of the boys. I knew he had little, if any, patience with Scott and Tyler and I worried about their happiness being tainted. Not to mention, I would have a lot less time to do all the day-to-day jobs at home. Not only would there be no help from Curtis, but I suspect he would make even more work for me. Well, there was only one way to find out. So that's exactly what I did.

It didn't take long for me to find a job. I had good experience in sales and the first interview I attended was for a full-time manager of a London-based fashion house that held a concession within a large department store in the city. I got the job and started the September that Tyler started school. I went in the deep end, with full time instead of part time. No point getting into a routine, just to change it later on. The job was amazing, I loved it. It actually made me smile to myself if someone called me. Just hearing my name was so liberating — I was so used to being either Mum or Curtis' wife. This felt like a totally new beginning for me. It gave me confidence and a whole new circle of friends and colleagues that didn't know Curtis, and this, I loved.

He did, however, turn up unexpectedly to my workplace on my second day at work. He said it was just to see where I was working but, watching him wander around the whole floor, I realised his excuse was just a pretence so he could check for any male members of staff. He had already asked about male staff when I got the job. He threatened that if he found out I was working with any men, he would make me leave. So, with his checks carried out, and satisfied there were no male workers in my vicinity, it just left him to deal with the fact that my boss was a man. However, being based in London, it would be only four times a year he came up to visit.

He did call me on our landline at seven thirty p.m. every working day to get figures and stock movement, etcetera. I would try and be the one to answer the phone, just to save any arguments, but on the odd occasion that Curtis answered it, he was very short with my boss and embarrassingly sarcastic when he shouted for me to come to the phone. My boss was constantly asking if everything was okay. I reassured him it was brilliant. On the occasions when Curtis was out, I would stay on the phone and have a good catch up with him, and make excuses for Curtis' rude behaviour.

The concession I worked on did really well. I overachieved all my targets and got some fantastic regular bonuses. I was given a very generous clothes allowance and my wages alone were very good. Curtis continued to make impromptu visits to try and catch me out. He was tiresome in his efforts but was always disappointed with no results. I wasn't stupid. I had male friends at work. They worked in different departments but we all shared the same staff room. This way, I made friends and was protected by the safe haven. The guys I befriended knew about my marriage to Curtis and I hadn't hidden how controlling and jealous he was. They knew not to come and chat to me on the shop floor, just in case, and were very supportive of my requests.

Meanwhile, the boys were enduring spending more time with their father. They told me that they didn't like being with him after school because, a lot of the time, he was late picking them up and then he would make them sit quietly in the back of the car while he drove around calling in to see people about things! When I arrived home and questioned Curtis about the time from three thirty p.m. to six fifteen, he just got angry. "It's all right if I'm only popping to see Ben and Allison or Gary and Susan because they're happy to play with the kids. But if I need to see anyone about business or any work I am doing, then what am I meant to do? If you weren't working, it wouldn't matter," he complained. "But they're either pissing about or annoying me, fighting in the back of the car. They do my head in, honestly."

He continued getting angry about me questioning him. "Why don't you just pack in work? I've changed my mind, we've got enough money," he suggested.

"Well, I could, but look what we have had. An extra holiday this year, and don't you still want to put some of your money back into the business?" There was no way I was stopping work now. Unbeknown to Curtis, I had started secretly saving money for my 'what if' fund.

"Yes, I do," he mumbled with acceptance. "It's just hard having the kids every day."

Mmm, I thought to myself. *For two hours, forty-five minutes a day! He should have tried twenty-four seven when they were babies.* But I knew better than to share my thoughts. If I'd learned anything over the years, it was to say the right thing and hide what I was doing to get my own way.

"Look, leave it for a week or so and let me see what I can do," I suggested. Which could have meant anything and would give me some breathing space. I knew Dad finished work at four p.m. so, at my next available opportunity, I drove down to my parents' home to have a chat. My mum was at work, her job, albeit it part time, took her all over the country.

Sometimes she was away for a night or two and sometimes she didn't work for a full week. She had worked at British horse racing venues for many years. She really, really loved her job too. So, I got the chance to speak to Dad alone.

I put the kettle on and told him my dilemma. Just as I suspected, he was more than happy to help. I asked him if he would be willing to have the boys at either his house or ours from four fifteen to six fifteen. I offered to pay him for doing this for us but, at first, he declined. I explained how much it meant to me for the boys to be with him. How much they loved spending time with him. I also shared my secret about having savings for myself and disclosed how much I got paid. I said I would only continue with the agreement if he let me pay him. Begrudgingly, he agreed. This made me so, so happy to be able to help Dad financially, and I knew the boys would be made up. This all made me feel much better. We agreed to keep the money side of the arrangement just between the two of us; it really was a win-win for me.

Curtis thought my dad was a saint for offering to do this and said he would get them from school and meet Dad at ours at four fifteen. I could either collect them from Dad's, or just see them all at ours at six fifteen. Curtis was in his element, being off the hook, so to speak, and consequently was hardly ever at home when I got in. As usual, I never questioned his whereabouts and he very rarely offered any explanation, much to my chagrin. It wasn't unusual for friends to say to me that they were always seeing Curtis' car here or there. More often than not, at Ben and Alison's.

Sometimes Curtis would tell me when he had been to visit Ben and Alison, but not always. Sometimes I would find out from Alison that he had spent an entire afternoon there, even staying for lunch. I knew Ben would be at work and Curtis would make football and talking to Joshua his excuse. Generally, though, he would go wherever he wanted and come home whatever time he chose and didn't disclose his movements.

I had spent over a year at my present job and, when petty rules started getting introduced in the store, I started looking elsewhere. Just across the road, a brand new five-floor department store had opened. So, one day, during my lunch hour, I decided to go and ask about positions available. To my shock, all positions had been filled, bar one. This was a full-time position on the brown goods department. I didn't even know what brown goods were but it didn't stop my mouth from saying, "Perfect." I was even shocked at myself for this reaction. I stayed chatting to the personnel manager for over half an hour. Turned out he lived in our village and we got on really well.

Basically, I bullshitted my way into this job. I made promises that I would be top sales person in the first month, if they would just give me an opportunity. I still had no idea what it was I would be selling until the very next day, when I called in with my CV and was offered the job. The store manager came to see me to show me around the department. It was on the top floor, alongside the restaurant. Brown goods, I now discovered, were home entertainment items. Televisions, audio equipment and video recorders. I tried not to look shocked and just braved it out, saying it all looked brilliant. There was only one major problem I could see here, and it was nothing to do with the work. All the staff were men. All five of them. This was not going to go down well. Understatement of the century.

Chapter 20

As predicted, my accepting this new position was about to start another massive wave in my marriage. I knew I had to tell Curtis that I had been offered the job. I had, however, handed in my notice at work and knew there was no going back, so I waited for a good time to tell him. There probably was no such thing as a 'good time' to tell Curtis this kind of news. I knew he would be furious. I just needed to choose the right words. I picked my moment one evening, three days into me working my notice. The boys were fast asleep and now, being in a bungalow, I was concerned about waking them when Curtis inevitably kicked off. So, as it was a warmish evening, I made a cup of tea and opened the patio doors onto the back garden. I wandered down to the dividing wall, which was thankfully not in immediate ear short of any neighbours. I managed to call Curtis outside on the pretence of looking at some frogs in the pond.

"So, guess what?" I asked with an excited smile.

"I give in," he said, smiling. "But whatever it is, it looks like good news," he continued.

"It is," I replied, "it's really good news. One of the girls at work got herself a job across the road at the new department store," I said enthusiastically.

"Oh yeah?" He was only half listening now. I was aware my work bored him, he was never really interested in anything happening in my work life.

"Yeah, she getting lot more money for less hours. Much better working conditions, too," I hurried on.

"Lucky girl." He tried to feign interest. "Maybe you should have jumped ship, too," he suggested.

"Well, that's just it, she put in a good word for me and I managed to bag the last position available. It's not really on the department I would have chosen but I can transfer when there is any internal vacancies. So, I start next week and I only just found out today." I was trying to look super excited and hoping it would be contagious enough to get Curtis on side.

"Wow, that was quick work, Ellie, you never mentioned it to me!" he countered, with a definite frown across his brow.

"Yeah, I know, I didn't think it would actually happen, to be honest, but the working hours are slightly less and the pay is quite a bit more. So when I was asked today if I would like the position, I just jumped at it," I continued, with a big smile on my face and kept up the excitement level for good measure.

"And which department is it exactly?" he asked.

"Oh, er, well, television and hi-fi systems... You know, stuff like that". I generalised, as if this was really not important. All the time, I knew exactly what question was coming next and, unfortunately, he didn't disappoint.

"And who exactly will you be working with?" He now raised his eyebrows and stared right into my eyes, totally unblinking in anticipation of my answer. I knew this look and it really said... 'You had better not have accepted a job where you will be working with any men'.

I chose my reply carefully... "Oh gosh, I have no idea, to be honest. I never thought to ask." I tried to sound nonchalant and carried on. "Just think of the extra cash, though, and I don't have to leave home until thirty minutes later than usual, so I will be here to get you all breakfast."

I tried to look at all the positives but I could still see the black cloud of doubt hanging over Curtis. "Well... We'll see, then, shall we?" was all he could muster up in reply.

I knew this was not going to be the end of it but I obviously underestimated Curtis' action. Why, I have no idea. I clearly knew what he was capable of but we had seemed to reach a plateau in our relationship recently and this had led me into a false sense of security. Maybe I had now overstepped the mark. We very soon found out.

Thankfully, Curtis was too busy over the following days to check out my new working environment, or, more precisely, my new colleagues. So it wasn't until my first day at work that he made the effort to drive into the city to check on me. I was on an afternoon break when he showed up and, when I returned to the shop floor, I spotted him chatting, in what looked like a very friendly manner, to one of the boys on my department. I say boys, as a couple of them were only in their late teens. They were all different personalities but all very friendly and helpful. Curtis was chatting to Steve; he was quite a techno, geeky kind of guy, with a funny, patchy beard and thick glasses. They seemed to be in quite deep conversation when I saw them, albeit Curtis was the one doing all the talking. As I approached, I tried to put on a happy smile but, when Curtis spotted me, he turned away from Steve, marched towards me and leaned to speak in my ear. He held my wrist so tightly I could feel pins and needles starting in my hand. His sentence rang loud and clear.

"I've had a chat with Steve." He said his name in a sickly manner. "And I think he's got the message. What the fuck did you think you were doing, taking a job here? You are the only girl here and you fucking know that this is not acceptable. I'm sure Steve will let all your work buddies know the score. As for you... Well, I'll see you later." With this he roughly released my arm, I felt all the blood rush back into my hand.

He just marched out and I had to bite my lip not to cry. I could feel bile rising in my throat. Steve stood stock-still and just watched the whole scenario play out. Curtis didn't even wait for the lift. He angrily punched the call button but didn't hang around, opting to get out as fast as possible, he set off down the customer stairs. It seemed to last minutes but, of course, it was only a matter of seconds.

When Curtis was well and truly out of the vicinity, Steve came over to ask if I was okay. He very tentatively placed an arm around my shoulder and walked me through to the back stock room. In here was our television rental department and this was managed by a really lovely middle-aged woman called Hazel. She immediately got to her feet and came over to see what was happening.

"Oh my God," said Steve. "What is your husband's problem?" He looked very pale in the face.

"I'm so sorry," I offered. "I had no idea he would actually come here and kick off. He's a very jealous and possessive person but, unfortunately, he is also very reactive and, even worse, aggressive."

"You can say that again, I hardly dare repeat in front of Hazel what he just said to me," he said under his breath. His worried face turned to me and then he shook his head. Hazel put her arms around me to give me a hug and then I couldn't hold back the tears. Steve wanted to get back out onto the shop floor and let the other guys know the score, just in case Curtis returned, but, thankfully, that didn't happen.

After the store had closed, Hazel called our department into the stockroom for a quick meeting. Just to say to the guys that they should call her if there was any repetition of the day's events. She was so supportive and said I should speak to my parents about Curtis' behaviour. She just didn't understand, I thought to myself, so I tried to play it down. I said it was a one-off and Curtis was just stressed at work. Unfortunately playing down how he had threatened Steve and told him to make sure all the other guys knew his message, wasn't easy. In between all the swearing he said that if he dropped in and so much as saw any one of them looking at me, he would make sure they were very sorry. Apart from the sheer embarrassment of the whole situation, I still had to go home and face the music. Something I definitely was not looking forward to.

I drove home thinking about how great all my brand-new workmates had been on such an uncomfortable first day for me. Mark, one of the older guys, probably a few years older than me and, incidentally, about six foot two, had been out in the loading bay during the 'Curtis Incident', as it was now known. He had come back upstairs and walked straight into the aftermath of the drama. "Fuck me, I wish I'd have been here. I'd like to see him threaten me," he had laughed. "I think you have the same days off as me, Ellie, so don't you worry, love, I won't let the bastard lay a finger on you." I thanked him and gave him a quick hug. But it wasn't my time at work I had to fear.

As I pulled into the drive, I'd decided to fight my corner, but not in the way I would have in the past. That kind of 'fight fire with fire' attitude had only ever got me in hot water. No, this time I would have to be a bit crafty. So I went in to find Dad was there. I knew nothing would be said in his presence. I invited him to stay for tea and, as luck would have it, mum was away at Ascot for two nights so he accepted the invitation. He bathed the boys, read them a story and even stayed for a quick can of beer with Curtis. Thankfully, the boys were sound asleep when he left.

I poured myself a glass of wine and went to sit outside on the patio. I heard Curtis open himself another can and then he came to join me. "So you think you're clever, do you, getting yourself a job so you can work with a load of letching men all day?" I just looked at him and burst into tears. I got up and went to sit on his knee flinging my arms around his neck. This was not what he expected.

"Oh, Curtis," I cried, "they all hate me." I continued sobbing. "The store manager introduced me to them all and said I had a fabulous CV and an amazing sales record. He bigged me up so much it was embarrassing. They have all been really horrible to me. The only person who was nice was Hazel, the lady in the rental department." He'd been shocked at my outburst and put his arm around me. *Great*, I thought, *it's working*. So I continued. "Oh, Curtis, what am I going to do? They are all so crap at selling. We work on commission, too, and I sold more on my own today than all of them put together. I wish I had never taken the job," I cried.

"Whoa, whoa, hang on… Shh, stop crying." He tried to placate me. "Did you really sell the most?" he asked.

"Yes, loads," I replied through my tears. "Those

guys are like morons, honestly, they are such dumb guys. And all so God damn ugly, as well. I can't believe they all have such pretty young girlfriends. Two of them actually work in the store.

"Mmm," murmured Curtis. "Well, I told them today, in no uncertain terms, that they had better not lay one finger on you."

I laughed wiping away my tears. "I know, Steve, the geek, told me," I said in a scornful manner. "He's a right know-it-all, honestly, Curtis, I think he thinks he's a professor," I scoffed.

"Yeah well, you just tell me if any of the fuckers so much as talk to you wrong. They will have me to deal with, and you can tell them that, too," he added.

"I hope I haven't made a mistake taking this job, I mean, I know the extra money will be good but, well, I just hope I can rise above them all."

"Don't you worry, Ellie, I will pop in as often as I can, you can tell them that, too."

Phew, I had gotten away with it, for now, at least. He did keep questioning me all evening about one thing or another. I had to lie like never before but it was all in the name of keeping the peace. I said that Hazel had befriended me and she was like a mother figure to me. So I said that I intended to take all my breaks and lunch hours with her. Everything I had told Curtis was a complete fabrication of the truth.

During my first weeks I formed a very close bond with my colleagues. They were all so lovely to me and,

250

in particular, the youngest one, Edward, who, at eighteen, was a very switched on, funny and very sensitive boy. He didn't have a girlfriend and had a very well-to-do family. His father owned very successful antique business. Edward wasn't interested in antiques and wanted to save enough money of his own to travel the world. "Good for you, you can do anything you want to if you put your mind to it." I always enthused his outlook and encouraged him to follow his dreams.

We became firm friends over the months and he was the only one I told the truth to about my marriage. He was such a lovely boy he seemed so young and innocent. I gave him loads of tips and help to encourage him to be a really good salesman. We took all our breaks and lunchtimes together. We never ever left the building or even the staff room, really. The other lads took the micky about our friendships and constantly tormented Edward about dicing with death.

And even though Edward had expressed his fear of Curtis ripping his head off, we were very careful not to mess around on the shop floor. We left separately to go to the staff room, but this didn't stop us from being inseparable. We would joke about going out to look around the shops at lunchtime, or going out for lunch, but we both knew that would never happen it was far too risky. It didn't matter, we were both happy eating our packed lunches and making each other cups of tea and coffee in the safety of the staff room.

We'd talk about anything and everything and, one

time, when Edward had had a really bad argument with his parents, he came to work looking really gloomy. I listened to the unreasonable attitude of his father, hating Ed working in a shop and felt really sad for him. So much so, that later that evening, after I had dropped Scott and Tyler off to Curtis for football training, I decided to try and give Edward a call at his home. He had an unusual surname and I knew he lived in a very small village on the outskirts of the Peak District so I came up trumps with directory enquiries. Of course, I didn't call him from home. I had driven to an almost hidden phone box to conduct my dangerous liaison. His father answered and I said I was a work colleague and needed to check some work-related matter with him. I tried to speak with a confident and posh accent. His father was a very polite and asked me to hold the line.

When Edward came on, I laughed and said, "Shh, don't laugh, it's me." Edward was shocked to hear from me and we had a lovely conversation. We chatted about how I was hiding in a phone box and he was talking in hushed tones so his parents couldn't hear him. It felt very naughty and secretive but also it made Ed happy, so I didn't care.

We carried on our innocent, but sometimes very secretive, friendship for the next few months. There was nothing at all happening that shouldn't have been. If I were married to a normal person, the secrecy would not have been a factor. One or two times a week, when it was safe to, I called him from the phone box in the evening. We were really good friends and really understood each other.

During the last couple of months, Curtis had managed to get himself a nice little photography number. It was taking property photos for an estate agent in the city. The guy that had just opened this new business was a guy that Curtis had already met. He lived only two minutes away from us so, when he mentioned needing a photographer, Curtis jumped right in there. On the odd days he was working for Danny at the estate agent, he would be in an around the city and, if he had time, he would call into work to see me to say hi. This would always be an unannounced visit and I was always cautious that he could show up so kept myself to myself on the shop floor as much as possible.

One morning, during a stock check at work, I looked up from the desk I was sitting at. Edward was counting all the small stock items such as Walkmans, headphones, and packs of VHS video tapes. He was shouting numbers to me to cross off on my list and, as I made eye contact with him, I noticed blood in one of his nostrils. I shouted him over and told him to sit down and put his head forward. "Really?" he asked. I thought you should put your head back if you have a nose bleed?"

"I've never had a nosebleed, Ed, but I'm sure putting your head back, you would swallow the blood. That can't be right, you might choke."

"Shall I pinch my nose?" he asked, smiling. "Come on, Ellie, you're a mum, you should know what to do," he teased.

The customer toilets were on the same floor as us because that's where the restaurant was too. I sent him in there so he didn't drip blood on his uniform. "Go and hold your head over the sink and pinch your nose, here." I demonstrated. "I'm going to go and check with Hazel, she'll know." So, after checking, I went to the men's toilet door, held it ajar and shouted. "Ed, keep it pinched where I showed you and don't let go. Even if it stops. Give it about five minutes and then get some wet tissue and clean your face up." He mumbled back some inaudible words.

After ten or more minutes had passed and he still hadn't surfaced, I got more concerned. I asked one of the other guys to go in and make sure he was okay. "Have a look and make sure there's no customers in there and then shout for me when it's safe to go in," I asked.

Steve rolled his eyes and went to check, taking the mick while he went. "Aw, is little Eddie having a nosebleed?" he laughed, entering the toilets but, within a second, he was bellowing my name. "Ellie, quick, come in."

Ed was trying to hold his nose whilst leaning on the sink. The sink was absolutely covered in blood. Clots of blood literally blocking up the plug hole. Steve gagged and ran out. "Get Hazel," I shouted after him. I sat Ed on the floor and, as he held tissue under his nose, I pinched it hard. Hazel came in and said we were doing the right thing. "You weren't pinching it properly, you nob," I joked to Edward. "You'll be okay, now, just stay still for a while."

We sat there for at least ten more minutes. The blood stopped, I washed out the sink and Eddie's face. He said he had had a headache all morning but it had gone now and, even though he felt a bit washed out, he said he felt better. He soldiered on through the day and the other guys just spent all day making jokes about it. Jokes about being five floors up and his blood pressure couldn't take it. He laughed with us and, later in the afternoon, he seemed back to his normal self. So, we decided to get the pricing label guns and get all the new stock we had counted priced up.

Ed crept up behind me at one point and made me jump and I turned around quickly, pretending to shoot him with my pricing gun. He took his gun and repeatedly clicked it, sticking the paper price labels that came out onto my back. I laughed and, as I turned to look at him, I saw standing about twenty feet away… Curtis. Ed had his back to Curtis and, as I had turned, he accidentally stuck the next label he clicked, onto my chest. Oh my God, this was not about to be a pretty sight. Ed turned following my stare and almost fainted. He was scared of Curtis, even though he had never even spoken to him. "Hi," I offered. "What are you doing here?" I asked in a surprised and fake-happy voice.

"Just wondering what the fuck you're playing at," he responded with a murderous look in his eyes.

I turned to Ed and said, "Oh, I think Hazel was looking for you, Edward. She's waiting for the stock sheets." I picked up some random papers off our desk and gave them to him, part-steering him in the direction of the stockroom. He took them and fled.

Curtis came closer to me and I thought he was going to just punch me in the face, there and then. Instead, he took hold of one of my wrists and pulled me towards him, whispering, "Edward your fuck buddy, is he...?" I really didn't know how to react to this situation. Being in public didn't make any difference, I knew Curtis was capable of wantonly inflicting pain on me, whether it was physical or psychological.

"No," I replied.

"Well, you could have fucking fooled me," he continued. "Looked like a nice, cosy lovers' play-fight you were having, from where I was standing." He tightened his grip; it was like a vice.

"Curtis, please not here," I pleaded.

"Why, don't you want your workmates to know what a slut you are?"

I tried to free my wrist and, at that instant, Hazel appeared. She marched over to Curtis and outstretched her hand, offering it to Curtis to shake, saying, "Hi, you must be Curtis, Ellie's husband. I've heard so much about you — all good." He shook her hand, momentarily dumbstruck. "Ellie spends so much time in the rental department with me," she laughed, "rather than having to put up with all these stupid boys." She waved, gesturing to the staff across the shop floor.

"Really?" he replied with a sarcastic edge to his voice. "Funny, she never talks about you, Hazel... I'll be waiting for YOU outside, Ellie." He shot me a look and turned to leave. I looked at Hazel, a pained frown etched across my brow. God, but he was a misogynistic bastard. I struggled to find one redeeming factor to his character.

"I'm so sorry, Hazel, but thank you for coming to my rescue," I offered, as I felt my whole body deflate and shake uncontrollably.

"Don't mention it, love, Eddie said he had looked like he might cause trouble, I just didn't want you to end up in a fight on the shop floor." She smiled.

"God, yes, I know," I stammered. My stomach was churning over. "What an absolute twat he is, though." I sighed. "Total disregard for anyone, Jesus, he makes my blood boil, he's such a fucking asshole," I spewed out.

Hazel laughed. "Feel better now you got that off your chest?" she said, peeling off the sticky price label that Ed had stuck on my blouse front. We laughed together at the unintentional pun.

But I knew my smile wouldn't last and I would be immersed in the wrath of my bullying husband soon enough. One thing I was sure of was keeping my close relationship with Eddie at all costs. I felt really close to him and cherished our friendship. I wasn't about to give it up.

Chapter 21

It was almost three weeks since Curtis had waited outside work for me that day. Poor Ed had gone home worried sick for my safety and was visibly relieved when I arrived in the staff room the next morning.

It had not been an attractive altercation. I tried to explain about Edward's scary experience with the nosebleed earlier in the day, but I may as well have not even bothered opening my mouth. Curtis was consumed with uncontrollable rage and he screamed, swore and shouted at me whilst we sat in his car in the car park outside the store. He was incensed and totally fixated with what he was convinced was us having an affair. He didn't want to hear anything I had to say. He raged on, saying he was going to kill Ed and then started thinking up ridiculous scenarios and demanding answers. "I bet you go out at lunchtime together, huh? And have sex in your car, eh? Shagging on the back seat, yeah? Where do you drive to? Come on, Ellie, I'm talking to you."

He raged on and on, with spittle starting to form in the corners of his mouth. He looked so distorted and ugly when he was ranting and, even though he was asking questions, he clearly wasn't expecting any answers as he didn't stop even to take a breath. "Well, don't think I'm stupid and can't see what's going on here, I'm telling you now, you will not be taking the car to work any more. You will go on the bus and I will be checking to make sure you haven't been shagging around with all your boyfriends at work."

"You are totally crazy and totally wrong," I said, just shaking my head in disbelief.

"Crazy, eh, you think I'm crazy? Well, we'll see who's crazy. You mark my words." With this, he leaned over and opened my door and told me to get out. I drove home, half-expecting the tirade to continue when I walked in, but it was totally the opposite. He didn't speak to me at all. Not one word.

This trend continued for weeks. He would leave the house as soon as I walked in and, on the days my dad was at ours with the boys, I would arrive to find Curtis was out. He kept up his pretence of being a great dad and husband in front of my dad. And my dad would say things like, "Oh, Curtis had to go out, he's really busy at the gym and asked if you would leave his dinner for him to put in the microwave later." This was not a surprise as we were hardly ever in the same room at the same time. Even in bed we were apart.

Now and again, Curtis would come in and get himself a beer from the fridge and sit and talk to the boys. They talked about training and some of their mates at football. Curtis would be all happy and laughing with them like, all of a sudden, they we're best buddies. Normally he hardly had ten minutes to spare for them. At least this was a bit of a positive that came out of the bad situation. Then he would enter the room I was in and quietly ask something like, "So which boyfriend did you fuck today, Ellie? Mark, maybe, in the stockroom?' I just ignored him and didn't rise to the confrontation. This kind of behaviour simmered for weeks and I just came to accept it but didn't expect it to take a sinister turn.

One evening I was jumping off the bus (yes he followed through with his threat of the car being off limits) when I noticed Curtis and the boys waiting to meet me. "Oh, hey, how lovely, what a nice surprise," I said, a little shocked to see them. The boys just said hi and gave me a kiss but looked a little questioningly towards Curtis.

"Hi, Ellie," he said in a kind but suspicious voice. "We just thought it would be nice to meet you off the bus and have a walk home together, didn't we boys?" The boys just raised their eyebrows in obvious lack of knowledge of this unique act.

"Really?" I answered tentatively. "How lovely to see you all. Come on then let's get going and get some dinner on. Who's hungry? And what shall we have?"

"Dad said we could have a Chinese takeaway if we came for a walk," piped Tyler innocently.

"Well, okay then, looks like I don't need to cook. Brilliant," I said.

Curtis put his arm around me and kissed me on the lips. "Yes, you must be tired. We thought you should have a night off." He smiled at me.

As we walked downhill towards our bungalow, we passed through a shaded area. There were a few big houses dotted around but you couldn't see them. They had big gardens, with very tall, old trees surrounding them and there wasn't a person in sight. Curtis then ordered the boys to walk a little way in front of us and told them not to turn around. When Scott started to question this request Curtis just bit his head off. "Just walk in front and do not turn around. It's quite simple. Just do as you're told," He growled at them. They knew him well enough to recognise this voice was not to be questioned.

I just looked at him with a curious frown on my face and he answered me by pulling my uniform skirt up. With one hand on the back of my neck, he proceeded to roughly push the other hand down into my pants and, in a harsh and violent manner, he shoved his fingers as far as a he could in between my legs. He jabbed them in, in a vigorous manner, two or three times as I tried to get him off me, without shouting or drawing the attention of the boys. It was all over in a couple of seconds and, as he withdrew his hand, he looked down and said, "Yes, just as I thought, nice and wet. Who is this who has been inside you?"

"What the fuck are you doing?" I demanded in a harsh whisper.

"Like I said, I would be checking, Ellie, you cheating slut. Whose is this?" he demanded, holding the intrusive hand in front of my face.

"You're a fucking psycho, Curtis... Mental... That's what you are." I walked a little faster and caught up with the boys. I smiled at them and held them both by the hand and chatted as we neared our home.

I got them in my car and drove to get them the Chinese takeaway they had been promised. When we got back home, Curtis had gone. He must have returned around eleven p.m. I was in bed but heard him using the microwave. I had left his dinner in the fridge. As I lay there, wondering how this ridiculous situation would ever come to an end, he came to bed. He had been drinking but wasn't totally wasted. Nevertheless, he had obviously been driving, too, which infuriated me. Then a thought just came into my mind. Imagine if he killed himself drink-driving. I continued the daydream, as long as no one else was involved but he actually died. I would have the rest of my life, just me and the boys. I would have some great friends and even probably a revitalised relationship with my family. I had to shake these thoughts from my mind as Curtis whispered to ask if I was awake.

"Yes, why?" I asked. He started cuddling up to me and started blubbing apologies about his bad mood over the weeks.

He said he was sorry for what he had done tonight and tried to justify his obscene actions by saying, "Ellie, I'm so scared I will lose you. When I saw you at work, you looked so happy and relaxed. You never look like that when you are with me. But I wouldn't be able to live without you. Please say you'll never leave me. Swear on Scott and Tyler's life that you won't leave me. Please, Ellie, say it." He waited for me to promise. I said nothing. My daydream of having a life without Curtis was exactly that — a daydream... Fictitious nonsense. Tears started to roll from the corners of my eyes and drop onto my pillow. I couldn't even think of anything to say. Curtis started to cry and sat up in bed. "Ellie, please, I'm so afraid. You have to promise," he begged.

"Curtis, I tell you what, I will swear on my own life I have never cheated on you. Never. I never have and never would. Even though you treat me as badly as you do and don't deserve the wonderful family that you have, cheating is something that people with no morals or values do. I am not that person, despite what you might think. Curtis, I love you, why is that not enough?"

"Because I know what men are like. I would be stupid to think that blokes don't look at you and want to sleep with you. It eats away at me every moment you're not with me. I can't stop it. If I lost you, I would kill myself," he groaned.

"Jesus, Curtis, that is just stupid. You need to get a grip. What am I meant to do, pack in work and spend all day with you?" I scoffed.

We lay quiet, in our own thoughts, for a minute or two and, just when I thought the conversation had drawn to close, Curtis sat up. "I want you to pack your job in," he blurted out. "That will be better. I can't stand the thought of you being with those guys every day. I hate it," he concluded.

I made no effort to reply because I had no intention of doing what he wanted. I loved my job. I was really good at it. Top sales every week, it was like having another life, a secret life, with secret friends. I loved it. Especially Eddie.

"Ellie." He nudged me. "So what do you say? You can spend more time with the boys and help me out when I need you to."

"Go to sleep, Curtis, we'll discuss this another time," was all I could offer.

When 'another time' reared its ugly head and Curtis brought the subject up again, it was about a week or two later. I had not changed my mind. He'd tried to be nice to me during this time, in the hope that he would get his own way. I was just shocked that he'd managed to hold off the temptation to question me, again, for so long. So I tried to buy myself some more time. "Look, we are already into November. I would be stupid to leave now with Christmas coming up. There is an absolute mountain of commission to be had and, also, I would lose my end-of-year bonus. Let's have a rethink in the new year, eh?" He just looked at me with hate in his eyes, turned and walked out of the kitchen, slamming the door aggressively behind him.

I expected him to take my decision really badly and was waiting for him to kick off again at any given moment. Suspiciously this didn't materialise. Instead, he was unusually calm. Very out of character for him. He kept talking about Christmas. How he was looking forward to putting the tree up and shopping for presents. He was a lot more tolerant with the boys. Normally they either played out at the park, just by our street, or, if the weather didn't permit, they would stay up in the bedroom, out of Curtis' way.

Since moving into the bungalow, we had done lots of work on it ourselves and slowly, slowly, it was being transformed. The boys now had a massive shared bedroom in the loft space. This ran the full length of the bungalow. The stairs we had installed midway gave them approximately half each of the upstairs space. Perfect for getting away from their dad's bad moods. But for the past six or seven weeks, they had spent more quality time doing things with Curtis. This, again, was unnerving.

Curtis himself had not made any more impromptu calls into my work, save for the day we arranged to meet in my lunch hour and do some Christmas shopping for the boys' gifts. He was actually in the city a lot more, as the photography for the estate agent he freelanced for was relentless. The property market was booming and he was in great demand.

Danny, who owned the estate agent, was a really funny man. Very quirky in his dress sense and a brilliant sense of humour. He called round to ours often to speak to Curtis and always stayed for a cuppa. His girlfriend was a stunner and quite a few years younger than him and they were about to have a baby together. They already had three other children between them, to two previous marriages. Danny was very forward and sometimes crossed the line but it didn't offend me in any way. He meant no harm and was always a gentleman, too. He seemed to have a soft spot for Curtis but, I have to say, Curtis did reciprocate this. He couldn't seem to do enough for him. I was never surprised when he was late home from doing work for Danny.

The time since the night he asked me to pack in working seemed ages. Too good to be true, it felt, a bit like the calm before the storm. I couldn't quite work it out and then, one evening the week leading up to Christmas, I found out why. I had just made dinner for the four of us and a friend of Curtis' from football training. Sean. He was one of the older teenagers who played football and he frequented the gym, also. He had become a firm friend and was always popping round to see Curtis, or the boys, even. At eight and six years old, respectively, Scott and Tyler were very grown up for their ages. They never misbehaved, simply because they knew it would not be tolerated. They were very happy to have Sean as company and he had walked round to bring a Christmas card from his parents. I asked if he would like to stay for tea. "Turkey burgers, chips and baked beans," I said, tempted him.

His reply was instant. "Ooh, yes please, go on then. But can you call my mum and let her know so she won't worry?"

"Yeah, okay, Curtis, can do that while I'm cooking? You boys go on and get on with your video games." They all cheered and dashed back into the lounge, playfully squabbling over who's go it was.

When dinner was ready, they begged to have it in the lounge on their knees, so they could carry on playing. I thought this request would be one step too far for Curtis. We had just had the whole place re-carpeted in a very pale greyish green wool carpet and Curtis went ballistic if they so much as sneezed near it. But he seemed to not even notice when I carried the dinners in on trays for the three of them. I served Curtis his and sat opposite him at the large breakfast bar. I sat opposite so that I would be facing the portable TV which was wall-mounted by the window. Coronation Street was about to start and Ken Barlow was about to destroy his wife, Deirdre's, Christmas by disclosing his affair with Wendy Crozier, his secretary. Curtis seemed to be poking his dinner around his plate but not particularly eating much of it. The adverts came on and I had wolfed mine down in ten minutes flat. I looked across at Curtis who was just staring at his plate of food.

"Oh no, naughty Ken," I said, laughing. "I bet Dierdre wasn't expecting that for Christmas." I looked at him, rolling my eyes. "Curtis?" I questioned him out of his muse.

"Oh yeah, sorry, what?" He came back into the room.

"Penny for them?" I offered.

"Aw… Don't ask," was all he replied.

"Hey, what is it?" I asked. "You have been really quiet all night, what's up?"

He looked up and then looked directly into my eyes. His eyes filled with tears and he just lowered his head and rested it in his hands. His elbows by the side of his barely-touched dinner. God, I really didn't know what to think. He sighed heavily and shook his head then unbuttoned the top few buttons of his shirt. I looked at him and he just looked broken. He had developed a red patchy rash on his neck and chest. "Curtis." I demanded his attention. "What the fuck? You're scaring me. Tell me what's wrong. Don't you feel well?" The colour had drained from him and he looked grey. He didn't move he just sat there. All sorts of things were shooting in and out of my mind faster than a Porsche. *Is he ill? Is he dying? Is he in debt? Oh God, please don't say he's done something completely stupid, like re-mortgaged the bloody house.*

Now I was starting to feel sick. "Talk to me, for God's sake. How can I help if I don't know what's wrong? Whatever it is, Curtis, we will be fine. We will be okay. You'll be okay. Is it money? Have you done something stupid? Tell me, we can work it out whatever it is."

Oh no, I thought, *what if he really does have cancer or something?* I put my arm around his shoulder and kissed his face two or three times. "Come on, love, do you want to sit in the bedroom and talk? Let me help you."

I just tried to help him to stand up and, as he rose to his feet, he stumbled over to the kitchen sink. He made a strange noise between a growl and a cough. Bent over the sink, retching and throwing up. I passed him some kitchen roll to wipe his mouth and ran a tea towel under the cold tap, gently placing it across the back of his neck. "Come on, Curtis, it'll be okay," I said gently as I put my arms around his waist.

He pulled me in and held me so, so tight and, after about thirty seconds of this vice-like embrace, he held me at arm's length, looked me in the eye and said, "Ellie, I'm so sorry, I have been seeing someone else."

Chapter 22

I had never really thought about the saying 'you could knock me down with a feather', until this moment when strangely it came into my mind. I took two or maybe three steps backwards where my back made contact with the kitchen door. The door gently clicked shut. I felt like I was in a slow-motion film. It took a few seconds but it felt like ten minutes. And then it hit me. I looked him directly in the eye and he looked like he was about to collapse. "You are cheating on me with another woman?" I asked, just for clarification.

"I'm so sorry, Ellie, I know you will hate me for this. I just want to explain—" I cut him off mid-sentence and now there had to be a look of murderous rage taking over my face.

I was thinking about ten things at once, not least of all the boys. These thoughts skid alongside the worry, for just a second or two, and then drown in it. I clenched my teeth together and snarled. "Who is she? Who the fuck is she? Do I know her? How dare you constantly accuse me, and all the time you're... How long has this been happening? Are you leaving? Yes, yes, you definitely are leaving. Get the fuck out of my life, you absolute bastard. GET OUT NOW," I screamed.

He was white lipped as he started to speak. "Ellie, please, I will do anything. It was a mistake. I hate myself." He tried to hold me and I just went crazy, pummelling my fists on his chest. When my strength left me and I was spent, I leaned back on the door and slid down it to the floor. I laid my head over my tucked-up knees and sobbed. Again, this could have lasted... I don't know, fifty seconds, one minute, whatever, but then, suddenly, the thought of the boys returned and also Sean being with them in the room. I quickly got to my feet and wiped my face.

I marched into the room and picked up the empty dinner plates saying, "Okay, guys, come on, bath time now, let's get going, come on." I smiled at Sean and ushered him into the hallway, handing him his coat, which was laid on the bottom stair. "Look, it's good to see you, Sean, we'll see you again soon. Say hi to your mum and dad."

He put his coat on silently and, with a look of disbelief, said, "Yeah, okay will do... Thanks for dinner, Ellie." And, as an afterthought, as he was being practically pushed through the porch doorway, he shouted, "See you later, Curtis." This deserved, but didn't receive, a reply.

I went into the kitchen and placed the plates on the side. Curtis had not moved an inch. I looked at him with sheer hatred and said, "I'm going to see to the boys and then I want some fucking answers, and no bullshit. I want the truth and, if you don't answer everything, I want to know, so help me God, I will ruin your fucking life." As I turned to leave, I swung my head around and added, "Don't just stand there like a prick, get packing your bags."

I closed the kitchen door behind me and got the boys into the bathroom. There were protests about getting in the bath together, as normally they would take turns, but, whether it was the tone of my voice or just a feeling they had, I don't know, they abated the protesting and got in together, chatting animatedly about playing the football video games with Sean. I just sat, dejected and deep in thought, on the toilet lid. All kinds of things rushed in my mind. *How will I pay the mortgage if Curtis is gone? Who will see the boys to school if I'm at work? What will I tell my parents? Oh, Jesus, my dad will go absolutely mental. He will kill him. Where will Curtis go? Oh, fuck, what a mess.*

After a while, I left the boys play-fighting in the bathroom and closed the bathroom door behind me. As I made my way to our bedroom, Curtis was just leaving with his training bag in his hand and another carrier bag tied to the handles. "Where the fuck do you think you are going?" I demanded. "Just happy to walk out at the first sign of trouble, are you, and happy to ditch us, eh? Oh yeah, that's right, you just run away and I'll see to the fall out. Pay the mortgage on my own, shall I?" I laughed, a crazy mental laugh. "Take the boys to school while I'm at work, shall I?" I was talking at a million miles an hour. "You'd better think again and put that back, you made this fucking mess," I spat at him. "And you're going to fucking stay here and sort it out."

He didn't even utter one word, just stared at me while I ranted, and turned to walk back into our bedroom.

"And while you're in there, you'd better get some answers ready and God help you if you lie to me, you cheating fucker." With that, I slammed the bedroom door. I was on a roll and somewhat shocked that he offered no resistance to my tirade of demands.

I sorted the boys out and got them settled in bed, then returned to our bedroom which he had not left since I slammed the door. He was sat on the bed leaning on the headboard, with his feet up and his head in his hands. I demanded that he started talking and my first question was her name. I needed to know if I knew her. Then I continued on with all the expected questions.

Her name was Lisa and she worked at the estate agent where he did the photography. She was twenty-three years old, so six years younger than me. Blonde hair, long. Obviously slim-figured and obviously very attractive. These things I just assumed to myself. I hit him, I swore at him, whilst sobbing all the way through the questioning.

He just kept repeating, "Stop now, Ellie, that's enough, I'm so sorry please can we just stop with the questions?" He snivelled through his tears.

"You must be joking, I haven't even started yet. Where did you fuck her? I hope you didn't bring her here. Was she better in bed than me?" I just continued to torture him and myself, too, for that matter.

Turned out he had sex with her in his car, or hers, if they went out together for work purposes. She was married, no kids, and her husband didn't yet know of the affair. She was making demands of Curtis and wanted him to leave me for her. She threatened him, that very morning, that if he didn't tell me about their affair she was going to come to my place of work and tell me herself. He was scared she would follow through with this threat so decided to tell me himself. What a typical coward, only coming forward when threatened and backed into a corner.

"So, do you want to leave us and be with her?" I asked.

"God no, Ellie, not at all. That's the last thing I want." He shook his head vehemently. "I love you, I always have and always will. I am a total dick for getting into this, I know that." He started to cry and made a funny coughing kind of sound as his whole body shook. "Ellie, I can't live without you, I need you. This whole thing was a stupid mistake. It just ran away with me. I don't want her, I never did. It happened when you started your new job and I was an absolute wreck every day. I had convinced myself that you must be having an affair."

"So you thought you would just have one, for good measure?" I whispered with a sarcastic edge.

"I know, I know, oh God, what have I done? Will

you ever be able to forgive me? I hate myself. Please, I will do anything, I will make it up to you, Ellie, please just give me a chance, please. I only love you, Ellie." He sobbed openly.

I was still crying, myself, and was really struggling with the whole thing. I needed time to think. "I can't deny that, at this precise moment, I actually want to kill you, Curtis. But I'm fucked if you are going to get off scot-free. I need time to think and I don't want ANYONE to know about this." I made my emphasis on the word anyone. "Unless, of course, anyone already knows," I continued.

"Only Danny at the estate agent. He tore a right strip off me when he found out and called me all the names under the sun. But he won't tell anyone and I certainly won't."

I walked over to the drinks' cupboard in the front room and poured us both a large brandy. Not something that we drank often at home but I think this was left over from last Christmas and it felt like an occasion for a stiff drink. Curtis didn't move from where he was sitting on the bed. I cleaned up the kitchen and tided the front room. He was still sat there like a statue. I took the boys a drink up. I got washed and ready for bed myself and he was still sat there. I got into bed and turned my back to him saying nothing.

I must have been tired because, as I mulled over the events and revelations of this evening, I fell into a fitful sleep filled with harrowing dreams. As I stirred the next morning, the memory of what had happened hit me right in the pit of my stomach. I stretched and looked over to Curtis' side of the bed. He was still sitting in the same position as last night and woke as I moved. "Have you actually been sitting up all night?" I asked.

"Yes," he answered, moving to sit on the edge of the bed. "I was afraid. Afraid you might have slid a kitchen knife under your pillow and decided to stick it in me while I slept," he said, looking completely serious.

"Yeah, well, I can't deny the thought had crossed my mind but what would that solve?" I looked at him and raised my eyebrows.

I had two more days at work and then I had booked ten days off to be with the children over the Christmas and New Year period. I was determined to go to work and keep things as normal as possible for the boys. "Right I'm off to work, boys, be good for Daddy, he's not feeling too well today, so make sure you look after him. Come and give me a kiss," I called. Scott kissed me and Tyler ran over for a cuddle. He outstretched his arms for me to pick him up.

"Mummy, can Daddy take us to McDonalds today? He said he would before Christmas."

"Yes, what a good idea, darling, and if you ask him nicely, he may even take you bowling and the cinema too," I added with a cheeky smile.

Curtis strode over to us and leaned in for a kiss. My look was enough for him to withdraw. I popped Tyler down and took the car keys off the kitchen side. This would be the first time I had taken the car in weeks, if not months. I just looked up at Curtis, willing him to challenge me. He said nothing. "See you tonight, then." I waved at the door and left.

I confided in Eddie at work and, while I was feeling brave and defiant, I insisted we went out for lunch later. I wasn't going to see him over Christmas and I knew I would miss him. We were very good friends, but that was all. We got on so well. I knew I would phone him over the holidays. We had a really lovely lunch-hour together in a posh restaurant in the city centre. Ed listened to my mess of a marriage story, without judgment and without comment. He just said he wanted to be there for me, whatever he could do to help.

Chapter 23

Although the obvious anger I was feeling was at the forefront of my mind, there were other emotions battling away inside me and surfacing. One in particular that I couldn't shake was the feeling of insecurity. Something I hated as I knew this had been a contributing factor in Curtis' infidelity. And now I was starting to feel like he only did this because I wasn't good enough. Not slim enough, not pretty enough, not fun enough and clearly not good enough in bed. So, as much as it took me a few weeks to even be able to talk to Curtis in a civil manner, inside, the sense of guilt became increasingly stronger. Curtis was continually apologising and, alongside this, professing his undying love.

Now and then, he would feed me snippets of how he got lured into the affair. He said it just happened on a day he was feeling low and his sadness encouraged this girl he knew to pity him and put her arm around him. He was slowly justifying his actions and making me feel like I had driven him to it. The longer term effects of all this were my losing weight, getting my hair dyed really blonde and making the effort to be the one to instigate sex.

Despite all this, on a cold February afternoon, when Curtis had picked the boys up from my parents' home, something strange happened. We pulled up in separate cars on the drive and I said I needed to go and do some supermarket shopping. It's not something I would normally do at six thirty p.m., but we were running low on lots of bits and pieces, so I told the boys to jump in my car if they wanted to come. "If not," I said, "you can stay home with Daddy for a while and I will bring something nice back for dinner." But, before the boys made a decision, Curtis jumped in with the suggestion that we all went in his car and he would nip round and pick up their favourite Chinese takeaway while I did the shopping.

"Yay!" Cheers all round. So, off we went. Thirty minutes later, when we were all done, Curtis pulled up near the doorway of the supermarket where I stood with four carrier bags of shopping. He jumped out and insisted I get in while he put the bags in the boot. This wasn't just out of character for Curtis to help me, but it was, in fact, an absolute first.

"No, I'm fine," I laughed. "I can manage." But as I approached the car boot, he moved so fast to join me. Hugging and kissing me, he steered me away from there towards the passenger door.

"Get in, get in," he encouraged. "I will see to the bags." He went back to retrieve them and stuffed them in the boot. Getting in the car, he pointed to the takeaway in my foot well and said, "There ya go, Ellie, you look after the dinner, make sure it doesn't spill."

We drove home and Curtis seemed in an unusually good mood. He asked me if I'd had a good day at work — that was enough to arouse suspicion on its own. "So, so," I replied. "Why do you ask?"

"Oh, no particular reason, I just wondered, just making conversation and, anyway, why can't I asked my beautiful wife how her day was?" He smiled, leaning a little and squeezing my thigh. I knew he was still trying to make up for what he had done but this was like a total personality transplant.

We pulled up on the drive and Scott and Tyler couldn't get out fast enough. "Come on, Mum, get the food, I'm starving," said Scott.

"Yes, me too," chipped in Tyler. "Can I open the prawn crackers, pleeease?" I laughed and walked to the back of the car to carry in a couple of the bags and Curtis stopped me.

"You go in, I will get these," he said, trying to stop me opening the boot.

"Now I am suspicious." I frowned "What's in the boot that you don't want me to see?"

"Nothing, no, nothing," he replied, but guilt was written all over his face and I knew there was something in the boot he didn't want me to see. I pushed him to one side and opened it. Apart from the shopping and an old jumper of Curtis', there wasn't really much else to see. So I pulled the jumper out to make sure it wasn't hiding anything. I held it close to me and a strong waft of — not my — perfume filled my nostrils. I wasn't going to say anything in front of the boys.

I passed the jumper to Curtis and said, "You can explain this later... Oh, and if you'd have let me put the bags in the boot, I wouldn't have been any the wiser. You gave it away yourself." I shook my head.

After the boys were in bed, I asked him if he wanted to explain without lying. He said that he'd bumped into Lisa in the office and she gave him back the jumper. It had been in her car for weeks, apparently. I asked him if he had seen her at all since Christmas, when he'd told me. He said no, not until today. And then I asked him if she still wanted to see him and carry on their affair. "I think so, she cried in the office today, saying her marriage was over and she was going to leave her husband. She says she's leaving him because she wants us to be together. But I swear, Ellie, I don't want to be with her. I want you, I love you." He looked tired and drained and then said, "I know it's hard for you to trust me just now but she is being a proper pain and insisting we should be together. I told her I'm sorry but I don't want to lose my wife and she got nasty, saying if I don't go back with her she will come to see you at work and tell you we are still seeing each other. Oh God, what have I done? She even said she would take an overdose if I don't leave you. Now he was holding his head in his hands, crying.

"Have you got a contact number for her? "I asked.

"Yes, why, what are you thinking?" He looked

nervously in my direction.

"Well, I could just call and say I'm aware of everything and ask her to keep her distance, as you have made up your mind." I shrugged my shoulders.

"Oh God, well, you could, but what if she hasn't told her husband and he answers the phone, then what will you say?"

"Well, if that happens maybe he should know anyway. They need to sort their own shit out, eh? I mean, this has been really hard for me but if we are going to get back on track this needs resolving."

Curtis wasn't keen but I insisted he give me the number, saying that if he wouldn't I would only take it as an indication he was still seeing her. Reluctantly, he gave in and I called that number. She answered and as soon as I said who I was she hung up.

We talked about nothing else for the next hour and when the phone rang, I jumped up to answer it. It was a man's voice. "Hi, is that Ellie?" he asked.

"Yes, it is," I said.

"I'm Lisa's husband... I believe she has been having an affair with your husband, Curtis?" he asked tentatively.

"That's correct," was all I answered.

He then continued with a long, drawn-out sentence without any pauses. "Okay, well Lisa has just told me about this for the first time tonight. But I don't know what to believe and what not to believe. I would like, if possible, to meet up with you to see what you know and

I would prefer you not to tell your husband, for the moment. I have been told where you work and I think there is a restaurant on the same floor. I believe you would want to feel in a safe environment, so how about if I meet you there tomorrow for a coffee, say… eleven-ish?"

"Okay," Was all I replied and hung up.

When Curtis asked who it was and what they wanted, I just said it was Lisa's husband and he had only found out about the affair today. "He said he was still in shock and just wanted it confirming, as Lisa had walked out after telling him," I told Curtis. "And he asked if he could call back if he had any questions, so I said okay." Curtis just digested this information, while I felt nervousness spreading through me at the prospect of the meeting tomorrow.

I had a really badly interrupted night and the next morning I tried to inject myself with an air of confidence that I really wasn't feeling. Who knew what this meeting would reveal, I was going to find out in a few hours. I couldn't concentrate on work and Ed was aware of the reason. I told him what had happened last night and he thought it was good that I was meeting her husband. "I will be watching all the time, and if anyone wants to know where you are, I will cover for you. Sit out of sight a little bit. But shout if you need me," he insisted.

"I will, thanks, Ed, you're such a good friend." I gave him a hug.

At ten fifty a.m., I saw a tall bloke walk into the restaurant alone. He walked over and took a seat at a table near the window. I watched him for a minute or two as he ordered two coffees. No one came to join him so I walked over. Ed nodded at me and smiled. As I approached the man, he stood up, proffered his hand for me to shake at the same time as asking if I was Ellie. I nodded. He said his name was Michael and asked me to call him Mick. "Sorry, I took a chance and ordered a white coffee for you, Ellie. I know that was a bit presumptuous of me, I just didn't want us to be disturbed. I hope you don't mind?" He sounded apologetic. His voice was deep and soft. I just nodded and sat down. "Shall I start?" he asked. "And then you can tell me what you know." Again, I nodded. "Just chip in, though, anytime, if you want to ask anything." He looked about mid- to late-thirties, I thought, as I studied his face.

He moved his hand across the table and placed it gently on my wrist saying, "Ellie, your husband must be mad to cheat on you, that's all I can say. Are you okay?"

"Yeah, I'm good, thanks," I said with a bravado I wasn't really feeling. *Likewise*, I thought to myself. Why would anyone in their right mind choose Curtis over this gentle, handsome man.

This question was answered, in a fashion, as we sat and talked. Turned out Mick was fifteen years older than his wife, which made him around thirty-eight. He had a very good, well paid and very much respected job. They had been married just shy of two years and he seemed amazed that we had been married over nine years. I felt safe confiding in a total stranger and we sat there for over an hour. We talked about our respective spouses and it was interesting to hear Lisa's side of the story. Well, the one she had told him anyway. But it rang true to me.

She claimed that Curtis was a real show off about being self-employed. Bigged himself up as a successful entrepreneur and, in her words, 'swept her off her feet'. She had confided in Curtis that she wanted to have children and said it just wasn't happening. Curtis had made her believe he was some kind of stud. So she wanted to leave Mick, marry Curtis and have a couple of kids, then live happily ever after on Curtis' fictitious bank full of money. Of course, hearing this made me feel sick and angry but I couldn't help but laugh. I put Mick straight on the state of our bank balance and even made him laugh out loud when I told him that Curtis had, in fact, had the snip.

We talked about ourselves, too, and the time passed quickly and enjoyably. Mick seemed a really nice guy and, apart from the circumstances which had brought us together, I can honestly say I was really glad to have met him. I never did tell Curtis about our meeting. It felt like something I should keep to myself. Like a trump card, should I need it.

The estate agent which Danny owned in the city, was, a few months later, renamed, and he opened a new office in the town near us. We were good friends with Danny and Wendy and we both frequented each other's homes. Even more so, now. We saw them almost as often as we saw Ben, Alison and their kids. Tanya and Josh had become best mates with Scott and Tyler. When Curtis gave my dad an afternoon off, he always took the kids to Ben's. It wasn't just the boys who were into training, even Tanya had got involved. Curtis loved spending time with their family. Ben worked away a lot and Alison, being a mobile hairdresser, did much of her work at home. She had a book full of regulars that came to her. Curtis was always round there for a cuppa and watching out for his best mate's family, as a good friend would. Well, with the estate agent's photography work now being local, Curtis had no need to drive into the city.

He all but stopped his visits to my work, surprise or otherwise. This didn't abate his obsession with me packing in my job. But I had absolutely no intention of doing it anytime soon. And, let's face it, at this point in our marriage, Curtis was most certainly not in a position to be making demands of me. I definitely had the upper hand at the moment. Don't get me wrong, Curtis wasn't about to win any titles, but he was much nicer to me in more ways than one. Our lovemaking was much more sedate and caring on Curtis' part. This turn of events, I was not complaining about. Recently, for obvious reasons I felt a little more in control and, added to that, I had lost quite a bit of weight — now a size ten. I was full of confidence. I was doing really well at work and having the extra money was nice, too. Of course, I still had my 'keep something back for yourself' fund. I always kept my hospital bed neighbour's advice in my mind and now, more than ever, having just ridden the marital storm of adultery. I was well aware of the need to have the means to care of myself and my boys, should the need arise.

My relationship with Edward was stronger than ever. We were inseparable and spent our breaks and lunchtimes together, only now we went out to eat and shop. I knew, in my heart of hearts, that there was never going to be a physical relationship, but this didn't matter. The bond of our friendship was the tightest. We had fun and never argued. We hugged often but only ever kissed on the cheek, when meeting or leaving each other. That said, it still felt like a betrayal to me, but a betrayal I felt justified in continuing with. I thought about Eddie a lot. He was my guilty pleasure. I knew we would, undoubtedly, eventually go our separate ways but, for now, I was going to revel in this warm and happy relationship.

Chapter 24

We were a very busy family, all told, that seemed to have very little time to relax. Having a night out with friends was something that we had religiously done almost every weekend for years. We did still have regular contact with Simon and Angie. Simon's poor mum was still holding out for a grandchild, that, as yet, had not put in an appearance, even though Simon and Angie had been married for six years. They had said, 'Never say never', so we were all thinking that maybe they had made plans but weren't ready to share them just yet.

On the other hand, our friends, Andy and Jenny, had separated. Andy had been having an affair. For how long, I had no idea, but it all came to a head when Jenny found out and she upped and left. Easier to do, I thought, when there are no children involved but, nevertheless, I admired her for not succumbing to Andy's promises. Just the same as I had admired Kelly for walking away from cheating Tony, even though she was pregnant.

So, why then, had I stayed with Curtis.? I didn't really know the answer to this myself. In the heat of the moment, I know I had panicked and had visions of me being penniless with two children to take care of. This made my decision for me, and, little more than eighteen months later, I was starting to regret that decision. The first incident that brought suspicion back into our relationship was during the summer of 1991.

Curtis was, by now, so inundated with work, both photography and the gym. He came home late in the evenings and, with my dad being relied on to have the boys, I started feeling guilty. They were passed from pillar to post and said they never had a chance to go and play with the school friends after school. I felt this was the right time to cut down my hours at work. So, I spoke to my boss about this, not Curtis. I wanted to have the choice that suited me and the boys and not particularly Curtis. My boss was very understanding and gave me the option to either work five days a week, for less hours, or work a three-day week. I gave it a lot of thought and, even though working the busiest times five days a week would be financially more beneficial, I decided against it for two reasons. Firstly, I didn't want to piss off my workmates, just walking in when it got busy and then walking out and leaving them with all the mundane jobs that needed to be done. And, secondly, having more full days off work would give me more opportunity to do things with the boys. We agreed on me doing Monday, Wednesday and Friday, which meant I would have every weekend off. When I told Curtis, he was happy but, again, tried to push me to pack in all together. I said I would see how the part-time worked out first.

I loved having four whole days off. I had time to visit friends after dropping the boys at school and, on Tuesdays and Thursdays, they got to choose what they did after school. Although Curtis was putting more and more pressure on them to do training. He wanted them to be the best and treated them as though they were a lot older. They never expressed any feelings to their father. They were too scared of him and it showed. He only had to look at them and they knew. He hated them making any kind of noise if he was in the house. They would go to their bedroom the minute they heard his car pulling up outside. He constantly criticized them, even when they were eating. On an occasion when we were all watching television, he totally lost it because they were eating crisps. "Do you have to make that much noise?" he shouted. They both looked at me wide-eyed, looking for an ally.

"What do you expect them to do, Curtis? Suck them until they are soggy and don't make a noise? Or smash them into bits and use a spoon?" I said this with such sarcasm that the boys both giggled, which infuriated Curtis further and he jumped up, snatching the crisp packets from both of the boys and threw them in the bin. I signalled to the boys to leave the room with me and I got two more packets of crisps from the kitchen and we all went upstairs together.

"I hate Dad," stated Scott.

"Me too," agreed Tyler.

What was I supposed to say? Defend his bullying

behaviour? I was mad that I did. "He's probably just tired, maybe he's had a busy day," I tried.

"No he hasn't," piped up Scott. "Cos when we went with him to Alison's to play with Joshua after school. Tanya said he had been there all day."

"And how does Tanya know that if she has been at school all day?" I smiled.

"Cos she's not been to school. She's sick," chipped in Tyler.

"Oh, okay, Dad never said anything. Is she all right?" I inquired.

"She didn't look sick to me but she was grumpy and kept crying," offered Scott.

"Oh dear, well we can pop up tomorrow, I'm not working." I finished the conversation.

When I returned downstairs, I asked Curtis if he'd been busy and he just nodded. Didn't offer any conversation and didn't even look at me. We sat in silence and, at around nine p.m., someone rang the doorbell. When I opened the door, one of the girls from football training was standing there in floods of tears. Her name was Rebecca, she was a very stern and aloof girl. Never really spoke to me, or Scott and Tyler. She was friends with a couple of the other girls at training, around her age group — fifteen.

Curtis appeared at the door and totally took over, shoving me out of the way. "What's happened, Becky?" He looked concerned, putting his arm around her. She glanced in my direction and Curtis walked her into the kitchen, closing the door behind them. I could hear her crying and talking quietly and, every now and again, I could make out Curtis talking to her. After about twenty minutes he popped his head round the living room door and said he was going to drop Rebecca back at home. She lived in a more run-down area of the village with her mum and little sister. I know her dad wasn't there but didn't know any more details.

When Curtis returned, I had already gone to bed. He'd been gone nearly an hour and I knew her house was only a two- or three-minute drive away. "Blimey, you took your time," I blurted out when he came into the bedroom.

"Yeah, bloody kids, ya do your best to look after them and… Well… I don't know, they're all as bad as each other," he grumbled.

"So what's up with her, that she had to come here?" I wasn't going to let it go that easily.

"Oh, something and nothing. She has a problem with bullies at school and one of them is another girl from the gym. Her mum doesn't give a shit, she's just a drunk. I think Becky ends up looking after her sister most of the time. I feel sorry for her. Suppose she didn't know who else to go to."

"So who's the girl who was bullying her? We should have a word. Don't want any problems at the gym, do we?" I pushed.

"Ellie, don't get involved." And, with that, he brushed me off. I knew there must be more to it than that but I also realised I wasn't going to get any answers from Curtis.

In fact, it was about a week later when I stumbled upon a little bit more information. We had arranged an evening at Alison's. All her family and the four of us. We decided to have a barbecue. It was a sunny Saturday afternoon and Ben and Curtis had moseyed off to get the meat. And obviously copious amounts of alcohol. I offered to pick up their kids from Alison's mum, who lived nearby. Alison had a cut to do in the village and then another client calling by her house for a cut and colour. So, we made a time, and, with Scott and Tyler in tow, I pulled up to get Tanya and Joshua. Outside their grandparents' bungalow, I gave a little toot on the horn. "Hi guys, how's things? How are your granny and granddad doing?" I enquired cheerily. Joshua dived into the backseat with Scott and Tyler and just shouted 'hi' to me.

Tanya sulkily opened the front door and got in. "Yeah... Hi, Ellie... Yeah, Grandma and Granddad are okay, thanks," she offered very unenthusiastically.

"I'm looking forward to the barby, eh. I'm starving, how about everyone else?" I ventured to the car in general. A few excited comments from the rear shot through the car.

Tanya just shrugged her shoulders. "I hate that Rebecca," she mumbled back with her chin almost on her chest.

"Ooh, Tanya, hate is a very strong word. What has

she done to you?"

"You'd hate her too if you knew what she was saying to the other girls at school," she insisted.

"Like what?" I tried to coax her.

"Try asking Curtis. I bet he'll know." She looked angry. "Just ask him what she's been saying about her sore knees," she exclaimed in a nasty voice. "She called me teacher's pet just because my dad is mates with Curtis and we had a fight."

"Jesus, Tanya, don't let people hurt you with words. She obviously has problems at home and this makes her an angry girl. And she's only fifteen — that's a really difficult age. Another two and a half years and you will find out for yourself," I mocked. "In the meantime, don't lower yourself to her level, just try and ignore her."

"Huh," she sighed under her breath.

We pulled up at the house and everyone jumped out. The boys were all over the place, just a bundle of energy. They ran straight through the house and out onto the long back garden, almost out of sight. Tanya sloped off to her room. Alison was just waving off her last client. A very happy client, by the look on her face as she passed the hall mirror and checked out her new hairdo.

"What's up with Fanny Adams?" asked Alison, nodding her head towards the stairs. "Honestly, she is so moody these days. Half the time she won't even speak to any of us and the other half she just angry and rude. She is forever fighting with Joshua. God knows what's got into her. I swear, Ellie, she's so bloody argumentative with me and Ben. She's turned into a terrible teenager a bit prematurely," she joked. She rolled her eyes.

"Yeah, looks like hard work, she was just telling me she has a problem with that Rebecca girl from football training. You know, she said something really strange."

And, as we poured ourselves a glass of wine, I filled her in on her daughter's gripes. "Funny thing is, though, Alison," I started. "That Rebecca was knocking on our door in tears last week and Curtis practically shoved me out of the way and took her into the kitchen to talk in private." I looked at her wide-eyed to see her response.

"I tell you what, Ellie, give me boys any day. Joshua is so easy, in comparison, and look at your two, they are amazing. Chuffing girls, they're just a bunch of raging hormones. Sometimes we nearly come to blows. Honestly, she's got a right temper. Don't know what we're going to do with her." She exhaled loudly.

"Who?" questioned Curtis as he came in, carrying a number of bags.

"Tanya, at a guess," offered Ben.

"Why, what's up with her and where is she?" demanded Curtis as he looked around.

"Upstairs, sulking… Seems she's had a falling out with that Rebecca girl. Bloody kids, or, more precisely, bloody girls." She tutted.

"Ellie, help Ben get the meat sorted and pour me a beer. I'll go up and see if she's all right," Curtis responded and quickly dropped his bags on the table.

Unbelievable, what's it got to do with him, I thought. "Curtis, wait, I was just speaking..." I trailed off. He wasn't listening, he'd gone.

"Ha ha," laughed Ben. "He's a braver man than me, either that or stupid."

Ben was such a laid-back guy. They say opposites attract and Alison and Ben were most certainly a couple of opposites. Alison was lively, always on the move and always laughing. Ben was thoughtful, quiet, unassuming and very placid. When all else were losing their heads, Ben was always the one with a gentle voice of reason. He never seemed to be in a rush for anything and, as long as Alison wasn't emptying his bank account, she could pretty much take the reins. He seemed quite happy with this.

"Yeah brave or stupid, I can think of a few more words to best describe him," I muttered under my breath but loud enough to be heard. Alison and Ben both let out a little giggle.

"He certainly takes the whole football thing very seriously," declared Ben "I know I couldn't be bothered with other people's annoying kids, it's hard enough having a couple of your own."

We got the barbeque underway, and I switched to juice. I did this, knowing Curtis wouldn't take a turn as designated driver, I mean, why change the habit of a lifetime? I only ever had a drink outside of the house if we were going out with someone who offered to pick us up and drop us off. Curtis never offered to drive, ever, but I always took my turn.

Now, Curtis was well on his way. On his sixth can of beer already. I knew he would totally overdo it, he always did. He had managed to coax Tanya out of her room and, indeed, out of her bad mood. She didn't want to join in with the boys playing rough in the trees at the bottom of the never-ending garden, but she was happy to sit with the adults. We had a lovely evening, which we always did up at their house. As usual, the only thing to spoil it was Curtis being drunk and not wanting to leave when the time came. I knew the boys didn't particularly need to be getting up early the next morning but, nonetheless, they were totally spent and were falling asleep on the sofas. Tanya and Joshua had long since gone to bed because I had started making noises of leaving over an hour ago. It was now getting towards midnight and I was more than ready for my bed.

I was helping Alison tidy up a bit in the kitchen when Ben came in saying, "Good luck with that lot, Ellie. They're all asleep. He was laughing, I was fuming. I woke the boys and helped them into the car. I went back inside to drag Curtis out and, no surprise, he was out cold. I was quite physical, trying to wake him up, and when he stood slightly, he just lashed out and told me to fuck off. I was so angry and, as much as I didn't plan the next move, his vile mouth just tipped me over the edge. I totally, involuntarily, lifted my foot and stamped really hard across his shin bone. He woke instantly, reeling in pain and was furious. He looked at me with hatred, while trying to roll up the leg of his jeans to assess the damage. He was so drunk he couldn't roll it up and instead stood with a wobble and pulled down his jeans. Alison had left the room whilst trying to stifle a giggle. I was not hanging about, I knew this wouldn't end well tonight and my consideration for the boys outweighed waiting for Curtis. So I bid Ben and Alison good night, thanked them for a lovely evening and apologised for my twat of a husband.

"Just leave him there to sleep it off when he gets over his sore leg."

I shrugged my shoulders. "Call me in the morning, I might pick him up," I teased. "Or might not!"

Chapter 25

We were sat having breakfast the next morning, enjoying the eggy bread that the boys loved to make, when the door opened and in walked Curtis and Ben. Curtis looked like shit and Ben just couldn't stop laughing. I was still angry and could see that, again, today was not going to be a day to tackle him about what Tanya had said yesterday. But it was really bugging me. I was aware today was only going to get worse. I knew I should just leave it until later today but still have it out while things were already grim. Curtis just looked at me with disdain and, for maximum effect, he limped into the bathroom. I thanked Ben and saw him out. We had a quick chat by the car and he agreed Curtis was going to be in a foul mood all day. "It's only gonna get worse. You know what Tanya has told me. I'm not leaving it, Ben, I can't." He wished me good luck and left.

I went back in to finish off with the boys' breakfast, to catch the back of Curtis limping to our bedroom. I ignored him. "Right, boys, come on, let's get dressed and why don't we go over to the ice-skating rink today? Maybe bowling afterwards," I enthused.

"Yay, yay… Yes, let's go," said the boys in unison.

"Oh, Mum, what about the cinema?" jumped in

Tyler. "I want to see *Problem Child 2*. Can we, can we, please, Mum?" he begged.

"Oh no… If we are going to the cinema, let's see, *Bill & Ted's Bogus Journey,*" suggested Scott.

"Let's just get ready and get going. We can see when we get there, depends what's on at the time. More important to get out of the house while your dad feels rough, so he won't want to come with us. Now, chop chop," I encouraged.

They shot off to get ready and I braved the bedroom. Curtis was just crawling into the unmade bed. "Oh," I tried to act surprised, "we're off out to go ice-skating, are you not coming?"

"Yeah, course I'm coming. I can hardly fucking walk, never mind skate, thanks to you," he added.

"Yeah, well… Time you learned to act like a responsible adult. Honestly, you drink way too much, Curtis. And, when you're ready, I want to ask you about Rebecca," I added, for good measure.

"Oh, just keep your fucking nose out, why don't you, it's nothing to do with you, anyway."

"Not according to Rebecca's comments… At school. Seems like it's a lot to do with me."

He turned around and glared at me. "Why, what do you mean?" he snapped.

"Oh, don't tell me the delightful Tanya didn't share information with you last night?" I asked sarcastically.

"Tanya?" He looked lost. "What's she got to do with Rebecca?"

"Yep, that's what I'd like to know, but you sleep off your hangover and we can talk later when the kids are in bed. See you later this afternoon." I turned on my heels and walked out.

Back in the kitchen, I rang Alison to see if Joshua wanted to come with the boys. They were just off out for the day to visit family but Alison asked Josh if he preferred to come with us and he said yes. So I picked him up on the way and they drove off in the opposite direction.

We had a great day. Nice and relaxed, no being nervous because you're being watched. We laughed and fell over on the ice. A very nice man gave me a hand up when I went flying. he helped me over to a seat and asked if I was okay. *How pleasant*, I thought, *if Curtis had been here and seen that, the poor bloke would be on his way to A&E by now.* We checked the cinema and, after seeing off a McDonald's, we went to watch *Bill & Ted's Bogus Journey.* Then finished off at the bowling alley, stuffing more fast food down us. Heaven. It was a perfect day.

Joshua came home with us and Curtis was up, watching rugby on the telly. He had a look of thunder until he clocked Joshua was with us, then he flipped his personality to being a saint. "God, he makes me sick," hissed Scott, noticing his dad's mood change instantly when he knew Joshua was with us.

"Ay-up, mate, how's it going? Have you all had a good day?" But he directed his question to Josh. Josh politely said he had and then the three of them disappeared upstairs. "What time do you call this? I thought you'd be back after lunch," he complained.

Now his genuine mood surfaced. "Yes we are," I answered. "It's ten past four. That's after lunch." I looked smug.

"Don't be clever, Ellie, it doesn't suit you. You know what I mean. I had to get myself a sandwich for dinner."

"Oh dear. Bet that hurt more than your leg." I thought that was a great reply and was just in the process of laughing at my own joke as I walked into the bedroom for my slippers. Curtis sprang into action and quickly followed me, shutting the door behind him. He pushed me with force onto the bed and consequently easily sat astride me. Grabbing my wrists, his pent-up anger exploded but not volume-wise, as the boys were upstairs. I was wearing a strappy vest top, not just because the weather was warm but since Curtis' affair admission, I had adopted a little bit of a rebellious attitude. Seemed his period of relenting was coming to an end. I had obviously milked it one step too far and Curtis was not happy. Grappling with the front of my vest, including my bra, he pulled downwards, exposing both my breasts. Then, squeezing them roughly, he snarled at me, "You think this is acceptable, wearing a revealing top like this when you're out without me? What did you do, leave the boys in the cinema and sneak off to meet lover boy? Find somewhere nearby for a quickie, eh?"

"Get off me, you lunatic." I struggled to try and get up. "Don't judge me by your own standards. And while we're here, what about Rebecca? Seems she's telling anyone and everyone she's hurt her knees while she was at the gym… With you… Care to explain?"

"Don't try and turn this situation around, Ellie. Becky has grazed her knees on the carpet at the gym and the girls at school were teasing her, saying they wondered how she got carpet burns. I've no idea how she has one on her back." He just came out with this sentence like it was pre-practiced.

"On her back?" I was stunned. "No smoke without fire, Curtis. Is there something you want to tell me? That girl is always mooching around you at training, looking sullen and moody. I hope you know she's only fifteen. A bit young, even for you, no?"

"Actually, she's just turned sixteen, not that that makes any difference. What do you take me for?"

I made a concerted effort to pull my top back up whilst struggling to sit up on the bed. "I don't know, Curtis, I just don't know. You tell me." I could, in my heart of hearts, imagine Curtis loving the adoration of these young girls.

"How sick are you? Surely you don't think… Ellie, I love you. I've made my mistake and I think I've paid for it, too. Things need to get back to normal around here and I'll be keeping a close eye on you. I know you will want revenge but if I ever find out you've cheated,

Ellie, so help me God, I will kill you and him. I will make sure you never see the boys again, got it?"

My bravado was diminishing rapidly and my next words spilled out. I intended them to be under my breath but Curtis heard. "I should have kicked you out when I had the chance," I thought, out loud.

"Yes, you probably should. But I can tell you now I'm going nowhere. You'd have to prove I was cheating now to get rid of me. And that will never happen. You are my wife, this is my house and they are my boys, so you'd better just start toeing the line." He made to leave the room. "And you can start by packing in work. I prefer you here where I can keep my eye on you." He pointed at his eyes and pointed back at mine with a real menacing look on his face.

"I could leave you today and take the boys." Words braver than I felt. He shot back in the room and grabbed a handful of my hair, yanking my head sideways. He whispered in my ear, "You will never be able to leave me, Ellie, I will find you and I will kill you, you know I mean it and you know I'm more than capable. So why don't you stop your stupid threats get them out of your head. Write out your notice for work and then make me a cup of tea." He let go of my hair, pushing my head at the same time and smiled an evil smile. I was shaking, not sure whether it was from rage or fright, probably both.

But one line he had just said was replaying in my head… 'You'd have to prove I was cheating'. Maybe he had just handed me my golden ticket of freedom. I would prove his infidelity, however long it took, whatever I had to do. I stopped for a few minutes and thought. Surely, he'd be bound to trip up sooner or later and lulling him into a false sense of security would be my only way of giving him enough rope to hang himself. And probably packing in work would be my first move in this chess game for freedom.

Chapter 26

I thought long and hard about my strategy. I didn't want to look too obvious, like I was just prepared to roll over and give in, so I made out to Curtis like I didn't want to pack in work. We discussed it a couple of times over the following months and I complained about the money I would lose. Curtis offered to employ me to do his books and other bits and pieces he needed. He was really bad at book-keeping anyway and I usually ended up sorting the mess out for him. He thought anything he didn't actually want to do, was beneath him. So many of the members at the gym and training, treated him like some kind of God. He really did have an inflated ego. His whole demeanour just got more and more intolerable. It was sickening to watch grown up, intelligent adults treat him like a celebrity. But he couldn't pull the wool over my eyes. I knew him better than he knew himself.

Eventually, when I felt the time was right, I gave in and finished work. It was very bittersweet. I knew I would love being a full-time mum again but actually saying goodbye to everyone, especially Edward, was wrenching. I cried on our last lunch hour together and so did he. When I left the building for the last time, with arms full of gifts, Edward gave me a hand and walked me to my car (yes, I won that battle, the car). He gave me a gorgeous bunch of yellow roses; he knew they were my favourite. We held each other in a strong embrace and Edward kissed my cheek. The last kiss off him ever. I really was going to miss him. I promised to call him when I had the chance but said I hoped he would heed my advice and, when he'd saved enough money, throw caution to the wind and get out into the world and have some fun. He agreed he definitely would.

Scott and Tyler were thrilled I had packed in work and we now began our little three-man army. We were so, so tight and, even though they weren't privy to my long-term plan, they seemed to know that we were on a crusade of some kind. They had seen many battles fought in the past and there was plenty more to come, I was sure. But, with my sons by my side, I was fearless and we stuck together one hundred percet of the time. Now, and at the ages of ten and a half and nine, respectively, Scott and Tyler had Curtis worked out for themselves. There had been so many occasions when they had compared him to their friend's dads, and realised the adoration he received from people was so undeserved. People didn't see the real Curtis. No one, except the three of us, knew the real Curtis. The selfish, disrespectful and deceitful sociopath that he was.

Scott was due to start the comprehensive School in September 1993 this was only a few months away. I needed to sort out all his compulsory uniform — blazer, tie, trousers, shirts and school badges, etc. We decided to take him shopping for all the extras he would need. Shoes, trainers, anything he could choose himself. We went on Saturday to a very large shopping centre and made it into a day out. We had a nice lunch and bought but some bits and bobs for each of us. We walked into a massive sports retailer and we all wandered off in different directions, looking at whatever took our fancy. Scott came over to me with a training shoe in his hand. "I like these ones, Mum, can I try some on?" he asked.

"Yes, sure, let's find someone to help us," I replied, looking round for a member of staff. We found someone and she brought us a pair in Scott's size. Curtis was with Tyler and came over to look. Scott was smiling, looking at the trainers in the mirror.

"Wow, they're nice, how much are they?" asked Curtis.

"Same as all the others if you're getting Nike, they're all around sixty quid." I smiled at Scott and Curtis just walked over to the adult section and picked up the exact same trainer.

"I think I'll get a pair of those. Put yours back, Scott, and choose a cheaper pair," he ordered nonchalantly, like it was an acceptable request to a child.

"You're joking… I hope," I said.

"Oh, Mum," groaned Scott. "Really!" His face just dropped. "Why does he always have to be such a nob? Don't bother, I don't want any others, I'll go without."

He left the shop and stood just outside the door, leaning on the window. Tyler just watched it all play out, his eyes wide open with shock. Curtis carried on, oblivious, tried on the trainers and, consequently, bought them for himself. I was stunned. Yet again, Curtis demonstrated his worsening sociopathic personality.

We three walked quite a way in front of him to the car, as this latest episode brought our shopping trip to an abrupt end. In the car, he more or less told Scott to stop sulking and get over it. "When you earn the money, mate, you can buy what you like, 'til then, I decide." This summed up his feelings in a nut shell.

Once home, Scott agreed that they were quite expensive for trainers. He didn't have a problem with not being allowed to have them. "I just thought buying them for himself was a spiteful thing to do, don't you, Mum? I don't know why we just don't leave him. He's never nice to us. Do you know, Mum, one day when you were at work and we were out with Dad? He locked us in the car while he went in an office to see someone. He said we were not to unlock the door in any circumstances and that he would only be ten minutes. He was gone for nearly an hour and Tyler needed a wee. He was so scared to open the door that he peed on the car seat. At first, Dad went mad, then, on the way home, he said we hadn't to tell you cos you'd be cross. So we had to keep it a secret."

"Yeah, and tell her what he said the other week about Josh," added Tyler.

"What? What did he say about Josh?" I was dumbstruck. How many more occasions had he silenced them?

"Oh yeah." Scott started remembering the details of what was said. "We had just had a training match at football and I had missed a chance of a goal. Josh scored two, but we still lost. Dad said to us in the car that he wished Josh was his son." The story tumbled out. My stomach just flipped over and I thought I might throw up. What a bastard he was. This was just fuelling my fire.

"Hey, listen, boys," I started, trying to keep calm, "don't you even worry about what your dad thinks or says… Do you love me? And do you trust me?" I looked into their eyes. They both nodded simultaneously. "Right, well, all we have to do is just carry on and don't let anything he says or does hurt us. I promise you one day soon he will be leaving us. It will take some time and you mustn't repeat this to ANYONE, but I promise I will make it happen. Do you understand?" They nodded again. "Good, okay. We will always stick together and I will never let you down. I love you very much. Just try to be polite when you have to speak to him but just try and keep away from him. Don't get into arguments with him. Got it?" I read them the rules. They both hugged and kissed me and it felt like we were all on a secret mission.

The days merged into weeks, merged into months. We carried out our mission with aplomb. Keeping our composure, even when some situations with Curtis had us boiling over with anger. It would have been so easy to retaliate. Instead, we did whatever he asked of us and had secret liaisons while he was out. And so, we went on.

Scott loved it at his new comprehensive school. He had a lot of friends, some who had moved up with him from the junior school and some new ones. He was a confident student and did really well in most subjects. He would come home and tease Tyler, telling him stories about how much harder the high school was. Tyler took it all to heart and, the nearer it got for him to go, the more nervous he became. He was a very sensitive boy. Not as academic as Scott, but excelled in other areas. Scott had boatloads of bravado and was sometimes overconfident. Tyler was the opposite, doubting his own ability. I worried that their personalities were being tainted by their father. I had to get away from him... The sooner the better.

I needed to keep vigilant and see what Curtis was up to. He had become totally obsessed about me getting my revenge, therefore questioning my every move. I had to be able to account for every minute of my day. Everyone I spoke to was a potential affair. It was so draining. Even when a friend of his, who, incidentally, I hardly knew, called into the gym one day to let Curtis know his wife had had a baby girl. He expressed that they liked the name Ellie for her, and wanted to check that I was okay with it. To be quite honest, I was flattered. Curtis kicked off like someone possessed. H accused me of sleeping with the guy, why else would he want to name his baby after me?

Time was closing in for Tyler, regarding the move up to high school. I could feel his anxiousness and suggested to Curtis that we check out the price of private schools. I was worried that the small amount of confidence Tyler did possess, would be dragged out of him in two minutes at the comprehensive school, with its two thousand students. Surprisingly, Curtis seemed right up for my suggestion, but for all the wrong reasons. I soon realised it would give him something to brag about. He even asked Scott if he wanted to go to a private school, but he declined, saying he was happy where he was.

We immediately got onto checking all the schools within a feasible distance. Tyler came with us to look at the three we had chosen to view. He ultimately had the final say. They were all pretty much the same cost and that was where Curtis' concern ended. It was an old house on very big grounds, and no more than eight pupils to a class. Tyler settled in really well and even went before he reached high-school age. It helped with his confidence, no end, and, even though he was never going to be the top of the class academically, he stood head-and-shoulders above all the other pupils in sport. He became very popular very quickly and excelled in all aspects of sport.

With both boys happily settled in their schools, I

concentrated on sorting out my marriage. I watched Curtis' every move whenever possible but he shook me off continually with every excuse in the book. He sent me on errands to get rid of me and then got angry if I was gone longer than he anticipated. In general, he just wasn't pleasant to any of us.

Late one afternoon, with all four of us in his car, he pulled up in a petrol station to fill up. It was lashing down with rain and he made me get out and do the honours. When I returned to the car after paying in the shop, Scott was in floods of tears. Tyler looked ashen and Curtis was shouting and swearing, his face as red as the mist that was beginning to wash over me. "Whoa, whoa, whoa, what the hell's happened here?" I demanded. Tyler turned his head away quickly as if to say he wasn't getting involved.

Scott tried to speak in between sobs. "I only asked a question and he bit my head off," he declared, nodding towards Curtis.

"Don't you fucking lie to me, Scott. I've told you before, if I find out you have been on a motorbike, you will be in so much trouble," he shouted in the general direction of the back seat.

"I only asked if—" But he got shot down by his dad.

"Scott. ENOUGH! Shut it, will ya? That's the end of it," he bellowed. He started the car and we drove home.

As soon as we pulled up on the drive, Scott jumped

out and slammed his door. He went straight upstairs with Curtis yelling after him, "Do not slam my car doors and change your fucking attitude, boy."

Gosh, this seemed really out of control. I followed Scott upstairs to get to the bottom of it, with Tyler hot on my heels. Behind me, Curtis was still grumbling and called after me, "Oh, that's right, you run after your baby boy. Little mummy's boy."

Turned out a friend of Scott's had an old motorbike of his dad's that he was allowed to ride up and down their huge back garden. He was telling his mates at school how he took an empty can to the garage to get petrol for it. Scott thought he was lying and that he was too young, at thirteen, to do this, so, innocently, he had asked his dad. Curtis just assumed Scott would have ridden the bike and went ballistic. "Why doesn't he believe me, Mum? I said I haven't ever ridden on it and I am not lying. He is just so unreasonable. I hate him, Mum."

Scott was wiping his eyes and Tyler added, "Yeah, me too, he nearly strangled Scott when he pulled him by the front of his coat." The look on his face was so serious.

"I don't want to be here, Mum!" continued Scott. "I've had enough, I feel like getting a rope around my neck and hanging myself." He threw himself forward onto his bed as a fresh bout of sobbing washed over him.

Oh my God, I had never felt so sad and helpless, not to mention scared. I pulled Scott into my arms and held him tight. Tyler joined us and, instead of explaining to them that Dad didn't mean to be so cross, and, therefore, defending his unreasonable behaviour, I just looked him in the eye and spoke slowly. "Never, ever, think those thoughts again. Do you hear me? Both of you. Your dad is not worth getting upset over. He's a bully and he only wants to listen to his own voice, he doesn't want to listen to anyone else."

Scott's interrupted by saying, "He doesn't love me; he wouldn't care if I were dead."

"I care… I care, Scott, and that's enough. We don't need his love we don't even want it. We have each other and that's what counts. He is not worthy of our love. Just keep your distance, as much as you can, and keep any conversation as minimal as possible. I'm sure he does love us all but he doesn't display it very well. He is an angry man and we need to try not to make him any worse. We need to be clever but, mark my words, this won't last too much longer, I promise."

"But, Mum, I've heard Dad say that he will kill you if you ever leave him and I believe him. He's a nutter. We should go to the police. Please, come on, why can't we just do that," Scott insisted.

I tried, as much as I could, to explain that, without any evidence, it would all just be a waste of time. That Curtis was manipulative enough to be really nice and genuine and totally dismiss any accusation I made as ridiculous. I sat with the boys for an age and even took them their tea up to bed. When eventually they got into bed, I slid to the floor and, with head in hands, I watched them for an interminable amount of time.

When I was sure they were sound asleep, I quietly tip-toed downstairs, where Curtis sat watching telly, can of beer in hand, and three empties on the floor. "Huh, thought you'd moved into their room," he commented sarcastically.

"Curtis, I'm not about to get into a fight with you but I think you are an absolute bastard. I have had to sit and listen to our son saying he wants to kill himself, because you don't love him. You are a fucking bully." He just laughed. "Is that it?" I continued. "Is that all you can do? Laugh? I can't believe you can be such a cruel person. They told me you wished Josh was your son… In front of them. Can you imagine how that made them feel?"

"Bollocks. I didn't mean instead of them," he countered, as if defending his words.

But I wasn't listening any more. I walked closer and leaned down to speak into his ear. "You know, successful relationships require kindness, commitment, appreciation and respect. All of which you have NONE OF, Curtis… NONE." I left the room.

A short three days after this latest episode, we were at Ben and Alison's. We had, all eight of us, been out to a big country park for a picnic and played cricket. We had had a fun day and now, back in Alison's kitchen, just her and I, I gave her a short version of what had happened at home a few days previous. She was disgusted and asked if the boys wanted to stay for a sleepover. Of course, they jumped at the chance.

Curtis had already had quite a few cans during the day, so was in good spirits. He was always happy when he was at Ben's. In fact, other friends of ours had confided in me that they saw Curtis' car outside Ben's most days and thought he had an unhealthy obsession with the family. I couldn't disagree. The boys, as always, shot off upstairs, but, Tanya, now almost fifteen, was intent on hanging around the adults. Her parents tried to encourage her to join the boys so we could talk in private but Curtis quickly jumped to her defence. "Aw, leave her alone, she's almost an adult now, aren't you, love?" he declared. She blushed and thanked him with a cheesy smile.

Curtis was like a knight in shining armour to all the kids. All except his own, that was. Other kids, boys included, treated him as a confidant. He enjoyed this and enjoyed the position of (how he saw it) an idol. Shame his efforts didn't extend to his own children.

Now he'd just found out the boys were staying over, he whispered to me in private, "I think we'll find a nice place to stop on the way home and have some lovin' in the car, eh?"

I rolled my eyes. "I think the chances of you being awake when it's time to leave are pretty slim," I retorted.

"I won't fall asleep, I promise. Not after last time," he reminded me. "Ben wants to watch *Tales of the*

Unexpected and it starts in a minute. Be a love and get us another drink and tell Alison to hurry up with the snacks or she'll miss the beginning." It was a very sinister storyline about a widow being haunted by her dead husband. She saw him in every mirror she looked in and he made sure no men came into her life. She killed herself in the end.

"Phew, that was scary," exclaimed Alison. "What a psycho."

Curtis went to the loo and Ben helped Alison clear the dishes. I stood up, stretched and looked in the mirror to tie my hair back up. All of a sudden, Curtis appeared behind me, his reflection in the mirror looking at me. He laughed at me for jumping. "Fuck me, Curtis, don't do that, you scared the shit out of me," I scolded.

"Yeah... Well, guess what? I would do exactly that if I died before you. I would haunt you until you killed yourself. No man will ever touch you, Ellie. You belong to me and we will never be apart. I know what you think about me, but it's tough, you will never be able to leave me." He grinned. "Come on, driver, get in the car. Let's see where we can go for a good time." His laugh was deranged and felt very threatening.

Chapter 27

The relationship between Curtis and Scott didn't seem to improve. Curtis was steadfast in his justification of the cause of the fallout. He had no intention of listening to anything Scott had to say and carried on his day-to-day life of selfishness without being affected. Scott, on the other hand, was still full of emotion. Angry, upset and a little unsettled. You could see his whole demeanour had changed. He spent a lot of time after school with his friends and he had taken up rugby in school. But I'm not sure that it wasn't seeing his mates' dads being normal, that convinced Scott his own dad was some kind of freak. He started to grow in confidence and nothing could have prepared me for the day he came home and announced he was packing in football. That he wasn't going to do any more training with his dad... Ever. Oh Jesus, I could only imagine how Curtis was going to take this. It would be a very public slight on him and I wasn't looking forward to the fallout of this decision. "Okay, love, so do you want me to tell him?" I asked Scott. "You know he is gonna flip out, no matter who tells him?"

"No, I can tell him myself. I'm not scared of him," he said with obvious fake bravado.

"Okay, if you're sure, love, do you want me to be with you?" I couldn't believe he was braving this out on his own. Maybe he was underestimating the reaction he was going to receive.

"No, I will do it. I don't need you to protect me. What's the worst he can do? He can't hurt me with words, he's already done that."

I could only watch and hold my breath when the opportunity presented itself. Scott just caught his dad in the lounge alone and informed him of his decision. As predicted, Curtis totally flew off the handle. He started to tell Scott what he thought of his ridiculous choice and said that Scott was throwing all the training he had given him back in his face. Scott must have turned to leave mid-confrontation and, as he opened the door to leave the room, I heard him say, over the top of Curtis' is ranting, "Well, I'm old enough to make my own choices so I don't really care what you think." And with that statement, he closed the door behind him and, raising his eyebrows at me, he disappeared upstairs. I felt like punching the air, go on, Scott, nice one.

Within a couple of seconds, Curtis bounded out of the same door, took one look at me and, totally engulfed in rage, he barked at me, "I suppose you put him up to this, eh? Think you're clever, getting him to ditch me and the gym. How's that going to look? What a bitchy thing to do."

"Actually, it was a Scott's own decision and nothing to do with me, but you can hardly blame him, the way you treat him." I was now expecting a full-on row, but, instead, Curtis grabbed his car keys and took off, out.

And it didn't end there. He actively ignored Scott for almost two weeks. He wouldn't sit to eat with us and, when the boys were watching television, Curtis would not stay in the room unless Scott left. It was so uncomfortable for Tyler. He kept asking me if it was going to be like this all the time. I tried to keep some semblance of normality, though it was a strain, being on your guard all time. I tried to have an adult conversation with Curtis in private, to make him see how ridiculous he was a being but it fell on deaf ears. He was mad like a spoilt child. Whereas Scott was just getting on with it. He kept saying to me, "Mum don't worry, I don't. He can blank me for as long as he likes. I'm not bothered in the slightest. In fact, it's better. No arguing and no sarcastic or demoralising comments. It's great."

It had to be said if Curtis wasn't speaking, it was definitely an improvement. He made a point of sucking up to Tyler more than normal and I think that just made Scott dig his heels in harder. Poor Tyler must have felt so pulled in this conflict. We continued like this for ages and it just started to feel normal. Curtis had to be the one to give in eventually, surely. He was the one with the power to change. But no, it seemed Scott was the adult. He had, on a couple of occasions, spoken to his dad, just to ask a question, or maybe even a hello or goodbye. But Curtis totally ignored him. So, Scott just gave up trying.

I juggled dropping off and picking up both of the boys to their training sessions.

The rest of the time, I spent working in whatever capacity Curtis chose. There were a few occasions where I bumped into the delightful Rebecca and she would just look at me like I was shit on her shoe. Then she'd sidle up to Curtis and adopt a comfortable position and start a cosy chat. It was an art. I just treated her with the contempt she deserved. I knew she was a child but, honestly, teenage girls just seemed to be a different breed these days. In the business we were in, we had so much contact with stroppy teenagers.

On the other hand, there were also the vulnerable ones too. None more so than Hannah, it seemed. Again, only fifteen years old, but with a strong personality. She always seemed a bit of a loner, which I thought showed her vulnerability, but one look from her, could make you stop in your tracks. She was very hard-faced. Her father, Pete, helped out with training sessions on occasions. He was a very unassuming man. Slightly reserved, when he spoke his eyes wandered upwards, a bit like Charlie in Casualty, he never really looked you in the eye. Almost as if he doubted his own words. He had another daughter, Sarah, who was a few years younger. Hannah was not like the other girls at the gym. She wasn't quite as pretty, which seems like an unfair assessment, but she didn't wear makeup or have the latest hairstyle. Her dress sense seemed very old fashioned, in comparison. She was pale skinned with freckles and her hair was almost black, and always tied in a ponytail.

This particular day was no exception. It was a Sunday afternoon and she was as inconspicuous as ever. Until Curtis called me over to go and speak to her. She was in the girls' changing rooms so he didn't want to go in. Some of the other girls had reported to him that she was sat, crying, and wouldn't come out. I asked her dad first if there were any kind of problems I should know about. He looked his normal, vacant self and shrugged his shoulders. Big help. So, I went in to see her. I sent out all the other nosey girls, who were looking like they were getting ready to watch a blockbuster movie. "Hey, Hannah, what's up, love?" She pulled her feet up onto the bench and held her bent knees close to her chest. But said nothing. "Okay, look I can't sit here all afternoon, and there's clearly something wrong, so, until you feel ready, I'm just gonna have a stab at guessing what's wrong."

I took a deep breath… "Is it the other girls?" I tried. She sniffed and shook her head in response. "Okay then, well, have you had an argument at home with your mum or anyone?" Another shake of the head. "Are you ill?" Now there was an instant response. She turned her head to look me in the eye and then shook her head again. "Are you sure?" I pushed, I thought I had touched on something.

"Not really ill," she offered. Then bent her head back down and started sobbing.

"Hey, come on, come on. If you're not ill it can't be that bad, can it? Look, there's no one else in here now." I stood up. "Let's go and see—"

She made to grab me and cried. "No, no… Don't get Dad… Please," she begged. This was an instant reaction and, as I slowly sat back down, she whispered, "I think I'm pregnant." Wow, another 'blow me down with a feather' moment, I couldn't help but think.

"But you're not sure, right? Have you done a test?"

She shook her head. "Dad can't know. Don't tell him, Ellie. Promise?" She looked sick to her stomach and her eyes were scared and pleading.

Think, Ellie, THINK! "Okay, okay, don't worry, Hannah. The first thing we need to do is a pregnancy test. Because if you're not, well… Then we can relax a little. But, Hannah, seriously what are you doing having sex at your age? And didn't you take any precautions?" She just clammed up at my questions. "Right, let's get going. I can't imagine it's gonna be easy finding a chemist open on a Sunday, but, well, we can try."

"What are you going to tell… Curtis? And my dad?" she questioned, as if her dad were an afterthought.

"Leave them to me. Come on. I have to get Scott from rugby in an hour, we haven't got long." I gave her my car keys and told her to wait in my car for me.

I spoke to Curtis and her dad quickly, as they were busy, and made an excuse for Hannah, saying she was ill and I was taking her for a drive and some fresh air. Not the best story I could have come up with, admittedly, but… Well, I was in uncharted territory right now. They just looked confused and I left hurriedly. But not without noticing a dirty look flashed at me from Rebecca. Jesus, that girl, spiteful child, I really didn't like her.

I met Hannah in the car and we drove to the nearest chemist. It was closed. I tried another two that I knew of, they too were closed. During our drive around, Hannah started to talk. Asking what I would do if she were pregnant. So, I asked her some more probing questions. "I didn't even know you had a boyfriend," I ventured, conversationally.

"I haven't," came her immediate reply.

"What, what do you mean, you haven't? Who got you pregnant then? Do you know who the father is? Look, Hannah. I need to know what I'm dealing with here." Did she even comprehend what was going on here? I didn't want to scare her even more, but I needed some answers.

"I don't have a boyfriend. And I can't tell you who did it. You have no idea how bad my life is, Ellie. You and Curtis, with your lovely house and three cars. Two perfect sons and loads of money. My life is shit. All the girls at the gym talk about is how fabulous Curtis is and what a great life you have."

I couldn't believe what I was hearing. *Just shows how much they know*, I thought. "Well, it's not as perfect as you might think. Curtis just likes everyone to think it is, so I suppose he must do a good cover-up job,"

I laughed.

"Yeah, all the girls love Curtis. I hate that Rebecca," she announced with venom. "She's always boasting to us about how much time she spends with Curtis. How he picks her up and drops her off at home. She makes me sick. She even made up some sick lies a while ago, that she was having sex with Curtis in the gym at nights. I mean, honestly, no one believed her, she's such an attention seeker."

"Well, don't listen to her." I finally chose some words. Though I wasn't as sure as she was about the gossip being fabricated. I would obviously have to look into those allegations a bit deeper, I pondered.

I got back to the more immediate problem of who Hannah had slept with. "Never mind that now, tell me more about why you think you are pregnant. How late is your period?"

"About three weeks."

"And does this boy, who isn't your boyfriend, live near you? Or is he a boy from school?"

"I was raped!" I almost crashed the car.

I pulled into a nearby car park, which was thankfully empty. I got out of the car for some air and leaned on the bonnet. Fuck me, how much worse was this situation going to get? A lot, I was just about to discover.

"Hannah, are you sure? I mean, do you know this person? You can't go around throwing accusations like that around, willy-nilly. If you agreed to sex, then it's

326

not rape. I'm sure you didn't plan to get pregnant, but you have to be sure of an allegation like rape. If this is true then we need to tell your mum and dad and go to the police." I exhaled long and loud. "What's the boy's name?"

"It was my dad. My dad raped me. He's been doing 'stuff' to me for ages." She just stared at me.

OH FUCK! Holy shit… What the fuck had I gotten into here? I nearly threw up. I gasped for fresh lungful's of air. I sat back in the car and hammered my fists on the steering wheel. Then, raking my fingers through my hair, I held my head as if it were about to explode. What now? Think, Ellie… THINK.

"It's time to pick Scott up." She pointed to the little clock on the dashboard.

"Right, yes, okay, we'll go for Tyler first, we're nearer to him, then go for Scott. You can stay with me while we decide what to do," I suggested.

"Thanks, Ellie. My mum is gonna kill me."

"Why? Surely, she's going to want to kill you dad, no? I know I want to," I declared.

"You don't understand my life. It's awful. Scott and Tyler are so lucky, they probably don't even realise what a wonderful life they have." She looked so sad.

After we had picked the boys up, I drove home and didn't speak to Hannah again until we were in the kitchen, alone. I had briefly told Curtis there was about to be a shit storm. I said she had accused Pete of raping her and thought she was pregnant. I left him to decide what to do about Pete, and, as I turned to leave, he just stared, open-mouthed, in shock. I knew I couldn't make Hannah go home but, by the same token, I wasn't prepared to deal with this alone.

As we sat together in the kitchen, I told her we had no alternative than to report this to the police. She nodded as if she were resigned to this action being taken and said, "Please don't send me away. Please let me stay with you, Ellie. I'm scared. I can't go home, please."

"Let's see what the police have to say," was all I could manage in reply. I dialled 999 and gave a brief outline of the situation. They said they would have someone over to the house soon.

Hannah relaxed into her surroundings a little and told me some of the things her father had done to her over the years. Scott and Tyler kept coming in and out of the kitchen for food and drinks. I didn't want them to know the details of what was happening here and just let them believe she was ill and waiting until her dad could pick her up later. "Do you want me to call Grandad and see if he can pick you up? I can come and bring you back later," I offered. They loved spending time with my dad and jumped at the chance. This helped me right now to keep them out of what was about to unfold.

Hannah's revelations were that Pete had started, years ago, just saying they were secret games. Moving on to more touching and then to the actual act of intercourse. Now pregnant... To her father!

Curtis and the police arrived within five minutes of each other. Thankfully, more than twenty minutes after the boys had left with Dad. Curtis admitted he had lied to Pete, so as not to arouse suspicion for the moment. "I thought we needed to buy some time and see what the plan was," he declared, shrugging his shoulders.

One of the police officers was a woman and she sat very close to Hannah throughout the questioning, holding her hand and reassuring her. She said that she was safe now and that no one could hurt her any more. The police needed her to go to the station and be interviewed in the appropriate manner. They said that would happen tomorrow. "In the meantime, we can't thank you enough for what you have done for Hannah, Mrs Parson, we will take care of her from here. She will go to social services, who will arrange an emergency foster home for her. We can keep you posted."

Hannah was panic-stricken. "No, no, no, I'm not going anywhere. Tell them, Ellie. Tell them I can stay here, can't I?" She lunged at me, wrapping her arms around me tightly.

"Er, well…" I looked at Curtis for some help. He shrugged his shoulders and nodded his permission. There weren't many situations that rendered Curtis speechless but this was definitely among them. "Yes, I suppose she can stay here, if that's allowed. And we can see what happens tomorrow," I said, resigned. "Will you be contacting her parents?" I needed to know. "They won't have a clue what's going on."

"Yes, we have enough details, don't worry, we will deal with that. And we will be in touch in the morning about picking Hannah up," said the WPC, smiling.

I told Hannah to have a nice hot bath while I found her some pyjamas. She wept on and off all evening and, when the boys returned, all fed and watered, they had a bath and went to bed. Hannah opened up a bit more with stories of the grooming she had been subjected to. We were so exhausted by the time we went to bed.

Hannah hugged us both and thanked us for letting her stay and for supporting her. She declared that if she had been taken away from us, she would have killed herself. At this point, I tried to explain that, ultimately, it may not be our decision what happened and where she would go. Curtis said that was nonsense and he would make sure she stayed with us no matter what.

Chapter 28

To say the following weeks weren't easy, was the biggest understatement ever. The very next day, Hannah had to give her statement, with representatives from social services present. I went with her, at her request, and tried to fathom out what all the implications of this situation were. The subsequent pregnancy test showed that she wasn't pregnant but still, she was adamant that she was. The doctor said it could be the shock of the events coming to a head that caused her periods to stop.

I took her home and we had constant contact with the police as they were bringing her father in for questioning. We were informed later that Pete had denied he had ever touched Hannah in any inappropriate manner. He had been more than cooperative with the police and had helped them as much as he could. They told us he was devastated and seemed totally perplexed at these allegations. So now it seems it was a case of 'she said, he said', and I even had Hannah's mum on the phone, calling me all the names under the sun, saying I planted these seeds in her daughter's head. Jesus, what had I gotten myself involved with?

I took Hannah out and tried my best to make her feel welcome and safe. I bought her new clothes, shoes and even asked her if she would like to have a visit to the hairdressers. Nothing drastic but just to help make her feel better. She seemed to be settling in and, to begin with, she got on really well with the boys. The investigation was ongoing and, the longer she stayed, the more phone calls and visits from authorities we had. Hannah attended her own school throughout the weeks and a taxi was arranged to pick her up from ours and bring her back home in the afternoons.

A few weeks had passed and, whilst we had never done any more pregnancy tests, Hannah insisted she was pregnant she still hadn't had a period. It was a mystery. She was using the boy's old bedroom (pre-loft conversion), and, one afternoon, as I was hoovering through each room, I opened the bedroom door to do her room. I tidied her clothes on the bed and then I opened the wardrobe door to put them away. An awful smell met me. It was pretty bad and I had visions of finding dirty socks, that the boys had stuffed in the back of the wardrobe from ages ago. I routed through all Hannah's bags and bits and bobs, looking for the offending article, but couldn't find anything. Strange, I thought. But the sickly, pungent odour suddenly got so much worse. The powerful, breath-taking smell was rancid, so much so, that I could almost taste it. I began searching through boxes and bags in the area it was emanating from and, when I opened a carrier bag, the smell just got stronger and more unpleasant. Inside the carrier bag was another carrier bag tied tightly at the top. I carefully untied it, all the time expecting some kind of dead animal, and when I looked inside, I found dozens of used sanitary towels. I almost puked. Gagging, I held my hands over my mouth and my eyes started to run.

After opening the window, spraying almost a full can of air freshener and tying the discovered towels in five or six more carrier bags, I went outside to put them in the dustbin. What in God's name was happening here? Hannah clearly had been having periods but not saying anything. I decided to ring the social worker we had been appointed and see what her take was on the discovery.

After a long discussion, we decided to talk to her together the next afternoon. I told Curtis when he got home, he just pulled a face like it was too much information for him to process and said he'd leave me to deal with it. As usual, supportive and helpful. When the social care woman came to talk, Hannah just clammed up and cried. She wouldn't answer any questions about hiding the used sanitary towels or about why she wanted us to believe she was pregnant. Eventually, I agreed to leave it. I let Hannah go to her room while we had a private conversation in the kitchen.

After the social care woman left, Hannah came to me and dropped to her knees. "Please don't send me back, I love you and Curtis. I will be good, I promise. Please, please say I can stay." She literally begged at my feet.

"Okay, okay." I helped her up. "Hannah, get up,

listen, nobody's sending you anywhere, we are just trying to understand what's actually happening here." I walked her to the sofa. "Why did you want us to think you were pregnant?" She just looked at the floor. "You need to tell me the truth or I can't help you. Did your dad rape you or not?"

"See, I knew if I wasn't pregnant nobody would believe me. Of course he raped me. He's been abusing me for years." She just started to cry again but now she seemed angry too. I decided to leave it for now.

Throughout the remainder of the day, she mooched around the house. The boys came home and she antagonised them while they were playing a video game on the telly. She kept pressing the buttons on the remote control and spoiling their game. Scott came to the kitchen to find me and said she was being a dick. "Mum, can't you tell her. She's just getting on my nerves." He looked at me with a frustrated frown. "When's she going home? I've had enough of her." As we walked back into the room, she was laying on the floor beside my large rubber plant bending over the ends of the leaves and snapping them in a line.

"HANNAH!" I shouted. "Stop that now. What on earth do you think you're doing?" I really did raise my voice.

"What?" she replied nonchalantly, as if she were doing nothing wrong.

"Bending and snapping the leaves on my plant, I just watched you do it, don't try and deny it," I scolded her.

"Mum, send her home," moaned Tyler. "We've been telling you for days that she's a nasty piece of work. Why don't you believe us?"

I felt like a rabbit caught in the headlights, not knowing which way to turn. I took the boys into the kitchen and reassured them that she would be leaving soon.

When Curtis walked through the front door an hour later, Hannah shot from the floor onto a small two-seater sofa. When he walked in the room, she looked at him through her eyelashes and patted the empty cushion next to her. He walked over and sat next to her putting his arm around her shoulder. He asked her if she'd had a good day. She leaned in putting her arms around his waist and, resting her head on his chest, simultaneously giving me a fleeting, but devious smile. Just enough for me to recognise it was intentional. As she sat back, her face changed, like butter wouldn't melt. Now I was angry.

On another occasion, I had to tell her off for putting her bare feet on the glass front of the gas fire. The fire was on and when she took her feet away it left skin marks on the glass. She said it didn't hurt, though clearly it must have. I just replied that I didn't care if it hurt or not, it was making a mess on the glass.

Although Hannah wasn't aware, we had been informed of an impending visit from the police to update us on the allegations and subsequent investigations. This couldn't come quick enough for me. It wasn't as straightforward as Hannah would have us believe.

The following Sunday evening, we were all in and around the house. Curtis was sitting on a breakfast bar stool with his head in his hands stressing about some stuff he had to pick up the next morning. He was sitting in the same chair, just below the portable television, where he had sat the evening of his affair revelation. That alone made me want to punch him in the face but I refrained. "Come on, Ellie, if you just come with me, I can park right outside, it'll only take two minutes. If I have to find somewhere to park, I could be bloody ages."

"Yeah, I've heard that before — two minutes. Last time you said that I was sat there for over an hour. Sorry, I have an appointment with the accountant and I can't be late. And I still have to sort out all the receipts you have stuffed in your car and in the drawer in the bedroom," I said, as a 'get-out' tactic.

"I'll go with you," piped up Hannah. She had an inset day at her school and I had already told her she would be spending the day with me.

"No, no, Hannah. You're coming with me tomorrow." To which, she stuck out her bottom lip and looked towards Curtis to save her. She had mastered a look of 'Bambi' and he fell for it every time.

He looked up and smiled. "Yeah, great, that's a brilliant idea," he enthused.

"Absolutely not," I cut in. "Like I said, you're with me, now skidaddle off to your bedroom and get ready to have a bath."

"But I can wait in the car, if it helps Curtis," she said, with a loving emphasis on his name.

"Yeah, course y'can, love," he said, putting his arm round her, much to her delight.

"Get in the bath, Hannah," I said in a very sharp tone, whilst directing a death-stare at Curtis.

Before anyone else had chance to carry on this discussion, the doorbell rang. Scott was obviously the nearest as he got there first and opened the door. Then he bellowing from the porch, "MUM... Cops are here."

"Scott," I chided. "Police, to you, if you don't mind," I corrected.

"Sorry about that." I smiled at the two regular offices who had been our contact throughout this whole debacle. They just laughed and said it was fine and they had been called a lot worse. I could only imagine.

I saw them through to the kitchen and closed all the kids out. They stayed long enough for a cuppa and filled us in on all developments. Hannah's dad had left her mum, though we weren't aware of where he was and whose decision that had been. The officers said there was no evidence at all to point toward Hannah's allegations being true and, in fact, quite the contrary. It looked like a full search of the house had brought up some interesting revelations but we were not given any details, and wouldn't be, until Hannah had been taken back in for some more questioning. I told them how she was starting to display a devious side and described some examples of her behaviour. Then I decided to explain, as much to Curtis as to them, about her trying to spend time alone with Curtis tomorrow, and why I thought it was a bad idea.

"Oh, for God's sake, Ellie, she only wants to sit in the car." Curtis rolled his eyes.

"And you think that's a good idea, do you? And what if she comes back and claims that you raped her, eh, what then?" I was angry with him for his naive stupidity where devious teenage girls were concerned.

"Actually, you present a very good point, Ellie," agreed the WPC. "If she is lying about her dad, what's to say she wouldn't do it again. I'd steer well clear of being alone with her at all, Curtis, if I were you." She nodded in his direction. He looked deflated to be put in his place by two women. I hoped I didn't look as smug as I felt.

"Honestly, she's an absolute nightmare she's causing me grief with the boys and, some days, I have to stop myself from punching her," I admitted.

"From everything you've told us, Ellie, I'm not surprised. Listen, you need to think of your own family and your own sanity, so we will speak to the care service department. Looks like she will be called into the station on Tuesday after school, around four thirty, so we'll see if we can get her moved after the interview. Okay with you, Ellie?"

"Perfect, the sooner the better, thanks. She's really treading on thin ice with me." I smiled but with a withering look.

The officers left and Hannah wanted to know what they said. I gave Curtis a warning look and he just up and left the house. The boys got ready for bed and, a little later on, I went up to their room to let them know she would be out by Tuesday evening. The look of relief on their faces almost made me cry. I felt so guilty for getting into this messy situation and the strain it had put on the family. I could only imagine what devastation it had ensued on her own family. Her poor parents, not to mention her sister. From the way the police had just spoken, it looked like something may have come to light in her father's defence. Shame it looked like it was too late to save the family from the destruction that already had a hold.

"Tyler, your bus is here." Monday morning, seven fifty a.m. and Tyler's plush little school bus pulled up outside. I kissed him goodbye and gave him a squeeze. He knew the meaning behind it. The boys couldn't wait to get Hannah out of the house.

Next, I bundled Scott and Hannah into the car and they argued as Hannah made to get in the front passenger seat. "Hey, I'm in the front," objected Scott, pushing her out of the way. She took a couple of unexpected steps sideways with the force of the push and Scott just jumped in and slammed the door. She reluctantly got in the back and slammed her door even harder.

"Now, now, that's enough," I said to no one in particular.

"Well, Scott is so rude. I'm the eldest. I should be in the front," she whined.

"Yes, well, it's my mum's car, not yours. This is not even your home. I don't know why you're here anyway, trying to shove your nose into our family." Scott had never sounded so cutting. "Being a creep around my dad all the time, don't think we can't see what you're up to," he finished off.

"You think I'm creeping around him? If you were that bothered, you'd be having a word with Rebecca, not me. She's the one that's going to destroy your precious little family," she announced with venom.

"That's enough, stop… Finished," I screamed.

I kissed Scott as I dropped him off and he slammed the door and gave Hannah an evil glare. For the remainder of the day, I kept her within arm's length, but she constantly and successfully irritated and undermined me. At the accountants, during supermarket shopping and everywhere we went. Thankfully, she was picked up the next morning for school.

Curtis just thought I was overreacting and said I would feel bad if it turned out that Pete was guilty. "I don't even care if it turns out she's telling the truth, Curtis. She's driven me to destruction over the weeks and I feel guilty enough for putting the boys through all of this. You're never in so you've no idea," I concluded.

Curtis had not let the imposition on our family stop his movements. He was either at work, whether that was at the gym or doing photography, or he was up at Alison's house. He treated there like a second home and, even though the Rebecca issue kept rearing its ugly head, I wasn't sure whether or not I should, in fact, be worried that he was getting too close to Alison. He spent so much time there. He always spoke highly of her and didn't care if Ben was in or out, he would spend more time there than at home.

When Hannah's car arrived to take her to school the next morning, I bid her goodbye and wished her a good day. I planned to tell her the police were coming to speak to her, but not until she came home from school. I didn't want her worrying at school all day. So, on her return, I took a deep breath, ready to have the conversation. I heard the distinct rattle of the diesel taxi pulling up on the drive. I waited to hear the front door open. I heard the taxi pull away and I stood, lacing my fingers together with nerves. *Come on*, I thought, *open the door*. I stood and I waited and eventually, getting frustrated with her for hanging around outside, I opened the door. I drew a deep breath to ask her why she didn't come in but she wasn't there. I knew I wasn't mistaken that she'd arrived, because, from the hallway, I'd glanced through her bedroom window and saw her in the taxi as it arrived. Where the hell was, she? It was as if she had disappeared into thin air. I shouted her name a couple of times and looked in and around the area.

Nothing. No sign of her. What was going on? Where had she gone? I nipped inside and, shouting the boys to join me, we got in the car. "Come on, boys, quickly, you need to help me look, while I drive."

"I don't care if she's run away," Tyler cried, getting in the car.

"Me either, good riddance to bad rubbish," Scott added.

"Yeah, well, I care. If she disappears, who do you think is going to get it in the neck? Me, yes, she's my responsibility while she's here."

"I thought she was going anyway," continued Scott.

"She is, the police are coming here in about thirty minutes and I need to find her. So, take one side of the road each and keep your eyes peeled."

Our search of the immediate surrounding area brought nothing and, as we returned, a police car was waiting on the driveway. They were about five minutes early for picking her up and now I had to tell them she'd done a bunk. *So help me God, if I get my hands on her I will choke her*, I thought. I explained everything to the police and they called it in to the local station to get any police, out and about in the area, to keep an eye out for her. As we stood there for a few minutes, making plans for when we found her, the police officer's radio crackled into life. On came a broken voice asking if she was in a school uniform but from a school in a different area.

"Yep, that's her," replied the PC. "Where is she?" Then another crackly voice but I couldn't quite make out all of it. The bit I did catch was that she had been spotted in a phone box. "Okay, check her name and take her to the main station, social services are waiting to sit in on the interview," was the reply from this end.

"Oh thank God for that," I said, exhaling. "I tell you, I was ready to throw a right wobbly. She's been a complete pain in my arse and then this disappearing act. Jesus, don't let me see her again."

"No, love, don't worry, she's already being placed in care, as from tonight."

I was still curious, though, and I asked, "So do we know what this interview is about tonight?" I was just looking for any snippet of information.

"Yeah, sorry, love, can't disclose." He looked apologetically at me. "Someone will be round in about an hour to collect her stuff, though, if you'd be so good as to get it ready for them."

"Sure, yes I will do." I nodded.

"Thanks, and I'm sure you will get to know the outcome, sooner or later." He smiled and gave my shoulder a light squeeze as he indicated to the WPC that they were leaving.

"Yeah, thanks, Ellie, thanks for everything, you really went above and beyond. Not many people would have done what you did," agreed the WPC. I nodded and smiled in response.

Chapter 29

Not having Hannah on the scene did free up a lot of time for me. It had been overly stressful and so emotionally exhausting. I'm sure Curtis just took advantage of me being occupied with all the appointments and reports I had to attend and write.

The fact that she had hidden all signs of her period, plus her antagonistic behaviour, had all added to a pattern that the social care team identified as habitual lying. They kept me informed, that even though there had been a search, of sorts, in her family home previously, another, more in-depth one, had now taken place. When they received the results of that search it turned out that they had found, under her mattress, which was a top bunk bed, a magazine with a true story in it. This story, pretty much word for word, what she had accused her dad of. When they questioned her about the find, she broke down and admitted what she had done. Using in her defence that she wanted a different life. The life she thought we had. How wrong could she be? I just prayed that it wasn't too late to rebuild her own family. But with her parents now separated I could only imagine it was going to be a long and rocky road. Oh dear, what a mess.

Meanwhile, I had my own issues to deal with. Mine and Curtis' relationship was as volatile as ever. He was out of the house more than he was in. This just maximised my suspicions of him being unfaithful. He bought me a mobile phone and had the audacity to wrap it up and give it to me as a birthday gift. Then told me it was only for him to track my movements. He said it was registered to him and I was not allowed to make any calls on it. The itemized bill was sent in his name and if I used it, he would take it off me. He had had a mobile phone for a few years, at this point, but always forbid me to have one. Now, though, he only wanted me to carry one so he could find me at a minute's notice. Typical, I thought, not that I went anywhere I wouldn't want him to know about but just the feeling of being on a long leash was enough to provoke me.

So, I gave the number to anyone I thought could benefit from it. Including our best friends and Curtis' and my family members. I never used it to call anyone, ever, and vowed to only use it in an emergency, which, thankfully, never occurred. The amount of times Curtis called me, however, was beyond ridiculous. Half the times, I never even heard it ring. If I was in the car with music on or, even just out shopping and the phone was in the bottom of my bag, it was easily missed. Curtis would go ballistic when he finally tracked me down. I can't even count the amount of times he came home and kicked off because I hadn't answered a call from him.

His behaviour towards me was quite intimidating

and I would be lying if I said I wasn't scared of him. I had seen how many times he'd punched a hole in a door and didn't want to push him into my face being that door. They say mobile phones were a godsend and made life much easier. Not for me. My already prison sentence of a life was now more like solitary confinement.

Curtis showed so many signs of infidelity and I even think he knew I suspected this to be the case. Never before had he gone out himself and bought his own underwear, for example. Now here he was with four expensive and up-to-date pairs of men's briefs from River Island. When I questioned his unfamiliar purchase, he claimed he was just saving me a job and smiled. As if Curtis had ever done that.

One midweek morning, we had just seen the boys off to school. Tyler, on his school bus and Scott, who had now taken to meeting his mates and either walking or catching a bus to school with them. Curtis told me to get ready — there was something he wanted to show me. He drove us to a massive building site and drove all the way through it, until we reach the sales office. "Fancy moving to a new house?" he asked, with a smirk on his face. I was totally taken aback.

Really?" I couldn't hide my shock at this suggestion. What a bizarre thing for him to want, given the state of our relationship. "What, here, are you serious? How much are they? Can we really afford it?" The pictures of the houses they were building did look amazing. I can't deny having a brand-new house would have been dream to me.

"Well, that's why I've brought you here, Miss Moneypenny." He kissed my cheek. "You know what we earn and what we have to pay out, so you can tell me what we can afford." He looked really pleased with himself. "Come on, let's have a look. Our bungalow is too small now the boys are growing up and, besides, I need an office at home. And besides…" He grinned with a cunning look on his face. "We need a house bigger than Ben and Alison's."

Oh… Oh, now this made sense. Keeping up with the Joneses. Why did I not guess that was the ulterior motive? Still, if he wanted a new house to show off, I would just love one for myself, so, tally-ho, I thought. Why not?

We looked at all the different styles that were being built and there was one in particular that caught Curtis' eye. It was going to be the biggest house on the estate. Built in an 'L' shape, with a double garage, four bedrooms, large lounge, separate dining room, massive kitchen and utility room. There was a downstairs toilet and a room adjoining the garage and house, which would make a perfect office. They didn't have a show house of this style, aptly named 'The Westminster', because there was only going to be that one built. So we were shown around a four-bedroom house with a separate garage.

The salesman did a great job on Curtis. He honed

in on his arrogant and opinionated attitude and just played up to him. Having discovered what we did for a living, the clever salesman just stroked Curtis' ego to the degree that left him no other option but to say yes to the house. We consequently did some number crunching and then went for a walk on the site to see the exact position of the house.

It all seemed to happen very quickly. The house was already more than half built and due for completion by July of that year. We were now almost at the end of February 1995, and therefore would need to get our bungalow on the market as soon as possible and secure a new mortgage offer. Of course, this would all be left to me. That said, we signed the necessary papers, there and then, at the site office that day and wheels were in motion.

The new house was much nearer to the high school for Scott and about a one-minute drive to the gym. Although, now, being closer to the gym wasn't really essential as Curtis had expanded his training into nearby towns and villages, anyway. He utilised the gym three days a week, so one night a week I took a step aerobics class and another night I did circuit training for ladies. It kept my fitness up and enabled me to add to my secret stash. I even stayed behind after the training sessions and did some working out in the gym with a friend of mine, Janet.

She was really unhappy at home and we used to daydream together about having a new life. She had a daughter and a son of similar ages to my boys. She was one person I had started to confide in. We both felt sorry for each other and for ourselves, how ironic, what a predicament.

The progress of the build was constantly monitored and I was trusted to make all the choices for fittings and fixtures. This I relished, and chose understated and minimalistic, that was my preference. On numerous occasions I had to drive past the gym and, once or twice or even maybe more, I would see Curtis with different women. Either chatting in the doorway or seeing them to their car, which did seem a little unnecessary, if you ask me. If I dared to question him about who he had seen during the day he just declared he had private training sessions booked in. Private training sessions, my arse. Did he think I was that much of a mug?

It didn't, however, lesson his paranoia about my whereabouts. He was constantly questioning and checking up on me. If ever I was seen by him talking to a male, he would go berserk. I tried not to let men stand too close to me in the gym as this would be misconstrued as them fancying me and, as Curtis so pleasantly put it, 'trying to get into my knickers'. If I laughed with, or smiled at, any bloke, it was deemed to be me leading them on. There was no let-up in his unreasonable jealousy and accusations.

We hosted a dinner party, of sorts, one evening for some people Curtis knew in the same business. He wanted to impress them and I had to make lots of nice food, buy flowers and stock up a ridiculous amount of alcohol. He chose what I wore, of course, and during the evening, while I was washing some glasses, one of the guys came into the kitchen for a drink of water. I laughed at him. "Water?" I exclaimed. "You must be the driver."

He came over to get a glass from me and, as he was taking it from my hand, laughed and said, 'How did you guess?'

Curtis opened the door. I can't imagine how he saw the situation as a threat but he embarrassed himself, me and the guy, by grabbing the glass from his hand, looking his most threatening death stare at me and saying to the bloke, in the most obnoxious manner, "I'll bring your water into the room." The bloke took the hint and disappeared. Curtis twisted my arm behind my back. "Just lining him up for a fuck later, were you?"

"Don't be so bloody ridiculous," I answered. "You just managed to make yourself look a right prick. Well done, Curtis." I left the room, shaking his grip from my arm, went into the lounge and wished everyone an enjoyable evening and excused myself with a fake migraine.

Later that evening, or, more probably, the early hours of the following morning, Curtis came to bed and forced himself on me. This wasn't unusual. It wasn't lovemaking and it hadn't been for a long time. He just took pleasure for himself in having the most aggressive sex he could. He was so strong and insistent it just made me cry. I was only thankful the boys had stayed overnight at Josh's.

The time came for us to move into the new house. It was stunning. I had chosen all the new furniture, all the furnishings to go with it and the colour schemes for all the rooms. The boys were totally thrilled to have a brand-new bedroom each and couldn't wait to have their friends' round. They had chosen everything necessary for their own rooms. It was so nice to see them happy and excited about something. But, I'm afraid, that excitement was short-lived. Curtis announced they were not to have any friends around to the house. Not only that, he forbid them from having any phone calls. He said it was a business line, now that he had an office, and the line needed to be kept clear for him. So, there we were, all in this new fabulous house that didn't even feel like home. I know I felt sad and miserable and I could see the boys did, too. They did and said everything they could to show their loathing and disapproval of Curtis' decisions.

Scott came home one day and said he had had an argument with a boy at school because the boy called his dad a paedophile. The boy lived across the road from Rebecca and he told Scott he saw his dad with her in the car all the time. I knew if I told Curtis this, he would go crazy and probably find the boy responsible and kill him.

I expressed my concern later that week to Janet, when we were in the gym after a step class. She offered to park up and hide to see if she could catch Curtis up to no good, but I declined the offer. I knew he would squirm his way out of anything without us having proof. So, on I battled. I normally enjoyed a glass of wine in the evenings and barely noticed when my drinking started to increase. Not only were the evening bottles being opened earlier, I had also taken to opening a bottle when I felt despondent and alone. Which was most of the time.

Winter was well and truly upon us and, with Christmas approaching, we had made an effort to go shopping together, just Curtis and I, to get some presents for the boys. Scott was past thirteen now and Tyler coming up to twelve next April. They weren't particularly difficult to buy for, but I wouldn't trust Curtis to choose. We'd arranged to spend Christmas day with Ben and Alison and their children so wanted to get some gifts for them too. Curtis was very overly generous when buying gifts for them. Not that I begrudged this, but he spent a lot of time choosing something special. He asked me what I wanted, so, as we were looking around, I chose a couple of bits for the house and a pair of shoes. Curtis just wanted me to have something expensive as well, so took me into a jeweller to pick something nice. He acted like the doting husband while we were in there and spoke loudly as he gushed, "Pick anything you want, darling, you're worth it." The staff in the shop smiled and commented on how lucky I was. What a joke. We spent some money and, while we were in there, Curtis spotted some little silver pendants and bought one for Tanya. She was the only one we were missing a gift for. So, all done, we made our way home. Curtis spent the whole journey home in a good mood and kept reminding me how much he loved me. Reminding me we were always going to be together, no matter what. He did this regularly and, every time, it came across as a threat. "It might not feel like it all the time but I really do love you, Ellie. I wanted the new house to be a new start for us. Business is doing so well and I think we should have a really big holiday next year, don't you?" I tried to look like I cared, but it was hard, because I didn't. "We could go with Ben and the family, it would be brilliant, what do you say?" He sounded excited.

"Yes, sounds good." I attempted to sound enthusiastic.

"Yeah, we're off out for a meal with them to a posh restaurant this weekend, we can ask them then," he decided.

And that's exactly what he did. We were getting ready to go and he chose which dress I should wear, as always. "Put your tight, black, lacy dress on, Ellie. You know Alison's a lot slimmer than you. It's your best chance of not looking too fat next to her." He somehow made this sound like a compliment.

"Gee, thanks," I offered.

"No, no, you've got a gorgeous figure, Ellie. You're so curvy in all the right places and that's why blokes always eye you up. Alison is far too skinny. I like a body to get hold of," he reminded me and started trying to take my bra off as I was getting my dress out of the wardrobe.

"Aw, no, not now, please… I've just got ready and done my hair," I tried.

"Won't take long and I won't touch your hair." He pulled me from the bedroom forcefully and pushed me against the long banister overlooking the stairs. "We haven't done it on the landing yet, so we can tick it off the list," he laughed as he bent me over. He pushed my shoulders forward and entered me roughly from behind. I just want to scream and fight but as usual I knew I wouldn't win and, in fact, I was afraid of ending up the injured party.

When he had finished, he told me to get him a big wedge of notes from the business money I had, saved for tax bills. I always over compensated for tax bills so we wouldn't get caught out. He knew this by now and always used this money to put in his wallet. I knew he wasn't going to spend it and would give it back when we got home. He just wanted it to be spotted in his wallet to make him feel good. I just had the secret wish, every time, that some thug that could outfight him, would spot the money and mug him as we left the restaurant. Bash him over the head with a rock and kill him. It would be worth losing all the cash in his wallet.

We had a nice evening with Ben and Alison. They were always so funny we had a good laugh, mainly because Curtis was on public display and played his part of a perfect husband very well.

Christmas morning arrived. We had visited Curtis' mum and Dave on Christmas Eve to exchange gifts and we were calling in at my parents' this morning for the same reason. I saw my family on very rare occasions, these days. Dad was still doing his job, which he loved, and getting very poorly paid for it. At least he was happy and that made me happy. Our family, my brother, sister and their families hardly ever spent time together. Christmas morning was when we made a special effort to make this happen. Everyone seems so busy, or maybe that was just an excuse. I was well aware that no one in my family liked Curtis but they disliked him on evidence of what little they knew of him. They didn't even know the half of it. The thought of the outcome, of me telling them the truth, wasn't something I could even bear thinking about.

As I got ready and put on my new shoes and jewellery that Curtis had bought me, he came over and said quietly, "Don't put your new shoes on, Ellie, or the jewellery, just looks like you're showing off. And you know Ben and Alison won't have spent as much on each other as I have on you. It might just spoil the day. Take them off and wear something else!" It was an order.

When we arrived at Ben and Alison's, late morning, all the festivities began. Josh couldn't wait to show the boys what he had received. Curtis dished out the presents he had bought for the family. When moody, sulky Tanya came downstairs in a too tight, too short, and too grown up dress, Curtis whistled and laughed. Ben just frowned at her. Curtis leaned over to give her a Christmas kiss on the cheek and whispered in her ear as he gave her the gift. She pulled a face at her dad and took her gift upstairs. Curtis gave Ben a man hug and tutted. "Daughters, who'd have em?"

"Yeah, tell me about it. I told her that dress was too short but she wouldn't listen to me, what did you whisper to her?"

"I just said it looked nice but might not be comfortable if we are going to play Christmas games." He winked at Ben like he was some kind of an expert on kids and went to help himself to a drink.

"Let's see if she listens to you, then, mate," Ben said, doubtfully rolling his eyes. "Hey, Ellie, you look lovely," he complimented. "Bet you're glad you only have boys, eh? Honestly, Josh is so easy in comparison."

"Do not talk to me about teenage girls." I slapped my forehead in mock horror. They were well aware of my history with Hannah. Mm, girls. Definitely not my cup of tea.

Chapter 30

Scott and Tyler looked more and more repressed. They just seemed to look sad behind their eyes, if that makes sense. Even in photos that had been taken over Christmas, they both had dark rings under their eyes and it made me want to cry. They knew exactly what was going on between Curtis and I. Now he had started not even taking into consideration that they could be in ear shot when he kicked off. Occasionally, worse, while they were even in the same room. Trying to protect them from this was increasingly more difficult.

It was a quiet Sunday morning and we were eating cheese toasties in the front room. The television was on in the background, some boring news programme. Then the presenter interviewed Jilly Cooper. I wasn't really listening as the boys and I were quietly discussing the possibility of picking up Josh and going out for a drive to the bowling alley. "Hey, look, aren't they the books that you've read?" Curtis pointed to a shot of her books, *Riders, Rivals* and *Polo* on the TV screen.

"Oh, yes." I glanced up unenthusiastically.

We carried on our Sunday outing plan and Curtis left the room. But, within two minutes, he had returned with my book off the bedside cabinet. I was about halfway through my copy of *Polo*. I had long since read the other two. "I didn't know that these books were just full of goddamn smut," he shouted in an irate manner. His face was flushed with anger as he flipped through the pages. Suddenly he started ripping and ripping at the pages. He was seething as he pulled more and more pages out, throwing them to the floor and ranting. "So this is what you read in bed, filthy disgusting pornographic rubbish." I chose not to dignify his comment with a response. He continued his tirade of bad language. "What, what... Do you pretend you're shagging the bloke in the book, Rupert whatever the fuck his name is? How dare you read this and then sleep with me, you whore." Vicious words just tumbled out of his mouth, accompanied by spittle foaming at the edges. Scott and Tyler just stood, open-mouthed, but took a protective step nearer to me.

"For God's sake, Curtis, listen to yourself, you're pathetic. It's a bloody book, you idiot."

He continued to rip out what pages were left hanging, including the cover, and threw it on the floor in his anger. "Don't you call me an idiot, you slag. Do you hear that?" He directed this question to the boys. "Your mother is nothing but a common slut. Don't you ever bring another book like this into my house, ever," he spat. "Do you hear me?"

I felt a muscle pulse furiously in my neck. "Fucking grow up, Curtis, you're a constant disappointment to me and the boys. Just get out of my sight," I cautioned in a monotone voice. I was just absolutely sick and tired of him. "I feel like I'm clinging to the last vestiges of sanity here." I felt quite confident he wasn't going to lay a hand on me in front of the boys; he never had done before. Instead, he almost imploded and, as he turned to walk out of the room, he swiped his hand across a small table, knocking my most prized piece of Lladró to the floor. It broke into three or four pieces on the carpet. For his final gesture, he slammed the door and left.

I told the boys not to worry and said that Dad was slowly losing control and he didn't like it. "The more we stand up to him, the madder he is going to get, so we just need to bear that in mind and stick together," I advised, hugging them.

We went out for our Sunday morning outing and had a lovely time. I don't know what had happened to me but I felt this burning fire inside me growing. More animosity and anger just grew over the following weeks. Normal day-to-day conversations became limited. An advertisement on the television sent Curtis spiralling out of control once again, as Tyler innocently made a comment. It was an advert for Gillette razors. Alison had, in front of the boys, one day, announced it to be her favourite advert. "It's funny, Mum, every time Alison sees this advert she says… 'Phwoar'." I laughed, agreeing the guy on the advert was handsome. Curtis picked up the remote control and turned the channel over. He just glanced in my direction and muttered the word 'tart' under his breath. From that day forward, he must have turned that same advert over at least ten more times. Idiot. Unequivocally an idiot.

Another evening, he came home and, when he saw Tyler cuddled up to me on the sofa, he sent Tyler to bed saying, "She's mine, not yours, now go to bed." He promptly sat down next to me. He had been drinking — I could smell it on his breath. He started trying to kiss me and aggressively undoing the front of my blouse. I stood up immediately to go after Tyler but Curtis pulled me back to the sofa. "You can go when I say you can," was all he offered.

It seemed, every day, situations were tearing us apart. Tension in the house was constantly palpable. It was early March and the weather was freezing. I had been spending a lot of time with Alison recently, she was completely at her wit's end with her hormonal teenage daughter. "She's so angry all the time, honestly, she threw a mug at Josh the other day and luckily he dodged it, but it took a right chunk out of the kitchen wall." Alison was tired with it. Ben was working away and I think Tanya took advantage of her mum being alone.

"I think Curtis asked her if she wanted to do some work for him and earn a bit of cash," I remembered. "He wants all his files and records changing from paper onto the new computer. Why don't you ask him, and give her something to do?" Tanya was at college now and was at the age where having money was important. Alison said she would try and arrange it.

Only a week later, Saturday morning, and Tanya was, in fact, helping Curtis in his new office at home. "Make us some sandwiches, Ellie," he demanded "Oh, and coffee." I heard Tanya giggling as he went back to join her in the office. He was just incredulous. Making demands in front of my friends' daughter. I wasn't about to embarrass myself, screaming like a banshee in front of her, so I went upstairs and told the boys to get their boots and coats on quietly and quickly. I took my mobile phone and, as a total act of defiance, stood it up on the chaise longue in the hallway by the front door. We crept out to my car on the drive and took off.

We just couldn't stop laughing. "He's going to go mental when he sees you left your phone at home," giggled Scott.

"I know, I don't care. I'm done. Your father is such a pig. We are not going back home 'til bedtime, see how he likes that. Maybe he can get moody Tanya to make him a sandwich." We all roared with laughter.

We had a full day doing all the things the boys liked to do. On the way back from McDonald's, we decided to call in on Gran and Grandad. My parents were going off on a trip next week with their friends, so just to kill some more time, we turned up on their doorstep and invited ourselves for tea, much to their delight. Dad said he was going to light a fire at the bottom of the garden later on. "Can't do it till after seven p.m.," he apologised to the boys, "but if you want to stay and give me a hand, you're welcome."

"Can we mum, please?" came the chorus in unison.

I laughed. "Yeah, why not." My dad looked pleased and said they should put the outside lights on and see if they could find any more sticks to add to his bonfire.

While they were outside, Dad told me Curtis had phoned earlier to see if we were there.

"Yeah, I forgot my mobile... But, anyway, no worries. If he calls again just do me a favour and say you haven't seen us." I winked at him.

"Is everything okay, Ellie?" He looked at me with concern.

"It is," I replied with confidence. "Nothing I can't handle." I sniggered conspiratorially. Dad gave me a fond hug and suggested a little tipple. I didn't want to 'drink-drink', so had a tiny tot of Tia Maria and, when seven o'clock came, the boys were excited to light the fire. Under the supervision of my father, they were allowed to poke the fire with a long stick. Yep, not really my thing. It seems all boys love a fire. Whatever.

As Mum and I watched from the dining room window, she suggested they stay overnight. "You can come for breakfast and pick them up in the morning."

"Okay not a problem. Don't let them put smelly, smokey clothes back on, I will bring them clean clothes here. Oh, and make sure they wash their hair in the shower," I finished.

"Don't worry, they have clean pyjamas here and I will make sure they are in bed at a reasonable time."

With that, I spoke to the boys and they were happy

to stay. Scott came over and whispered to me, asking if I would be okay going home to Curtis alone. I assured him I'd be fine. How thoughtful. The gratification and love I felt for my boys. Their understanding and support knew no limits. "Don't worry, love, I can always come back if I need to." He seemed happy with that and they both kissed me goodbye.

On the way home, the song, 'The Sign' by *Ace of Base*, came on the radio. I really liked this song and, as I sang along, I realised a lot of the lyrics were very poignant to me. The more I listened, the more I knew this was my song, my life, my new life. I felt strangely empowered. I sang along.

I kept singing. The more I sang, the more I knew this song was about me. I needed to get me a new life, and soon. I was sick of the one I had...

I pulled up on the drive and knew I was about to face the music. *Bring it on*, I thought. As I'd anticipated, Curtis was home alone and, by the looks of him, already half a dozen cans of beer down. He erupted. "How dare you just fuck off like that and leave your phone here?"

"Easy, when you speak to me like you did," I replied.

"Where have you been? You've been gone all bloody day. I called your dad's and he said you'd not been there. Where are the kids? Who the fuck have you been with?" He shot this tirade of questions out. I just walked away. "Don't you fucking walk away from me, Ellie," he almost screamed.

I walked upstairs with a bottle of wine from the fridge and a glass.

"Where do you think you're going? I want some answers and I haven't even had a proper meal today."

I had to bite my lip so I didn't laugh. What a twat. "I'm going for a bath. The boys are at my parents' and get your own fucking dinner." I felt so brave but knew he wasn't going to take this lying down. He threw my phone at me but missed. I locked myself in the en suite bathroom. He banged on the door, shouting insults and threats at me, nothing I hadn't heard before. I poured myself a large glass of wine and filled the bath, adding a large amount of bubble bath. In this time, Curtis had found something to turn the screw in the lock to let himself into the bathroom. I was just getting in the bath. He was beside himself with anger. "Straight in the bath, eh, washing off your whoring around, are you?" I just ignored him. I thought, being in the water with a glass, he couldn't really start a fight physically. "Who is he? Where have you been?" he tried again. Again, I didn't even open my mouth, apart from taking a large gulp of wine. "Oh, I know how much you hate me, Ellie. But you can't leave, can you? No, cos you will look like the guilty party. I will tell everyone you were cheating on me. You know how much everyone respects me. They will always believe me over you. You daren't leave cos you're spineless. And you know I will find you and kill you. You might think I'm exaggerating but, trust me, I'm not. You're my wife, you belong to me, and if I find anyone has so much as touched you, I will kill them too."

"Get out," was all I could muster up.

He left, but not before pointing his index finger inches from my face and saying, "Be careful, Ellie, and be afraid."

These were the last words we exchanged for days. I picked the boys up the next morning and, with it being Sunday, we did a full day of visiting friends. Anyone and everyone. If they weren't in, but most were, being a cold Sunday in March, we just put them back on the bottom of the list and called back later. We three were in good spirits and, if anyone asked about Curtis, we just said he was working.

We ordered takeaway pizzas for tea later on and ordered one for Curtis. He wasn't speaking to any of us and refused, silently, to eat the pizza we bought him. "What a loser," stated Tyler.

"What a tosser, you mean," challenged Scott, enjoying the joke being on Curtis.

"Hey, hey, language, please. Remember, if you haven't got anything nice to say, don't say anything at all."

"Pity Dad's mum never told him that," came the reply from Scott. "I hate him, Mum, he is horrible to all of us and what makes it worse is everyone we know loves him. It makes me sick. They don't even know him." He ended his speech.

"Exactly, so just bear that in mind. We know him

365

and that's why we stand strong together, okay?" They nodded in agreement.

Monday, Tuesday and most of Wednesday were so quiet it was deafening. The boys were at school. I, home alone. On Wednesday evening I had a ladies circuit training class at the gym. That was from seven until eight and usually after this, Janet and I would carry on and do some extra training alone. But this particular Wednesday, I was too frustrated. We just sat in the reception and chatted. "Honestly, Janet, I just wish I would get home tonight and some copper would come and knock on the door and say, 'Mrs. Parson, I'm sorry to tell you this, but your husband has just been killed in a car crash.' I swear to God I would jump up and down, singing Hallelujah."

Janet laughed. "That's a bit extreme, Ellie, chances are someone else would get hurt."

"Yeah, true, maybe not that, then. But I just don't know what I can do. You know he just threatens to kill me if I leave him. No one would believe what an absolute bastard he is." I sighed heavily.

"Come on, let's fuck the training and get a takeaway and a bottle of wine. We can have it here and you'll still be home in time for the boys at nine p.m."

The Chinese was about three hundred yards left out of the gym entrance and our house was about double that in the opposite direction. "You get us a curry and I'll walk to the offy for a bottle."

"Cool, okay, here's some money, get three bottles

and we can take one each home.

"Lovely, okay."

I picked up our Curry and rice and ordered the usual takeout for the boys and Curtis that we had religiously every Wednesday. By eight twenty we were back in the reception, having a good old bitching session, fuelled by a couple of glasses of wine. Janet wasn't happy at home either but her husband was the polar opposite of Curtis.

At nine p.m., I turned off all the lights, set the alarm and locked up. There was a single bar barrier that swung round and closed the car park of the gym. I made sure that was secure and headed back to the Chinese to pick up my order for the boys. It was literally five minutes later, as I drove home back past the gym, that I noticed Curtis' car parked outside. Half on the path and half on the road. I just continued driving home but couldn't help wondering why there were no lights on in the gym. He wasn't in his car, so I presumed he had gone in to the gym for something.

I pulled up at home and knocked on the door, as the boys always kept it bolted if they were alone. "It's me," I shouted as they approached. Still a little miffed about Curtis being at the gym, potentially in the dark, I decided to call the telephone in the reception. We hadn't spoken for days but I thought, when he answered, I would make an excuse and say I thought I'd left some paperwork under the till in the reception area. The phone rang a few times and then our answering machine kicked in. *That's really strange*, I thought, so I left a message. "Oh it's only me, I only rang on the off-chance you were there, I've left some papers in reception but they're not urgent so I will get them tomorrow." I sorted the takeaway cartons and left Curtis' on the side. "Listen, boys, I just need to pop back to the gym to pick something up, I will only be five minutes. Just call my mobile if you need me, as always, okay?"

"Yeah, no problem." They were too busy tucking into their midweek treat.

I decided to drive back and see if his car had gone, to explain why he didn't answer the phone. But, as I approached, I saw his car hadn't moved. I don't know what I was expecting. Such a frisson of excitement rushed through me; my tummy seemed to flip over with the fear of the unknown. As I got closer, I turned off the car lights and, a little nearer, I turned off the engine, then rolled as near as I dare. I got out and gently pushed the door to, without making a noise. I didn't want him to know I was checking up on him. As I approached the reception door, I thought maybe he's parked here and walked somewhere else nearby. All the lights in the gym were off. I bent down and, using the meagre light that came from the small screen of my phone, I looked in the keyhole. I could just make out there was a key already in the other side.

All that was now running through my mind was to make as little noise as possible and get in there as fast as possible. I don't know exactly what I was expecting to find, but a funny kind of six sense had taken me over.

The fear and excitement was mounting inside me and I could hear blood pumping in my ears. I took my own key to the door and carefully pushed it into the keyhole. With a little bit of jiggling I managed to get his keys to fall out the other side. They fell with a crash and then it was all systems go. I knew the noise would have alerted him and he would know it was me as we were the only two key holders.

Within a millisecond, I had turned my key, opened the door and dashed through the dark reception. I wasn't sure exactly where I was heading but as I drew close to the office door, I heard a noise. I quickly turned to the door and made to open it, grabbing the handle. At that instant he threw himself heavily against the other side. "Curtis... What's going on?" I demanded. I pushed heavily with my shoulder, adrenaline now surging through my body. "Open this fucking door now," I screamed. I kept ramming with my shoulder and the door continually opened an inch and banged shut again, with his obvious weight against it the other side. "You had better open this door now, I'm not going to stop, what are you doing in there, you bastard?" I shrieked. My emotions were all over the place. I felt like I was going to swell and burst, like The Incredible Hulk. I stood back a couple of steps and, thankfully, still wearing training shoes, I started to kick at the door with the bottom of my foot. I was screaming and shouting and swearing for him to let me in. I was so pumped up and the kicking was relentless. I was making progress, though. Curtis was losing his grip on the door and, after what was probably only about one minute, he shouted to me.

"Okay, okay, Ellie, I give in. Stop. You caught me. I was cheating. Stop kicking and I will open the door."

I stood for a second and then went in again with my shoulder. The door burst open and the sight that met my eyes just sent me spiralling out of control. Curtis was stark bollock naked apart from his socks, which, incidentally, had a bloody hole in the toe, and behind him stood Tanya... Tanya! Jesus Christ... She was naked on the top half and holding her top up against her chest, whimpering and trembling.

Sometimes it's hard to guess how you'd react in certain circumstances but I'd been here before. Aside from a few minor differences, I had been here before and now was the time to make sure there wasn't going to be a repeat performance. Oh no, that ship had well and truly sailed. I just let it rip and kicked and punched Curtis everywhere and anywhere. The first one straight in the bollocks, which doubled him over, and, from there on, the others made satisfying contact with his face. When I needed a breath, I stood there looking at the pair of them like I was standing knee deep in shit. "You disgusting bastard," I screamed at Curtis, panting.

"I know, I know, please, Ellie, I can explain... Listen, please." He was so used to me being pliable, malleable, getting his own way, whatever the situation. Not this time. His voice stammered; he was struggling to keep his composure. He repeated my name, trying to pull some of his clothes back on at the same time.

"And you." I looked at Tanya with loathing. "You had better watch your back. The pair of you are just low-life. Lower than a snake in the grass… Lower than a worm under the fucking ground." I was totally erupting. And then a striking realisation hit me like an epiphany. So clear, it was. I heard a voice above me, *Go on, then. What are you waiting for? This is what you asked for.* I looked up and, dazed, I blurted out, "Yes, yes, okay."

Curtis' face creased up in a mystifying and curious manner as he looked above me, confused. "Right. Okay." I looked at my watch. It was nine thirty p.m. "You've got one hour to get the hell out of my life. If you want to pick anything up from the house, you've got one hour, 'til ten thirty. Don't just stand there. Get dressed," I barked. "NOW."

I turned and left the office, then, for good measure, I picked up the reception telephone and called Alison. On her picking up, it just spilled out. "Alison, you'd better get down to the gym. I've just caught Curtis and Tanya at it. In the office!" And hung up. I sat down on a chair in reception to catch my breath.

This was it. This was my golden ticket. This was my new life. Divorce, definitely divorce. I was smiling to myself when Curtis and Tanya appeared, dressed, in the doorway. "You disgusting pair of fucking idiots. You're old enough to be her father."

Tanya now started crying, then came out with

something in an attempt to justify this insane situation. "It's your fault. He's been upset for more than two weeks because you're not speaking to him." What an absolute crock of shit she'd come out with. Now I was awash with indignation.

"Oh dear, poor Curtis. So he thought... 'I know, I'll shag Tanya, that'll make it okay'. Just shut up, you tramp." I stared at her repulsed.

The next minute, Alison turned up with Josh in toe. They burst through the door and gave Curtis his second beating of the evening. He just held his arms in defence but didn't retaliate. I stood and turned to leave.

Alison was screaming at Tanya to get in the car. She flatly refused and Curtis added, "She's sixteen and old enough to leave home. She's staying with me." He moved her behind himself, in the doorway, and held a protective arm in front of her. "I'm leaving... Remember, Curtis." I tapped my watch face. "Tick tock. Ten thirty. Then I never want to see you again."

As I drove home, too fast, I felt delirious. Whether that was delirious with shock or happiness I couldn't decide. Both, maybe. Euphoric, even. At home, rightly or wrongly, I told the boys everything. I probably should have dealt with it a little differently, but, well, I didn't. I just told them the whole sordid story and asked them to stay put with me in the lounge while he collected what he needed. They couldn't speak. They were stunned.

In the kitchen I pulled three or four black bin liners

from a roll. At ten past ten, Curtis pulled up on the road outside. Not in the driveway. He strode towards the house, accompanied by two of his gym buddies. I laughed to myself. He'd brought protection. Hilarious. I opened the door, said hi to the two guys and thrust the handful of bin liners into Curtis's chest. I made a point of looking at my watch. I said nothing and he said nothing. I closed the lounge door behind me and waited quietly, with the boys, for him to leave.

One of the guys, who I liked, opened the door to ask if we were okay. "Never better, thanks," was my instant and unwavering answer. "Oh, and give this to Curtis, would you? After you have driven away from here." I had written on a piece of paper:

YOU LOSE, YOU BASTARD. YOU HAVE LOST EVERYTHING.

Inside the message, I placed my wedding ring and wrapped it up tightly.

"Yes, with pleasure." He took it from me with a wink and squeezed my hand.

It was 10.28 p.m. Curtis left without a word. I saw him carrying two bin liners full of stuff. I had no idea what he had put in them. I didn't care, either. I just kept my eyes on him until he drove away in his car. I locked the door behind him and closed all the curtains in the house. I sat with the boys and assured them there was nothing at all to worry about. "This is what we wanted.

What we needed. Tomorrow morning, I will be filing for divorce and we can start our new life. A great life. A happy life."

I knew it wasn't going to be an easy road, this was, after all, Curtis we were dealing with, but I was determined to give my gorgeous boys a better life. I felt so proud of them. They sat there, both holding my hands in a show of solidarity. We were ready for our fight for freedom, whatever it took. "We're a great team, we will look after each other," I promised them, in a three-way bear hug squeeze.

"Mum, is Dad definitely never coming back... Ever... Ever?" asked Tyler.

"Never, EVER," I answered with certainty.

"Can I get a cat then?"

Scott responded, ploughing in with, "TYLER."

Oh dear, I thought. The indignation in Scott's tone of voice. Was he upset at Tyler's request, was it inappropriately too soon? But... No.

Scott continued, "That's not fair, you know I wanted a cat!"

With uncontrollable laughter, I declared, "Okay, two cats, it is."

CPSIA information can be obtained
at www.ICGtesting.com
Printed in the USA
LVHW050204090921
697353LV00001B/118